www.brindlebooks.co.uk

AVARICE of EMPIRE

C.Q. TURNSTONE

PROLOGUE

*"Pride, Envy, and Avarice are the three sparks
that have set these hearts on fire."*

Dante Alighieri

1865

It is the twenty-eighth year of Queen Victoria's rule over the sprawling British Empire. Three winters have passed since the death of her beloved husband, Prince Albert of Saxe-Coburg and Gotha, the Prince Consort.

As Europe enjoys a period of relative peace during an era of dramatic technological, economic, and political change, the seeds of maelstrom are being sown by Prussian ambition.

Across the Atlantic the American Civil War is drawing to a bloody and bitter end, and four million people are gaining a fragile emancipation.

Thanks to demand from Arabia and elsewhere, the African slave trade continues to flourish on the profits of misery.

France is constructing a canal between the Mediterranean and the Red Sea, whilst the French public is reading *Journey to the Centre of the Earth* by Jules Verne.

India and the opium trade with China, the jewels in Britain's imperial crown, are still feared to be the objects of Russian desire.

AVARICE OF EMPIRE

12

PART ONE

CHAPTER ONE
THE ANTRIM COAST ROAD, IRELAND
FRIDAY, 28TH APRIL 1865

Charles Agnew needed surprise on his side. He brought momentous news and a plan for mischief, though one thing had nothing at all to do with the other. Black Arch tunnel framed the promontory of Ballygally Head like a window into a better world, and it beckoned Charles homeward. Home to Cairncastle Lodge and the Carnfunnock estate he would one day inherit.

Arriving from the direction Harriet won't expect will be the key that unlocks the gate of success, Charles concluded as he pictured how he would play a trick on his sister. It made him smile to imagine her feigning momentary outrage and rebuking his folly before surrendering to joyful, carefree laughter. Whimsical pranks had been an expression of their solidarity and mutual devotion since childhood, and they never tired of making game of one another. Charles liked to stage ambitious performances with theatrical flair, while Harriet's talent lay in careful observation and quiet subtlety. Charles always felt at liberty to be himself with his sister, unmasked and without pretentions, and he missed Harriet's open-minded company whenever they were apart. He knew she would be just as eager for their impending reunion.

Charles was the only passenger in a landau carriage meant for six. Beside him on the back seat lay his duck's head cane, top hat, and a small bouquet. Though the day was far from warm, he'd insisted on the top being down so that he might enjoy the invigorating sea air and an unobscured view to his right of the flood tide sparkling in the spring sunshine. The driver, a middle-aged man of few words and conservative temperament, had obliged without comment. He kept the pair of blinkered horses at a trot through Black Arch, which had been an aesthetic indulgence on the part of the road builders and cut a brief but defiant path through the cliff. The drumming of hooves echoed off its vaulted masonry like a timpani roll rising to a crescendo. When the carriage emerged back into the light on the north side of the tunnel, the next bend revealed distant rolling hills and the broad sweep of Drains Bay with its shoreline of boulder-strewn grey sand. In the glens far out of sight to the left, black cattle grazed, lambs frolicked, and crops of winter oats swayed in hedge-lined fields cultivated by Agnew tenants.

Cairncastle Lodge nestled amongst trees in a wide hollow on the seaward side of the ridge, about half a mile south of Ballygally Head, from where it commanded a majestic view over the bay. It was a modest, five-bedroom home built in the contrasting stonework of the Tudor Revival style, with high gables, tall chimneys and ornate decorative flourishes. Despite still being invisible from the road the house loomed over Charles's thoughts like a menacing storm. The closer he came to it, the more anxiously he anticipated his father's habitual disapproval and criticism, and the more irritated he was with himself for still labouring under their yoke at the age of nearly twenty-nine. Charles was entertaining the optimistic idea that by seeding uncontentious conversation he might stand a chance of avoiding the usual paternal interrogation regarding his cavalry career, finances and marriage prospects. To that end, since Belfast he'd been carrying a copy of *The Times* of London. Charles thought its shocking front-page report was bound to prompt lively discussion.

The horses were being reined to a walking pace before negotiating the left-hand turn into the Carnfunnock estate. Stone gate pillars, neither of which had ever borne the weight of an actual gate, marked the threshold between public and private land. As he crossed it, Charles wrestled his attention back to Harriet and the plan.

Of the two roads that led to the house, the shorter southern loop was reserved for the Agnew family and their guests. Harriet would be watching for his carriage to arrive that way, so Charles instructed the coachman to take the north road used by servants and tradesmen instead. It curved along an ascending route through the musty tranquillity of mature woodland, hidden from view for six hundred yards. Charles was confident he could jump out before reaching the house and without being seen from its south or east-facing windows. Of course, the ruse would fall flat on its face if Harriet was already outside waiting to greet him, but that seemed unlikely and they would laugh about it in either case. Charles explained what he required of the driver and secured his complicity with a generous tip paid in advance. It was clear from the man's incredulous expression that he considered the whole silly enterprise a most peculiar way for a gentleman to carry on.

Leaving the shroud of trees behind, Charles was pleased to find the gravel driveway deserted. The driver steered as far to the right of it as was practical, while Charles slipped off his frock coat and picked up the bouquet. He opened the low door of the carriage and crouched at the opening until a cluster of bushes had passed by. Then he took a great leap, landed in a run, and made straight for the kitchen door at the north-west corner of the house. He was through the kitchen before a startled Mary O'Hara, the cook, could say a word. Stopping to catch his breath, he peered around the corner into the hallway. The front door, studded oak with a Gothic arch, was open and he could see Harriet outside speaking to the coachman. Charles rushed to the door and slammed it shut.

"You wicked devil, Charles!" Harriet scolded.

He paused.

"Open this door at once!" she ordered, rapping the brass knocker.

Charles waited a little longer. Then he lifted the latch and opened the door in the unhurried manner of a servant. "Hello little sister," he said in a tone of mock bemusement. "Whatever are you doing out there?"

Harriet was exaggerating a frown and had her hands on her hips. She stepped forward and stood on tiptoe to kiss his cheek. "Hello big brother, you awful man, you," she teased. Her expression relaxed into the happiest of smiles and then laughter overcame them both.

Charles presented Harriet with the bouquet he'd been concealing behind his back and she lifted the petals to her nose to appreciate their delicate scent.

"They're wonderful, thank you," she said. "And for all your letters too. It was so exciting to hear of the regiment's move to Dublin and that you'd not be so far away."

"My pleasure, and thank you for yours as always," Charles replied. "Dublin's by far the best place yet, that's for sure," he added, taking Harriet's hand and leading her in a comic waltz around the panelled hall. Charles was an accomplished tenor and he sang as they whirled. *"Mid pleasures and palaces though we may roam, be it ever so humble, there's no place like home.* That's a fizzing dress, by the way."

"I'm delighted you think so," Harriet beamed, proud that the time spent selecting the pale-yellow gown hadn't been wasted. "Mother and I both acquired new things especially for your visit."

"I'm honoured! *A charm from the skies seems to hallow us there, which seek thro' the world, is ne'er met elsewhere.* How's she been keeping? And father?"

"*Sweet, sweet home...*" sang Harriet, joining in. "Oh, Mother's quite well, but father has seemed rather out of sorts these past few weeks."

"Is he ailing?"

"I'm sure it's nothing. He'll never say so of course, but I know he's missed you just as much as mother and I have."

"I somehow doubt that," Charles replied with raised eyebrows, "but it's gracious of you to suggest it. *There's no place like home!* When will O'Hara be serving lunch do you suppose?" he asked, bringing their dance to an end with an extravagant bow.

"One o'clock as usual, I expect. Shall we take a stroll out to the walled garden in the meantime?" Harriet suggested. "It always looks so pretty when the sun's shining."

Her brother was about to agree when Hugh McNally appeared from the drawing room. The butler's hair was whiter than Charles remembered and his posture a little more stooped.

"My dear chap, it's marvellous to see you. How are you? And Mrs McNally?" asked Charles with affectionate warmth.

McNally had served the Agnews for a quarter of a century, ever since the house was built and the family first took up residence. Like Mary O'Hara and Sarah Duff, the lady's maid, Hugh was part of the family in all but name and social class.

"And to see you, Mr Agnew, sir. Thank you. The wife and I remain in fine health, touch wood," he replied, tapping his forehead with two fingers. "I trust you had a pleasant journey up from Dublin, sir?"

"Indeed I did," said Charles. "The railway delivered me to Belfast in good time yesterday, and again to Larne this morning."

"Very good, sir. Shall I inform Mr and Mrs Agnew of your arrival, sir?" McNally asked, referring to Charles and Harriet's parents, James and Catherine.

Harriet answered on her brother's behalf, as was often her habit when excitement got the better of her patience. "Please do, McNally, thank you. My brother and I will be in the garden."

"Very well, miss. And I'll fetch your things from the carriage as well, sir."

"Let's fetch them together," Charles replied, halting Harriet's advance and strolling back outside. He thanked the coachman for his indulgence and retrieved his hat, coat and cane, while the butler loosened the straps of the luggage rack.

"Tell me, McNally, has my father read the London papers yet today?" Charles asked once the carriage had departed.

"I don't believe so, sir, no. Not yesterday's at any rate."

There was always at least a day's delay between the broadsheets being published in London and them reaching newsstands along Ireland's east coast. *The Times* Charles had purchased at Belfast railway station this morning was only the Thursday edition. He opened his bag and unfolded the paper so that Harriet and McNally could read the sensational headline:

ASSASSINATION of PRESIDENT LINCOLN
The intelligence of the assassination of President Lincoln and of the attempt to assassinate Mr Seward caused a most extraordinary sensation in the city yesterday.

"Oh, how awful!" exclaimed Harriet, covering her mouth with her hand.

"Happened a fortnight ago, on Good Friday of all days, at a theatre in Washington," Charles explained. "Seems the poor man was shot in the head by a scoundrel loyal to the southern rebels."

"Terrible sad news, sir," said Hugh. "I wonder who the new president will be?"

"Vice President Johnson will have to take over, I imagine," Harriet suggested, impressing Charles with her knowledge of such things.

"Apparently," Charles continued, "we're only learning of the tragedy so quickly because some fellow from Reuters happened to intercept the mail ship from North America while it was in Irish waters and telegraphed the story to London. Quite remarkable, don't you think?"

"It is that, sir," agreed McNally. "Your father is in his study. With your permission, sir, I'll convey the newspaper to him right away."

James Agnew was a man of business with ten thousand acres in Ireland, other property in Cheltenham and his native London, and had at one time served as the High Sheriff of Antrim. He was now in his seventieth year and prized his reputation and that of the Agnew family name above all else.

James had given his son an unusually warm welcome and, as Charles had hoped it would, the foreign news helped conversation flow during the course of an excellent O'Hara roast lunch. However, it was obvious that the master of Carnfunnock was perturbed, and by far more than the demise of President Lincoln.

"Forgive me for asking, sir," Charles ventured, "but is something troubling you?"

James looked down the table towards Catherine, who was ten years his junior, and found the encouragement he sought in his wife's reassuring gaze. Harriet glanced at Charles, perplexed. James cleared his throat and took a mouthful of wine while he marshalled his thoughts before answering.

"I had hoped that Easter would provide the opportunity for this discussion, which I regret is now past overdue," he began, looking at Charles as he spoke.

"My apologies once again," Charles responded, feeling the familiar sting of his father's apparent disappointment. "As you know, I was unable to take leave of the regiment until this weekend."

"I meant only to make clear that my intention had been to speak to you and your sister about a number of matters before today. And so, on that account, it is I who must apologise." James stroked his white moustache. "These matters to which I refer will affect us all and I confess, to my eternal shame, that both fault and responsibility are mine." He paused and sipped his drink. "You're both aware of my investments in the Carrickfergus to Larne Railway. In fact, you travelled along its iron road only this morning, Charles." His son nodded in acknowledgement. "And you may also know that the steamer service from Stranraer was suspended indefinitely some fifteen months since. Well, I'm afraid that has had a rather unfortunate impact on the financial stability of the company. As a result, towards the end of last year, the directors were forced to call in promises of capital from most of the investors, myself included."

"Father, I'm so sorry." Harriet began, but Catherine cut her off.

"Please, Harriet, let your father say what he has to say."

James carried on without losing momentum. "The long and the short of the situation is this: I have no alternative but to sell Cairncastle Lodge and a large proportion of the surrounding estate."

Tears filled Harriet's eyes and she held her head in her hands. Charles restrained himself, not allowing his expression to reveal the outrage and disbelief running riot in his mind.

"Negotiations for the sale have already been concluded with Mr James Chaine, of Ballycraigy Manor, who'll be taking possession before the end of next month. Harriet, you'll be coming with your mother and I to the residence in Cheltenham."

"Forgive me," sobbed Harriet, throwing her napkin on the table and rushing from the dining room without saying more.

Despite her charming nature, attractive features, and the fact that she came from a respected landowning family, Harriet was still a spinster. Her parents had often arranged introductions to eligible, well-bred gentlemen, but romance had never blossomed. She'd spent almost all her twenty-seven years at Cairncastle Lodge, which was her sanctuary as much as her home. Not that Harriet disliked Cheltenham. She'd been there many times. It simply didn't compare with Carnfunnock and the fertile Antrim coastline she adored.

"I'll go after her and leave you two to talk further," Catherine said, her poise unwavering as she left the room.

James pushed back his chair and walked to the bay window overlooking the south lawn. He stood there in silence for more than a minute before asking if Charles would care for a cigar.

"I would, thank you," Charles replied, grateful to share the ritual.

James retrieved a walnut box from the cabinet on the other side of the room, opened the lid, and offered it to his son. Charles selected a cigar and removed its cap with the brass cutter he kept in his pocket. James followed suit and struck a parlour match for Charles before lighting his own.

"I appreciate your candour in explaining the situation," Charles said after the first drag clawed his throat. "The strain of these past months must have been intolerable."

"Trying times to be sure," said James. "One never knows what unexpected fences one will have to hurdle. The important thing is to face them head on with confidence and good spirit, and with faith that the course ahead will offer good running."

"You still have faith in the future then?"

"Of course. One must always have faith. Things may well get worse before they get better, but I'm sure we'll prevail in the end, God willing."

"Get worse?" queried Charles with alarm.

"Possibly, yes. You see, whilst the sale of the house and grounds is raising a sum of £12,800, my commitments to the railway far exceed that. I suspect we'll need to sell most of our holdings in Ireland before long, and certainly Larne harbour."

This was a devastating revelation, as if the implications of losing Cairncastle Lodge weren't serious enough already. Charles swallowed a barrack-room curse. He thought of all the times he'd endured lectures about being more responsible, and the bitter arguments that invariably followed them. Now his father was tumbling from the moral high ground as dramatically as the family was about to fall from grace and fortune. Charles seethed with resentment at the hypocrisy, and wanted to express it, but as he stalked around the room he realised he felt sorry for the old man. There was nothing to be gained by being churlish. He tried to say the right thing instead.

"I won't deny my surprise at learning of such catastrophe, nor my concern for what the future may now hold – especially for poor Harriet and the staff – but I'm sure you've always acted with the best of intentions. The railway was a gamble, I suppose, but you can hardly be blamed for circumstances beyond your control."

"Thank you for your understanding. It's more than I deserve," said James, returning to the window. "As for Harriet, I imagine she'll settle in to Cheltenham life easily enough. But let's talk of other things for a while, shall we?"

Charles sat down, drained his glass and refilled it.

"I've never told you this before," James continued, "but one of my few regrets is that estate business kept me from the army."

"I had no idea you ever entertained such an ambition."

"Of course. What young man doesn't long for adventure and to test his courage? Which is why I wonder if your expectations of military life are being fulfilled with the 9th Lancers?"

Charles sensed a veiled criticism. "We both know that's a rhetorical question," he snapped back. The answer was long and painful.

Charles and Harriet had worshipped their elder brother, but Charles never doubted that William was their father's favourite. William had been three years older and could never do wrong, whilst Charles could rarely do right.

In early May of 1857 indigenous troops serving in the army of the East India Company began a revolt that threatened British interests in the sub-continent. It had to be quashed at all costs. After reading the first reports of what was dubbed the Indian Mutiny during June, by the middle of August William had purchased a commission with the 2nd Dragoon Guards and was soon travelling to northern India to join the fight. On 5th March the following year he took part in a valiant cavalry charge to repulse an attack on British infantry outside *Lucknow*. The regiment paid a heavy price for its success that day, with rebel musket fire claiming many lives. Cornet William Agnew was amongst the fallen.

Charles had just begun his final term at Trinity College when word reached Cambridge that his brother was dead. Any notion of sitting exams and graduating then seemed futile, trivial and meaningless. Driven by grief and a smothering sense of being powerless, Charles was overcome with fury. Vengeance was on his mind and within a day he'd left the university to seek it.

A letter received only a week earlier, and at first thought to be as inconsequential as it was brief, pointed to the opportunity Charles needed. It was from Samuel Pretor, an old friend from Rugby School, who was now with the 9th Queen's Royal Lancers in India. Samuel wrote of how he'd been promoted to the rank of lieutenant following the demise of another officer, opening a place in the regiment for a new cornet. Swift enquiries revealed that the vacancy remained unfilled, and Charles seized upon it without hesitation. He would join the cavalry, just as his brother had done, and deliver brutal retribution.

But dispatches from India took many weeks to arrive and by the time Charles was wearing uniform the fighting was already as good as over.

During the seven years since then, the regiment was kept on home soil between barracks in Maidstone, Aldershot, Brighton and Dublin. It hadn't taken long for Charles to become thoroughly bored and disillusioned. Frustrated by inactivity and robbed of purpose he soon developed notoriety for finding distraction in the most inventive and entertaining of ways, often in mocking contempt of ineffectual senior officers and authority in general.

Out of face-saving necessity he'd purchased his lieutenancy only a year ago after remaining a cornet, the lowest officer rank, for nearly three times longer than was typical or seemly. Given he lacked nothing in ability, flair, or financial means, his overtly intentional slow progress was baffling to his family and colleagues. When challenged about it Charles would say, not untruthfully, that he simply had no enthusiasm for investing capital in a status he didn't need. The heart of the matter was something he never voiced, not even to Harriet, and barely even admitted to himself. Until he'd faced battle with the same courage as his brother, Charles felt unworthy of a rank higher than William's.

James returned to his chair and poured what little wine was left in the decanter into his son's glass. "Rhetorical perhaps, but I meant no slight in it," he said. "Just the opposite, in fact. I know how much you admired William and his gallantry. And your grandfather's time at Saratoga too, I'm sure. My point is that I understand your motives better than you realise and I have the utmost respect for them."

Charles was confounded and heartened by his father's words. "Oh, I see. Then, thank you. It means a great deal to hear you say that. But why are you bringing all this up now?"

"Do you recall meeting my friend, Major Gavin, at a dinner here some years ago?"

"I believe so. Of the 16th Lancers, retired?"

"Yes, that's right. We've been corresponding recently about his political ambitions – he intends to stand as the Member of Parliament for Limerick in the near future – and he often asks after you. I received another letter from him the other day, the thrust of which may interest you."

"How so?"

"Firstly, it seems almost certain the 16th Lancers will be shipping out to India this season. And secondly, that, for reasons best known to themselves, a number of its gentlemen are seeking to exchange their commissions with officers in regiments remaining at home. Like the 9th, for instance. Major Gavin wondered if you might consider such an exchange? And, if you did, he'd be pleased to help expedite the formalities on your behalf."

James could see the embers of renewed hope smoulder in his son's deep brown eyes.

"There would appear to be some truth in that old saying about silver linings and every cloud," said Charles.

CHAPTER TWO
COLCHESTER CAVALRY BARRACKS, ENGLAND
SATURDAY, 17TH JUNE 1865

Scarlet tunics, tobacco smoke, and exuberant conversation filled the Officers' Mess. Attendance was mandatory for a special dinner arranged by the 16th Lancers' commanding officer. Morgan Farrell was one of the last to arrive.

In keeping with regimental hierarchy his fellow lieutenants were seated halfway up the long table. Morgan strolled in their direction and stood behind the vacant chair, casually folding his arms atop its high back. The scene before him offered amusement and intrigue in equal measure.

Fair-haired Augustus Dobrée, who cultivated a reluctant wisp of a moustache and an air of arrogant superiority, was twenty years old and came from a family of merchant bankers in Walthamstow. His posturing rarely escaped Morgan's teasing, which he took in good sport, and what he lacked in modesty he made up for with cheery optimism, an enquiring mind, and genuine promise as a capable officer. Morgan liked him for that, as did most of the others, but there was no denying Augustus appreciated the sound of his own voice.

He was indulging that pleasure at the expense of three of his immediate neighbours at the table. To his right was the amiable John Barker, a wiry, hard-working twenty-four-year-old from Cumberland, while in the seat opposite was the pallid son of a cross-Channel packet service entrepreneur from Dover. Charles Carrington Churchward was a year younger than John and insisted on being called *Carrin*. He always had a face as solemn as a mule at a funeral, which Morgan found peculiarly at odds with his otherwise gregarious and good-humoured nature.

Augustus was endeavouring to impress the broad-shouldered gentleman to his left. From across the table Morgan paid close attention to the new officer's face as Augustus neared the familiar anti-climax of a tale about his grandfather having been Governor of the Bank of England. It was a healthy face, handsome in its proportions, with strong features framed by hair that had a rebellious natural wave and the hue of dark mahogany. The groomed sideburns and moustache were flamboyant, though by no means ostentatious.

Even for an astute observer of character like Morgan, the man's composed expression was hard to read. He was giving Augustus the courtesy of his undivided attention, showing almost paternal tolerance and no hint of impatience or disinterest. There was gentle kindness in his eyes, certainly, and verve in abundance, but was there a restless scepticism too? Morgan wasn't sure.

As soon as Augustus stopped for breath and received the subdued plaudits of his audience, Morgan wasted no more time in asserting his presence. "You'll be Mr Agnew then?" he began with a welcoming smile, "Morgan Farrell. Pleasure to make your acquaintance."

"Likewise, Mr Farrell," Charles replied as he stood to lean over and shake hands. "Yes, I'm Charles. It's good to know you. Is that a touch of Dublin I hear in your voice?"

"I see already there'll be no out-foxing you," Morgan quipped as he took his seat. "You're quite right. Born in County Kerry, but educated in Dublin. Playing at soldiers for coming up four years. You know Ireland yourself, I take it?"

Charles had a typically upper-middle class English accent polished by his time at Rugby and Cambridge, but one that never entirely lost the influence of time spent in Antrim. "In Dublin myself of late, but the family estate is in the lands around Larne," he replied, using the present tense out of habit and feeling no obligation to correct himself.

"That's beautiful country up there. Not like Kerry of course, but very pleasant nevertheless. I see you've been introduced to these disreputable gentlemen already," Morgan said, the jest evident in his striking green eyes.

"Best to ignore this rogue, Mr Agnew," said Carrin before Charles could respond. "He'll lead you down the path of ruin given half a chance."

"We'll get along famously then."

"Speaking of ruin," chimed in Augustus, "are you still tupping that pretty wench from The Three Cups?"

Morgan laughed and tasted the claret. "The Three Cups is the hotel next to the town hall on the High Street, Charles, and serves an excellent pint of pale ale. I can recommend it, and its billiard table. As for pretty wenches, I can't begin to imagine what Mr Dobrée is talking about."

Charles liked Morgan's sense of humour and could see straight away he lacked the pompous sense of entitlement that was typical of so many officers. His appearance was out of the ordinary as well. He was clean-shaven for a start, shunning the fashion for generous whiskers, and kept his thick black hair in an unruly mop rather than short and neat with a centre parting. His gold-braided uniform was immaculate though. The 16th (The Queen's) Lancers was the only cavalry regiment still permitted to wear traditional red instead of the new regulation dark blue. It was a source of great pride and earned them the nickname the Scarlet Lancers.

"I bet that tunic still feels like a stranger? Is it from Hawkes on Saville Row?" asked John Barker.

"A distant cousin at least, but it'll soften up soon enough," Charles replied. "Yes, Hawkes, and a fine job of tailoring they did too. Took a while, but it was no hardship to enjoy London's many diversions for a few days."

"Colourful diversions, by the looks of it," said Morgan, who'd noticed Charles had stubborn traces of several colours of paint on his hands.

"Ah, yes. Life should be a colourful business though, don't you think?"

"I do indeed. So, what's the story?"

"Did you ever visit Wyld's Great Globe in Leicester Square?"

"No, but I've heard it was quite a marvel. I'm partial to some of the Square's other attractions, mind you," Morgan winked, in reference to its theatres and brothels.

"I did once," said Carrin. "It must've been a good sixty feet across. One climbed its internal stairs to view a scale model of the surface of the Earth from the inside out. Rather staggering really."

"Yes, that's it," confirmed Charles. "Well, after the thing was demolished a few years ago, the old statue of King George I on horseback was found buried underneath. It's been resurrected to reign over the gardens again, but in a far from regal state of repair. I thought it only right and proper to restore the German to his former splendour."

"Jesus wept!" Morgan exclaimed. "You didn't?"

"I most certainly did, and adorning him rainbow-like improved his appearance no end," said Charles with pride. The others laughed and applauded.

"Make a note, gentlemen, there's a new rogue in town!" joked Morgan. He was looking forward to getting to know the unpredictable Mr Agnew better in the days that lay ahead.

The regiment's conscientious adjutant was an Irishman called Robert Maillard. He occupied the chair on Morgan's right and had been engrossed in conversation about horse racing with his friend Maurice, Captain Fitzgerald. Diminutive and quietly spoken, though not without bearing, Robert compensated for his lack of good looks through sporting prowess at the crease and on the track. He was ideally built for a jockey. "Did you find your tent without any trouble, Charles?" he checked.

"I did, yes, thank you. I was a little surprised we're not in the barracks, but it makes a pleasant change to be under canvas in the fresh air."

"Quite so. It's all part of our preparations for departure, as I expect you appreciate. We've been out there on Abbey Farm Field for ten days or so now, but hopefully not for much longer."

"That was a busy time," commented John.

"Wasn't it just!" agreed Augustus, all too happy to recount it for Charles. "We had two troops in Norwich and another two in Ipswich, you see, and they all had to rejoin headquarters here after it was confirmed we'd be going overseas. Captain Riddell's troop rode directly from Norwich, while I led the other one to Ipswich. All the Ipswich horses were handed over to the 17th Lancers, and then we marched the twenty miles to Colchester under the command of Major Burnell."

"That's Hugh," said John, pointing out the officer near the top end of the table. He was the same age as Charles and Robert, a year older than Morgan. Charles had met Hugh earlier in the day and formed the opinion that the major's serious disposition was a disservice to his affable personality.

"All four troops arrived the same day, on the 6th," Augustus continued, "which is when the 17th took over the rest of the horses and saddlery, and we relocated to the tents in the field. We slept well that night, I can tell you!"

"I should imagine you did," said Charles. "Which troop are you with?" he asked Morgan.

"Captain Whigham's. We were part of the Ipswich mob."

"We'll need to find you a suitable *bâtman*, Charles. Do you chaps have any suggestions?" asked Robert.

"Solomon Smith is a good soul," offered Morgan. Private Smith was the best friend of Morgan's own servant, John Gantz. Both men were steady, dependable sorts from the shires of Lincoln, and Morgan could foresee advantage in them having equal duties.

"Very well. I'll see about arranging that tomorrow, and I'll get you a copy of Standing Orders as well, Charles. Nothing you're not already accustomed to, of course."

"Much appreciated, thank you."

Robert wanted to ask Charles about his successes as an owner of thoroughbreds in Antrim and whether, like Maurice, he had any experience as a trainer. But his questions would have to wait for another time. Colonel William Dickson was entering the room followed by Brevet Lieutenant Colonel Thomas White. Chairs were hastily scraped back and the whole assembly stood to attention.

Both men were in their mid-thirties and came from distinguished military families. They were close friends as well as trusted comrades, having served in the regiment together for eighteen years.

William was the taller and broader of the pair. Jovial by disposition and benevolent in his countenance, he was known for his fair but forthright style of command, a love of cats, and the substantial income he enjoyed from estates in Limerick and Tipperary. The colonel was a Dickson from Berkshire, a servant of the Crown, and considered himself blessed to be a God-fearing Englishman.

Thomas was two years older, but had purchased his first commission a fortnight after William back in the spring of 1847. He'd long since learned to accept subordination with equanimity. Like Hugh Burnell, the place he called home was in the heart of Nottinghamshire's Robin Hood country. Unlike the major, Thomas had the self-assured demeanour of a man who knew he would one day inherit the baronetcy of Tuxford and Wallingwells. He'd already inherited his mother's strawberry-blonde curls.

Colonel Dickson invited everyone to sit as he strode to the head of the table. He came straight to the point in a voice deep with authority. "The news we've all been expecting arrived this morning, gentlemen.

Allow me to read from the official orders," he said, holding up the all-important telegram. "*The 16th (The Queen's) Lancers to hold themselves in readiness to embark for Madras per S.S. Golden Fleece about the 27th*."

Everyone cheered and got to their feet again. There was loud applause and William beamed. He couldn't wait to return to the land of his birth, a land that had done so much to shape his family's fortunes. "India beckons, gentlemen. Join me in a toast," he said, lifting his glass from the table. "To the 16th..."

"The 16th!"

"And to Her Majesty the Queen..."

"Her Majesty the Queen! Huzzah! Huzzah! Huzzah!"

As seats were taken again amid a wave of feverish chatter, a callow young man named Charles Pulteney Chaplin whispered an anxious question to the doctor beside him. "I say, how long will we be in India for?"

Assistant Surgeon Charles Alexander Innes was a proud Scot in his thirty-third year. Like many of the more experienced officers, he was a veteran of the brutal Crimean and Indian Rebellion campaigns. He'd only recently joined the regiment from the 16th Dragoons, but had already gained the admiration and respect of the men in his care. They called him Doctor Alec, which he preferred, or Surgeon Innes when an officer was in earshot. "Eleven years," Alec whispered back, "but don't you fret laddie, it'll be 1876 before you know it," he added, nudging the cornet in the ribs. Chaplin downed a full glass of wine.

"Gentlemen, if you please," said the colonel, bringing the room back to order. "I'd like to take this opportunity to welcome Lieutenant Charles Agnew to the regiment. Mr Agnew joined us earlier today and will be in Captain Battine's troop. He comes to us from the 9th Lancers via exchange with Mr Bingham who departed last week for Dublin."

Charles thanked the colonel and acknowledged the smiles and hearty foot stomping of his new brother officers.

"However," the colonel continued, "with my permission, and as you will observe, Captain Battine is absent from this gathering. The reason being thus – which will no doubt come as little surprise to most of you – that having already served his country with distinction in India, and now wishing to fight life's battles side by side with his fiancée – the very charming Katherine – William's preference is to continue his career here at home." A chorus of knuckles rapped their understanding along the length of the table. "It will take some weeks to be confirmed through the official channels, of course," the colonel explained, "but I have it on good authority that William will exchange with Captain James Goldie of the 17th Lancers and previously of the 9th. Mr Goldie has very considerable experience on the sub-continent, and has only recently returned from whence we are about to go, so I'm sure he'll be a most valuable asset to the regiment." Knuckles rapped again, but the colonel hadn't finished. "I gather that, aside from waiting for exchange bureaucracy, Captain Goldie is also about to tie the dreaded knot. He and his bride will therefore be making their own way to India at a later date."

"Where are we to be stationed, sir?" piped up Cornet William Bovill.

"The colonel was just coming to that," said Thomas White, letting the interruption go unchastised.

"Upon reaching Madras – which, for those of you whose geography may be lacking, is on the east coast of southern India – we will proceed inland by railway to the cantonment at Bangalore."

Bangalore had a reputation for being the finest of all the military garrisons in India, and the one with the most comfortable climate. The room buzzed with enthusiasm at the news.

"Like all the regiments there," William continued, "our duty will be to protect British interests and the British population throughout the region – and beyond if called upon. Now, Major Burnell, perhaps you'd carry on?"

"Certainly, sir," said Hugh Burnell, getting up from his chair. "As you're already aware, gentlemen, Captain Riddell's troop has been broken up and re-distributed amongst the other seven. A new depot troop, consisting of thirty-nine men of all ranks, has been formed under his command. It will be stationed at Canterbury and brought up to the full strength of seventy with new recruits over time." The major then addressed Captain Riddell directly. "George, you'll be departing on Tuesday morning and travelling to Kent on the railway."

George Riddell thanked the major, offered his best wishes to all those going abroad, and made a tongue-in-cheek promise about keeping the home barracks well-stocked with brandy ready for their return. Though he wasn't yet of a mind to leave the army, George had no desire to go to India and was relieved when the colonel had offered him the depot role.

Hugh picked up from where he'd left off. "A handful of you are following the colonel's example and planning to travel by independent means via the overland route across Egypt rather than enjoying troopship hospitality. As things stand, in addition to Colonel Dickson, that's Captain and Mrs Fitzgerald, captains Gooch and Whigham, lieutenants Maillard, Churchward and Duke, and Cornet Peacocke. Oh, and now also Captain and Mrs Goldie. If anyone else is thinking of doing the same, please inform Mr Maillard before the end of this weekend. It goes without saying that surgeons Macbeth, Innes and Farmer, and our paymaster, Mr Dynon, are required to be part of the *Golden Fleece* contingent."

"Aye, we wouldnae dream o' missing it," said Surgeon Major James 'Pills' Macbeth with mock ambivalence. Alec Innes and William Farmer both chuckled. Dublin-born Thomas Dynon was impassive.

Infantrymen fighting in the Punjab were the first to bestow James with a sobriquet that favoured brevity over unoriginal exploitation of his surname. Now even the most senior officers called him *Pills* and nobody thought anything of it. India had become his home since then and he was almost as devoted to it as he was to Thomasine, his wife of nearly twenty years. James transferred from the 74th Highlanders last December, the third time in his career a change of regiment had been necessary to continue their life in India. Formidable in both intellect and stature, with hewn features a walrus moustache and penetrating stare did nothing to soften, his next birthday would be his forty-eighth.

William Farmer was the newest member of the medical department. Though a couple of years younger than Alec Innes, he had been an assistant surgeon for just as long. A son of the Poplar Hall estate in County Kildare, and lately of the 29th infantry garrisoned at Newry, he was eager to see the world with Louisa, his wife of not yet four full months.

Turning to Charles, Hugh said, "Because Captain Goldie won't be on the *Golden Fleece*, Mr Agnew, your command of the troop in his absence would be welcomed. Will that suit your plans?"

"Of course," Charles replied, "It will be my pleasure." His tone was sincere, almost grateful, and Morgan saw a dormant longing flash across Charles's eyes. He really means it, Morgan thought to himself.

"Thank you. One further point to note, gentlemen," Hugh continued, "Since Lieutenant Maillard is travelling via Egypt, Quarter

Master Fuller will be acting-adjutant in his stead during our voyâge and until we reach Bangalore. Are there any questions?"

Riding Master Thomas Brown, who'd served in the Afghanistan campaign of 1839 and once gave the Prince of Wales riding instruction, and Tom Richardson, the veterinary surgeon, had both been wondering the same thing. Thomas enquired on their joint behalf. "I have one, major. When will the regiment take possession of new mounts?"

"Thank you, Mr Brown. We understand that we're to inherit horses and saddlery from the 18th Hussars who are moving to Secunderabad from Bangalore around the same time we're due to arrive. I'm sure they'll be happy for you and Mr Richardson to inspect them as soon as you wish."

"Understood, sir, thank you."

"Now, gentlemen, I suspect the first course is ready to be served. Let me finish by offering another toast. Raise your glasses with me and drink... to India!"

"To India! Huzzah! Huzzah! Huzzah!"

There was a tense atmosphere at breakfast the day after the depot troop left. Everyone could feel it. Even those a little worse for wear after too many pale ales at The Three Cups the night before.

As adjutant, in charge of regimental administration, Robert Maillard was tasked with drawing a lottery to decide which of the wives would be going to India with their husbands. The lucky ones, who'd be able to take their children too, would be regarded as *on the strength* of the regiment. As such, they'd be entitled to weekly pay and rations in return for washing uniforms and other domestic duties.

A list was posted outside the Sergeants' Mess by midday. For some it brought happiness and relief, but for many it was the harbinger of cruel heartbreak. By any standard, eleven years is a long time for a couple to be apart and an eternity for children to be separated from a parent. Though they never talked of it, except amongst themselves, all the wives knew there was no guarantee their men would ever make it home and making ends meet in the meantime would require ingenuity and endurance.

"Are you a married man, Smith?" Charles asked his new bâtman. They were sitting outside Charles's tent, enjoying the warmth of the mid-summer sun before beginning their afternoon duties. Charles was reading a telegram from Harriet. Pressing business was apparently going to prevent their father reaching Colchester in time to say farewell, but Harriet and mother hoped to be there. Private Smith was polishing his lieutenant's boots.

"Heck no, sir, not I," said Solomon. "Perhaps one day, mind."

"Probably just as well. It must be dreadful for those poor families being torn apart like that."

"Yes, sir. These coming days will see many a tear shed, and not just by the women, I'll wager."

A year younger than Charles, Solomon Smith had already proved to be an eminently capable and willing servant. He had a dour expression much of the time, but was friendly enough. He spoke at a gallop, in a broad accent that was sometimes hard to follow. Charles assumed the urgent pace of his speech was a symptom of an equally quick mind. He liked Private Smith, and had thanked Morgan for suggesting him.

"Have you wondered what the Indian women will be like, Smith?"

"Can't say I've given it much thought, sir. Happen they'll be much the same as women everywhere."

"But speaking a language we don't understand."

"Do you reckon that'll matter, sir? Haven't met a man yet who truly understood a woman's thinking."

Charles laughed off Solomon's question and returned to Harriet's telegram.

The final transport order had been expected by the weekend. It was four o'clock the following Tuesday afternoon before it came through the wire. The regiment would take the ten o'clock train the next morning.

Quarter Master James Fuller spent the evening overseeing the movement of baggage to the station. It included the silverware from the Officers' Mess and all the unissued clothing and equipment from the store. Then there were the lances, carbines and ammunition, all manner of horse accoutrements, and the soldiers' own kit. There was so much of it, Tuesday had turned into Wednesday by the time the task was complete. James had been to India before, serving with the regiment in the 1846 war against the Sikhs. It was there that the 16th Lancers distinguished themselves in a decisive charge against enemy lines during the Battle of Aliwal. Mr Fuller was an unflappable man, with a barrel chest, drooping moustache, and a dry wit. The whole barracks agreed he'd performed a miracle in getting everything ready for departure.

Each soldier had been issued with a trunk for his belongings. Most of the space was taken up with uniform, not least of which was the black *czapka*, the four-pointed Prussian-style helmet with its horsehair plume. Full dress, including white leather gauntlets, a blue and gold forage cap shaped like a pill box, and steel spurs, would be worn for embarkation. That still meant packing overalls, a second pair of trousers, stable jacket, patrol jacket, frock coat, mess dress, and cloak. Then there were the brass spurs, jack boots, undergarments, a variety of pouches and other accessories, and a sabre in its scabbard with accompanying sword belt. All the officers had acquired white pith helmets, so they had to be packed as well.

The twenty-eighth day of June dawned cool and clear. A parade was called at nine o'clock to assemble the men, each of whom carried a day's ration of bread and beef, along with their personal items, in a white haversack. By quarter past the hour, led by the regimental band, six hundred and seventy-six people, including sixty-four women and eighty-eight children, were turning right out of the barrack gates on to Butt Road. The folk of Colchester waved and cheered as the procession marched through the town in a column six abreast, its formation resolute over the uneven, dung-covered cobbles. They passed the High Street and crested North Hill, from where it was downhill all the way to the bridge spanning the River Colne. The railway, where a new white-brick station building was being constructed, lay not far beyond it.

The southbound platform was a sea of families and friends. The cavalrymen flooded in to say their goodbyes. An agonising mother clung to the neck of her only son. Lovers savoured a last embrace. Proud fathers strove to keep a stiff upper lip as they shook hands with the boys they cherished. It was a heartrending scene and no less emotional for the soldiers without anyone to bid them farewell.

Charles found his mother and Harriet near the rear of the train by the First Class carriages reserved for officers. They hugged him and apologised for his father's absence.

"Can't be helped," said Charles. "We'll see each other again and I'm looking forward to regaling you all with tales of heroic derring-do."

"That's the spirit," Catherine said, squeezing her son's arm.

"Allow me to introduce my good friend, Lieutenant Morgan Farrell," Charles said, turning to Morgan who'd been maintaining a polite distance. "Morgan, this is my mother, and my sister, Harriet."

"It's a privilege to make your acquaintances. Ma'am. Miss," Morgan said, bowing to each of them in turn.

"Likewise, Mr Farrell," Harriet replied, dabbing her cheeks with a lace handkerchief.

"I do hope you'll take good care of Charles for us, Mr Farrell," said Catherine, looking Morgan square in the eyes.

"I'll certainly do my best, ma'am."

"Thank you."

"Yes, thank you, Mr Farrell. Charles means the world to us," added Harriet. "Be sure to write as often as you can, big brother."

"Of course I will, don't worry. And you too, little sister."

"All aboard!" bellowed the station master. "All aboard!"

Charles kissed Harriet and Catherine one last time, before pushing his way through the throng.

"Ready for an adventure?" Morgan asked, holding open a door in the last but one carriage.

"Always," replied Charles as he climbed inside.

The six-wheeled W-class locomotive of the Great Eastern Railway hissed in readiness. The band of the 17th Lancers was playing *Auld Lang Syne*, and capped heads leant out of every carriage window. The station master blew his whistle and two shrill replies came from the engine. Couplings clanked apart as the long train began to move and steam billowed over the platform like clouds across a threatening sky.

As the waving hands at the station disappeared from view, the soldiers settled into their seats. Boisterous chatter hid the sadness and fear being felt by most.

Sergeants and corporals, collectively known as Non-Commissioned Officers or NCOs, along with the privates and most of the wives and children, were packed on wooden benches in the Second Class carriages. There were four compartments in every carriage, each one accessible only from the outside doors. In First Class, where officers had a more comfortable ride, each compartment accommodated six people in upholstered seats with armrests.

"Pretty girl, your sister," said Morgan, idly, as they chuffed through Witham station.

"She is indeed," Charles replied. "Good thing you're leaving the country," he added.

Morgan laughed. "I don't know what I've done to deserve such a reputation."

"Of course you don't."

"Ha!" scoffed Morgan.

"If it's not impertinent, I noticed you weren't met by anyone back there."

"Charles, I doubt you could be impertinent if you tried. A horse's arse, certainly, but never impertinent." There was no malice in Morgan's words, but that was all he said, and he turned to stare out the window. Charles decided not to press the matter further and changed the subject.

Chelmsford, Brentwood, and Romford all came and went as the train rolled its way through the pastoral landscapes of Essex. The locomotive was changed at Stratford, reversing the direction of travel and taking a different line to Forest Gate, Barking, and the first glimpse of the Thames at Purfleet. By half past the noon hour the carriages were jolting to a halt at Tilbury station.

Sergeants wasted no time forming the men into ranks on the platform and the quarter master and his staff got to work with the baggage. Bâtmen found their officers, and the wives and children tried to avoid being trampled. The station was just across the road from the riverbank and the mass of people was shepherded in that direction. An elegant paddle steamer called *The Earl of Essex* was moored at the pier. It would convey passengers across the river to the steamship *Golden Fleece* waiting on the Gravesend side.

Surveying the scene, Morgan reckoned it would take at least several hours and many trips back and forth for the small ferry to move the whole regiment. There was time to kill.

"Who fancies one last pot of beer to steady their sea-legs?" Morgan asked the officers standing nearby.

"Tempting though that sounds, I think I'll pass," replied Charles, to Morgan's surprise. "I need to stay with the troop and I'm keen to see the ship."

With some reluctance, the others came to the same decision. Morgan wandered off on his own, undeterred, leaving Private Gantz with instructions to wait at the pier for his return. He tipped a station porter a penny for directions to the nearest tavern, a place about four hundred yards down the road to the east.

CHAPTER THREE
THE WORLD'S END, TILBURY, ENGLAND
WEDNESDAY, 28TH JUNE 1865

The World's End was a spartan building. Whitewashed timber shielded its walls from the ravages of wind and rain and creeping decay. With the river only a stone's throw to the south and man-made swamp on two sides, the rotting armour was fighting a losing battle. The tavern stood alone near the heavy gun emplacement of Tilbury Fort, one of a number of such defences along the Thames that guarded London from seaborne French assault. In earlier times, when the threat of invasion came from Spain rather than France, Elizabeth I, the virgin queen, had graced it with her presence and delivered a rousing speech to her troops. Cromwell's forces occupied it during the Civil War, but desolate obscurity had become the fort's defining characteristic in the two centuries since then. It was no place for virgins, royal or otherwise.

A handsome pair of black geldings whinnied to a standstill behind Morgan as he approached the tavern door. They were drawing a carriage with an odd collection of bags and boxes strapped to the roof. Without waiting for the coachman, two female passengers stepped down. The taller one began issuing assertive requests about how the luggage needed careful handling. Morgan was intrigued. She was a winsome lass, he observed, with a soft Highland accent and dark red hair.

"Pardon me, ladies," he ventured with a courteous bow. "Lieutenant Farrell of the 16th Lancers. May I offer any assistance?"

The second woman turned around and studied him for a moment before answering with a disarming smile. "That's very kind of you, Lieutenant Farrell of the 16th Lancers, but I believe we have everything under control."

Both women appeared unorthodox in almost every regard. They were clearly ladies of some status, but were travelling without male escorts. In place of gowns bloated by crinolines, they wore straight, dark brown skirts and simple blouses that were flattering yet practical.

Beneath wide-brimmed hats, more suited to hunting than socialising, their hair was left unbound rather than disciplined by an army of pins.

It was the petite woman though, the one with the smile and provocative wit, who most captivated Morgan's curiosity. He thought she was probably about his own age and a little younger than her companion. Her hair was a lustrous black and tumbled to her shoulders in natural waves. She too had the gentle, melodic voice of a Highlander, and her eyes were pale blue. Not glamorous in the fashionable way, Morgan found her singularly beautiful.

"Very well, miss," Morgan replied, somewhat lost for words.

"The ladies may not feel the need of your help, squire, but I won't turn down a hand with this," the driver called from the roof as he struggled with a heavy-looking square box.

"Do take extra care with this one," the redhead repeated, reaching up to receive it.

Morgan rushed over and helped her lower the box to the ground. It wasn't heavy at all, so he presumed its contents must be fragile. "Might as well pass down a few of those others now I'm standing here," he offered. The luggage was soon unloaded and the coachman waved in gratitude as he wheeled the horses to the right and trotted away.

"Thank you, Mr Farrell. It seems you appeared at exactly the right moment after all. Forgive me if I sounded less than gracious."

"You're most welcome, miss. There's nothing to forgive, I assure you," he replied, removing his cap.

"Presumably you're a stray from the chaos we passed on the way here?"

"I suppose I am. The regiment is preparing to sail for India, miss."

"Then we're all to be seafarers for a while. But I'm forgetting myself. I'm Mrs Munro and this is Miss Steward."

"Mrs Munro? Oh, I see," said Morgan, disappointed. "Then apologies for my impoliteness, ma'am."

"Och, how could you possibly know one way or the other? No apology is necessary, really. To be perfectly honest, we prefer to avoid all those boring airs and graces whenever possible. Let's begin again simply as fellow travellers, shall we? My name is Sophia and this is Janet," she said, holding out her gloved hand for Morgan to shake.

"How very novel!" Morgan replied, astonished, but gladly taking her hand in his. "And I'm Morgan."

"Well, Morgan, perhaps you'll allow Janet and I to procure you an ale, by way of thanks for your gallant labour?"

"That's kind of you, but I couldn't possibly..."

"Och, of course you could," Sophia insisted before he could finish his sentence. She picked up one of the boxes and headed for the door, which she opened herself without waiting. Janet followed, carrying the precious square box. Morgan laughed to himself and grabbed another canvas-wrapped parcel from the pile, this one about four feet long.

A haphazard arrangement of worn tables and chairs littered the dark interior around a central fireplace. The aroma of stale beer, wood smoke, and roasting beef hung in the air between the low ceiling and the flagstone floor. There were only a handful of customers, all artillery men or dock workers, and they paid surprisingly little attention when two young women stepped inside followed by an officer of the cavalry.

Sophia rested the box on a table in one corner and invited Morgan to take a seat. She took off her gloves and hat, and ran a hand through her hair. "I just need a wee word with the landlord," she said as she turned towards the bar.

Morgan propped the strange parcel against the wall and waited for Janet to sit before occupying the chair across the table. He removed his gauntlets and loosened the neck of his tunic. Janet was smiling, as if at a private joke, as she placed her own hat and gloves on a chair.

"If I may say so, you look like a man with many a question on his mind," she said.

Morgan laughed. "Indeed I am, chief amongst them being why a young married lady and her servant would journey here, of all places, unaccompanied by her husband?"

"Society's unwritten rules about such things are rather tiresome, don't you find? First of all, I'm not a servant. Servitude goes against all Sophia's principles. Strictly speaking I'm her employee, but she treats me very much as an equal and a friend."

"My apologies. I meant no offence."

"That's quite all right. It's what people are conditioned to assume."

"Yes, I suppose they are. So is that why Sophia is speaking with the landlord, rather than you?"

"Either of us might have done so. She just happened to be first through the door. As for husbands, Sophia is a widow, and a very independent one at that."

"She certainly is," Morgan said, his earlier disappointment evaporating. "Very..."

"Progressive?" Janet offered.

"I was going to say liberated, but progressive, yes, that too. And as for yourself, Janet?"

"I was engaged once upon a time, but a fever took my fiancé before we could marry."

"Oh dear, I'm sorry to hear that."

"It was years ago, but thank you."

"There's something else I'm curious about," said Morgan. "Outside, Sophia said we were all going to be seafarers. What did she mean?"

Janet laughed and was about to reply when Sophia returned to the table. She was followed by George Farr, the landlord, carrying a tankard of ale and two glasses of wine.

"Mr Farr has been most helpful. Our room is ready when we are, Janet, and the rest of our luggage is being brought inside."

"No trouble at all, ma'am," said George, setting down the drinks and handing Sophia a key, before walking back to the bar.

"I was just putting Morgan's conscience at ease about not having to expect a pair of furious husbands to burst through the door," Janet explained with a mischievous glint.

Sophia Munro's laugh was as carefree and playful as her reply. "Aye, fear not Lieutenant Morgan Farrell of the 16th Lancers, your honour is quite safe with us."

Morgan laughed too and raised his pint. "I'll drink to that. *Sláinte!*"

"*Slàinte mhath!*" Sophia and Janet replied in unison, touching their glasses to Morgan's beer.

"So, about seafaring?" Morgan prompted.

"Aye," said Janet, "I'll let Sophia explain. Morgan was wondering what you meant about us all being seafarers."

"Well, like you, Janet and I are about to embark on our own wee voyage. I'm a photographer, you see. I've been commissioned to record the *Great Eastern*'s attempt to span the Atlantic with an under-sea telegraph cable."

In truth, both the telegraph company and the ship's captain had taken months of persuasion to allow the two women on the project. But Sophia didn't dwell on minor details.

"That's... that's really quite astounding. I didn't know women could be photographers," Morgan said, eliciting raised eyebrows from across the table. Realising too late that the clumsiness of his words had obscured his meaning, he made haste in trying to correct himself. "What I mean is... well, I just mean I've never heard of any female photographers."

It surprised Janet that Sophia was so forgiving in her response. "There are perhaps only a few of us. I'm of the firm opinion that women can be whatever they choose to be, though it's true to say we have far fewer opportunities than men. I'd like to think that will change in time."

"That's an interesting thought. Perhaps it will," Morgan pondered, though he couldn't imagine how. "Either way, I have the greatest admiration for what you're doing. Truly. And now I think I can guess what's in some of these boxes."

"Thank you. Aye, the camera itself is in that one," Sophia said, pointing at the fragile square box. "Under all that canvas you carried in is a tripod, and these boxes contain glass plates and other paraphernalia. It's a lot of equipment to lug around, but we usually manage quite well."

"I seem to recall reading something about the Atlantic cable in the press. Where are you sailing to?"

"A place called Heart's Content in Newfoundland, if all goes well. It's a mission of science of course, but I've no doubt we'll have a memorable adventure whatever happens."

"Goodness me, that's tremendous. I'm sure you will."

"I'm glad you think so," said Sophia. "What's the name of that sandbank again?" she asked Janet.

"The Nore."

"Aye, that's it," Sophia continued, turning back to Morgan. "The *Great Eastern* is anchored there, downstream in the estuary, and is due to depart any day now. We're staying here until we receive word to join her."

"You'll be sailing right past," said Janet.

"I'll keep a look-out."

"Now tell us about India. To what exotic location are you destined?" Sophia enquired with genuine interest.

"Well, I gather we'll reach Madras in a couple of months or so and then we'll travel inland to Bangalore. As you can probably imagine, we're all looking forward to discovering what the place is like."

"How wonderful. I'd like to visit India myself one day."

"Stranger things have happened," said Morgan.

The trio talked more about India and expectations of their respective journeys, inevitably soon returning to the subject of photography. Sophia was animated in explaining how much she admired the portrait work of Julia Margaret Cameron, which she and Janet had seen at an exhibition in London the year before. Morgan remembered that Pills Macbeth and Robert Maillard were keen amateurs and how the adjutant planned to photograph the pyramids en route through Egypt. Both women were openly envious about that. Morgan wanted to know more about where Sophia came from and how she was able to pursue such a fascinating career, indeed any kind of career at all, but the opportunity vanished when Private Gantz stormed in looking hot and flustered.

"There you are, sir," he said, saluting Morgan and looking at Janet's chest. "I had a devil of a job finding out where you'd gone. I'm sorry to intrude, but I'm afraid your presence is requested at the ferry."

In the privacy of his own thoughts, Morgan swore all the worst curses he knew. "Ah, hello Gantz," he said in a practiced even tone. "Thank you for finding me. I'll join you outside presently."

John Gantz saluted again, nodded politely to Sophia and Janet, and retreated back out into the sunshine.

"Thank you for the drink and your charming company. Time to go and do some soldiering, I'm afraid," said Morgan, before downing the last of the beer and pushing back his chair to stand up. "It's been an absolute pleasure meeting you both. You've given me much to think about. I do hope you have a safe and successful voyage to Canada."

"Thank you, and likewise. It's a rare treat to talk to a gentleman blessed with an open mind," Sophia smiled. "Our best wishes to you for India and your safe return."

"Aye, good luck to you," added Janet, extending her hand to shake.

"Despicable airs and graces, I know, but if you'll permit me..." Morgan said, bowing to kiss her hand instead.

"Of course," invited Sophia, offering her own as well.

As he held her outstretched fingers, Morgan promised himself he'd remember the softness of Sophia's skin against his lips and the delicate scent of her bergamot and lemon perfume. "I hope our paths will cross again," he said.

"I hope so too," she replied.

*   *   *

The S.S. *Golden Fleece* still hadn't moved by the evening of the following day.

Bureaucratic delays caused the troopship to miss the afternoon tide, and its passengers faced a second night of restless anticipation. Officers enjoyed the relative privacy and comfort of cabins off the saloon deck. Everyone else, crammed like cattle in the troop deck down at the waterline, shared the challenge of sleeping in hammocks. There was unanimous agreement that perseverance was needed to master the art.

Lieutenant Ker of the Royal Navy Reserve had been tasked with commanding the vessel to India. Shortly before four o'clock in the morning on Friday, 30th June, he gave the order to weigh anchor. The eager thumping of the ship's twin engines reverberated inside the iron hull. Deprived of sleep, tired bodies stirred into movement and climbed the companion stairs to the chill air above. Few wanted to miss the moment of departure.

There was no wind in the half-light of dawn and the first quarter of the moon still hung low in the sky over the city to the west. Smoke belched from the squat funnel just forward of the mainmast. The smell of burning coal helped to mask the stench of the Thames, which reeked of London's filth. A pair of gulls mewed to each other as they circled the bow and settled on the murky water.

Charles was leaning against the port rail near the foremast when a bleary-eyed Morgan found him.

"Any sleep?" Morgan yawned, pulling a blanket tighter around his shoulders and casting a glance at the building with whitewashed timber on the north bank. Lieutenants were allocated twin cabins and Charles and Morgan had agreed to share on the condition that Morgan took the top bunk.

"Not much," replied Charles. "Here, have some coffee to warm yourself up," he added, passing the steaming brew he'd brought up from the galley.

Morgan wrapped his hands around the tin cup. "Good man. Just what the doctor ordered."

"Not unless there's a wee dram in there," joked Alec Innes, overhearing their conversation.

"Good morning, doctor. Looks like this is it," said Charles.

"Aye, any moment. We've just slipped our moorings, so it's too late to change your minds now," said Alec, lighting his pipe. The surgeon spoke with his deep-set brown eyes as much as with words. He was of average height and lean build, with receding dark brown hair and a prominent nose. Above a bearded chin, a thick moustache cut past the corners of his mouth. It concealed a gentle smile and exaggerated his hard features, making him appear far sterner than he really was.

A sturdy tug was taking up the strain and all on board felt the initial jolt of its powerful tow. The mood on deck was subdued and thoughtful. Nobody cheered when the *Golden Fleece* slid away from the dock towards the main channel, its three masts bare of canvas. Gravesend's New Tavern Fort passed by on the starboard side just as the sun greeted the day above the Kent marshes.

Henry Wilkinson had begun a circuit of the deck to rally the subalterns – the junior officers – and the senior NCOs. Accompanied by Walter Bagenal and Bill Wauchope, he spoke to groups of them in turn. The three captains were shouldering responsibilities usually shared by seven. Henry wanted to re-assert their authority and begin the voyage with a spirit of optimism.

One of twelve siblings born to a Durham clergyman, Henry's star was in the ascendency. He was considered the regiment's most naturally gifted officer, albeit a notoriously vain one. He was the same age and height as Morgan, but there the comparison ended. He cut an unusual figure by any standard. The shape of his skull resembled a wide plateau, unassailable above the escarpment of a high forehead and the sharp ridge of his nose. Youthful features narrowed to the promontory of his chin. His chestnut brown hair and whiskers were in the de rigueur style and groomed with excessive care. But it was perhaps the arching eyebrows that left the strongest impression. They made it seem as if Captain Wilkinson viewed everyone with supercilious disdain.

The contrast with his colleagues couldn't have been starker. Shorter than Henry in stature and experience, and three years his junior at just twenty-four, Walter and Bill entertained less conspicuous ambitions and always appeared friendly and approachable. Unlike Henry, they came from wealthy, landed families and had never had to fight, either literally or figuratively, for attention, status, or their lives. They both deferred to Henry without question. Walter had been a captain for nearly two years and was the eldest Bagenal son from County Carlow's Dunleckney Manor in the south-east of Ireland. Tender-hearted and mild of manner, he had a riot of fair hair that was hard to miss. Stocky Bill Wauchope from Niddrie Marischal Castle on the east side of Edinburgh, on the other hand, had held the rank of captain only since April and was still acclimatising to its demands. To the amusement of some, and the imitation of others, he waxed the ends of his moustache into extravagant points. It was always easy to tell when Bill had something on his mind, because he'd twist the creations between finger and thumb.

When they made it round to Charles, Morgan and Alec, John Barker and Augustus Dobrée had already joined the conversation.

"Hello gentlemen. A fine morning to go for a little sail, wouldn't you agree?" Henry began.

"Morning," replied a sullen Morgan.

"Aye, a fine morning indeed," said Alec. "Next stop Madras."

"I imagine this must bring back memories for Surgeon Innes and yourself?" wondered Charles.

Alec and Henry exchanged a knowing glance. Before transferring to the cavalry, Captain Wilkinson was an infantry soldier and had fought in eight bloody battles in India during 1858. He was a strong leader who'd earned the unswerving trust of the men under his command.

"Inevitably so, Mr Agnew," he answered. "Leaving the shores of home to serve one's country is always a proud moment."

"Are there any special duties we should be carrying out, sir?" asked Augustus, eager as always to impress.

"I admire your enthusiasm Mr Dobrée, well done. As you'll soon discover, the novelty of a long sea journey is fleeting. Needless to say, discipline must be maintained. However, I'd like you all to devote particular attention to the morale of the men. The NCOs will have a vital role to play in that endeavour. It's important to remember that boredom and drunkenness make easy bedfellows. Do your best to guard against them both."

The four lieutenants acknowledged Wilkinson's request, which they took to be an order.

"I might add," said Alec. "If you haven't already, make sure you locate the sick berth in the stern so you know where to find it if needed."

"The stern, doctor?" asked John Barker, confident that Alec wasn't the kind of man who'd mock his ignorance.

"Sailors have their own peculiar names for things, much like the army does in its own way. The stern is the rear of the ship and the other end is the bow. Beams are sides, port is left, starboard is right, the heads are... well, you'll soon get the hang of it," Alec explained. "Anyhow, the sick berth. Other than the *Mal de Mer*, which only time and patience can remedy, even the slightest injury or complaint of sickness needs reporting at once."

"Ah, yes, good point. Thank you. Now, if you'll excuse us, gentlemen. We must get on," said Henry, turning on his heels to continue his motivating mission elsewhere. Bill followed him, but Walter took the time to shake each of them by the hand. "God's speed, gentlemen, God's speed."

The ship had reached the final bend in the Thames and was turning eastward towards the wide expanse of the estuary. It soon approached the mouth of the river and the North Sea, where the tug released the towlines and left the *Golden Fleece* to continue under its own steam.

Off the port beam, some distance to the north of their position, Morgan could make out a small fleet of craft anchored at the Nore. There were all shapes and sizes, and among them was a lightship that warned passing vessels about the lurking sandbank. The sight lifted his mood.

"You see that enormous one in the middle," he said to Charles, pointing at a four-funnelled steamship more than twice the size of the *Golden Fleece*. "That's the *Great Eastern*. It's going on a mission of science to Canada with a telegraph cable."

"How in heaven's name do you know that?" asked Charles.

Morgan smiled to himself. "You'd be surprised what a man can discover at The World's End."

CHAPTER FOUR
200 NAUTICAL MILES OFF THE PORTUGUESE COAST
SATURDAY, 8TH JULY 1865

"We therefore commit his body to the deep, to be turned into corruption," said Lieutenant Colonel White, reading from the Book of Common Prayer. *'Looking for the resurrection of the body, when the Sea shall give up her dead, and the life of the world to come, through our Lord Jesus Christ..."*

John Reynolds hadn't died a hero's death. There was no battle cry or daring charge, no enemy slain or victory won. It wasn't even disease that killed him. He simply had a weak heart.

The twenty-eight-year-old private had been walking to the galley when he dropped stone dead. That was at half past five in the afternoon. Now it was eight o'clock the next morning and his corpse was wrapped in sailcloth weighted with ballast. His comrades from Captain Wilkinson's troop stood shoulder to shoulder near the starboard rail with their heads bowed in mournful respect.

As Thomas White completed his solemn duty, and Trumpeter William Dolan began *The Last Post*, the mortal remains of John Reynolds made a dull splash in a calm sea. It would be many weeks before Mrs Reynolds and her three young children learned of their loss.

Tragedy was commonplace in the lives of everyone on board the *Golden Fleece*, but witnessing a funeral at sea was a new experience for most of them. The necessarily brief lapse of time between death and burial prompted quiet reflection on the fragile uncertainty of life. Home felt a long way away.

No matter where each soldier came from, watching the Cornish coast disappear beyond the horizon was a poignant moment they'd not soon forget. The seven days since then had been something of a baptism for those on their first voyage.

Officers dressed however they wished, as was their privilege, while the men of the regiment were ordered to wear 'sea kit' for the duration. Feet had to be left bare at all times, neckerchiefs were adopted, and white smocks replaced regular tunics. Never washed, they had to be whitened every day with pipe clay.

A summer storm in the English Channel had introduced people to the discomfort of a heavy swell and the salty hazards of being on deck in a high wind. A lucky handful found they were blessed with an enviable immunity to the *Mal de Mer*, Morgan Farrell and John Gantz among them. For the rest, seasickness brought nothing but misery for several days.

The regiment had the freedom of most of the ship, although the quarterdeck at the stern was strictly out of bounds. That was the exclusive domain of Lieutenant Ker and his officers. Navigation, steering, and the overall operation of the vessel were controlled from its vantage point.

In a simplistic way at least, the more observant cavalrymen soon learned how the steam engines and sails were employed in a cunning partnership. Lieutenant Ker would order sails to be set or lowered depending on wind speed, direction, and untold other factors only a sailor could comprehend. When the wind was judged favourable, relying more on the sails conserved the coal supply. At other times, when the wind was too light or too gusting, the burden of propulsion would fall on the engines. Charles noticed that Solomon Smith had an instinctive aptitude for understanding these things.

Crossing the Celtic Sea, porpoises were sighted near the starboard bow. William Bovill suggested they'd make good sport, but the school had swum to safety before a carbine could be found. Sergeant Major Burrell's young daughter gave everyone cause for concern the next day when she began complaining of a sore throat and rash. Alec Innes diagnosed scarlet fever and the girl was quarantined in the sick berth until she recovered.

Other than the coarse food and living at close quarters in a confined space that never stayed still, the most notable thing about being at sea was the change of routine. None felt that more than the men of the ranks. They were accustomed to being worked hard from five o'clock in the morning to nine in the evening, breaking only for three square meals a day. The absence of stable duty, riding school, and kit drill had been a welcome relief at first, but idle hands were already beginning to breed restless minds.

The ship's bell dictated the tempo of life on board with metronomic regularity, and the passengers were learning to anticipate its sound every half an hour. Eight chimes signalled the end of a four-hour watch for the crew, and one chime the first half hour of the next. At eight o'clock in the morning eight bells also meant the children's breakfast was being served, with adults following at two bells. Lunch coincided with the next eight bells at noon, whilst dinner was at the six o'clock four bells for children and six bells for adults. Officers were seated in the dining saloon, while occupants of the troop deck had to collect their ration from the galley and return below. Morning prayers were held at four bells every day for those who felt the need or obligation, and there were two Divine Services on Sundays. Lights were extinguished in the saloon at the four bells of ten o'clock each evening and the officer of the watch would call for all lights out at six bells. All of which left upwards of fifteen hours every day to fill with recreation. As Captain Wilkinson had predicted, the novelty didn't last long.

After dinner on the evening of the funeral, a rigged barque called *Look Out* pulled alongside. Its captain spoke to Lieutenant Ker and explained they were eighteen days out from Liverpool. Glad of the diversion, people rushed on deck to see what was happening. They exchanged greetings with the *Look Out*'s crew and offered three cheers when the merchant ship pulled away to continue on its course towards Brazil.

Morgan missed all the excitement. He was down in the troop deck, which was almost deserted, where Corporal Cook was talking to him about his ferrets. Nobody was entirely sure how he'd managed to smuggle them aboard, but they provided no end of entertainment for the children. Cook was in the process of explaining how Mrs Ferret was about to make Mr Ferret a proud father, when an argument broke out further down the deck. Fists were flying by the time Morgan got there. Without a second thought, he launched into the mêlée and separated the two combatants.

Morgan was neither as tall as Charles nor as robustly built as most of the sergeant majors, but he had a powerful physical presence and a reputation for fearlessness. For all his blarney and casual attitude, everyone knew Lieutenant Farrell was a conscientious officer they could depend on. They also knew he wasn't a man to pick a fight with.

"All right now, gentlemen, that's quite enough of that," Morgan said with calm authority, his arms outstretched to keep them apart.

The older and wiser of the two privates immediately took a step back and lowered his guard. His adversary, however, was still seeing red. He sprang forward and tried to get past Morgan to land another punch. Morgan saw it coming and pushed him back.

"I recommend you consider your next course of action very carefully, private, before this goes any further."

He didn't. Instead, he swung at Morgan's head with a flailing fist. Morgan dodged the blow with ease and delivered a swift, bone-breaking head butt in reply. The private crumpled to his knees, clutching his bloodied nose.

"That's called the Kiss o' Kerry where I come from. Now get up before I lose my temper with you."

The man was submissive and did as he was told.

"Both of you, stand here," Morgan instructed, pulling the two men within striking distance of each other. "You know that brawling is a punishable offence?"

"Yes, sir. I'm sorry, sir," the older man replied.

"And that striking an officer earns you a flogging?" he asked the other soldier, who remained silent.

"Well, here's the thing, gentlemen. We've all had a pretty rough time of it this past week, and there's a long way to go in this tub before we get to where we're going. So I don't give a galloping shite what petty nonsense started all this, it stops here. And make damn sure it doesn't happen again. I won't be making a report to the major. I trust you'll not be in any rush to tell him either. Do we understand each other?"

"Yes, sir, thank you."

"Aye, understood. Sorry, sir."

"Good. Now shake hands and find Corporal Cook some grog. He's celebrating."

Walter Bagenal hurried into the saloon a little after six bells the next morning. "Hello gentlemen," he said, taking a seat amongst a group of his fellow officers. "The major's just been telling me some splendid news."

"Good morning, Walter. What might that be then?" asked Henry Wilkinson, looking up from his book.

"We're in sight of Madras already?" scoffed Thomas Dynon.

"Not quite that splendid I'm afraid," Walter laughed. "The ship's purser, Mr Mills, spoke to Hugh before Divine Service earlier. It turns out the *Golden Fleece* has a small printing press aboard. Apparently on previous voyages it's been used to publish contributions from passengers in the form of a weekly gazette. The purser was wondering if we'd like to continue the tradition. What do you all think? Might be an entertaining way to keep minds occupied. Good for morale and all that."

"That sounds like a marvellous idea," said Henry with enthusiasm. "Who would run the press?"

"I gather we would. Once the purser had shown us how to use the thing, that is. The major thought a few volunteer editors would likely be needed to sort the wheat from the chaff, and to do the typesetting and so forth."

"Perhaps an officer, an NCO, and a private joining forces to represent the spectrum of views?" suggested Charles.

"Rather egalitarian but, yes, that's a sensible proposal. They could each come from a different troop as well," said Henry, thinking aloud.

"If nobody minds, I'd be happy to do it," offered Augustus.

"Good for you," said Henry, sincerely.

"I'm sure you'll do a fine job," said Walter. "Private Parnham from my lads would be an appropriate choice, I think. He's a most eloquent and witty fellow."

"Which just leaves an NCO to find," said Augustus.

"I'll track down Bill and explain what we're planning. I'm sure he'll think of someone," confirmed Walter.

By mid-afternoon a box had appeared outside the galley to collect submissions from willing contributors. Charles was reading the notice beside it when Alec Innes walked past, filling his pipe with tobacco. Charles called after him as he climbed the companion stairs. "May I join you for a smoke, Alec?"

"By all means, Charles. I'd welcome the company."

There was a freshening breeze up on the weather deck. Some of the junior officers were playing a game of quoits. Others lounged in deckchairs, basking in the heat beneath a cloudless sky.

"How's the Burrell girl faring?" Charles asked as he lit his cigar, wasting a few matches in the attempt.

"Showing signs of improvement, thankfully. She's a brave wee lass."

"That's good to hear. Terrible shame about Private Reynolds though. I hadn't got to know him, but from what I've been told he was a good soldier."

"Aye, that he was, and a popular one. Our first casualty, poor lad. I dare say he won't be our last."

"Some sort of heart complaint, I understand?"

"A ruptured left ventricle to be precise. I performed the post mortem, you see. He was in the peak of health in every other respect. Just one of those things, sadly."

"Yes, very sad indeed," agreed Charles, staring out across the emptiness of the ocean. "I've been meaning to ask, by the way, why do you permit the men to call you Doctor Alec?"

Alec laughed. "Too informal for your taste, Charles?"

"Heavens, no, it's not that. I'm just curious. It is rather unconventional after all."

"Aye, I suppose it is. Well, as you probably know, my given name is Charles Alexander."

Charles nodded.

"My father is called Alexander, and so was his father. Up in Moray, and no doubt elsewhere in Scotland, Alec is a common abbreviation for Alexander. My father has always been known as Alec, and since I was a *bairn* he's liked to call me that too."

"Oh, I see. But what of Doctor Alec?"

Alec looked wistful and he puffed on his pipe a few times before answering. "Not long after I arrived in the Crimea in '55, I was attending an artillery gunner – no more than a boy really – who'd taken shrapnel in the chest. He was delirious in his agony and there was nothing I could do to save him. Just before he expired, he took my hand and called me Doctor Alec. That was all he said. I'll never know why, though I've often wondered if he was remembering an Alexander from his own family. I don't know, but the name followed me around after that."

"I imagine a soldier might feel more at ease if he's on familiar terms with the man trying to relieve his suffering. That can't be a bad thing," Charles thought aloud.

"I'd like to think you're right," said Alec.

The second week of the voyage passed more easily than the first. The *Golden Fleece* made swift progress southward, averaging around a hundred and eighty miles a day thanks to the trade winds. The temperature rose perceptibly, and Pills Macbeth issued a warning to all passengers about the dangers of sunstroke. By the middle of July the complexion of the ocean had changed from deep blue to green, the trade winds were lost, and the ship was back under steam again.

On 15th July, just as four bells rang out for the children's dinner, a great commotion on deck sent almost everyone rushing topside. Twenty days out from Sierra Leone on her way home to Falmouth, the merchant ship *Emma Goodwin* was steering to come alongside. As soon as lines were secured, her captain and a few of his senior officers came on board offering to carry mail back to England. Lieutenant Ker invited them to stay a while and share a meal, which gave the whole ship's company time to gather letters and write new ones. When the visitors were ready to depart a few hours later, the regimental band played the national anthem, followed by *Home, Sweet Home,* to rapturous applause from the decks of both vessels.

The next day was Hugh Burnell's twenty-ninth birthday and was marked by the publication of *The Golden Fleece Gazette.* One hundred copies of the inaugural, double-sided edition were distributed throughout the ship.

Not surprisingly, the editors hadn't had much to work with for the first issue. There was a memorial to Private Reynolds, the amusing story of an unnamed NCO having a mishap with a hammock, some verse, and an announcement about the birth of three ferrets. It achieved the goal of sparking imaginations, even if the content was on the sparse side, and that was all that really mattered. Setting the satirical tone for future issues, the introduction by the editors read:

In commencing a public journal like the Golden Fleece Gazette it is necessary to announce our political creed and to put before our readers the programme by which we hope to gain their confidences and ensure our success. We beg distinctly to state that we shall not pledge ourselves to either party, conservative or liberal. We hold ourselves radically free to think and act for the good of our subscribers, be they patrician or plebeian.

We certainly have not so extensive a field as the other great leading journals of the day to glean matters from. Our Political horizon is summed up in the mornings and evenings. 'How's her head', those few words do not probably at present engage so much attention as they will when sailing through the Bay of Bengal. Besides the want of subject matter we have had many difficulties to contend against with our printing machinery, having had no place to set it up.

We hope, having engaged the fertile brains of most, and surely the good wishes of all, with God's blessing and a little management, to rise superior to every obstacle and yet electrify the world with the wit and talent of the Golden Fleece.

The programme we propose to submit is to set before our readers a resume of the weeks transactions under the head of our log. The space for foreign interlude will be devoted to passing ships. There will be a column for original communication and in writing them we would strongly urge upon our contributors to look always on the sunny side! Ample space will be provided for births and marriages. In our answers to correspondence, we beg distinctly to state that we will not adjudicate between man and wife as to who is to wear the breeches, nor shall we give any reasons why crinolines have been discarded on board.

By the end of the following day the box by the galley was overflowing with anonymous envelopes.

Cornet Bovill had the sport he'd been hoping for on the afternoon of 22nd July. A large school of porpoise raced the ship, leaping from the waves and diving beneath the keel to cross from port to starboard and back to port again. Their playful company lasted nearly half an hour, which was time enough for William to locate a carbine and start shooting from the bow. His aim found its mark at the fourth attempt and he was very pleased with himself.

Early that evening, under sail and with a steady breeze, the *Golden Fleece* entered the South Atlantic.

There were no initiations into Neptune's Dominion, because every member of the ship's crew had crossed the equatorial line before. The passengers who'd hoped to watch the traditional ceremony were disappointed. However, the sailors had just been paid and that was cause enough for celebration.

"Burying the Dead Horse can be a rather entertaining nautical custom. I do hope you'll enjoy it," said Lieutenant Ker. He'd granted all the officers special permission to join him on the quarterdeck to observe the spectacle. It was a great privilege, and one which the old campaigners of the regiment particularly appreciated. Men like Quarter Master Fuller and Riding Master Brown stood a little taller than usual, their chests swelling with pride at the honour. The other passengers filled the length of the weather deck. All except for Mrs Eacleston and Mrs Tapper, whose pregnancies were both nearing term.

Nobody quite knew what to expect, but a loud cheer went up when a procession of crew appeared from the starboard companion stairway. The leading men were carrying a crude effigy of a horse. It was fashioned from sailcloth stuffed with straw, and had a flowing mane and tail of teased manila rope. They picked their way through the crowd towards the quarterdeck, accompanied by a merry jig from a fife and drum.

"Allow me to explain," continued Lieutenant Ker, raising his voice to be heard. "A crew is said to work for nothing during the first month of a voyage, having drawn a month's pay in advance and spent it all ashore before sailing. The handsome creature you see paraded before you represents that period of unpaid work. The crew now being in receipt of a second month's pay means their proverbial horse is dead. Hence its burial."

Clapping and laughter and the stomping of feet followed the horse to the capstan, where it was hoisted aloft. One of the sailors climbed up next to it. He addressed the whole assembly with witty verse to invoke fair winds and health and happiness for all. Then the horse was ceremoniously thrown overboard and an extra ration of rum was issued to all hands.

It was long after midnight before the revelry stopped, and everyone staggered to their cabins and swinging hammocks for the first time in the southern hemisphere.

Charles was drifting into an afternoon snooze when Morgan burst through their cabin door.

"Wakey-wakey, old boy," said Morgan, imitating an upper class English accent with aplomb. He handed Charles a copy of the latest *Golden Fleece Gazette*.

Charles swung his legs out from his bunk. "Scant chance of sleep with friends like you," he said.

"Still limp and staggery after last night, are we?"

"Possibly," Charles replied, glancing at the paper. "Ah, the second issue. Rather more substantial than the first, isn't it. Anything good?"

"There's a clever acrostic, and the answers to correspondence are amusing. Listen to this one," Morgan began. "*To D, K, A and M. The shape of your feet and ankles is a point upon which we decline to give an opinion. For shame, gentlemen never take notice of such things.*"

Charles laughed as he scanned the pages to catch up. "Very good. Oh and this one to Mrs O'Callaghan. *Pimples on the face may be removed with a spoke shave and freckles may be mollified by a diligent use of sand paper.*"

"And we now have a regimental library," said Morgan.

"Really?"

"I thought it was a joke at first, but apparently it's true. Well, in a way. Folk can take along books they've finished with and exchange them for ones they haven't read."

"What a fizzing idea," said Charles. "I have a few to swap, myself. Wait, what's this? Is this your handiwork?"

"Is what my handiwork?" Morgan queried as he climbed up to his bunk.

"This poem, entitled *The Lancers*?" Charles read it aloud.

I am a Lancer bold and gay,
As any Lancer of the day.
For to every noted place I go,
And end, always keep it up you know.

With the fair sex of Ipswich town,
I've had my fair share of renown.
For I was the Lion of the day,
The reason why I will not say.

I've a fast friend who keeps a yacht,
Another who a drag has got.
To Whitehart Feeds at Harwich, we,
Are often going on a spree.

I'm an handsome dog as you must know,
And always welcome where I go.
And at the opera oft I'm seen,
Beside, o' such a crinoline.

I'm off to India you must know,
But a few more words before I go.
I hope your pleasure will never cease,
As I sail away in the Golden Fleece.

Our ship has sailed, I join again,
The Sixteenth Lancers Royal train.
And come to India you will see,
No jovial fellows on the spree.

"Ha! I hadn't spotted that. And sadly I can claim no credit," said Morgan, wondering who might've written it. "The bit about a fast friend with a yacht – that's likely your predecessor they're referring to."

"Mr Bingham?"

"The very same. He was always off sailing in some regatta or other. The 16th had the better of the bargain when he exchanged with you."

"Decent of you to say so. Thank you."

They both read on for a while and then a thought crossed Morgan's mind. "I'm wondering if I owe you an apology?"

"Why, what have you done?"

"Do you recall on the train from Colchester when you asked me about not having anyone there to say farewell?"

"Yes. You seemed a trifle irked," Charles remembered.

"Not really, no, but I may have been short with you. It just wasn't the time or the place to explain."

"Don't worry your head about it."

"I was an only child, you see, and my parents were killed when I was a lad," Morgan elaborated. "Hence the absence of teary-eyed family at the station."

"Goodness, I'm sorry. When you say *killed?*"

"They were on a train to Dublin, coming to visit me at Belvedere College just before my 18th birthday. Along the way, there was an accident at a place called Straffan. You might have read about it at the time. This was October '53. Anyway, they perished in the wreckage along with sixteen others."

"How thoroughly awful. I believe I do remember hearing about it. I can't imagine what a difficult time it must've been for you."

"I've had better birthdays, I must admit."

"You know, I don't think you ever told me exactly where you're from – other than Kerry, that is."

"Have I not? Oh, well that's easily remedied. It's a place called *Dromquinna.*"

"Drom-what?"

"Quinna. Dromquinna House. A magical place it is too, overlooking Kenmare Bay. I never went back there after the accident, though perhaps one day I will. It is my inheritance after all."

"Sounds delightful. So it turns out I'm sharing a cabin with landed gentry? Who'd have thought it?" joked Charles. He was happy his friend had a home he could choose to return to, although it reminded him about the loss of Cairncastle Lodge. He thought of Harriet and how she might be adjusting to her new life in Cheltenham.

"Hard to believe, eh?" Morgan laughed and returned to the *Gazette*, though he couldn't concentrate on the words. He was thinking back to happier times. Going to the monthly livestock fairs in Kenmare with his father, a respected solicitor, and learning the value of wit and favours owed. Skimming stones on the glowing ebb tide before sunset. His mother's infectious laugh. The rugged beauty of the mountains. One day, he thought to himself. One day.

The sea was dead calm on the 27th July and the *Golden Fleece* was under full steam to make headway. The smooth passage was suiting Private Cooper. He'd fallen down a hatchway two days before and broken his arm. Without the benefit of a breeze, however, the tropical heat had become intolerable for most people. It was hardly more comfortable below decks, especially in the fetid, stale air in the bowels of the ship. Sweating bodies, unwashed clothes, tobacco smoke, children crying, sergeants barking, couples grunting, and tempers fraying all conspired with the ever-present noise of the engines to make the troop deck a miserable venue for a birth. But that's where Mrs Eacleston was when labour began late that afternoon, and that's where Alec Innes concluded she needed to stay. Things were progressing at a pace and the Farrier Sergeant's wife was in no condition, or mood, to be moved to the sick berth.

The weather had changed by the evening, with a squall blowing in from the west. It came as a welcome relief for those seeking fresh air and many chose to escape to the open deck for a while. A little after eight o'clock, Alec Innes joined them.

"What's everyone looking at?" he asked as he walked up to Charles, who was standing in a group at the port rail.

"Our first whale," Charles replied over his shoulder.

"An auspicious omen, perhaps?" said Alec, peering over the side to see the tail of the majestic creature arch and dive.

"Auspicious? How so, doctor?" wondered John Barker.

"Mrs Eacleston has just been safely delivered of a daughter and I'm happy to report they're both in fine fettle."

"That's fizzing news," said Charles.

"And it evens the tally," noted Paymaster Dynon.

Three days and a shark sighting later, another squall rolled in during the morning. It was much more powerful than the last and tore away some sail. The wind settled down to only a stiff breeze by lunchtime, bringing with it noticeably cooler temperatures. Most of the passengers remained below deck during the afternoon. Charles was halfway through the second chapter of *Ivanhoe* by Walter Scott. Morgan was winning at pontoon. Private Daley carried his five-year-old daughter, Mary, to the sick berth. Pills Macbeth diagnosed a case of pneumonia.

Thomas Brown, the riding master, enjoyed being outside whatever the weather. Every day since leaving Gravesend, he'd spent as much time as he could strolling back and forth along the length of the ship.

"Pardon me, sailor," Thomas said to one of the crew near the quarterdeck. "What kind of bird is that?"

"Bird, sir?" questioned the young man, squinting into the sun.

"Over yonder," replied Thomas, pointing to a distinctive, black and white bird. It was gliding fifty yards off the starboard beam and looked about the same size as a seagull.

"Oh, aye, sir. Well spotted. That be a Cape Pigeon. See its white belly and speckled wings, sir?"

"Thank you, lad," said Thomas. "So does that mean we're nearing the Cape itself?"

"Oh no, sir, I don't think so."

Lieutenant Ker could hear the conversation. "Always a joy to see wildlife appear as if from nowhere, is it not, Mr Brown?"

"Most certainly is, sir. She's a beauty, too."

"That species is also called the Cape Petrel. They're quite common in the South Atlantic, though not usually this far north."

"You know your birds then, lieutenant?"

"Only as passing interest really. One learns these things along the way. You were asking about the Cape of Good Hope, I believe?"

"I was, sir. Does the presence of the bird suggest we're close?"

"Not quite yet, I'm afraid. Our current position is very much closer to the coast of Brazil than it is to Africa. Perhaps another couple of weeks or so, God willing."

CHAPTER FIVE
SOMEWHERE IN THE NORTH ATLANTIC
WEDNESDAY, 2nd AUGUST 1865

Sophia Munro woke with a peculiar, uncertain sense that something was about to change. Unable to quite put her finger on it, she mentioned the instinct to Janet over their early morning coffee in the grand saloon.

"Neither of us has been sleeping as well as we might like, what with the clank and beat of the machinery and so forth," Janet observed.

"True – it never stops! But, no, I don't think it's that."

"Perhaps you were being haunted by the disembodied spirit of the poor plate-riveter the crew are always talking about?" Janet teased.

Staff-Commander Moriarty was coming in from the weather deck and overheard them. In imitation of the riveter's hammer, he rapped three times in quick succession on the table behind Sophia.

"Och, away with you!" Sophia laughed, turning to see who it was. "Ah, good morning Henry. Don't tell me *you* believe the ghost story?"

"Good morning to you, ladies. We seafaring types tend to maintain a prudent respect for the supernatural," he replied with a wry smile. "One is tempted to make jest of such a *riveting* story, but that might be judged poor taste."

"And that would never do," Sophia replied, frowning in mock chastisement.

Ordinarily a captain in Her Majesty's Royal Navy, Henry Moriarty, like the rest of the ship's company, was on secondment for the voyage to Newfoundland. Now in his fiftieth year, his distinguished career had included service on HMS *Agamemnon* during previous attempts to bridge the Atlantic with cable in 1857 and 1858. His superlative navigation skills were vital and he provided regular updates about the ship's position, distance travelled and expected arrival timing.

"I notice the wind has picked up. How are we getting along?" enquired Janet for the journal she was keeping.

"Indeed it has – rising from the west earlier and now from more to the north. Despite the high sea, I'm happy to say we're continuing to make a steady seven knots."

"I do find it remarkable how impervious the ship seems to be to the temperament of the ocean," noted Sophia.

"A wee island of terrestrial stability," said Janet, gaining agreement from Henry and a raised eyebrow of admiration from Sophia.

Sophia was about to offer Henry coffee when the kindly chief officer rushed in looking agitated.

"Mr Moriarty, sir, your presence is required. There's been another fault."

"Thank you, Mr Halpin, I'll be right along. Forgive me, ladies," Henry said, already moving towards the door. "Here we go again!" he added over his shoulder.

Sophia and Janet had spent several days at The World's End tavern before being invited to board the S.S. *Great Eastern*. They'd known in advance that the timing of its departure was uncertain. The technical preparation and complexity of the whole operation was staggering. Nevertheless, they hadn't expected to have to wait a whole fortnight. It was noon on Saturday, 15th July, when they finally got underway.

Their time at the Nore as captives of Brunel's mammoth creation had been useful in many ways though. It provided ample opportunity to photograph the ship when it was stationary and to ingratiate themselves with the crew. Sophia particularly appreciated getting to know Henry Moriarty and hearing his stories about the appalling West African slave trade. The seamen, cable gangs, and the fifteen electricians under the leadership of Mr Charles de Sauty, had all been flattered to join group portraits. There were several young gentlemen with an interest in engineering and science who'd been accommodated with a passage on board as well. One appeared to have taken quite a shine to Janet, though he was too bashful, or preoccupied, to venture into conversation.

Many of the original crew berths and passenger saloons had been sacrificed to make room for three cavernous tanks. Between them they held twenty-three hundred miles of coiled marine-grade telegraph cable. Located fore, aft and amidships, they were a little over twenty feet deep. At fifty-one feet in diameter, the forward tank was the smallest and carried nearly seven hundred miles of cable. The other two were about seven feet broader and were loaded with just under nine hundred miles each. Demonstrating the scale of all this was a challenge from a photographic point of view and Janet volunteered to stand in some of the scenes as a human yardstick.

The crucial paying-out machinery, on the starboard side at the stern, was the dominion of Mr Canning and Mr Clifford, ably assisted by Mr Temple, Mr London, and a corps of eight other engineers. Sophia hoped her compositions would do justice to its ingenuity, and to the striking resemblance of Samuel Canning to Napoleon III. The cable was supported on its journey from the hold by a wrought-iron trough with jockey wheels at intervals. This led to an arrangement of six large wheels, each with a V-shaped groove around the circumference, which in turn rolled the cable to a final V-wheel overhanging the stern. Friction wheels controlled from a master tiller wheel modulated the speed of rotation. Between the third and fourth V-wheels was the dynamometer, which by its rise and fall indicated the strain on the cable. It was said that the brakeman, responsible for constant adjustment of the tiller in response to the dynamometer, had the most skilled and important task of all the engineering staff.

Despite his original misgivings about having women on board, Captain James Anderson proved to be generous and accommodating. He was a fellow Scot, in his early forties, and was genuinely interested in how pictures of the expedition could benefit the telegraph company and perhaps his career. A handsome, well-built man standing six feet tall, with auburn whiskers below a profusion of brown hair, his eyes were blue and he was blessed with the most pleasant of smiles.

As well as a berth and private bathroom each for Sophia and Janet, the captain allocated a third berth for all their equipment. He granted them the complete freedom of the ship on the condition they neither obstructed anyone's work nor put themselves in peril. He even obtained special permission for them to enter the electricians' testing room, a darkened chamber situated between the grand saloon and the bridge, and extended an open invitation to visit the latter whenever they wished. They did so at least once every day. Located forward of the middle of the weather deck, and flanked by the two gargantuan paddle wheels, the captain's position had a commanding view fore and aft.

Aside from everything to do with the cable project, the S.S. *Great Eastern* was a mine of photographic possibilities in her own right. At six hundred and ninety-two feet long, with four slender funnels and six masts, she held the current record for being the world's largest ship. Designed as a liner, she'd been capable of travelling non-stop from Britain to Australia with four thousand passengers.

The landward end of the cable had been hauled ashore from S.S. *Caroline* at Foilhummerum Bay on Valentia Island on Saturday, 22nd July. Valentia was the most westerly point on Ireland's Kerry coastline with a telegraph station, and the elaborate enterprise attracted crowds of onlookers. Twenty-six miles of cable was run out to sea and buoyed by half past ten that evening.

The *Great Eastern* had been harboured in the sanctuary of Bantry Bay, a little further south past Kenmare Bay, and rendezvoused with the *Caroline* just after seven o'clock on the morning of the 23rd. Most of that day was spent splicing the landward and *Great Eastern* ends of the cable together and testing that everything was working correctly. At quarter-past seven in the evening, the *Great Eastern* set off on a north-west-by-west course flanked by its escort vessels, HMS *Terrible* and HMS *Sphinx*. The paying-out machinery came to life, wheels whirled, and out had spun the black line of cable in a graceful curve that extended two hundred feet astern. The nine days since then had been nothing if not capricious.

The westward advance was generally rapid with the *Great Eastern* making light work of even the most turbulent conditions. So much so, in fact, that HMS *Sphinx* couldn't keep pace and had to drop back on 26th July. HMS *Terrible* fared better and maintained its watchful position two miles off the port beam, ready to divert any ship that might inadvertently stray across the path of the cable.

However, the monotony of progress was punctuated by drama with alarming frequency. The electricians operated a strict testing schedule, which continued day and night. When the connection to shore was lost they'd order the 'picking-up' routine, which was as laborious as it was hazardous. It involved retrieving submerged cable, sometimes many miles of it, testing section by section to find the source of the fault, cutting, re-splicing, and testing again. Finding and fixing a particularly devilish 'dead earth' fault on 29th July saw Captain Anderson endure twenty-six hours on duty without a break.

"One feels so powerless, because one can do so little to govern events," he'd commented to Sophia and Janet during one of their visits.

Two days later, the same day the aft tank released its last mile of cable and supply was switched to the fore tank, sabotage was detected. At least the electricians inspecting a section of faulty cable believed it to be. A demonstration of villainous design, they called it. One of the cable gangs that worked in the tanks was suspected, though nothing could be proven, and a motive was far from obvious. Nevertheless, erring on the side of caution, Captain Anderson drew up a roster of volunteers to act as tank watchmen.

Janet recorded all these events in her journal, along with notes about how she and Sophia occupied their time. They took brisk walks around the deck, usually several times a day. In part they simply enjoyed the fresh air and the chance to talk without being overheard. As had long been their habit, they shared even their most private hopes and desires with one another. The exercise also allowed them to judge if the activity, light, and conditions lent themselves to more camera work. They allowed their easy curiosity to take them on explorations of every recess of the ship, including the lightless crypts discovered beneath the cable tanks. Sometimes they'd hear the echoes of a piano from a neighbouring saloon. Occasionally the melody would be entwined with notes from a violin.

The labour of the engineers during picking-up had been worth photographing the first couple of times. There was fascination in all the scientific apparatus used during testing too. But there was little to be gained by repetition.

"Shall we follow him?" Janet wondered, as Henry Moriarty disappeared from view.

"How's our stock of glass plates?" evaded Sophia.

"Beginning to run low."

"Then let's enjoy a leisurely breakfast and catch up with all the commotion later on."

It was a few minutes past noon when they ventured topside and headed towards the nest of machinery at the stern.

Samuel Canning, the chief engineer, called across to them as they approached. His usually friendly tone was brusque. "Now's not a good time, ladies. Keep your distance, if you please."

Sophia and Janet retreated to huddle by the companion stairs and get the measure of what was happening. Another picking-up routine was in progress, but something was evidently amiss. Looking forward along the deck, they could just make out engineers and crew engaged in frantic activity.

"Ah, hello again," said Henry Moriarty, breathing hard as hurried up the stairs from below deck. The women returned his greeting and asked about what was going on.

"We're picking-up a loop from the bow," he explained, "but the cable has snagged on a hawse-pipe and now it's chafing against the hull. The ship is drifting to port, creating a terrific oblique strain on the line. Apologies – I must get to the captain with a report of our position."

Just as he finished his sentence, they all had to steady themselves in reaction to a sudden, uncharacteristic heave of the *Great Eastern* to port. Samuel Canning cursed and the brakeman fought the tiller control in vain. The cable ripped from the V-wheels and snapped with a pitiful twang – the untethered end vanishing beneath the waves.

None of those who witnessed the tragedy said a word. They simply gazed at the tortured strands of the parted cable in despair and disbelief. Tears came to Sophia's eyes. She gripped Janet's arm. Henry removed his cap and looked down at the notebook he'd been clutching. "We'll not feel much interested now in knowing how far we are from Heart's Content," he said quietly to himself.

Janet was the first to regain some composure. "I think we'd better fetch the camera," she whispered in Sophia's ear.

In the days that followed, repeated attempts were made to retrieve the broken cable with a pair of five-armed anchors acting as grapnels. None were successful, which left Captain Anderson with no alternative but to abandon the expedition one thousand and sixty-two miles from Valentia and six hundred and six miles from their destination. He turned the *Great Eastern* around and steered a course back to Ireland. The transatlantic telegraph would have to wait.

*   *   *

The south-east trade winds propelled the *Golden Fleece* towards the Cape of Good Hope with mixed fortunes.

On Tuesday, 1st August, the saloon deck hosted an evening of songs and skits under the musical direction of Corporal Thornhill. The Sable Minstrels had blackened their faces with burnt cork and featured Private Griffin as the interlocutor, Private Sielkford as Bones, Private Allan on concertina, and privates Deare and Short playing other roles. Everyone in the audience agreed the caricatured performances were jolly entertaining and worthy of reprise. Some even praised the plantation melodies, as Corporal Thornhill called them, for their undoubted educational value.

Joy and grief fought over the hearts of the passengers during the week that followed. Mary Daley lost her five-day struggle against pneumonia, Sergeant Major Tapper's wife gave birth to a healthy son, and Sergeant Major Chester's child became the last fatality of the voyage. Grief had won the battle and it cast a lingering shadow over the whole ship.

With the intention of expressing his condolences, Major Hugh Burnell went to visit the troop deck early the next morning. The mission ended prematurely when he missed his footing on a hatchway and fell a considerable height. A prompt examination by Alec Innes confirmed that only his pride had been injured.

Most of the officers had brought tinned food and other luxuries, and Walter thought a hamper of treats might be an appropriate way to help the families in mourning, as a token gesture of support if nothing else. He asked all the officers to contribute, which most of them did without complaint. The tins included corned beef, pea soup, apples, pears, sardines, and an assortment of vegetables. Tobacco and even some toffee were donated as well. The collection was divided in half and placed in a couple of pillowcases, hamper baskets being in short supply. They found their anonymous way to the hammocks of Mrs Daley and Mrs Chester, and it was later reported that they'd been received with much gratitude.

The first vessel seen for nearly a month appeared off the starboard bow on the morning of 12th August. The Dutch merchant was called

Grondwet, meaning *Constitution*, and was fifty-one days into a journey to Indonesia. It pulled alongside for a parley with Lieutenant Ker during the afternoon. After it left, morale on board began to improve again. Perhaps it was just a coincidence, or the reminder that they weren't alone in the world after weeks of isolation, but it was almost as if the noble *Grondwet* had snared the passengers' grief and towed its shadow far out to sea.

Two days later the *Golden Fleece* rounded the southern tip of Africa and entered the waters of the Indian Ocean with a west wind in her sails. Squally weather followed, building into a frightening storm so ferocious that the port lifeboat was carried away during the night of the 19th.

After breakfast on Saturday, 26th August, Lieutenant Ker ordered the ship thoroughly scraped and cleaned. All the passengers naturally took this as a sign that their destination was near at hand. In reality Madras was still more than twenty-seven hundred miles away, which the lieutenant knew all too well, but his announcement buoyed people's spirits with renewed optimism. Recognising the benefits of the men having something new to do, Lieutenant Colonel White issued a supporting order that called for ten volunteers from each troop to assist the ship's crew. Once the work was complete, attention fell on the baggage. Several hours went by with people sorting through their belongings and polishing buttons, buckles, spurs, and sabres.

Sunday brought a strong headwind that slowed the ship's progress and made time on the open deck a chore. The morning's Divine Service was held in the troop deck as a consequence, and the smoke-filled saloon remained fully occupied by officers for most of the day.

"How many times have I read this now?" John Barker pondered aloud. The fifth issue of the *Golden Fleece Gazette* had been old news for a fortnight.

"Too many," said Charles. "Was that the one speculating about what might be going on in the world?"

"It was. Let me see... the start of the stalking season and the harvest. The fate deserved by the rebel Jefferson Davies in America. The *Great Eastern* taking its cable across the Atlantic..."

"I wonder how they're getting on?" said Morgan, more to himself than the others.

"Who?" asked John.

"The *Great Eastern*. Never mind."

"Not long now, gentlemen," Alec Innes assured them. "We'll soon be refreshing our general knowledge with newspapers bought with rupees and letters delivered by turbaned *coolies*."

"I can't wait. Especially for letters!" said John. Everyone agreed with that sentiment.

"Strange to think that we're already on the other side of the world," mused Charles, "and yet the colonel, Robert, Carrin and the others probably haven't even left yet."

"I bet they'll have a more interesting journey than we are," said Morgan.

"Shorter and more varied, certainly, but not necessarily any easier," pointed out Alec.

"Do you and Pills expect to have your work cut out when we get to Bangalore? With the hospital and such, I mean," asked John.

"Aye, no doubt, but we'll take things as we find them. You can all help us by staying well."

"We'll do our best. Do you have any advice?"

"Well don't go drinking dirty water, no matter how thirsty you may be. That's essential. And if – or more likely, when – you seek out the company of the local women, remember you always get what you pay for," Alec replied, his expressive eyes full of concern and humour.

"So, we should stick with ale, hard liquor, and the most expensive whores we can find?" suggested Morgan, only half joking.

"Aye, that's about right," Alec laughed. "I mean it though. Water and women. You should make sure the ranks know too. I'll be telling them myself often enough, but you gentlemen can lead by good example."

The conversation drifted on and John Barker went to talk to some of the junior officers. Then Charles remembered something he'd been curious about for a while. "Alec, how did you come to be an army surgeon in the first place?"

Alec was filling his pipe. "It hadn't been my intention," he began. "Growing up listening to my father's stories about fighting at Waterloo, I'd imagined being an infantry soldier like he was."

"Your father was at Waterloo?" Charles interrupted with reverence.

"Aye, he was, and very proud of it he is too. Anyhow, by the time I finished my studies at King's College in Aberdeen, I'd become fascinated with the sciences. Instead of going to the infantry, I decided to train to be a doctor. It was '55 by the time I was qualified. By then of course the Crimean campaign was in desperate need of medical staff. So the army ended up with me after all."

"And very glad it is to have you," responded Morgan, sincerity obvious in his tone.

"Indeed," agreed Charles. "I'm inclined to think you have the hardest job in the regiment."

Alec was touched by their words, and took his time lighting his pipe. Combustion achieved, he had a question of his own. "Are you both looking forward to India?"

"Apart from the water and the women," Morgan joked.

"Very much so, of course," said Charles. "I'm sure we'll get used to it soon enough, but to begin with it'll all be new and fascinating – what with the customs of the people, strange food, seeing elephants and tigers and so on."

"I'm looking forward to meeting a camel. Although I've heard they spit a great deal," said Morgan. "I should imagine India will come with its fair share of challenges, one way or another," he added.

"Aye, there'll be plenty of those," said Alec.

"I hope we don't have to wait too long to see some real action though," Charles admitted.

"Impatient for a slice of the glory pie, Charles?" asked Morgan. He already knew what his friend would say.

"Unashamedly so. Aren't we all eager to test our mettle?"

"I don't feel the need to prove anything, to myself or anyone else. I'm certainly hoping we'll have some grand adventures though. If it takes a good ol' glorious war to get them, that's fine with me."

"Don't be too impatient for war, gentleman," interjected Alec.

"Why do you say that?" Charles asked.

"Well, you talk of glory, but I can assure you there's precious little of it around when the intestines of some poor laddie are spilling out into the mud, or when a fellow's leg is being amputated with a blunt saw. It's a grim business. If you don't believe me, just ask the likes of James Fuller, Thomas Brown, Henry Wilkinson or Maurice Fitzgerald – and watch the look in their eyes when you do."

Charles thought of his brother, William, and how he might have suffered before he died. "But you believe in doing one's duty – for the Empire and so forth?"

"My first duty is to my patients, not to Her Majesty and her ministers. Should you ever find yourselves in a front line, the only real duty you'll feel you owe is to each other and the men around you. Don't mistake me, I believe in the Empire as much as any man here, and there's certainly honour and purpose in giving service to one's countrymen. But as for glory, you'd do yourselves a kindness by seeing that for what it really is."

Charles and Morgan looked at Alec with blank expressions.

"I mean that it's an illusion," Alec went on. "A sleight of hand that distracts the eye from the real purpose of fighting wars and subjugating colonies."

"Which is?" prompted Charles, leaning forward in his seat.

"Ultimately, to create more wealth and power for an elite few. War and conquest are expensive ventures after all, and somebody somewhere has to finance and profit by them. It all boils down to controlling trade and natural resources. That's not to say we don't all benefit from the table scraps, because we surely do. I just think that if a man is going to throw himself into harm's way, he should understand why he's really doing it. And that has nothing to do with glory."

"I've never thought about it like that before," said Charles, suddenly feeling rather naïve.

"Nor I," Morgan concurred. "So, are you saying the Empire exists only for the money that can be made from it?"

"Aye, that's exactly what I'm saying. India is the prime example. It's rich in profitable commodities like cotton, spice, tea, and of course opium, and it's the gateway to the east. Opium alone earns Britain a Queen's ransom, because we're the only ones who can sell it to the Chinese. The role of the army is to protect all those assets from dangers within and without. We don't want the Indians upsetting the party, like they nearly did in '57, and there's always the threat of the Tsar deciding he wants to take India for himself."

"That's not really likely though, is it?" asked Morgan.

"Who can say, but don't forget it's only three months ago that Tashkent was being overrun by Cossacks."

Alec believed very strongly in everything he was saying, though he feared he might have said too much. He was thankful that Thomas Brown's arrival interrupted the conversation.

"Afternoon," he said, blowing into his hands to warm them after another bracing walk up top. "This sounds like a rather serious debate. What are you gentlemen talking about?"

"Dirty water, dirty women, and the avarice of empire," said Morgan, shuffling a deck of cards.

CHAPTER SIX
MADRAS, INDIA
SATURDAY, 9TH SEPTEMBER 1865

After seventy-two precarious days on board, all of a sudden the *Golden Fleece* felt like the safest place everyone could possibly be. It was as if leaving the familiarity of its decks meant plunging into the unknown towards certain doom.

In the dark of yesterday evening, when the crew dropped anchor three quarters of a mile from the coast and Trumpeter William Dolan sounded *Dismiss*, the passengers' first vivid taste of Madras had been the mosaic of scents carried on the offshore wind. It beguiled their imaginations with spices and the richness of the earth.

Since Madras possessed no harbour, and without a pilot to guide him, all Lieutenant Ker's experience had been brought to bear on navigating between the other vessels clustered in the open sea haven known as the Madras Roads. He was thankful only three nights had passed since the last full moon.

Now at half past six in the morning, soldiers crowded the port rail to feast anxious eyes on an unfolding drama. The sun was just emerging from the horizon behind them and lavished Madras with a russet-ochre hue. Boats launched from the beach were pitching over the distant breakers. The sight of their struggle stoked the coals of collective trepidation.

The flotilla of small craft covered the distance to the *Golden Fleece* in less than quarter of an hour. They jostled about the hull, embraced in its long shadow, and vied for position at the foot of the accommodation ladder. There were about thirty high-sided rowing boats, all of them painted white and many with colourful decoration, each with a steering oarsman and a crew of between a dozen and twenty. They were strong, lean men, and without exception wore white cotton loincloths and voluminous crimson turbans. Having ferried countless Europeans to and from ships in the roads before, they showed little interest in the waving caps and shouted greetings from the deck above them. They were impatient to get on with the job and get paid. Other ships would need their services today and there was fishing to be done if they wanted to feed their families.

"They're called *masulah* boats," Lieutenant Ker was explaining to some of the officers. "Observe the flat-bottomed design, gentlemen, and how the lack of bracing endows suppleness upon the hull. The natives build them that way for this very purpose."

"For carrying passengers?" asked John Barker.

"To run the breaking waves and land on the beach. The surf can be as high as ten feet here, sometimes even higher."

"Oh, I see!"

Augustus was pointing at one nearby. "Those coolies appear to be bailing!" he said. "That doesn't bode well."

"If you'll permit me, Mr Dobrée, the boatmen are called *lascars* rather than coolies. Every masulah has a couple of men dedicated to the bailing task. Fear not, I assure you it's perfectly normal." Augustus thanked the lieutenant for setting him straight, but looked far from reassured.

Morgan and Charles had been taking it in turns to watch the approaching boats through a telescope borrowed from the ship's boatswain. Now Morgan trained it on a man beginning to climb the steps of the accommodation ladder. To Morgan's unaccustomed eye, the individual's attire suggested he was neither a lascar nor a general labourer. "Who's that smartly dressed fellow?" he asked Lieutenant Ker, who peered over the side to look.

"Ah, yes. He's a *sepoy*, a soldier of the native Indian army. Carrying a dispatch for your commanding officer, I'll wager."

The sepoy was followed on board by members of the boat crews bringing bread, fruit, and eggs, which they traded for items of regimental sea kit.

"I think I might go and find out," Morgan replied. He handed the telescope back to Charles and set off down the deck.

Charles turned the lens shoreward. An imposing curtain wall dominated his view. From a protruding bastion almost directly opposite the ship's anchorage, the structure ran parallel with the beach for the best part of two miles to Charles's left. It was hard to judge scale from so far away, but he guessed it might be twenty feet high. More bastions and a gatehouse were just visible in the farthest reaches of the wall. Charles could make out rooftops, the steeple of a church, and an unmistakable Union Jack whipping on a flagstaff that nearly matched the spire in height. Beyond the town, verdant hills lay inland to the west.

"Seen all you need to, sir?" asked the boatswain, eager for the return of his telescope.

"Yes, thank you. You're most kind," said Charles, handing back the instrument. "Are you familiar with Madras?"

"Been here many times, sir, aye."

"I assume that's Fort St. George down there in the distance?"

"Aye, sir, it is."

"Then tell me, what's protected by the rest of the wall – this whole section ahead of us here?"

"Black Town, sir. That's what they calls the native warren where the bazaar is. Rough old place, sir. Filthy as sin."

"I see. And the railway station?"

"On the north side of Black Town, just outside the wall there," said the boatswain, pointing off to their right. Charles thanked the sailor again and wished him a safe onward journey.

"A dispatch for Mr White indeed. Something to do with the railway, apparently," Morgan confirmed when he returned. "Thomas is ordering the regiment be divided for reasons of practical necessity. Captain Wilkinson will lead the left wing to Bangalore at six this evening and then the right wing will follow on Monday morning."

Augustus was quick to ask the obvious question. "Which troops are to be in the left wing?"

"Henry's, Bill's and Walter's, along with the quarter master and the baggage. So you and John better get a move on – you'll be among the first. Pass the word as you go."

"Did you discover anything about where the rest of us are going in the meantime?" asked Charles once Augustus and John had hurried off.

"We're to have the undoubted pleasure of a couple of nights at the fort."

"Time enough to explore then."

Charles and Morgan found their respective troop sergeant majors and explained how things were being organised. The NCOs would take care of putting the ranks in order, and Solomon Smith and John Gantz could be relied on to fetch their possessions, which left the officers free to return to spectating from the port rail. Charles lit a cigar. Only one more remained of those he'd purchased in London. He wondered how palatable the tobacco sold locally would be.

For the sake of efficiency, a few days previously Lieutenant Ker had briefed Thomas White and Hugh Burnell about the way the transfer from ship to shore would work. The details were passed down the chain of command so that nobody was left in any doubt about what to expect. Nevertheless, what sounded only vaguely hazardous in theory looked potentially suicidal in practice.

With Henry Wilkinson leading from the front, soldiers were queuing down the accommodation ladder and doing their best to retain some dignity as they clambered into the waiting boats. The masulahs seemed perilously unstable and rocked from side to side with aggressive zeal. At around thirty feet long and ten feet across, they could each carry at least twenty passengers. The cavalrymen were wearing their forage caps and scarlet dress tunics, and many had to cut their boots to make them fit their now swollen feet. Officers donned their pith helmets, and the regimental wives were in their finest crinolined dresses and dainty bonnets. Mrs Eacleston and Mrs Tapper swaddled their newborn infants close to their chests and understandably looked quite petrified. The older children held hands with protective parents and tried to put on their best brave faces. The moment one boat was fully loaded and rowing away it was replaced by another at the bottom of the ladder. The whole process was clumsy, chaotic, and often darkly comical, but a ragged line of masulahs soon began to stretch towards the beach, waved and cheered away by those still on board.

"Can you swim?" Morgan asked.

"No," replied Charles.

"Me neither."

After depositing the regiment's left wing on dry land, the masulah fleet was back again within the hour. Quarter Master Fuller was already prepared. He supervised the loading of baggage in his usual calm and methodical manner, employing the ship's cargo nets and cranes to lower trunks and crates over the side. More manageable items were simply carried down the steps by hand. It was a laborious task and only when it was complete to his satisfaction did he and his staff venture into the boats themselves.

The sun was high on its arc by the time empty masulahs were flocking to the *Golden Fleece* on their third visit. NCOs immediately took charge of disembarking the men and families in the four troops that made up the right wing, while Lieutenant Ker invited the remaining officers to the quarterdeck for a farewell toast. Thomas White expressed his sincere thanks for the crew's generosity and seamanship, the lieutenant wished the regiment success in its posting, rum was downed, formal salutes were exchanged and there was much shaking of hands. When all else was done and the last boat was ready to depart, Lieutenant Colonel White considered it his duty to be the final man to descend the accommodation ladder.

The masulah was no respecter of rank. Charles and Morgan shuffled sideways on the low bench they were squatting on to make room for Thomas as he climbed in. Hunched in a cramped space ankle-deep in seawater, it was even more demeaning and uncomfortable than expected. Above their heads, seated on planks that rested between the beams, the rowing crew faced the steering oarsman. He stood on a platform at the stern and dictated the rate of stroke with a call and response chant. Every roll and pitch of the boat threw passengers together, against the rough timbers of the leaking hull, or cursing to their hands and knees in the sloshing bilge. All they could do was try to hold on, hope for the best, and listen to the crashing surf grow louder with every drive of the oars. As they approached its thundering crescendo the boat seemed to stall momentarily before succumbing to the inexorable power of a cresting wave and surging forward in a fearful rush. The wife of one of the sergeants shrieked as the bow plummeted and the stern soared, but her terror was mercifully brief. The masulah levelled off and glided to an almost casual halt in the shallows at the edge of the tide. Not one person on board wanted to go back and do that again.

Battered and briny, and exhilarated by the triumph of their survival, the passengers hauled themselves over the side and took their first stumbling steps on Indian sand. The lascars received no word of thanks from anyone, although a few, Charles and Morgan amongst them, did acknowledge the part the steering oarsman had played in their deliverance with a nod or a smile or a raised hand. He returned the gestures, but was evidently unmoved.

How unsteady they all were on their legs after ten weeks at sea was a source of amusement for some and embarrassment for many.

Staggering like drunkards was a disconcerting experience when sober. They trudged up the slope of the beach to where their comrades were waiting in a ragged parade formed either side of an arched gateway. Alec Innes confirmed that no serious injuries had been sustained during the landing. He was being kept busy administering aid to those who needed it for scrapes and sprains. All along the line as he went about his task, grateful eyes were looking out to the roads and the sleek lines of the ship that had carried them halfway around the world.

A portly Englishman in an ill-fitting suit strutted through the open gate from Black Town. He introduced himself to Thomas White as the Master Attendant in charge of all things connected with shipping in and out of Madras. Superficial courtesies of greeting were followed by an explanation of how the regiment's left wing had already cleared off the beach and was making its way to the railway station.

"If you'd be so kind," the man said, "to similarly vacate the area and get your men to the fort without delay, it would be appreciated."

Such apparent indifference to the arrival of the regiment's commanding officer didn't endear the Master Attendant to Thomas or any of the other officers close enough to hear, but the desire for shade and refreshment overcame their impulse to put him in his place. They listened to his simple directions and were pleased to learn that a dozen sepoys would be providing an escort.

Wheeling left through the gate, the detachment marched down a broad dirt road for a thousand yards. After the Master Attendant's office, they passed a boatyard and a substantial warehouse with four loading stages piled high with sacks and boxes. The craftsmen and labourers were all too engaged in their work to care about being stared at. The function of the ramshackle buildings that lined the rest of the street was uncertain, but more impressive structures rose behind them.

"I hadn't expected such fine architecture," Charles commented to Morgan.

"Or for it to be so white. The place hardly lives up to its name," Morgan replied. "This damp heat is intolerable though, don't you think?" he added, wiping the streaming sweat from his face.

"Let's hope Bangalore is more agreeable."

The sea wall robbed them of the mitigating breeze that was now all too conspicuous by its absence. Despite how well the voyage had acclimatised everyone to the tropics, the torment of humidity, hanging acrid smoke, reeking excrement and the ubiquitous predatory flies came as a debilitating and most unwelcome surprise. As did the relentless persistence of the begging children who ambushed from alleyways with outstretched hands and over-practiced patter. "*Baksheesh, sahib!* No father, no mother, no sister, no brother. Every day never coming," they parroted, bounding from one person to the next and tugging at tunics and dresses. Their efforts were entirely in vain, not least because the regiment had yet to be issued with any local currency, and caused great distress amongst the women. More than one NCO had to remind his men that striking the natives was frowned upon.

A cacophony of trade hustled their attention away from the disappointed beggars as they neared the end of the road. Open ground could be seen up ahead and beyond it the stout walls of the fort. The onslaught of noise was coming from the great China Bazaar to the right of the junction. Thomas White signalled a halt so the officers could satisfy their curiosity, even if only from a distance for now. The dense crowd moving between the stalls made it hard to tell how far the street extended. Hugh Burnell guessed three hundred yards. Charles reckoned it was more like four hundred. He was looking forward to finding out.

Before moving on, Thomas wanted to know about the obelisk on the corner. It was about fifteen feet tall and rendered in the same glimmering white plaster as many of the buildings. He asked one of the sepoys what it represented. The soldier understood the question and knew the answer well enough. They'd reached the liminal southern edge of Black Town. The cleared ground bordered by the market was an uncompromising no man's land, three hundred yards across. Originally conceived for its defensive value, it kept the Indians and mercantile nationalities a comfortable distance apart from the governing British population in the fort. The sepoy's competent grasp of English had factored in him being chosen for escort duty, but his vocabulary was no match for his eagerness to explain settlement divisions. He ushered Thomas closer to the structure and showed him the bronze plaque set into the east side of its base. It read: *Boundary of the Esplanade 1ˢᵗ January 1773*

"The esplanade, sahib," he said, pointing at the open ground. Then he turned to face the bazaar and pointed again with a counting motion. "Twelve more, sahib."

Thomas wasn't quite sure what the sepoy meant at first, but when he looked again he realised there were identical obelisks at regular intervals all along the street. "Thank you, my good man. I quite understand," he said, before bringing Hugh, Charles and Morgan up to speed and ordering the march to continue.

The column crossed the esplanade and entered the relic of East India Company rule through its forbidding Middle Gate. Ahead of them, flanked by a retinue of clerks, a man of military bearing dressed in expensive civilian clothes was waiting to greet the regiment in person. He raised his white cloth top hat once Thomas and the other officers were standing before him.

"A very good afternoon to you, gentlemen," he began. "It is my great pleasure to welcome you to White Town, as we like to call our little corner of civilization here in the fort. My name is Sir William Denison, Governor of Madras."

Thomas tucked his pith helmet under one arm, pushed sweaty strawberry-blonde curls from his forehead, and bowed respectfully. "Lieutenant Colonel Thomas White, at your humble service, Sir William."

Before his knighthood and a career serving the Crown as governor of some of its far-flung colonies, Sir William had held the rank of captain in the Royal Engineers. He was tall and broad chested, with receded grey hair, and an expression in his blue eyes that projected a certain conviction of moral character. If judged by his youthful complexion alone, nobody would have guessed that he was now in his early sixties. He stepped forward and shook Thomas's hand with firm enthusiasm.

"I'm delighted to make your acquaintance, colonel. I dare say you were expecting to be met by the army's new commander-in-chief, or at least a representative from his senior staff, but I'm afraid Sir John Le Marchant is away up-country this weekend, so you'll have to make do with me in his stead."

"We had no expectations one way or the other, Sir William, I assure you. On behalf of the 16th Lancers, please accept my grateful thanks for your most gracious reception," said Thomas. Then turning in Hugh's direction, he added, "May I present Major Hugh Burnell."

"Welcome Major," said Sir William. "I trust you and your men are still hale and hearty after your long voyage?"

"Thank you, sir. Yes, all fighting fit and ready to do our duty," Hugh replied, stiffly.

"Excellent, excellent. I'm very glad to hear it."

Charles and Morgan were presented as well, each receiving the same courtesy of a handshake and interested enquiry. Then, with proper protocol satisfied, Sir William was eager to move on to matters of a practical nature.

"I'm given to understand, Colonel White, that your stay here will be rather brief?"

"Indeed so, sir, yes. Half the regiment is making its way to Bangalore this evening, and we're to follow them on the first available train on Monday morning."

"Ah well, time enough to get your land-legs back and enjoy our Christian hospitality. But first you'll no doubt be anxious to get your men accommodated and in order. The sepoys will lead the way to the barracks," he said, gesturing vaguely to his left, "where there's ample room and the cooks have been forewarned to expect a ravenous influx. Of course, you and your officers will be my guests at Admiralty House."

"You're most kind, Sir William, thank you," Thomas replied.

The curtain wall of the original fortress, about a hundred yards square with bastions at each corner, occupied the centre of White Town and dominated the view at the end of the wide street. Sir William directed the group's attention towards it.

"The old fort now houses the government offices and provides residencies for many of our civil servants. To begin to give you your bearings, gentlemen, the steeple you may observe behind it belongs to St. Mary's Church and immediately beyond that you'll find Admiralty House, which I'm blessed to call home. May I suggest you join me there in an hour? I'd like to show you around and hear something of England and your journey before we dine this evening. Would that be agreeable?"

"Certainly, sir. That would suit us very well. We shall look forward to it," said Thomas, happy to indulge the ennobled administrator's desire to ease their arrival.

"Excellent, excellent. Well then I'll leave you to get your men settled in."

The presence of a permanent garrison meant that Sir William's idea of ample room was either ill-informed or wildly optimistic, but everyone made the best of it and NCOs were quick to establish a semblance of organisation and discipline. The barracks were adjacent to the arsenal on the west side of the fort, and sported *verandahs* on all three floors. Many of the regimental wives and children took refuge beneath their shade.

The governor was as good as his word and devoted more than two hours of the late afternoon to giving the officers a personal tour of not only his grand residence, but almost the whole of White Town. They were rightly impressed by the magnificent architecture of its public buildings, the handsome private houses, and the breezy panorama on offer from the cannon embrasures. As they walked, their guide needed no invitation to volunteer his opinions about the state of affairs in England, why the Indian natives couldn't be trusted, and how his irrigation and town improvement projects were under-appreciated.

The Cooum River swept below the western section of the outer wall before emptying into the sea about a thousand yards to the south. Further upstream, it forked to create a large island that was easily accessed from the West Gate. Sir William took pride in describing how successive generations of the White Town community had tamed the island with hedges, groves and landscaped flower gardens. He omitted to mention how much of the actual labour they took credit for.

"Do you suppose he'll run out of steam soon?" Morgan whispered to Charles. "Fascinating though all this is, I'm parched and my stomach thinks my throat's been cut."

"Same here. I suspect we're about to get the *pièce de résistance*."

The group was approaching the base of the gargantuan flagstaff that Charles had spied from the *Golden Fleece* before they disembarked. It was braced in position by elaborate rigging more substantial than on any ship.

"And this, gentlemen, is of course our mighty flagpole," said Sir William. "Its teak reaches a hundred and fifty feet towards the heavens, which I'm reliably informed makes it the tallest in all of India – if not the world."

"Quite astonishing," Thomas acknowledged on their collective behalf. "And the flag is uncommonly large as well."

"Perhaps forty feet across, lest anyone approaching these shores be in any doubt about who governs here."

"No chance of that," said Morgan more audibly than he intended, earning an amused frown from Thomas and a stifled laugh from Charles.

"We're most grateful to you for giving up your time this afternoon, Sir William. It has been an education," said Thomas, hoping to prompt an end to the tour.

"Oh it really is my pleasure, but perhaps I've got a little carried away. I'm sure you must all be feeling fatigued and in need of refreshment?"

"Your thoughtfulness is appreciated, sir," said Thomas, diplomatically. "Our first day ashore has been as exerting as it has been memorable."

Returning to the revitalizing cool of his room at Admiralty House, Charles was pleased to discover that Private Smith had been as diligent as ever in anticipating his needs. A clean shirt was laid out on the bed, and beside it his wash kit and clothes brush. There was a box of *cheroots* as well. Charles wondered how on earth his bâtman had procured them. It was probably best not to know, but he would thank Solomon for his kindness later.

There was an hour and a half to kill before his presence would be expected at dinner and Charles planned to make good use of the gift of solitude. He took off his uniform and brushed the dirt from it as best he could, lit one of the slender cheroots, and sipped the tea he'd been brought by a maid. It did little to quench his thirst. Then he bathed before writing in his journal and penning a brief letter to Harriet. A third and a fourth cup of tea. Another cheroot. He was already acquiring a taste for their coarse character and unfamiliar sweet aroma.

Closing his eyes and listening to the distant sound of breakers as he sank back into the luxurious comfort of the bed, Charles savoured what he knew would be a rare and fleeting moment of tranquillity.

Sunday was tiresome and the regiment was restless. Having become so accustomed to hammocks on board ship, the men of the ranks and their families had slept fitfully in the barrack cots. Most woke with sore heads and aching bellies. The latrines would be busy all day.

Sir William's determination to monopolise the officers' time was becoming rather a bore, though no one could argue with his unwavering generosity. During the lavish meal he'd hosted the previous evening, he insisted on them joining him for an early breakfast and of course for lunch and a farewell dinner. It was also made clear, in the gentlest of terms by his charming wife, Lina, that he'd be disappointed if the whole regiment didn't attend the ten o'clock Divine Service at St. Mary's Church.

Thomas had forbidden anyone from leaving the fort, which had come as a bitter disappointment to all those excited about visiting the bazaar, and he needed to keep the men occupied. The interminably long church service took care of the morning, and an improvised parade and drill practice passed some time in the afternoon until monsoon rain forced everyone back inside. Sir William had warned the officers to expect it – after a dry day yesterday, it was a God-given inevitability today, he'd told them – but the suddenness of its arrival and the force of its deluge took everyone by surprise.

Spirits were high at seven o'clock on Monday morning as the wives and children were helped into requisitioned bullock carts. Hardly anyone complained about the soaring temperature or how their clothes were already soaked with sweat. Ahead of them, led by the now familiar sepoy escort, a column of officers and men preceded out of the fort through the Middle Gate. Everyone was glad to be leaving and impatient to reach their destination. The cart drivers twisted the tails of their beasts to make them keep pace with the march.

Crossing the esplanade and not pausing at the bazaar, they continued north to the end of Middle Gate Street, through another gateway, and onward along a street lined with haphazard shanty dwellings. A few of the juvenile beggars tried their luck again without success, but for the most part the local population paid little attention to the British passing by. The same could not be said in reverse. The convoluted way the Indian men wrapped themselves in cotton robes was a source of fascination, and people were astonished by the variety of rich colours worn by the women.

Within the hour the 16th Lancers' right wing was forming up outside the grandiose entrance to Royapuram railway station. Painted crimson, with white Corinthian columns and pilasters either side of a tall archway, the building stood in vivid contrast to the neighbouring poverty and dilapidation.

Order was maintained as they filed through to the bustling platform, but there it became obvious the waiting train wasn't for their exclusive use. Discipline disintegrated into noisy chaos as people elbowed their way aboard. When a conscientious corporal attempted to intervene, he was saved from certain humiliation by the wisdom of his sergeant major. "Let 'em go, lad," he said. "Know when to pick your battles."

The locomotive getting up to steam at the left-hand end of the platform was much larger than its English counterparts. It reminded Charles and Morgan, who were standing back to watch all the pushing and shoving with amusement, of illustrations they'd seen of engines in America. Indian railways operated on broad gauge tracks, which meant the lines were set further apart than at home. The carriages were wider to match, though they were divided into compartments in much the same fashion. The distinction between First and Second Class appeared to be one of name only, all the carriages having identical wooden benches and the Indian passengers evidently being accustomed to sitting wherever they liked. Some even took precarious rooftop positions, which Charles and Morgan admired very much for its audacity and daring.

Once the initial rush subsided, the two lieutenants strolled towards the furthest carriages and found a couple of empty spaces in the last but one.

"*Déjà vu*. After you this time," said Charles, opening the compartment door for Morgan.

They squeezed past two girls aged perhaps five and seven, the young couple who were presumably their parents, and an elderly man with red-stained teeth and a caged chicken on his lap. Stowing pith helmets in the netting above their heads, Morgan took the vacant place by the window and Charles sat down beside him. Opposite them was a gentleman reading the *Times of India*.

It was torturously stuffy in the compartment, and Morgan looked forward to a breeze coming through the window grill once they were moving. He eyed the front page of the man's newspaper. There was a headline about a famous British explorer visiting Bombay.

"A rather remarkable chap," Morgan commented.

The owner of the newspaper seemed to be in his early fifties and wore a smart brown suit, with waistcoat, wing-collar shirt, and black tie. He had a noble, almost hawk-like face with a high forehead leading to a bald pate. What hair he had was thick and prematurely white, as were his burnside beard and moustache. He looked up to see Morgan pointing at the paper.

"Doctor Livingstone? Why yes, quite so. Recruiting staff for another civilising expedition apparently. He hopes to discuss the African slave trade problem with the government while he's about it. Arrived yesterday," the man replied. He had a deep, clear voice and there was a hint of northern Irish in his colonial accent. "My name's Doctor John Orr. It's a pleasure to meet you both, gentlemen," he said, leaning forward to shake hands.

"Lieutenant Morgan Farrell, and this is Lieutenant Charles Agnew."

"You're with the new batch of cavalry griffins, I take it?"

"Griffins, doctor?" queried Charles.

"John, please. My apologies. Griffins are what we call newcomers to India during their first year in the country – when they're still acclimatising to the culture and language, the customs, and so forth."

"Oh, I see. I don't think we've heard that expression before. And after the first year? What are we griffins called then?"

"Home sick," John replied with a wry smile.

Charles and Morgan laughed, relieved to have happened upon someone who would make a fine travelling companion.

"To answer your question, John," Charles continued, "guilty as charged. We're with the 16th Lancers, heading to our new barracks in Bangalore."

"Splendid. I can tell you there's much excitement about the arrival of such an esteemed regiment. The place could do with livening up a bit."

"We'll do our best not to disappoint," Charles promised.

"You reside in the cantonment yourself, I take it?" asked Morgan.

"For many years, yes. I hope you'll learn to enjoy it as much as I do."

The old man with the chicken stood up and spat a dark red wad of something out the window. He sat back down and cleared his throat.

"Seems to be a common habit around here," Charles commented in John's direction.

"And a thoroughly revolting one, if you ask me," said Morgan. "The station platform is covered in red stains from all the spitting."

"The colour comes from the betel nut, gentlemen, the chewing of which is popular across the country," John explained. "It's said to have stimulating medicinal properties, and is often used as a mild narcotic, but it's never swallowed and does terrible damage to the teeth."

"I think I'll stick to tobacco," said Charles.

"A much healthier choice," John replied. "Stains aside, has Madras been to your liking?"

Morgan and Charles described some of their other first impressions and recounted the governor's hospitality in the fort.

"It sounds as if your transition from ship to shore has been a gentle one. I'm glad to hear it," said John. "I've met Sir William on a few occasions, though I don't pretend to know the man. And I'm not convinced I'd wish to. In person and by reputation, I'm afraid to say he's always struck me as being a humourless Bible-thumper of the worst sort, and I find his views about race and the rights of the local people most troubling."

"He's vocal about them, that's for sure," agreed Morgan.

"Perhaps a new broom will sweep change for the better?" Charles suggested. "He told us, at great length, about his plans to retire to England next year."

"Perhaps so, yes, perhaps so," John mused.

Carriage doors were being slammed shut all along the train and somewhere out of sight there was a commotion of shouting.

"Tell me, John, would we be correct to assume that you're an army doctor?" Morgan was wondering.

"For my sins. Started as a surgeon of course, but that was nearly thirty years ago. I'm the deputy inspector general of hospitals these days."

"Goodness me," said Charles. "Are there many of them? Hospitals, that is."

"There are five in the cantonment alone, one of which is dedicated to the cavalry," John replied. "I'd recommend you try to keep out of it if you can."

"We certainly hope to," said Morgan. "One of our own doctors, a fine fellow by the name of Innes, has been telling us to be cautious about the water supply – amongst other things."

"That's very sound advice. If I might offer further guidance... Always insist that your coffee or tea is made piping hot, and at the old barracks only drink water that's been drawn from the *dhobies'* well."

"Thank you. We'll pass that along," said Morgan. "One thing though, if you'll forgive a griffin-like question, what's a *dhoby?*"

"That's quite all right, it takes a while to learn these things. A dhoby is an Indian who provides a laundry service. There are a number of water sources, but only their well is reliably clear and unpolluted. Not that you'll need to worry about that where you're going."

"Useful to know, thank you," said Charles. He was about to ask what John meant by his last sentence, but was interrupted by the carriage lurching forward. The late departing train for Bangalore was clanking away from the platform.

"Off we go, at last," said Morgan. "Somebody said it takes eight hours. Is that about right?"

"In theory, yes," replied the doctor. "In practice it's a rare journey in India that doesn't include delays of one sort or another. All being well, we should arrive by sunset. That's around half past six at this time of year."

The train moved westward from the station at a slow but steady pace. It passed the outlying villages of Madras, and clattered across the flat farmland beyond. The landscape was an abundant patchwork of fields and lakes that teemed with stork, heron, and pelican. Mud-walled hovels, thatched with reed, clustered in the shade of palm trees. The breeze Morgan had hoped for ventilated the compartment with only warm, moist air scented by the vegetation. He loosened his tunic in vain.

"Was it a hospital inspection that took you to Madras, John?" asked Charles.

"Partly, yes. I had to give a lecture at the Medical College as well, and yesterday I was at the races. I'd have stayed a little longer, but I've a gathering to attend this coming weekend."

"I think we might've seen the Medical College during our tour of the ramparts," said Morgan. "Is it the grand-looking place just north of the island?"

"Yes, that's it," John confirmed. "Well remembered. The race course is further away to the south – a good six miles from the fort."

"There's been much debate in the regiment about the kind of sport we can look forward to in Bangalore," explained Charles. "None of us are really sure what to expect, but we gather there's a race course there too?"

"You'll not be disappointed. There's no end of enthusiasm for cricket – particularly from Major General Haines, the new commander of the division – and naturally we have a polo club. Hunting parties sally forth into the hills on a regular basis, but most importantly are the not one, but two race courses."

"Oh that's fizzing news!" said Charles. "Clearly you're a man who appreciates the turf."

"Most definitely," John beamed. "The main course is about a mile west of the old barracks. I steward there from time to time. And then there's the steeplechase course on the other side of town on the Agram Plain. That's where the new cavalry barracks are being constructed, and where I believe you're destined to end up this evening."

"Reckon we're in for a fine old time in that case," said Morgan, not hiding his delight.

"That we are," agreed Charles. "*Reveille* might be sounding," he added, "about something you said back at the station, John. I mean about us not needing to worry about the water where we're going."

"I'd almost forgotten. Yes, Agram's wells tend to be pretty reliable. Which isn't to say you shouldn't still exercise diligence with regard to water purification, of course."

"Of course," said Charles.

"And you mentioned a gathering?" prompted Morgan.

"A gathering? Oh at the weekend, yes, quite so. Michael Lavelle, a very good friend of mine, is throwing a modest garden party on Saturday. Fascinating fellow, actually. He was a sergeant in the 43rd Foot during the Sepoy Uprising, and later at Madras, then Rangoon and Bengal. A couple of years ago, instead of leaving the army as he could have done, he went with them to New Zealand to fight the Māori."

"A man with many an adventurous tale to tell, I'll wager," said Morgan.

"An inexhaustible supply," John confirmed with a laugh. "And his story doesn't end there. Once the Māori were dealt with, Micky stayed on in New Zealand for a while to prospect for gold. He became quite the expert, so he tells me, and did well enough to make his way back to retirement in Bangalore."

"Mr Lavelle sounds like quite a character, and an Irishman too I'm guessing?" said Charles.

The conversation turned to Ireland and John explained that Micky Lavelle was from Mayo on the west coast. His own family came from County Tyrone, in the north around Omagh, although he was born in Ceylon where his father had been stationed. Morgan shared stories about Kenmare and Dublin, and Charles spoke with great fondness about Antrim and the Carnfunnock estate.

The railway line turned south before *Arcot*, where a bridge spanned the half-mile-wide *Palar* River with a string of elegant stone arches. The view from the unglazed windows began to change dramatically. From amongst banana and jackfruit plantations, steep hills rose towards a glowering sky. They were blanketed in forest, and a nebulous purple haze seemed to hang above the canopy. In the valleys, colourful parakeets and cuckoos called from banyan trees and aromatic sandalwoods. Monkeys scurried for cover, and an elephant was spotted hauling lumber. Even from a distance, Morgan and Charles were astounded by the size and strength of the strange animal.

John was talking more about horses and racing when the train slowed to halt in the middle of nowhere. The old man with red teeth opened the carriage door and hurried out, followed without hesitation by the two sisters and their parents. It appeared that all the compartments were emptying into the long grass beside the track, and the passengers up on the roof were climbing down too.

"Welcome to India," said John, laughing at the confusion on the faces of his two new friends. "We still have at least another couple of hours before Bangalore, so I'd recommend taking advantage of this brief stop to stretch your legs and so forth. Just mind where you step."

The comfort and circulation of its passengers restored, the train resumed its journey ten minutes later.

"I'm not sure which is more remarkable," said Morgan, "the spectacle of so many people squatting in a field, or that we're all back in the same seats again."

"And with not a hint of bashfulness," observed Charles. "Such breaks along the way are common, presumably?" he asked John.

"Yes, all perfectly normal. Rest stops aren't scheduled or official, and can occur just about anywhere at the driver's discretion, but everyone knows to expect them."

"I rather like the unpretentious honesty of it," Morgan decided. Charles nodded in agreement.

"I was thinking..." said John, returning to their previous topic of conversation. "Once you gentlemen are settled in and ready to acquire personal mounts, I'd be happy to introduce you to a reputable trader."

"That's very kind of you," replied Morgan.

"You're most welcome. There's a well-respected Persian fellow called Agha Aly Asker whom I'd particularly recommend if your preference is for Arabs, and there's plenty of choice when it comes to Australians."

"It's been months since we were last in the saddle, so the sooner the better as far as I'm concerned," said Charles.

"And another thing... you remember the party I mentioned earlier? Perhaps you'd both like to come along as my guests?"

"We'd like that very much," Morgan replied, confident Charles would feel the same.

"Splendid. It'll all be quite informal and it'll give you a chance to meet some of the old hands. I'm sure Micky will be delighted to have more fellow Irishmen there. I'll sketch some directions for you."

John took a notebook from the briefcase at his feet and spent a few minutes deep in concentration as he drew a simple map of central Bangalore. He tore out the page and turned it around for them to see.

"Not exactly to scale, of course, but hopefully this will suffice as a guide," he said. "From left to right is roughly three miles. Over here to the south-east is the Agram Plain with the steeplechase course and your soon-to-be new home. A little north and west of there you'll find the infantry and artillery regiments in the old barracks adjacent to the parade ground. And this road here," John said, pointing with the tip of his pencil, "along its southern perimeter – and appropriately called South Parade – is one of the main thoroughfares across town. As you can see, there's an area of parkland at the western end of it and the main race course is but a short distance beyond that."

"And are those lakes?" wondered Morgan, referring to several large oval shapes. One of them was close to the old barracks.

"They're called *tanks* in this part of the world, but yes. They act as reservoirs and provide Bangalore with most of its water. Up here at the top of the page is the railway line, with the station in the middle," John continued, "and then this curving road running north-south near the park is where Micky Lavelle has his house. You can't miss it."

"We're grateful to you. I've no doubt a map will prove invaluable in the coming days," said Charles, sincerely.

"No trouble at all. You'll get the lie of the land soon enough, I'm sure."

"What now?" asked Morgan. The train was stopping again.

"This'll be *Jolarpettai* station. The locomotive takes on water here," explained John.

Some of the Indian travellers left the train and new faces rushed on board to occupy the vacated seats. Local traders were flocking to the carriage windows to tempt hungry and thirsty passengers with all manner of supplies. Doctor Orr purchased three clay cups of tea, three bananas, and some flatbreads he said were called *chapatis*. Strictly not to be reused for the sake of caste purity, the cups were to be thrown from the windows.

Charles was intrigued by the leaf-wrapped parcels of pungent, orangey-brown food the girls and their parents were tucking into with their fingers. He asked John what it was.

"Curried *dal* and rice by the looks of it," said John. "Tasty and full of goodness, I assure you."

The elder sister noticed the men staring at her meal and guessed what they might be talking about. "Sahib?" she said to Charles, offering the open parcel in his direction. Charles looked to her father for consent and received a proud smile in reply.

"Thank you, my dear. I'd love to try some," he said to the girl, knowing all too well she was unlikely to understand his words. Trying his best to copy the method she used, he took a tentative scoop of the mixture. Everyone in the compartment waited for his reaction. Both sisters giggled.

"Goodness, what an extraordinary taste!" he said with wide eyes just moments later. "It really is delicious, and with a curious heat too."

The girl was delighted by his expression and seemed thrilled when Charles gave her a whole chapati to share with her sibling.

"The universal language of kindness," John thought aloud.

"Not tempted?" Charles asked Morgan.

"I'm still trying to work out what to do with this banana."

Within twenty minutes the train was ready to leave again. Just as the last carriage was clearing the platform, the monsoon clouds gave up their burden for the afternoon. An hour of torrential rain followed, which did nothing to cool the temperature or make the steamy humidity any more comfortable for the remainder of the journey.

It was past seven o'clock and already dark when the 16th Lancers stepped on to the platform at Bangalore's Cantonment Station. Charles and Morgan waved goodbye to the sisters and thanked John for his generous company, saying how much they looked forward to seeing him again at Mr Lavelle's party.

Developing a meaningful first impression of Bangalore was difficult. Apart from the absence of sea air it smelled much the same as Madras, though the temperature was certainly milder. The station buildings, with their brick arches, kerosene lamps, and latticed ironwork, were reminiscent of many a provincial station in England. What lay beyond them would mostly remain an enigma until daylight. The waning half-moon was obscured by the overcast sky, and none of the buildings offered more than a dim glow from their shuttered windows. The only useful illumination came from oil lamps carried by the sepoys sent to guide the regiment on its three-mile trek across town.

Augustus Dobrée was in nominal charge of the escort, having volunteered for the duty with typical eagerness. In reality all the sepoys from the infantry garrison looked to their *havildar*, or sergeant, for command.

"Well, it's all right for some!" Augustus scoffed when he learned how the officers of the right wing had passed the time in Madras. "We've spent the last two days working hard to get the camp organised. Henry has been quite the taskmaster, I can tell you!" he added.

"Quite right too," said Thomas White, unsympathetically. He was enjoying the simple movement of walking after the discomfort of the journey. "Wait, did you say *camp*, Mr Dobrée?"

"I did, sir. It's rather like being back on the Abbey Farm Field, except the tents are more spacious and there's no shortage of willing servants."

"From what a gentleman we met on the train told us, we were under the impression that new barracks were being built. Perhaps we misunderstood?" said Charles, exchanging vexed looks with Morgan.

"Being built, yes," Augustus confirmed, "but still quite some way from being finished – as you'll see for yourselves in the morning."

"Ah well, no matter," said Thomas. "How has the quarter master been getting on? Any problems to report?"

"Mr Fuller's wizardry is as legendary as ever," said Augustus. "He already has an equipment store organised, and all the baggage has been distributed. There were a few issues with food supplies yesterday, but they were quickly resolved."

"And have the ranks been behaving themselves?" Hugh Burnell wanted to know.

"There's been a little boisterousness. Nothing out of the ordinary though. Henry has confined everyone to camp until the regiment is all back together."

"Good. That's sensible," said Thomas.

"What about letters?" asked Charles.

"Oh yes, stacks of them."

"Wonderful! And any news of Colonel Dickson and the others?"

"Not that I've heard, no, but they must be well on their way by now I should think," said Augustus. "Oh, and we've established the beginnings of an Officers' Mess in one of the larger tents. Henry hopes you'll all join him for a somewhat improvised dinner there in an hour or so."

PART TWO

CHAPTER SEVEN
THE LAVELLE RESIDENCE, BANGALORE, INDIA
SATURDAY, 16TH SEPTEMBER 1865

Eight-year-old Michael was on lookout duty. To pass the time between guests arriving, he imagined the marbles he rolled down the verandah steps were cannonballs. A line of redcoats stood their ground on the bottom step. He'd painted the little tin figures himself and couldn't decide if it was more fun to bounce over their heads or knock one flying.

Michael was excited about meeting the last two people he'd been told to welcome to his home. When at last he saw the pair of real-life soldiers approach the front gate in their smart uniforms, he jumped down and ran along the path. He stood to attention and offered his best salute.

"Hello, sirs. My name's Michael Lavelle," he said, confidently.

"Well good morning to you, Michael. How do you do?" Morgan replied, returning the salute as genuinely as if to a colonel. "I'm Lieutenant Farrell and this is Lieutenant Agnew."

Charles returned the boy's salute as well before bending down to shake his hand. "Pleased to meet you, Michael," he said in his usual friendly manner. "You make a fine guard. May we have your permission to pass?"

Michael smiled at the praise. "Thank you, sir. Oh yes, of course. Please follow me." He turned on his heels and marched around the side of the bungalow, leading the way to the back garden. Navigating past groups of adults engaged in their conversations, Michael headed towards the man at the head of a long table. It had been laid with a crisp white tablecloth and on it was an abundance of cakes, pastries, fruit, and cold meats, all protected from the flies by dainty lace. There were jugs of lemonade too. Michael's brother and sister were sitting on their father's knees and sharing a popular song.

"*Then to the east we bore away...* your turn David."

"*To win a name in sto-ry...*"

"*And there where dawns the sun of day...* go on Anne."

"There dawned our sun of glo-ry."

Charles and Morgan applauded. "Brava, bravo!"

"Papa, may I introduce Lieutenants Farrell and Agnew," Michael said, gesturing at each man in turn and feeling very grown up. Micky Lavelle acknowledged them with a nod and continued the song. Charles joined in too.

"The hope of final victory,
In my bosom bur-ning,
Is mingling with sweet thoughts of thee,
And of my fond retur-ning."

"Well done my darlings," Micky said, kissing the children's foreheads before turning his attention back to Michael, Morgan and Charles. "Thank you, son, you've done a grand job. Welcome gentlemen. I'm honoured you could join us, so I am."

Charles crouched down. "And how old are you two?" he asked.

"I'm four," said Anne.

"Two!" beamed the boy.

"No, David, you're three now, remember?" Micky corrected him gently.

David was thoughtful for a moment and then he laughed. "Yes, papa. I'm threeee!"

"Well, you both sing most sweetly, wouldn't you agree?" Charles said, half to Morgan who reiterated the compliment.

"You must be very proud, Mr Lavelle, and of young Michael here too," said Morgan.

"Micky, please. Everyone calls me Micky. And yes, thank you, a prouder father there's never been."

Charles and Morgan returned the courtesy of their given names and thanked their host for his hospitality. Micky suggested that Anne and David go and play with Michael, and they all ran off into the house. Then he stood and gave the two men firm handshakes. He was wearing a collarless shirt, open at the neck, with the sleeves rolled up past the elbows. His physique was lean and muscular, and he was about the same height as Morgan. He wore a full beard, which was heavily flecked with silver, and his dark brown hair was neatly trimmed with a parting on the left. A lively intelligence was unmistakable in his grey eyes, which betrayed the suffering they'd witnessed during a life of military service. Charles estimated him to be in his mid-forties. He was thirty-four.

"So how are your bowels, gentlemen?" Micky enquired with disorienting bluntness. His Mayo accent was still strong and he pronounced 'so' like 'sho'.

Morgan chuckled, admiring the candour. "There's barely a man amongst us not suffering a watery constitution, but no doubt we'll soon be recovered."

"It's to be expected," commented John Orr who'd wandered across the garden to greet them. "Regimental guts often take a while to adjust to new circumstances," he added as he shook hands. Charles and Morgan both expressed their pleasure at seeing him again. "Mind you look after yourselves though," John continued. "A dose of the squits won't kill you, but it can be the harbinger of more troublesome complaints."

"We'll certainly try," said Charles.

"Good, good. Mr Lavelle here remembers an epidemic of cholera on a march across the country in '58, don't you Micky?"

"It cut men down like a scythe at harvest, so it did. We couldn't dig graves fast enough. But that's not a memory I care to dwell on today, if you don't mind."

"Of course. My apologies," replied John, changing the subject. "So you gentlemen found the place without any difficulty?"

"No difficulty at all, thank you," Morgan confirmed. "The map you drew was most helpful."

"We detoured via the park," said Charles, "and we're very glad we did too. It was a welcome oasis of calm after the last few days. This is the first chance we've had to explore this side of town."

A tall woman with a generous figure, dark blonde hair, and a happy disposition put a familiar hand on Micky's arm. They were the same age and her accent was as strong as his. "Rather charming it is, so," she agreed about the park. "Now since I'd wait all day for this husband of mine to do the necessary," she went on, "I'll introduce myself, so I will. I'm Mrs Lavelle, but please do call me Augusta." Micky kissed her on the cheek.

"Our pleasure, ma'am," Charles replied. "You have a lovely home, Augusta, if I may say?"

"You need never restrain a compliment with me, and I thank you for that one. We've not been here long, so, only since Micky's return from New Zealand. Did you pass that impressive new building on your way here, the one they're painting bright red?"

"We did indeed," said Morgan. "What is it?"

"That's *Attara Kacheri*. They only started it last year, but it'll be the public offices once it's complete," Micky explained.

"And the lake – or should I say tank – at the southern end of the park where six roads meet?" asked Charles.

"*Sampangi Tank*. Much of the water for this area comes from there, although we have our own well now, so we do."

"Which was a very wise investment," John interjected. "Most of the tanks are notorious for being polluted."

"Oh John, really, that's quite enough about pollution," said the petite woman who'd come to stand beside the doctor. There was gentle affection in her chiding tone. She was carrying glasses of lemonade on a tray and offered them around. Charles and Morgan were grateful for the refreshment.

"Quite right, my dear, quite right. Gentleman, may I introduce my wonderful wife, Emily."

"I've been very much looking forward to meeting you both," she said to the officers. "John was telling me all about your journey here from Madras."

Emily asked about how the regiment was settling in to its new station. Charles assured her that everything was going well, all things considered. As the conversation continued, Morgan noticed Emily's strong brow seemed set in a permanent frown that was out of step with the rest of her cheerful expression. Her high forehead was accentuated by wearing her dark brown hair up in the fashionable style. She had defined cheekbones and a small, sharp nose. Her crinolined dress, with its delicate embroidery and satin bow, was a pale blue that matched her eyes. Morgan thought she was pretty, albeit in a slightly severe kind of way. Given she could only be a few years older than he and Charles, and therefore a great deal younger than her husband, he also thought John had done very well for himself.

"And this is Katherine, the other woman in my life," John said, beckoning his six-year-old daughter over from further down the table where she was helping herself to another slice of cake. She skipped towards them and curtsied to Charles and Morgan.

"Hello," she said with her mouth half full. She blushed a little when they bowed in reply and Morgan commented on how handsome her dress was.

"Thank you, sir. Do you have a wife? I should very much like to marry a soldier when I'm older," she said, quite earnestly. Morgan explained that he didn't. Emily put a reassuring arm around Katherine's shoulder and smiled. Her frown evaporated when she did that. It was a beautiful, carefree smile. It reminded Morgan of someone else.

*   *   *

When Alec Innes walked up to the Officers' Mess tent just after ten o'clock the following Wednesday morning, he found Morgan and Charles lounging outside in its shade. They were nursing hangovers cultivated the night before with *arrack*, the potent locally distilled spirit.

Known throughout the cantonment as *Blackpally*, the bazaar district had become the regular and all too frequent haunt of officers and men alike ever since Thomas White lifted the ban on leaving camp. It was a densely populated Tamil area that spread down the gentle slope immediately north of the old barracks. *Ulsoor Tank* lay on its eastern flank. The two lieutenants had stayed in one particular joint for longer than they'd intended and were now paying the price.

"Good morning Alec," said Morgan with more cheer than he was feeling. "To what do we owe this pleasure?"

"Morning gentlemen. Not so good though, I'm afraid," Alec replied, as he lit his pipe. "Have either of you seen Mr Wauchope in the last wee while?"

"Not yet this morning, no, sorry," said Charles. "Is something the matter?"

"Aye. We have our first case of dysentery."

"Oh dear, that's unfortunate news. Who is it?"

"Private Claypole from Bill's troop. He fell ill during the night. I was hoping to advise the captain of the lad's condition before I continue my rounds."

"He can't be far," said Morgan. "We can let him know for you when he turns up if you like?"

"Thank you, aye, please do. Are you both feeling well?"

"Oh yes, quite well," Charles lied.

Morgan stifled a laugh at that. "We were just going to have some more coffee, Alec. May we offer you a mug?"

"Aye, go on then, twist my arm."

"Out of curiosity, how do you treat cases like Claypole's?" asked Charles, while Morgan instructed the mess steward to fetch the coffee.

"I've administered Castor oil and will keep monitoring him during the day. Depending on how he fares, I'll begin Ipecacuanha infusions at intervals tomorrow."

"I see. And is that likely to restore him?"

"Not immediately, no, but it may help to purge him of the illness," Alec explained. He sipped at the coffee he'd been handed. "If he doesn't show signs of improvement, or indeed if he deteriorates further, then treatment progresses with beef tea enemas and the application of leeches."

"Leeches?" Morgan checked.

"Around the anus. It's a grim business."

"Jesus wept!"

"Well, let's hope he gets better before that becomes necessary!" said Charles.

"We can hope," said Alec, trying to sound optimistic.

*   *   *

Sunday, 24th September, was Charles Agnew's twenty-ninth birthday. At Lieutenant Colonel White's behest, in between the interruptions of Divine Service, meal times, and monsoon downpours, much of the day was spent drilling the troops and carrying out the most thorough of kit and tent inspections. A telegram received on Friday reported that Colonel Dickson had landed in Bombay and hoped to reach Bangalore within a few days. Thomas wanted to make sure there was no room to question the diligence of his temporary command, and that everything was ready for William's reunion with the regiment.

In keeping with tradition, all the drinks in the Officers' Mess that evening went on Charles's tab and his good health was rewarded with toast after toast.

Private Claypole died the next morning and was cold in the ground before sunset.

Colonel Dickson arrived at the Agram Plain after dark on the Tuesday, tired but triumphant and wearing civilian clothes. With the exception of Captain Goldie, who wasn't expected for another week or two, William was accompanied by his fellow overlanders and they all sought out the Officers' Mess tent.

"Good evening, gentlemen. Has dinner been served?" William said with a straight face as he made his nonchalant entrance. Caught off-guard by the surprise, all the officers jumped to their feet to applaud and cheer.

"Welcome to Bangalore," said Thomas, shaking the colonel's hand. "It's a great relief to see you're all safely here and looking well. I trust your journey was a pleasant one?"

"Thank you, it was. And I'm very glad to see you too, my friend," William replied with sincere warmth, before turning to address the whole assembly. "Thank you, all, thank you. Please, do sit down. May I say how delighted I am to be finally here – indeed we all are – and to find you all in such good spirits. Now, if someone can find another eight chairs, a small mountain of food, and even more brandy, we'll happily exchange tales of Cairo and Bombay for news of everything that's been happening while we've been missed."

"Three cheers for the colonel!" Henry Wilkinson called out.

"Huzzah! Huzzah! Huzzah!" everyone returned, banging their fists on the table in unison.

Servants brought the necessary chairs and Thomas vacated the head of the table for William to occupy. The colonel was as hungry for details of how the regiment had been faring as he was for a decent meal. Thomas happily obliged.

Carrin and Robert Maillard took seats by Charles and Morgan. Carrin looked no less solemn than when they'd last seen him, and Robert's vitality was as boundless as ever.

"We hadn't expected you to all turn up at once, but about time too," joked Morgan, shaking their hands in turn.

"Entirely by luck rather than judgement," Carrin replied. "We went our quite separate ways from Colchester, but somehow managed to converge on Suez within a couple of days of one another. Fate having brought us together, naturally we boarded the same steamer and have been travelling as a group ever since."

"How long did it take to reach Bombay from there?" asked Charles.

"Twelve days," said Robert, "most of them made uncomfortable by a heavy sea. But what of you chaps and your voyage around the Cape?"

"Twelve days? Ha!" Morgan scoffed with a grin. "You should try six times that!"

Charles offered a brief account of the journey to Madras, but swiftly steered the conversation back to how Carrin and Robert had spent the past three months.

"Well, I imagine Mr Maillard's adventures will make for a better story than mine," suggested Carrin, "but I did enjoy a fine leaving party the week before sailing. My father spared no expense in arranging a ball at Kearsney Abbey in my honour. It's a grand old mansion house that he intends to purchase before long. I have a clipping here," he added, fumbling in his pocket book. "Would you like to hear some of it?"

"By all means," said Charles.

"All right then. It's from *The Kentish Gazette* and begins with mention of the many distinguished guests and so forth. Then it goes on to say: ...*carriages began to arrive within the gates before ten o'clock, and the guests, after passing under an awning outstretched from the portico, were ushered into a scene of gaiety such as it were enchanting even to witness. Dancing was commenced to the strains of a charming quadrille band from Dover, and was continued until midnight, when the company partook of supper, which was of a recherché character, and was spread with surpassing elegance. The ball was afterwards resumed, and maintained with increasing spirit until Phoebus rose and betokened the hour of departure.*"

"With increasing spirit, eh?" Morgan teased.

"In more ways than one. Drunk as lords we were. Everyone seemed to enjoy themselves."

"Good for you Mr Churchward. I'm sure they did," said Charles.

"And did Egypt live up to your expectations?" Morgan asked Robert.

"In so many fascinating ways, yes."

"Spill the beans then."

"Well, I made my way to Cairo via the train from Alexandria and took a room at Shepheard's Hotel. A remarkable place, I must say, much favoured by European travellers of status and of course by us military types on our comings and goings. To call it opulent would barely begin to do justice to its grandeur. Anyway, do you recall my ambition to photograph the pyramids?"

"Certainly," said Morgan. "There was a great deal of envy about it."

"Oh, was there? Well, in the hotel bar on my first evening there I had the good fortune to make the acquaintance of a gentleman from one of the Highland regiments. He also intended to make the trip and we agreed to share the cost of hiring a *dragoman* and porters – Nubians, I was led to believe – and a couple of horses and a donkey. He was far more skilled than I at negotiating a fair rate – or at least more determined to get one – and I was glad of his company. We set off at dawn on my second day, crossed the Nile on a small ferry boat and then rode the eight or nine miles to the Sphinx."

"But did you get the photograph?" Morgan was impatient to know.

"Of course I did. Would you like to see it?"

Not waiting for a reply Robert delved into the satchel he carried and fished out the treasured print, which he'd mounted on card. The Sphinx, long-since deprived of its nose, stared out into the desert that lay beyond the right-hand edge of the image. The Great Pyramid of Giza towered behind it, dominating the scene. The dragoman and five porters all faced the camera in the foreground, some standing, some sitting on their heels, and just to the right of centre, holding the bridle of a horse, was a man wearing a kilt and white pith helmet.

"My word, Robert," said Charles. "That really is tremendous!"

"Thank you. I think it was worth all the effort and expense of getting there."

"Without a doubt. And clearly you have a rare talent for the photographic art."

"A rare talent indeed," said Morgan. "To be admired."

*   *   *

Charles was wrestling with mixed feelings about the impending arrival of his new captain. After leading a troop for the past three months or so, it would be strange to relinquish some of that responsibility again. Not that doing so would make much difference to the daily routine, at least not while the regiment was still without horses. The question that troubled Charles the most was how he and James Goldie would get

107

along. More specifically, whether James would allow any memories of the past to cloud his view of Charles in the present.

Charles considered discussing his thoughts with Morgan, but in the end decided against it. Don't rush your fences, he reminded himself.

If Colonel Dickson's transit time from Bombay was anything to go by, the telegram received from Captain Goldie on Tuesday, 3rd October, meant he would likely reach Bangalore on Friday or Saturday. Charles reasoned it might be politic, quite apart from being courteous, to be ready to greet James and his wife at the station. He set about arranging for a suitable carriage to be made available, and instructed Solomon Smith to prepare the couple's tent.

When Friday came, Charles made sure he was on the station platform by sunset. As he paced its length, he hoped he wasn't wasting his time and that a repeat performance wouldn't be necessary on Saturday. The anxiety of waiting was cut short by the sound of an approaching locomotive just after a quarter to seven. Charles found a convenient vantage point near the middle of the platform from which to observe the disembarking passengers. As he half-expected, James had chosen one of the last carriages in the train. Being the same height as Charles and wearing a scarlet dress tunic made him easy to spot in the crowd.

"Captain Goldie, sir," Charles began, saluting at attention. "Lieutenant Agnew. May I welcome you to Bangalore. It's a pleasure to see you again, sir."

James Goldie returned the salute and then held out his hand to shake. "Thank you, Charles. It's good to see you again too." His voice was uncommonly deep and powerful, yet neither loud nor forced in its projection. "I appreciate the welcome, but we can drop the formalities now."

Charles was surprised and heartened by that.

"I'm truly delighted," James continued, "to be able to introduce you to Mrs Magdalene Goldie," he said, turning to the elegant young woman holding his arm with one hand and a parasol with the other.

"I'm honoured to make your acquaintance, ma'am," said Charles as he bowed politely.

"Thank you, lieutenant. Or may I call you Charles?" she replied.

"Certainly, ma'am."

"Then thank you, Charles. I'm very pleased to meet you. It would put me at ease if you returned the compliment and were to call me Magdalene. Would that be all right?"

"Of course, as you wish."

"Marvellous. There, you see, I feel more at ease already!" she said, lightly. "So I'm to gather you and James know each other of old?"

"We were in the same regiment for a short while," Charles explained, hoping he wouldn't have to say more.

"Much water has gone under the bridge since then though, my darling," James said to his wife. "I'm sure we're both quite different men now. We're certainly a long way from Maidstone, thank goodness! Wouldn't you agree, Charles?"

"I would. Wholeheartedly so."

"As far as I'm concerned, Charles, we're on the threshold of a bright new beginning for all of us and I'm looking forward to serving with you again. It's my intention that, working together, we'll muster the finest troop in the regiment."

"I'm gladdened to hear that. Rest assured you have my full and undivided support." Inwardly, Charles breathed a great sigh of relief. "Shall we away? No doubt you're both rather tired and hungry after your journey. I have transport waiting outside."

"Lead on, Charles, lead on," said James.

As the carriage made its way across town in the dark, Charles did the best he could to point out some of Bangalore's more significant landmarks. He congratulated the couple on their marriage and asked after their journey, which Magdalene said she'd found thoroughly enjoyable for the most part. She explained that she was no stranger to long voyages, having travelled to England from Van Diemen's Land as a child, but that this was her first time in India.

"Am I correct in understanding that Alec Innes is with us?" asked James.

A man with an open, honest face and a gaze that'll go right through you was how James had often been described in the past. In appearance, if nothing else, Charles thought the captain had changed little in the intervening years since their last encounter.

"Yes, that's right. You know Alec then?"

"I had occasion to meet the good doctor outside the walls of Delhi once upon a time. His dedication and compassion left a lasting impression."

"I feel most fortunate to call him a friend," said Charles.

"Quite right. And what can you tell me about where we're going?"

Charles described something of the regiment's status and the nature of their tented accommodation on the Agram Plain. Whatever Magdalene's expectations may have been, she appeared to take the news in her stride.

"You look like the weight of the world has been lifted from those broad shoulders," Morgan observed when Charles retired to the tent they shared later that evening. "Your excursion to collect the new captain went well, I take it?"

"That obvious?"

"I couldn't help noticing that there's been something on your mind for a day or two."

Charles sat on the edge of his bed and lit a cheroot. "Mr Goldie and I have met before, and I've perhaps been entertaining some concerns about how that would affect things here." He could see that wasn't enough to satisfy Morgan's curiosity, so he laid out the bones of the story. "When the 9th Lancers returned to England after the Indian Uprising, it was to the depot at Maidstone. I'd been there nearly a year by that stage. The repatriated officers and men were all battle-hardened of course, and I suppose one might say that many were dwelling in their memories. They certainly had no patience for the bluster and antics of fresh-faced new volunteers. James Goldie was still a lieutenant then, and in a different troop than I, but he quickly took a dim view of me."

"He was amongst those who returned from India?"

"Indeed. I don't recall the names of all the engagements he fought in, but the list is long and impressive and includes the relief of Lucknow where my brother fell. From all I heard about him, and having seen his style of command myself, it's fair to say James is what you'd call a soldier's soldier – and an officer to easily equal or surpass the likes of Henry Wilkinson. He exchanged into the 17th Lancers at the first opportunity and returned to India less than a year later."

"If you have such a high opinion of the man, why was there no love lost between you?"

"Have you ever looked back on things you said or did in the past and been ashamed of your younger self?" Charles asked.

"Not ashamed, I don't think, but doubtless there are situations I might handle differently if I had my time over."

"Well, let's simply say that Cornet Agnew of the 9th Lancers was a rather less conscientious officer than Lieutenant Agnew of the 16th tries to be."

"You're hardly alone in that failing," consoled Morgan.

"No, but added to that was the way some officers – those of lesser ability or courage or experience – would make game of Mr Goldie's family background in cynical attempts to undermine his authority and honourable reputation."

"I don't follow. What do you mean?"

"His father was a colonel in the army and came from Scotland, if memory serves, but his mother was Anglo-Indian."

"Oh I see. And has he inherited his mother's complexion?"

"Not that you'd notice, but resentment and spite made a habit of turning even that against him. In retrospect, his time in Maidstone must have been quite awful."

"Sounds like it. And you used the past tense about his parents?"

"The story I heard was that they both perished in the Cawnpore massacre along with two of his sisters. He was there himself only six months afterwards. Goodness knows what that must've been like. I believe another sister was killed while trying to escape down the Ganges as well."

"Jesus wept. But despite all that's gone before, after this evening your concerns have been allayed?"

"It was rather like he read my mind. He certainly wanted to wipe the slate clean, and aims to make his troop the best of the bunch while he's about it."

"Good, I'm happy for you. I look forward to meeting this Mr Goldie tomorrow. And what about his new catch? There's a rumour going around that she's his cousin."

"She may well be, I don't know. Magdalene seems like a very fine lady."

"Magdalene is it already?" Morgan teased.

"You'll like her. Just remember she's taken."

*   *   *

James and Magdalene's first few weeks in Bangalore coincided with the comparatively dry interlude between the south-west and north-east monsoons. Campaign veterans instinctively gave the new captain the respect he'd more than earned. His fair but firm approach was appreciated by men of all ranks, and the regimental wives took Magdalene under their collective wing with cautious enthusiasm. James turned twenty-nine on Sunday, 5th November, the same day the rains returned.

The following Friday morning William Dickson called all the officers to a meeting at his tent, which doubled as regimental headquarters. Like the mess tents, it was about forty feet long and twenty feet in both width and height. Held up by a pair of substantial teak poles, the roof canvas overhung the tent walls to create a kind of verandah and had a dark blue liner to reduce glare from the sun.

"There are a number of matters to discuss, gentlemen," William said, "beginning with an exciting telegram we've just received from Madras. Sir John Le Marchant, our illustrious commander-in-chief, will be gracing Bangalore with a visit a week today and intends to inspect the whole garrison on the parade ground. I would therefore ask all you captains, under the watchful eye of Major Burnell, to devote as much time as possible between now and next Friday to drilling the ranks. We might still be dismounted, but that doesn't mean we're going to be outdone by those infantry boys down the road!"

There was unanimous agreement about that. Everyone knew that preparing for an inspection, and the healthy competition between regiments it would inspire, could provide a useful focus for men fast becoming bored by inactivity.

"I suggest, major, that we have a full practice parade on Wednesday morning to give us Thursday to play with as well. Needless to say, the band should be pitch perfect."

"Consider it done, sir," replied Hugh Burnell.

"Thank you. Moving on then, I know you all share my frustration about the lack of news regarding horses and accommodation. As you're aware, the original expectation was that we'd take over the 18th Hussars' horses and saddlery before they departed for Secunderabad. That plan having changed, we may now be waiting for the 1st King's Dragoon Guards to return to England."

The majority of officers had already purchased their own horses, most within the first couple of weeks of being in Bangalore. Some, like Charles and Morgan, had done so with the expert help of John Orr. In lieu of proper stables, they were all kept in a makeshift paddock in the camp. It wasn't an arrangement that anyone was fond of. However, there was growing discontent in the ranks about the lack of troop mounts, and that was a more serious issue. Riding Master Thomas Brown asked the question on everyone's lips. "Given where we are in the season, sir, might we assume the King's Dragoons aren't likely to be going anywhere until the new year?"

"That's entirely possible, yes. The situation is far from ideal, but there's nothing to be done about it. Now, regarding the barracks, we can all see how fine the new buildings are going to be," William said, gesturing towards the construction work adjacent to the camp, "indeed I'm sure they'll be the envy of the garrison, but for the time being our village under the stars needs to maintain its patience. That said, as officers and gentlemen we're naturally required to find separate accommodation at our own expense. Whilst there need be no immediate hurry to vacate your tents, we should all be setting about finding suitable lodgings in readiness. In fact, I believe a few of you have already begun to do so."

The adjutant concluded the meeting with a few other minor points on William's behalf, before pulling Charles and Morgan to one side as everyone else dispersed. "I've been making enquiries about available housing in the vicinity, and have an idea I wanted to put to you both," Robert began.

"We're all ears," said Charles.

"Well, I was thinking that a bungalow with stables could serve as a *chummery* for likeminded subalterns – half a dozen of us dividing the running costs equally. There are a few such places close by. Would you be interested?"

"Who else have you asked?" wondered Morgan.

"Nobody yet. You're the first."

"That's very sporting of you. Count me in if Charles agrees?"

"Of course. It's a fizzing idea and very kind of you to invite us," said Charles.

"Good, I'm pleased. And you're most welcome. I'll sound-out a few others and then we can all go to look at some places and decide what'll best meet our needs."

*   *   *

On the morning of the inspection, South Parade swelled with onlookers raring for the noisy display of colonial might. Two hundred yards opposite them, columns of soldiers were wheeling right from the barrack gates and marching to their designated positions. Last to arrive, and receiving the loudest cheers from the crowd, the 16th Lancers cut their scarlet dash from the Agram Plain to the parade ground with the sun behind them.

Troops were called to attention by a succession of sergeant majors barking incomprehensible commands, and then an expectant, hushed silence descended as Sir John Le Marchant took his place on the inspection dais. The commander-in-chief was in all his finery, with an array of medals and badges of rank shining across his chest. Forty-five years had passed since he began his career at the age of seventeen in the 10th Regiment of Foot. It came as no surprise that the resident 2nd Battalion, led by their band, had the honour of being first to march past and give the salute. Once they were formed back in ranks at attention, Sir John walked the lines of redcoats accompanied by the regiment's commanding officer, Lieutenant Colonel William Fenwick.

The garrison's contingent of Madras Native Infantry was next in the running order. The sepoys wore turbans rather than *shako* caps, but in every other regard their uniform was largely indistinguishable from that of their British counterparts. With a vanguard of thundering drums, they replicated the march past and received the same scrutiny during the inspection.

As did the 16th Lancers when they took their turn. The regimental band played *The British Patrol* with gusto, and William Dickson's pride was clear for all to see when he introduced the commander-in-chief to his officers. It didn't go unnoticed that Sir John made a point of shaking hands with Captain Fitzgerald, Quarter Master Fuller, Assistant Surgeon Farmer and Lieutenant Dobrée, exchanging a few words with each of them before moving on down the line.

The gun carriages of the Royal Artillery's D Horse Brigade, C Battery, arguably created the most impressive spectacle for the audience on South Parade and certainly kicked up the most dust. They were followed by the 1st (King's) Dragoon Guards, in their dark blue tunics, whose troop horses were the objects of envy for the men of the 16th Lancers.

By noon the parade was finished, the crowd dispersed, and Sir John retreated to the barracks for lunch with the commanding officers of all the regiments.

When William Dickson returned to camp at the end of the day, he reported that the commander-in-chief had said he was, *"greatly pleased with the soldier-like bearing of the men and the general appearance of the regiment."*

*   *   *

Preparations for Christmas were in full swing in the Officers' Mess when Robert Maillard wandered in with Augustus Dobrée after a meeting in the colonel's tent.

"Gather round please, gentlemen," said Robert.

"You look chuffed about something, Augustus," Morgan teased. "What have you been up to?"

Augustus didn't reply and Robert continued. "I have some news to share with you all. Allow me to read this message received a short while ago from Madras," he said, referring to the note he was holding. *"This day, Friday, 22nd December, 1865, Lieutenant Augustus Dobrée, 16th Lancers, hereby appointed aide-de-camp to Sir John Le Marchant, commander-in-chief Madras Army."*

"Good for you, Augustus. I knew we'd find a way to get rid of you eventually," said Morgan with unrelenting banter.

"That's marvellous. My congratulations to you," said Charles. All the others reiterated the sentiment, shaking the new ADC's hand and clapping him on the back.

"Thank you, all. I must say this honour comes as a great surprise," said Augustus with uncharacteristic humility.

"Sir John and Madras will be fortunate to have you," noted Henry Wilkinson with sincerity.

"Hear, hear!" called out Walter Bagenal, who then led the gathering in a round of *For He's A Jolly Good Fellow*.

Augustus didn't take much persuasion to stay a while and talk about how much he was looking forward to his new role.

115

"How do you suppose he managed that?" Morgan asked Charles. They were out of earshot of Augustus, but not of James Fuller.

"I dare say Sir John recognises the merits of a fellow Brother when he sees them," hinted the quarter master.

Charles and Morgan looked at each other in puzzlement for a moment, before Morgan remembered the inspection parade.

"A fellow Brother? Do you mean Sir John and Augustus are both Freemasons?"

"Who did meet upon the level, and part upon the square? It's not for me to say, gentlemen, but I suppose you might be right," James replied, any suggestion of a smile obscured by his drooping moustache.

"I've known Augustus for more than two years, and I really had no idea," said Morgan, astonished.

"But then why would you? It is something of a secret society after all," noted Charles.

"One might say discreet, rather than secret," James suggested.

"A mystery to me in either case," said Morgan.

"It's a fraternity, Mr Farrell. One that seeks to make good men better, and provide relief to those in distress," explained James.

"That certainly sounds noble," said Charles.

"And so it is," James continued. "Brothers are encouraged to live by the virtues of temperance, fortitude, prudence and justice, and to extend the hand of friendship to all men regardless of race or creed. If either of you would care to know more, may I suggest a visit to the Victoria Hotel where the local Lodge gathers on the first Saturday of each month."

"We'll give it some thought," said Charles.

"Did you say temperance?" asked Morgan.

Christmas Eve brought with it news of a different and less welcomed kind, dampening all but the most optimistic festive spirits. The regiment's time under canvas was coming to an end. They were ordered to relocate to the old cavalry barracks on New Year's Day.

CHAPTER EIGHT
SOMESHWARA TEMPLE, BANGALORE, INDIA
TUESDAY, 9TH JANUARY 1866

The world always looks a brighter place when viewed from the saddle, Charles thought to himself as he ventured into new territory on *Woodman*, his Australian bay gelding. Riding for pleasure was an escape from regimental life and often somehow meditative in its nature. A time to relax in one's mind with clarity and perspective, or to simply let instinct take over and become immersed in the rhythm and harmony of motion. It had been a frenetic couple of weeks, so even a brief ride like this one was a welcome tonic.

The bungalow Charles now shared with Morgan, Robert, Carrin, and John Barker, was tucked away amongst trees in spacious grounds between the Agram Plain and the old barracks, a few hundred yards south-west of Holy Trinity Church. It was in a good state of repair, with plenty of well-ventilated rooms, and a colonnaded verandah on two sides. The defining feature of the place, its crowning glory, was the stable block, which could accommodate sixteen horses in two rows of stalls. In time they planned to fill it, but five was a good start. Along with *Woodman* there were two grey Arabs, *Taj* and *Greyling*, owned by Robert and Carrin respectively, a brown Arab that John Barker had named *Southern Cross*, and Morgan's chestnut Australian called *Lucifer*. They were cared for by a Tamil groom, known as a *syce*, chosen for his knowledge and experience of working with thoroughbreds. A dhoby and a couple of general domestic servants had been employed as well, and the subalterns were already realising they needed more.

Charles had left the bungalow after a light lunch and headed towards the south side of the Tamil-populated Ulsoor district, turning right at the church instead of left as he would if going to the barracks. Despite its close proximity, he'd not had a reason to explore that part of Bangalore before. He found what he was looking for after only about half a mile.

Seeking out the Someshwara Temple had been the suggestion of one of the assistant stewards in the Cavalry Officers' Mess. Yadhu

Nayak was a tall man of slender build, with a fine moustache and a placid disposition. He was required to be servile and quietly efficient, but in the presence of the more liberal-minded officers he allowed his intelligence and playful sense of humour to manifest. Charles liked him and had asked if he'd be willing to explain a little about his *Hindoo* faith and the caste system. Charles confessed he was entirely ignorant about both subjects, but was keen to learn. Sensing the lieutenant's interest was genuine, Yadhu had agreed with great enthusiasm. "One will do one's very best, but first sahib must go to Sri Someshwara," he'd said. When Charles asked why, Yadhu's reply was as confident as it was intriguing. "Go to Sri Someshwara and sahib will see."

Dismounting, and tethering *Woodman* to the post of a bullock shed, Charles began to understand what Yadhu had meant. Tapering to a height of perhaps eighty or ninety feet at the western end of the scruffy courtyard was an ancient stone tower.

A massive pair of studded doors bisected its pilastered base, which was around fifty feet square and twenty-five feet high. Above them, the structure ascended in five tiers of bewildering iconography towards a final level surmounted by seven cupolas. At the centre of each lower tier, life-size sculptures stood or danced in strange contortions to the left and right of a doorway. There were male and female figures, and a few that appeared more animal than human, all of whom seemed to be wearing elaborate jewellery. Some had four arms, while others were carrying what looked like instruments or weapons. Charles assumed they were important Hindoo deities, and he couldn't help noticing how the sculptors had accentuated the breasts of all the feminine characters.

Although the tower's honey stonework had weathered back to its natural state, the lower half of the base had been painted white and there was the faded suggestion that the mythological hierarchy had once been adorned in primary colours. Charles appreciated the thought of that and tried to imagine how spectacular it must have been. He wondered if any part of the seventy-foot pillar that stood in front of the tower had also been painted, and what the meaning of the carvings and inscriptions might be.

Two men in their middle age appeared from the street and strolled towards the tower. They were both barefoot and wearing the turbans and simple white robes that were the typical attire of the local people. Charles watched them spit out the betel nut they were chewing, push open the great doors and step inside. Before the doors closed again, he caught a brief glimpse of the temple sanctum and the golden shrine at its heart. He wanted to see more, but felt it wasn't his place to intrude.

Was there a single Hindoo god or a multitude? What did the five tiers represent, and why was the sculpted figure near the top of the tower seated in a giant flower? Charles had no end of questions to ask Yadhu later, and when he next saw Robert he'd recommend the temple to him for its photographic potential.

Afternoons usually remained dry this early in the year, and by Indian standards the temperature was comfortably mild. Nevertheless, Charles was still sweating beneath his tunic. Realising he'd rather lost track of the time, he mounted up and began the walk towards town.

Thanks in the main to the sober diligence of James Fuller, the New Year's Day move to the old barracks had been completed swiftly and with little fuss despite a regiment-wide epidemic of hangovers. The majority of officers kept out of the way during the day, only making an appearance when the work was over to praise their NCOs for a job well done. Charles and Morgan had made a point of locating the dhobies' well and instructing their troops to rely on it for their drinking water. It was exactly that topic, and William Dickson's thirty-sixth birthday celebrations this evening, that necessitated Charles riding to the barracks. He wanted to check that his instructions were being followed.

Eight single-storey barrack buildings were allocated to the garrison's two cavalry regiments, which was at least a couple of buildings shy of what was really needed. John Orr had mentioned on the train from Madras that they'd been there for fifty years and were past their prime. That had been something of an understatement.

Each barrack was around two hundred feet long, with Venetian doors and windows, and a high roof that looked like an upper floor when viewed from a distance. To the front and rear were wide verandahs lined with once elegant Doric columns. One hundred and eight men could be accommodated in each building, which were divided into three barrack rooms, three dining rooms, and three day rooms used for reading and recreation. Dim oil lamps provided the only illumination after eight o'clock in the evening when the ranks were supposed to be back in their quarters. One of the eight buildings was designated as the sergeants' married residence.

There were no stables, for which nobody had a sensible explanation, and so horses were simply tethered to stone blocks outside. The rooms occupied by the Dragoon Guards demonstrated how saddles had to be slung over the ends of beds when not being used.

Returning the salute of the sentries on duty at the gate, Charles made his way across the open ground past the Guard House. About fifty feet long, it contained a twenty-foot square main cell and three solitary cells for defaulters. Evil odours emanated from its privy, though they were no more offensive than the stench from any of the latrine blocks. There was one of those between each barrack building, and their cisterns and drainage were woefully inadequate.

Close to the Guard House was the coffee shop run by a Tamil man nicknamed John Bull. Though no more than a covered stall, the enterprise was accepted as a permanent fixture and relied upon by men of the ranks for hot beverages and glasses of ginger beer. The proprietor had apparently furnished the British with useful intelligence during the Mutiny, for which he was rewarded with a pension, his trading pitch in the barracks, and the mortal hatred of his fellow countrymen.

Charles thought back to the conversation with Solomon Smith about the wives' lottery before they'd left Colchester. At the time it had seemed the greatest unfairness was to the families being left behind in England, and perhaps it was. But now he wondered how those *on the strength* in Bangalore viewed their current fortune. Their husbands had more time on their hands than any of them were used to, and filled much of it with drinking. There was no drainage in the sergeants' married quarters, spaces for bathing and cooking had to be improvised with cloth screens, and wastewater carried away in buckets. The washhouses, two of which were reserved for the women, offered no privacy at all. And since the troopers' wives had to share their rooms with other married couples and their children, there was no privacy for intimacy either. They were used to that of course.

Glad of the privileges associated with his rank, Charles left *Woodman* tied-up near the Officers' Mess building, lit a cheroot, and went off in search of Cornet Chaplin and his troop's sergeant major.

*   *   *

A rumour began to circulate around the barracks during the morning of Wednesday, 17th January, and by the time Robert Maillard was buying everyone's drinks in the Cavalry Officers' Mess that evening it had become official news. The 1st (King's) Dragoon Guards would be handing over their horses and saddlery on Wednesday, 21st February, prior to departing Bangalore by the end of the month. It was the best thirtieth birthday present Robert could have wished for.

The carousing continued back at the subalterns' bungalow long into the night, with conversation dominated by how the regiment should celebrate its impending re-mounted status. Two ideas emerged from the brandy fumes as clear favourites. Carrin suggested a grand ball at the Public Rooms near the parade ground, while Robert was set on the notion of a day of races. "Why not do both?" said Morgan.

William Dickson was delighted by the proposal Robert put to him the next afternoon. He gave it his wholehearted approval on the understanding that he'd oversee the ball's guest list and be chief steward on race day. Bookings were made straightaway with the Public Rooms and Turf Club, and Robert and the others set to work on a plan. The ball would take place the evening before horse-handover and the races would follow the day after.

Compiling the guest list for the ball was the first priority, since invitations would need to be sent out as quickly as possible. The officers of the 1st (King's) Dragoon Guards and other regiments of the garrison were all included, along with Major General Haines and his HQ staff. It went without saying that Chief Commissioner Bowring and notable members of Bangalore society would be asked to grace the gathering. Robert wrote to Augustus to ask for his recommendations regarding who they should invite from Madras, and to let him know about the racing. Charles and Morgan requested that John and Emily Orr, and Micky and Augusta Lavelle, be added to the list as well.

Organising the regimental races was far easier and the subalterns had everything almost finalised within a single evening at the bungalow. The meeting would begin early in the morning, when the temperature was comfortably cool for both horses and riders, and feature a total of eight events. James Goldie's troop was rostered to be on duty that day, along with Henry Wilkinson's, which meant Charles would miss out on all the excitement. He was disappointed, but there was still the ball and there'd be future races.

The others convinced themselves that preparing for the race meeting was all the excuse they needed to acquire more animals. During the course of the next fortnight, John Barker continued his celestial theme with another brown Arab he named *North Star*, Robert found an Australian bay gelding called *Screwdriver*, and Morgan bestowed the name *Gunner* on a grey Arab. Carrin thought it would be fun to be represented in the pony race, and so a willing bay called *Mr Stiggins* became the ninth resident of the stables.

Although the ordinary troopers of the regiment had no part to play in the ball, all those not on duty would have permission to spectate at the races. Such a lively distraction from dull routine was of course welcomed, especially given the gambling opportunities, and everyone was looking forward to it almost as much as they were to inheriting new horses. Private Earnshaw of Bill Wauchope's troop was amongst them, but time proved not to be on his side. He succumbed to the ravages of dysentery on Friday, 9th February, and was buried that afternoon.

"I am most heartily grieved that such a thing should have occurred," said William Dickson a little after seven o'clock the next morning. He was addressing the whole regiment, which had been ordered to parade in the racket alley of the barracks, and was speaking not of Private Earnshaw's demise but of the flogging of Private Davis of B Troop. A court martial had found the man guilty of desertion and habitual bad character, and sentenced him to fifty lashes from the cat o' nine tails. "I tried hard to have the sentence remitted," the colonel continued, "not for the prisoner's sake, as he richly deserves it, but for the sake of the regiment. I sincerely hope this will never occur again. If any man amongst you ever feels aggrieved, your duty is to present yourself to me and state your complaint so that I may use all the influence in my power to right things. Make no mistake, however. Discipline must be maintained, for without it the service could not carry on."

Private Davis had been stripped to the waist and his wrists tied above his head to a tripod of lances. One of the regimental farriers wielded the cat with diligence, and everyone was under orders to watch every last one of the flesh-ripping strokes. Several fainted at the sight, but Davis took his punishment without flinching. When he was released from his bonds, he accepted a glass of water from Alec Innes and promptly threw its contents in the doctor's face.

*   *   *

"Are we ready, Mr Maillard?" asked William Dickson a minute before nine o'clock on Tuesday, 20th February.

"As we'll ever be, sir," Robert replied.

"Then we'd better let them in."

Robert gestured to Sergeant Majors Chester and Burrell who pulled open the heavy doors and bowed to the guests waiting impatiently in the dark.

The Public Rooms were to Bangalore's cantonment what the village hall was to the likes of Castle Combe, Baslow or Little Missenden. Located directly opposite the barracks on a side street off South Parade it was ideal for all manner of community gatherings, including galas like this one where top hat and tails and the finest crinolined gowns were the order of the evening.

Eighteen NCOs, specially selected for their good manners, formed an honour guard inside the doors. The guests walked between the two lines of immaculate scarlet uniforms to the anteroom where the colonel, Thomas White, Hugh Burnell, and all the other officers of the 16th Lancers were waiting to greet them. By half past ten the last of more than two hundred guests had arrived.

They hailed the ballroom as a victory of extravagant decoration and illumination. Around its walls, fresh flowers surrounded the handsome scrolls that commemorated the regiment's achievements, most notably its role at the Battle of Aliwal. The pillars were each hung with a sabre star and wreathed with evergreens and artificial flowers. And naturally there had to be lances, lots of them, standing in proud bundles of deadly ash and steel at intervals around the room. Every candle in every chandelier and candelabra had been lit, which left only a few shadowy corners available for provocative assignations.

A supper feast was revealed in the Reading Room at eleven o'clock, and by midnight enough Champagne had been consumed for nobody to mind the regimental band's interpretation of dance music.

Augustus had made the journey from Madras and was staying at the subalterns' bungalow for a few days. He and Morgan had been talking with Captain Richard Marter of the Dragoon Guards about their ambitions for Thursday, and now they wanted to hear about his leaving plans.

"Most of the regiment is returning to England by troopship, of course," said Richard. "However, as I imagine you know from experience, such an environment is hardly ideal for small children."

"It certainly isn't," agreed Augustus.

"It's my son's fourth birthday today as a matter of fact, and his sister, Emily, will turn five in a couple of weeks."

"Well, many happy returns to the young man. What's his name?" asked Morgan.

"Thank you. He's Richard, after me. Salome and I decided it would be best to travel independently and to take the children's *ayah*, their nanny, with us. We're scheduled to sail from Madras on March 14th, heading first to Suez, then Cairo, Alexandria, on to Italy, and eventually home to London."

"That sounds like a wise plan, and no doubt a fascinating route," said Augustus.

"I hope so. It means I'll miss the ceremony on the 16th, but that can't be helped."

"What ceremony?" asked Morgan, perplexed.

"Haven't you heard?" Augustus crowed.

"Apparently not."

"An equestrian statue of Sir Mark Cubbon is to be installed in the middle of the parade ground."

"Oh really. He was the chief commissioner before Bowring, is that right?"

"That's the chap, yes," confirmed Richard.

"And both Sir John and Sir William will be coming here from Madras to do the unveiling. The whole garrison will turn out for it," explained Augustus.

Morgan thought Charles should hear all this and managed to extract him from the polka he was dancing with Emily Orr.

"News to me too," said Charles once Morgan had brought him up to speed. He took another glass of wine from a passing waiter. "And you said Sir William? As in, Denison? He of the tedious monologue and distrust of the natives, whose company we enjoyed so much?"

"The very same."

"I dare say it'll be his last official engagement before he retires back to England at the end of March," suggested Augustus.

Morgan saw the sparks of invention flare in his friend's eyes.

"Then we should go above and beyond to give the man a memorable send-off," Charles smiled.

Dancing and revelry had continued until gone four in the morning. The honour guard was sent back to barracks long before that and its members awoke none the worse for wear after their brush with the great and the good. Most of the officers, on the other hand, weren't seen by anyone before noon.

Thomas Brown, James Fuller, and Veterinary Surgeon Tom Richardson had meanwhile supervised the handover of horses and saddlery, assisted as ever by the senior NCOs. Old habits needed to be re-sown after lying fallow for nine months, beginning with the cleaning of saddles, bridles and accoutrements before a thorough kit inspection. Thomas took responsibility for the initial pairing of riders to horses, using his experience to judge the best match of skills and temperament, before leading the first of the troops to the parade ground for some basic drills. Each horse was identified by a number prefixed by the letter of the troop to which it had been allocated.

Many of the men had still been novices before they left England, and all the rest were woefully out of practice, so Thomas wasn't in the least bit surprised by the disarray of their mounted ranks when they attempted a few simple manoeuvres. Nothing a few weeks of daily riding school can't put right, he thought to himself.

Unaccustomed to their new partners, and sensing anxiety, the horses were skittish and testy. Private Cooper was struggling on H6, a gelding that was being particularly obstreperous. He yanked at the reins in frustration and used his spurs in a manner that earned the ire of the riding master.

"Private Cooper! What kind of saddle is your flabby arse currently occupying?" bellowed Thomas, as he cantered nearer to Cooper's position in the third rank.

"A Nolan saddle, sir."

"A Nolan saddle, quite so. Named after the esteemed horseman who designed it. Captain Nolan, late of Balaklava. And what is our golden rule, Private Cooper?"

"Gentleness not harshness, sir."

"Well said, lad. Horses are taught not by harshness but by gentleness." Thomas was addressing the whole ragged formation and he trotted back to the front of it. "Troopers, you are riding upon hallowed ground! This is the very place where Captain Nolan first conceived of that golden rule. So mind it well. Gentleness not harshness. Now, let's try again shall we. Heels down, hands light."

The stands at the main race course were rowdy despite the early hour when Thomas Brown brought runners and riders under orders just after half past six on Thursday morning. The right-handed track was renowned for being a demanding test of horse endurance and jockey skill. It was a ten-furlong oval with a pronounced downhill backstretch and a climb to the finish. Captain Gooch was acting as judge, and Colonel Dickson's wish to be chief steward had been granted.

The opening half-mile Charger Race was a closer contest than expected, with Robert Maillard on *Taj* only beating Maurice Fitzgerald on his grey Arab, *Foreigner*, by a neck.

The Garrison Open came next, a once round the track affair that saw Walter Bagenal's black Australian mare, *Enchantress*, ridden by a Mr Shaw, winning by a length from Richard Marter on his grey Australian called *Albemarie*.

Carrin's *Greyling*, being ridden by Robert, was generally considered the favourite for the three quarters of a mile Subalterns Cup, but John Barker and *North Star* took it by half a length from Cornet Harrie Reid's brown Arab, *Take Care*. The adjutant came in a distant third.

Although jockeying was strictly a job for men, the race card included the quarter-mile Diana Stakes for horses regularly ridden by ladies resident in Bangalore since the New Year. Salome Marter's grey Arab, *Restoration*, ridden by her husband, won it easily from Captain Fitzgerald riding Mrs Geddes's brown Arab, *Dancing Master*. The winner's prize was a bracelet, which Arthur Gooch presented to Mrs Marter with a theatrical flourish.

William Bovill and *Assassin* romped home to win the half-mile Hack Selling Stakes. Charles Chaplin's *Finger Post* came second, ridden by

Cornet William Hill, and Morgan finished an uncharacteristically lacklustre third on *Lucifer*.

Maurice Fitzgerald and *Foreigner* claimed their only win of the morning in the Regimental Challenge Cup, before the crowd was treated to some post-finish excitement from the half-mile Lilliputian Race for ponies of thirteen hands and under. Cornet Peter Peacocke's *Flirt*, ridden by John Barker, won from Harry Reid's *Tomtit* in second, and Robert riding Carrin's *Mr Stiggins* in third. For no apparent reason, the moment *Flirt* passed the winning post he bolted across the course and unseated his rider straight into Major General Haines's carriage. No harm was done and John remounted to cross the line for a second time, receiving loud applause and cheers from everyone behind the rail.

Alec Innes would have cheered as well if he could have been there. Instead, he was at the Cavalry Hospital writing his post mortem report about Private Leach who'd gone the same way as Private Earnshaw.

The Consolation Handicap rounded off the morning with a three-quarter mile decider for horses beaten in previous races. John Barker won that too, this time on *Southern Cross*, with Robert, once again on Carrin's *Greyling*, taking second.

He didn't let on to his friends, because to do so would be unseemly and not at all sportsman-like, but Robert was bitterly disappointed by his performance. Even though he'd claimed victory in the first race of the day, he felt he really should've done better in the others. Back at the bungalow in the evening, he went to bed early leaving John Barker still re-living his successes. Charles had other things on his mind.

"Did you notice what's arrived in the parade ground on your way past earlier?" he asked Morgan.

"The plinth? No doubt the statue will be turning up soon as well. An inconvenient obstacle, if you ask me."

"It will rather get in the way during drill. I've been having some thoughts about it as a matter of fact."

"I reckoned as much," smiled Morgan.

"There's something I'd like to show you," Charles whispered. "Come this way." He led Morgan into his room and opened the trunk sitting in one corner. It was one of those that had come with him from

Colchester, and was now empty save for a rectangular wooden box. He took it out and placed it on the floor. "Open it," invited Charles.

Morgan roared with laughter when he saw what was inside.

*　　*　　*

On the afternoon of Friday, 16th March, one man in every eight from each regiment in the cantonment marched on foot from the barracks to the parade ground. They formed up in reluctant squares on the north side of the veiled statue and waited for the dignitaries to take their places on a temporary dais. Sir John Le Marchant led the way, followed by Major General Frederick Haines, Sir William Denison, Chief Commissioner Lewin Bowring, Assistant Commissioner Vijayendra Rao, and a few other senior civil servants from both Bangalore and Madras.

Sir John offered a few words of thanks to Major General Haines and the garrison, and then Chief Commissioner Bowring gave a speech about the life and good works of his predecessor. Everyone was grateful he kept it brief, especially those too far away to make out what was being said. A reporter from the *Bangalore Herald* scribbled notes at the sidelines, and a photographer by the name of Barton made ready to capture the scene.

At the appointed hour of four o'clock the parade was ordered to begin its march past between the statue and the dais, the cloth was removed, and the command was given: "Eyes left!"

At first Sir William and his colleagues assumed that the broad smiles marching by them were provoked by admiration for a great man. But when smiles gave way to unrestrained laughter that spread through the ranks like an infectious yawn, Sir John was the first to spot the outrage. The bronze likeness of Sir Mark Cubbon, sitting astride a powerful thoroughbred and gazing west across his beloved Bangalore, had been daubed across the forehead with three stripes of white paint — a Hindoo symbol for Shiva's power.

Sir William was utterly crestfallen by the humiliation. Bowring was cross. Frederick Haines thought it was hilarious, but was obliged by duty not to show it. He dismissed the parade with haste and apologised unreservedly to the guests.

By the evening, notices were being posted all around the barracks. Charles smiled with quiet satisfaction when he read one on his way to the Cavalry Officers' Mess. A reward of £100 was offered for information leading to the discovery of those responsible for the heinous act of vandalism.

It was never claimed.

CHAPTER NINE
HEART'S CONTENT, NEWFOUNDLAND
SUNDAY, 29TH JULY 1866

Sophia Munro wanted one more photograph. A final image to draw the story to a close. Something that would represent both a triumphant end and a significant new beginning.

The *Great Eastern* was anchored out in the harbour behind her. She'd already captured the resting leviathan from down on the grey shingle beach, where the Atlantic cable had been hauled in on Friday morning, and from a low hill on the south side of the bay. There was no need to repeat those compositions.

The obvious choice, she decided, was right in front of her. Janet agreed, and they began setting up the camera.

The telegraph station was a two-storey building with whitewashed timber cladding stained and faded by the elements. Six tall sash windows gazed out to sea. A large Union Jack whipped in the wind high above the steeply pitched roof. Two lines of signal flags fluttered either side of it like bunting. To the front was a goat paddock enclosed by tall, rough-hewn fence posts that cast a photogenic shadow across the path leading the hundred feet or so to the shore. To the rear, the silhouette of a wooded ridge ascended towards a fickle sky. It was from this humble building that North America was now connected to Ireland – and in turn to London, Europe and beyond – at the rate of a few words per minute. The second attempt at the mission of science had been a success.

Reprising the route of the previous summer, the *Great Eastern* had travelled from the Thames to Bantry Bay with five hundred and two souls aboard. Sophia and Janet were among them, having been asked to repeat their photographic study by the Telegraph Company. On Thursday, 12th July, in thick fog outside Valentia, the ship was reunited with HMS *Terrible* whose escort duties were to be shared with the steamships *Albany* and *Medway*.

Many lessons had been learned from the first voyage. The method of electrical testing had been improved, and much more robust and powerful picking-up equipment had been fitted fore and aft. *Festina lente* – make haste slowly – was the motto of Captain Anderson and his crew, who maintained an average speed that was a couple of knots per hour slower than last year.

With the exception of the small hours of 18th July when the cable running out of the tank became a tangled mess, none of the problems that so characterised the first attempt were experienced again. Everything worked to perfection, the weather and sea were kind for the most part, and paying-out of the cable continued with uniform certainty throughout the fortnight to Newfoundland.

The delightful monotony of the whole expedition was a mixed blessing for Sophia and Janet. On one hand the absence of drama made for less varied and arguably less interesting photography, while on the other it allowed them far more time to relax, socialise, and think to the future.

Henry Moriarty was once again acting staff-commander in charge of navigation, and Sophia enjoyed renewing their friendship. Henry spoke with great fondness about his wife and family, and invited both Sophia and Janet to visit them upon their return to England. As it had last year, conversation frequently returned to the topic of the slave trade. Henry explained that Zanzibar, off the east coast of Africa, was the abomination's commercial heart. It was there that slaves were sold to Arabian masters. The seed of an idea already sown in Sophia's mind was beginning to take root.

Another notable and very welcome difference on this journey was the daily publication of the aptly named *Great Eastern Telegraph*. Every twelve hours or so Valentia would transmit Reuters' reports via the cable. They were then reproduced in the form of an onboard newspaper for distribution among the passengers, as well as being posted outside the ship's telegraph office. The Austro-Prussian War and the riotous protests of the Reform League dominated the headlines. There was a cholera outbreak in Liverpool that claimed fifteen lives in the space of a couple of days. In Norway, a fire left six thousand people homeless. Soldiers fought with former slaves in Atlanta. There were stock market updates and the latest odds on the favourite for the Goodwood Cup. Enfield rifles were to be converted to breech loaders. Colonel Tom Sweeney was urging the Fenians to continue preparations despite their failed invasion of British Canada.

The House of Commons was discussing turret-gun ships and how England was lagging behind some other nations in their use.

After dinner on Thursday, 26th July, the *Great Eastern* passed a lone iceberg at a distance, and then the fog returned. It lifted shortly before eight o'clock the next morning to reveal Heart's Content Bay, and the passengers and crew were treated to the first sight of their long hoped for destination. As well as the one above the telegraph station, flags were being flown from the church and many of the sixty houses that made up the village. Most of its hardy inhabitants were fishermen and they'd come out in their boats to welcome the great ship and its escort.

At lunchtime that day, the onboard telegraph office received a message from Queen Victoria on the Isle of Wight for onward transmission to Andrew Johnson in Washington:

THE QUEEN CONGRATULATES THE PRESIDENT ON THE SUCCESSFUL COMPLETION OF AN UNDERTAKING WHICH SHE HOPES MAY SERVE AS AN ADDITIONAL BOND OF UNION BETWEEN THE UNITED STATES AND ENGLAND

A rowing boat was being landed on the beach and Sophia and Janet both turned around at the sound. Samuel Canning and Henry Moriarty climbed out and crunched across the shingle towards them.

"Good morning, gentlemen. How are you?" said Janet.

"A very good morning to you too, ladies. Still buoyed with joy at the achievement," Samuel replied.

"And so you should be," said Sophia, "It really is a wonder!"

"I'm glad we happened upon you," Henry began, "Mr Canning and I were just talking about you both."

"Oh, really? Should we be concerned?" Sophia asked with a mischievous smile.

"No, no. It's just that we've had an idea. You see, although the cable office will be busy tomorrow and the day after with replies going back and forth between Washington and England, it's likely to be quite quiet today," Henry explained.

Samuel continued. "We've come ashore to send a message or two of our own while the window of opportunity is open, and we wondered if you'd care to do likewise? After all, you've been with us from the beginning."

"That's so thoughtful and kind. Thank you, both of you. We'd love to," said Sophia.

"Capital!" Samuel exclaimed. "Of course, we could all be sending transmissions from the office on board, but somehow that no longer seems to have the same gravitas as the place where the cables meet."

"We quite understand. It's a wonderful idea," said Janet.

"And a great privilege," added Sophia.

"Well, have a little ponder about what you'd like to say and to whom. We'll be in the telegraph station when you're ready," said Henry.

"You'll need to keep them quite short though, I'm afraid," added Samuel. "Perhaps about half a dozen words? Don't bother with punctuation and abbreviate as much as possible. It makes the telegrapher's task easier."

The camera was in position and everything was just right for the picture Sophia wanted to take. The flag was fully unfurled in the breeze, the sun was peeking between the clouds to cast the shadow along the path, and a goat was grazing in the paddock. She waited for Henry and Samuel to disappear inside the building and then began the exposure.

"What will you send?" she asked Janet as she replaced the lens cap.

"A wee hello to my mother in Pitlochry, I suppose. And you?"

Sophia wrote in her notebook, tore out the page and handed it to Janet. Janet laughed.

TO LT M FARRELL 16TH LANCERS BANGALORE WITHOUT AIRS OR GRACES HEARTS CONTENT S MUNRO

*   *   *

As grand as the chief commissioner's residence near the race course, albeit on a more modest scale, the Polo Club building sat in immaculate landscaped gardens a few hundred yards from Micky Lavelle's house. The Polo Club itself had relocated to new grounds north of Ulsoor Tank several years before. The unofficial gentlemen's club established in its place was now the favoured haunt of officers and civil servants from the cantonment community. Micky Lavelle was neither of those things and nor did he fit the definition of a gentleman. However, as a respected acquaintance of John Orr and many others, he'd been accepted as almost an equal.

Friday tiffin had become a regular fixture at the club. Over time it had evolved from a simple luncheon to a gathering that sprawled through afternoon tea towards an evening drinks reception. Its popularity was due in no small measure to the open invitation extended to members' wives, and children of sociable age. Most of the rooms in the building naturally remained exclusively male territory, but all expatriates regardless of gender were welcome in the main lounge and on the oval lawn.

Carrin was being fussed over by regimental wives in the main lounge when Charles and Morgan entered through its arched doorways a little after one o'clock on 3rd August. The lieutenant had been afflicted by jungle fever more than once during his time in Bangalore and had not long got over the worst of the most recent bout. The doctors usually referred to the condition as malaria, but whatever it was called it left Carrin pale and exhausted.

Morgan spotted John and Emily Orr with Micky and Augusta Lavelle in the far corner of the room. He and Charles strolled in their direction after ordering glasses of pale ale from an attendant waiter. John and Micky were admiring one of the many hunting trophies that adorned the double-height walls. Emily and the heavily pregnant Augusta were talking amongst themselves. After the usual pleasantries, John asked after Alec Innes.

"He was, and I believe still is, planning to attend," explained Charles, "but he's been delayed by matters requiring his attention after another unfortunate death this morning."

"Oh, how very sad," said Emily.

"Another dysentery case, one assumes?" asked John.

"Yes, as far as I know. Private Ware, poor soul."

"How many's that now this summer?"

"Seven?" Morgan suggested, looking at Charles.

"Yes, seven," Charles concurred. "Nine altogether this year. Aside from Farrier McCarthy last weekend, all the rest have been privates. I've begun to wonder why that is, although I doubt the answer involves any great mystery."

"I suspect you're right," said John.

The waiter approached with the requested beers and Morgan signed the proffered chit to add them to his club tab. "Have you done much hunting, Micky?" he asked, cocking his head towards the stuffed head that looked down on them with glassy eyes.

"Aye, on occasion, but 'tis more of a gentleman's pastime, so it is," Micky replied, too modestly for Augusta's liking.

"Don't be hiding your light under a bushel now, husband. Tell them the alligator story, so," she insisted with an encouraging raise of her eyebrows.

"That was hardly hunting, my love. A simple necessity for a comrade in peril, so it was." He kissed her cheek.

The group of friends smiled expectantly at Micky and waited for the tale to be told.

"Aw, very well," he relented. "It was the day before we reached *Saugor* on the torturous march north in '58. My good friend, Isaac Tyrrell, was sergeant of the baggage guard at the time and bringing up the rear. As he was making his way along a particular riverbank, he found himself being pursued by an alligator of some considerable size. Now whether the beast was amorous or hungry, I wouldn't care to speculate, but Isaac was *quare* panicky, so he was. Anyhow, I happened to be up on the suspension bridge that spanned the river just ahead of the unfolding drama, so I levelled my Enfield and squeezed off a shot."

"And Sergeant Tyrrell survived the encounter?" asked Morgan.

"Well, I did consider putting him out of his misery," Micky replied with a wink, "but aye, I was aiming for the alligator, so I was."

They all laughed at that. "An impressive feat of marksmanship!" praised Morgan.

"Aw, I don't know about that. More luck than judgement, I reckon," Micky replied.

"Did the 43rd go all the way to Lucknow that year?" Charles asked.

"No, only as far as Cawnpore. And that was plenty far enough. This was the summer after the terrible sieges, so it was, and things were beginning to settle down. Nevertheless, we saw some sights I'll not soon forget. That sorrowful well... mutineers hanging from trees in such numbers that... aw, never mind."

Charles was silent. Morgan regretted him asking and was grateful to John Orr for changing the subject. "Ah, I see General Marshall has arrived," said the doctor, gesturing towards the doors. The group turned to look.

"And he's brought Jessie along for the first time. How delightful! She's such a charming young lady," said Emily, referring to the retired general's demure sixteen-year-old daughter.

John caught the general's eye and made the usual introductions when he walked over to join them. "I'm looking forward to that billiards re-match you promised, Hubert," he said.

"Happy to oblige, my good fellow. One never objects to thrashing a chap a second time," joked the sixty-two-year-old, his deep voice hinting at Midlothian ancestry.

"Will we be having the pleasure of Susanne's company? She's well, I hope?" asked Emily. Jessie Susanne Marshall was younger than her husband by twenty years. Like Augusta whose first name was really Harriett, she went by her middle name and bestowed Jessie on her eldest daughter.

"Quite well, yes. Thank you for asking, my dear. She decided to remain at home with the children. Little Charlotte is feeling a touch under the weather, you see."

"Nothing serious, I trust?"

"No, no, just a four-year-old with a sniffle. I'm sure it's nothing at all."

Augusta was keen to bring Jessie into the conversation and asked about her first impressions of the club. Miss Marshall was slim and nearly as tall as Augusta. She had a strong jaw with an ever-present, broad smile that made her cheeks look full and rounded. Youthful vigour shone in her deep-set, expressive brown eyes. She blushed at becoming the centre of attention, but retained her poise. "It's a little like going down the rabbit hole, ma'am," she replied in a soft voice after a moment's thought.

"The rabbit hole, my dear? And please do call me Augusta."

"Thank you. Yes, like in Mr Carroll's book when Alice finds herself in a curious hall and goes on to meet so many fascinating characters. It's terribly exciting."

"There are certainly plenty of characters here, so there are," jested Micky. "I fear we may be behind the literary times though."

"My apologies. It's called *Alice's Adventures in Wonderland* and it really is marvellous. Father was able to obtain a copy for me from London after Christmas last," she said, squeezing Hubert's arm and looking up at him adoringly. "I must've read it at least a dozen times by now. Would any of you care to borrow it?" she added.

"That's very kind, Jessie, thank you. I'm sure Augusta and I would enjoy it," said Emily.

The ladies chatted further about literature and children, and what Augusta might call her baby if they both survived labour. The men returned to more martial topics and added to their club tabs.

"I was pleased to see the Cubbon statue being cleaned up and moved to take pride of place outside *Attara Kacheri*," commented the general. "A much more fitting position than the parade ground. The whole damned park should be named after him in my view."

"Did you know Sir Mark?" asked Charles with a straight face.

"Oh yes, very well. A gentleman of remarkable fairness and intellect, and a great reformer to boot. The Empire lost an invaluable servant when he passed away. Such a pitiful end to a glorious career though."

"I confess to not being familiar with the story," Charles prompted.

"Well, he'd suffered with his liver for quite a spell, you see, and had to resign as chief commissioner because of it. He was returning to England for the first time in sixty years to convalesce, only to succumb while at that infested den of iniquity – Suez."

"An inglorious end indeed," Charles remarked. None of the first-hand descriptions he'd heard endeared him to the place.

"Quite. Now about that game of billiards, John" said the general.

Micky followed the two men down the corridor, leaving Charles and Morgan, the wives and Jessie to mingle amongst the club's guests. These sorts of gatherings were useful opportunities for making new connections and developing old ones. Emily was particularly conscientious in showing Jessie how it was done.

By the time a weary Alec Innes arrived later on, the afternoon monsoon had been hammering down for an hour. He was drenched through and in need of a stiff drink. Dripping across the marble floor, he made a beeline straight for Morgan.

"I have something for you," he said, fishing a damp envelope from an inside pocket and handing it over. Morgan looked utterly bemused.

"Afternoon, Alec. What's this then?"

"A telegram. It was delivered to the Mess just before I left to come here."

"Are you making game of me? You know I don't get letters, never mind telegrams. It must be for someone else, surely?"

"Well, it's got your name on it. See for yourself."

Morgan was just about to do exactly that when Emily came over to introduce Jessie to Alec.

"Oh bless your heart, you're soaked to the skin," said Jessie before Emily had even begun the formalities. She'd instinctively taken Alec's hand in both of hers as she spoke. The unconscious, tactile gesture disregarded the protocols of etiquette and expressed her empathy and depth of compassion all the more for doing so.

Neither Charles nor Morgan had ever seen the look in Alec's eyes that they were witnessing now. He was captivated by Jessie's gentle serenity and evidently lost for words.

Emily watched with a knowing smile. She had a suggestion. "Jessie, why don't you and I go and find the good doctor some brandy?"

Jessie nodded without looking away from Alec. "We'll return in just a moment," she said as Emily began to lead her by the arm.

"Jesus wept, Alec. If you could only see your face!" Morgan teased as soon as the women were beyond hearing distance.

Charles clapped Alec on the shoulder. "I think we'd better leave you to the ladies' tender mercies."

Alec's gaze was still following Jessie across the room.

"Aye, do that," was all he could say.

Charles and Morgan walked outside and sheltered from the rain beneath the carriage porch. Charles lit a cheroot. Absorbed in quizzical procrastination, Morgan was turning the envelope back and forth.

"Well? Are you going to open it?"

Morgan hesitated a moment longer before slowly extracting the telegram. It was almost as if he was suspicious, or even fearful, of the contents.

And then he laughed.

"What on earth is it?" asked Charles.

"It's a very welcome surprise. Here, see what you make of it," Morgan replied, passing the paper to his friend.

"Dashed cryptic. Who's this Munro fellow and why will his heart be content without airs or graces?"

"It's a place. And it's not a fellow."

Morgan had never told Charles about meeting Sophia at The World's End. Now was a good time.

*   *   *

Sabina Augusta Lavelle came into the world on 20th August, the same day Corporal Brice departed it. A week later, Lance Sergeant Courtney followed him. His would be the 16th Lancers' last death of 1866. Disease was once again the Reaper's agent. Seven months would pass before it claimed its next victim.

As well as the first anniversary of the regiment's arrival in Bangalore, September brought with it a daughter for James and Magdalene Goldie, another for William and Louisa Farmer, impatience for the end of the south-west monsoon, and a letter for Charles from his sister.

"Fizzing!" Charles thought aloud as he read it in the Cavalry Officers' Mess.

"What is?" asked Walter Bagenal, looking up from his newspaper.

"I feared it might never happen, but it seems Harriet has finally found herself a husband."

"Good for her," chimed in Morgan. "Who's the lucky man?"

"A chap by the name of George Cracklow – previously Captain Cracklow of the Bengal Horse Artillery no less."

"So perhaps you'll soon be Uncle Charles?" said Morgan, with an exaggerated wink.

"Oh yes, I suppose I might be in time. How peculiar that will be!"

"What else does your sister say?" asked Walter.

"Let me see... well, he lives off London Road by Oxford Street in Cheltenham, which is just a short walk from my father's residence, and they plan to have a ceremony at the abbey in Great Malvern on Valentine's Day next year. Oh, and she hopes I'll forgive her for not waiting until I'm able to be part of the day."

"Which goes without saying," said Morgan.

"Naturally. It's a shame I won't be there, of course, but I'm delighted for her."

"News deserving of a toast, me thinks," suggested Walter. "Yadhu! Be a good fellow and fetch four *pegs* of brandy, if you please."

The assistant steward brought the drinks and Walter signed the chit. "Raise your glasses, gentlemen," he began. "To the future happiness of Mr and Mrs Cracklow."

"To Harriet and George," Morgan called. Charles and the others repeated him and downed their brandy. Yadhu was told to fetch another round, and to bring an extra dram for Doctor Alec who was just walking in. Charles explained the reason for the impromptu celebration and Alec offered his warmest congratulations, as did Yadhu.

Although he was well known for his generosity of spirit and sense of humour, it hadn't gone unnoticed that Alec had been particularly cheerful of late. Everyone knew he'd begun to court young Jessie Marshall, but nobody pried into how the romance was blossoming. The consensus of whispered opinion was that if anyone in the regiment was deserving of affection it was Alec Innes.

Walter said cheerio on his way out. He was going to join some other officers venturing to the old city, known as the *petta*, which lay to the west of the cantonment by the fort. With time to kill before lunch, Alec, Morgan and Charles chatted on. They reflected on their first year in the country and how the reality of colonial life compared with the assumptions and expectations they may have once held. Alec and the other medical staff had been occupied with their unpleasant work in the hospital almost all the time. For Charles and Morgan and their fellow officers, infrequent regimental duties punctuated long days of leisure. They'd enjoyed riding and occasional hunting trips, the social life offered by the club, monthly quadrille parties, and going to the races. The regiment's Dramatic Society organised regular fundraising performances, usually in aid of the cantonment's orphanage. Charles was due to play the part of the foundling, Corin, in a burlesque production of *Once Upon A Time There Were Two Kings* at the end of the month. There were the many pleasures of the flesh too, with Bangalore catering for every conceivable taste and peccadillo, but there was no adventure. It was worse, they conjectured, for the fighting men of the ranks with no fighting to do except amongst themselves. They had morning and evening stables, roll calls, inspections, parades, and other routines, but only the intoxicating and erotic temptations of the bazaars to interrupt the tedium.

Then Charles noticed the title of the booklet Alec had arrived with. *"The Madras Quarterly Journal of Medical Science,"* he read with curiosity.

"Aye. Not exactly bedtime reading, as you can perhaps imagine, but terribly informative. I have a short piece in this edition myself, as a matter of fact."

"Fame at last, eh?" quipped Morgan.

Alec laughed. "Hardly. It's only a wee report on the facts and figures of this summer's dysentery epidemic. It offers some opinion about the causes as well."

"May I take a look?" asked Charles.

"Be my guest, though I'd caution you. As I've said before, it's a grim business and the report is rather detailed from a medical point of view."

Charles thumbed though the pages until he found Article Eleven. Morgan looked over his shoulder as he began to read. There were tables that summarised how many men had been admitted to hospital with diarrhoea or dysentery, which troops they came from, and how many had died. It seemed Bill Wauchope's troop was the worst afflicted by quite some margin. Charles and Morgan's own troops had suffered the least with fewer than half as many cases. They were both relieved to discover that. The report continued with Alec's observations and hypotheses about factors that might influence a trooper falling foul of disease.

"*Early morning parades, without any thing on his stomach except, perhaps, arrack saved from last night's allowance,*" Morgan read aloud.

"*The sudden and frequent chills from the nature of his duties,*" Charles continued. "Given the climate here, what sort of chills do you mean there, Alec?"

"Well, you know how the men strip to the chest to clean their horses after parade? In doing so, they're exposed to the sun, and of course the nature of the work itself is strenuous. They perspire a great deal and understandably seek shade or a draught to cool themselves once their duties are complete. That's when a chill can set in and cause mischief in the liver or bowels."

"Oh, I see," said Charles, not entirely truthfully.

They carried on reading about the unwholesome leanness of the ration-meat, the correlation between the monsoon and the outbreak of disease in Bangalore generally, and the close proximity of the barracks to the bazaar. And then there was the impurity of the water sourced from Ulsoor Tank.

"*It contained an average of five grains of organic matter per gallon, even after passing through the filters, as well as a large quantity of chlorine,*" Morgan quoted. "Jesus wept!"

"Thank heavens for the dhobies' well!" said Charles.

They continued reading until they came to graphic descriptions of treatments in four fatal cases of men they'd known and the subsequent post mortem examinations.

"That's enough for me, I think," said Morgan.

"And I," said Charles, handing the report back to Alec, who suppressed a smile at their squeamishness.

"The disagreeable water is also an influence on some of the other conditions we have to contend with," he said, turning to Article Six. "Doctor Lowe, of the Sappers and Miners, talks here about the *bad water, bad air, and peculiar atmospheric states* around the barracks. He goes on to suggest that, together, they excite a variety of malarial fevers."

"Of the sort that's been plaguing Carrin?" asked Charles.

"Aye, amongst others. Our collective welfare should be greatly improved by the more salubrious environment of the new barracks on the plain. I do hope the move there will be sooner rather than later."

The doctor's train of thought was interrupted by the looming presence of Yadhu Nayak, who dispatched the mosquito biting his neck with an efficient slap of his palm as he spoke. "Sahibs will be having more brandy?"

CHAPTER TEN
SALEM, INDIA
MONDAY, 19TH NOVEMBER 1866

What constitutes an adventure? That was the question still preoccupying Charles when the road emerged from the long shadow of the hills south-east of *Thoppur* and the expanse of the plain came into view.

Robert Maillard reckoned an adventure simply had to involve some sort of journey, while William Dickson defined it as endeavouring to accomplish something extraordinary in the face of danger and uncertainty. Pills Macbeth and Maurice Fitzgerald were reticent, but both seemed to agree that venturing into the unknown and returning to tell the tale were vital elements. Last night's discussion had gone round in circles and Charles was none the wiser for it. He supposed they were all right in their own way.

Their current expedition promised to fulfil all the suggested conditions, though it didn't yet feel very adventurous to Charles. He wondered what Solomon Smith and his fellow bâtmen would say on the subject, if the syces even gave it a second thought, and whether Corporal Thornhill and the other members of the string quartet had a different perception altogether. Perhaps adventure was no more than an illusion of expectation and hindsight. Perhaps, in fact, it really didn't matter.

Adventure or not, the irony wasn't lost on Charles that in being here they all had reason to be thankful to a tax collector. They were on their way to the Salem Races at the invitation of the Honourable David Arbuthnott, the eleventh son of a Kincardineshire viscount, a respected magistrate, and the collector of revenue in the kingdom of Mysore. A circuitous route home by way of the hill-country to the west was planned for afterwards.

This morning was the group's sixth away from Bangalore and they expected to make Salem before nightfall. Their luggage, supplies, camera equipment, a bullmastiff puppy called *Bulger*, and the quartet's instruments, were hauled in two carts, each drawn by a pair of ponies and driven by the syces. Everyone else was riding troop horses, including the officers who'd been given special permission to do so by the colonel. Tethered behind the officers' cart were *Woodman* and Maurice's Australian bay mare, *Cobweb*, and grey Arab, *Foreigner*. All three were unmounted to save their legs for the racing.

They'd travelled between twenty and thirty miles every day, always setting off well before dawn to make the most of the cooler early hours. The landscape varied from partially cultivated and gently undulating, to vertiginous hills cloaked in dense forest. Only once had a river crossing presented a challenge, and the carts forded it without incident. Low cloud was a constant companion.

Each day's ride was taken at a leisurely pace and spanned a convenient distance between *dâk* bungalows, the ubiquitous resthouses that acted as relay stations for the government's postal service. Found every ten to fifteen miles on all the main routes across the country, the majority were cramped and dingy. Yesterday's was amongst the exceptional few that resembled modest, well-maintained barracks. Whatever their size, on the inside they offered no more than bare cot beds in bare rooms. Guests were expected to fend for themselves and rely on their own servants to do the cooking, which wasn't thought unreasonable given lodging was free for soldiers and other Crown employees.

William's decision to take the band along made for a more entertaining journey. On the road they were never short of a song, Private Griffin could whistle any requested tune with the same finesse with which he played the cello, and when the instruments were unpacked in the evening impromptu recitals helped to pass the time and ingratiate other travellers. *Bulger* had a role in that as well.

Maurice's bâtman was unforthcoming about how he'd acquired the dog, but a game of dice or a barrack-room debt was assumed to have something to do with it. Either way, the captain's servant found the puppy's devotion and protective instinct an irritating nuisance. In search of affection elsewhere, the inquisitive bullmastiff padded around the dâks with furrowed brow and was rewarded with petting and kind words from almost everyone he jumped at. Privates Allan and Deare, who played the viola and second violin respectively, grew quite attached to *Bulger* and made sure he was properly fed and watered.

Robert was riding ahead of the group. When he stopped just past a fork in the road, Charles cantered to catch up.

"We continue on this main road south," said Robert, anticipating Charles's question.

"Right you are. We can't be too far away now."

"Only another few hours by my estimation," Robert confirmed. "You see those hills over there?" he added, pointing towards the substantial range about five miles away to the east. "They're the Shevaroys. If you follow the ridge line as it descends to the south, your eye will fall upon Salem."

"Ah yes, I see. But we don't go that way?"

"The turning we've just gone by leads in that direction, but I imagine the gradients would be a chore for the carts. If we carry on due south the road should be easier."

Robert's predictions were accurate. At *Omalur* the route turned south-east, the horses and ponies were rested, and the officers and men ate an unhurried lunch. By late afternoon the weavers and grain merchants in Salem's outskirts were witnessing the eastward procession of fourteen riders, two laden carts, and three racing thoroughbreds.

Now that they were in the town, navigational reference was made to directions provided by David Arbuthnott. He'd described how they needed to turn north at a crossroads and ride a short distance on the *Yercaud* Road. Someone would meet them outside the Central Jail.

The couple of miles to the junction were like an abbreviated tour through the ascending strata of Salem society. Construction materials changed from mud and thatch to brick and tile, huts became houses, and the scrummage of private dwellings gave way to grand public buildings in spacious gardens.

Bearing north as instructed, the group passed the District Court on their right and glimpsed the Central Jail's high curtain wall through the trees on their left. After another two hundred yards it veered away from them to form one side of a triangular esplanade. The jail's gatehouse stood at the apex of the open ground about forty yards from the road. Painted white and topped with a flagpole, the entrance façade was styled like a barbican with arched galleries on either side.

Everyone dismounted to stretch their legs, Private Allan took *Bulger* for a walk to restore his comfort, and William instructed Corporal Thornhill to announce their arrival at the gate. He returned to report that a Captain Gordon was being sent for and would join them presently.

Charles lit a cheroot. "Quite a place," he commented to Robert while they checked on *Woodman* and the other horses. "Surprising to find such a large jail in a small town like this, don't you think?"

"Indeed. And it looks recently built. I suppose it must serve the whole region," Robert replied as he inspected one of *Foreigner*'s hooves.

A narrow wicket door was set in the main gate and the sound of it being unbolted drew Charles and Robert's attention away from the horses. A tall man in a plain uniform ducked through the opening and raised a hand in greeting as he made his approach. He was followed by a subordinate of similar height who looked a little older and heavier set.

"Good afternoon to you, gentlemen," said the first man. "My name's Captain Gordon. I'm the superintendent here."

"Colonel Dickson, 16th Lancers. It's a pleasure to make your acquaintance, captain," William replied, stepping forward and shaking hands.

"Likewise, colonel, and may I say how delighted I am that you've mustered in such force."

"Think nothing of it. We appreciated the invitation and were only too happy to make a good showing. I take it you have some involvement with the race meeting?"

"Oh yes, quite so. In fact, I'm proud to be partly responsible for its conception. A couple of gentlemen from the Survey Department and I came up with the idea a while back, you see. Lieutenants Walker and Edgecombe are looking forward to meeting you at the Collector's Bungalow this evening. I expect Mr Shaw, the inspecting veterinarian, and Colonel *Foord* and his son, both of the engineers, will be there too."

"Excellent! I'm sure it'll be a credit to you all. Is the bungalow nearby?"

"Thank you. Yes, only half a mile up the road. You and your officers are to be Mr Arbuthnott's guests, and we have accommodation for the rest of your men within the jail. Mr Tyrrell here will show them the way," said Captain Gordon, gesturing towards his colleague who smiled and doffed his jailor's cap.

"You're most kind," said William.

"We wouldnae mind if you threw away the key to save us from Corporal Thornill's singing," teased Pills as he filled his pipe.

"And save me from your snoring," retorted the corporal. Pills laughed at that.

"Fear not, lads. You won't be seeing the inside of the cells today," indulged Mr Tyrrell, addressing the band members and bâtmen. "Mind you watch out for the deadly snakes and scorpions though." He had the authoritative, good-humoured tone of someone experienced in dealing with men of the ranks, and what sounded to Charles like the remnants of a Suffolk accent.

William expressed his gratitude again and took the opportunity to introduce Maurice, Pills, Robert, and Charles.

"Your reputation as a trainer of winners precedes you, Captain Fitzgerald," said the superintendent after the formalities were out of the way.

"You flatter me, sir," dismissed Maurice, taking a comb to the hair that failed to conceal his baldness. "The lion's share of credit must go to Lieutenant Maillard and the artfulness with which he jockeys."

"Oh I don't know about that. The horses do all the work," said Robert, modestly. "Will you gentlemen be riding?"

"Not personally, no," Captain Gordon replied, "but I'm in The Exiles syndicate, and we have a handful of decent runners on the card."

"I've been thinking I may get one of the local Eurasian boys to ride my *Shut-Em-Up* in the pony race. Just to enter into the spirit of things, you understand," said Mr Tyrrell.

Private Allan was making his way back to the group and let *Bulger* off his lead at the edge of the esplanade. The puppy spotted the two strangers and bounded towards them with volleys of suspicion-laden barks.

"And who's this handsome beast?" asked Mr Tyrrell, crouching down to mollify the animal.

"His name's *Bulger*, sir," explained Private Allan. "I'm sorry he jumped up at you like that." The puppy had reverted to playfulness and was enjoying the attention.

"He'll likely make a fine guard dog when he's grown," observed Mr Tyrrell. "You're lucky to have him."

"Oh, he's not mine, sir, but yes, I'm sure he will."

"Probably best to keep him on the leash, and be wary of other dogs when you're exercising him. Rabies is all too common hereabouts."

"Thank you, sir. I didn't realise."

Captain Gordon returned his attention to Maurice. "I wonder, Captain Fitzgerald, since your horses aren't racing until Wednesday, would you consider being one of our stewards tomorrow? I'm sure we'd all appreciate having your experience on hand to ensure fair play and so forth."

"Certainly, of course. I'd like that very much."

"Marvellous, thank you. Are all three of those yours?"

"Two of them are. *Woodman* is Lieutenant Agnew's. Come, captain, allow me to show you," invited Maurice, strolling towards the horses. William and Robert went with them, but Charles was more interested in talking to the jailor.

"If you don't mind me asking, Mr Tyrrell, does your given name happen to be Isaac?"

"Well bless my soul! It is, sir. How on earth did you come to guess that?"

"I believe we may have a mutual friend. Do you know a fellow called Micky Lavelle?"

"Why yes, we served together in the 43rd some years ago. Last I heard he was in New Zealand."

"He's settled in Bangalore since then. I thought there was a sporting chance you might be the same chap he's talked about. After all, I don't suppose there can be that many Tyrrells in this part of the world. It's good to put a face to the name."

"How about that. Please do give him my regards. I shall have to pay him a visit when I next go to Bangalore. And he's talked about me, you say?"

"I will, happily. Yes, a story about you being chased by an alligator and Micky shooting it from a bridge."

Isaac chuckled. "I've told that tale myself often enough, I must confess. In my recollection it was an altogether different alligator that fell under Micky's aim, but perhaps I've been mistaken all this time. No matter. It makes my day to hear that he remembers me."

"I've no doubt he'll be equally pleased. Has Salem been home to you since leaving the army?"

"No, no, only these past few months. I was an inspector of police for some years – in *Nellore* under Captain Gordon. When he left the force to take up his position here as superintendent, he offered me the job of jailor."

"Oh I see. Working with a man you already know and trust must be an advantage in your profession."

"Very much so."

"And Nellore? Is that around here?"

"It's near the coast about a hundred miles north of Madras. Not unlike Salem in size, but quite different in its climate. My wife, Rebecca, and both our children seem to prefer it here. I think the move will be good for all of us."

"I'm glad for you. When we first arrived at Madras in September last, the heat and humidity seemed quite overwhelming. It was a relief to discover how moderate Bangalore is in comparison."

"You've been fortunate to find yourselves in the garrison there, that's for sure. There are plenty worse. I was stationed in Bangalore myself for a couple of years before the Mutiny, though it's a very different place now and much changed for the better."

Isaac talked a little about his seventeen years in India and how, having travelled all over the country at one time or another, he could vouch for Bangalore's comfortable virtues. He asked after the regiment's health and was sorry to hear Charles describe the losses they'd suffered.

"Sadly, it's the way of things in India," said Isaac. "I recall how cholera took four of my friends within just days of us landing at Calcutta in '49. Many more went the same way."

Pills had been leaning against one of the carts and paying more attention to his pipe than the conversation, but the mention of disease nudged his professional curiosity. "What provision does your jail have for the sick, Mr Tyrrell?"

"None to speak of for the moment, doctor. However, our building works include the construction of a hospital for the inmates and it shouldn't be too long before that's complete."

"And how many do you have locked up?"

"Usually about six hundred, most of them native men. Some are awaiting trial, others have long stays ahead of them, and a goodly number are for the rope. There are women here too, of course. Before my time they were confined together with the male prisoners, but they have a new cell block of their own now."

"So, the jail really is as new at it appears from the outside?" asked Charles. "We were speculating about that earlier."

"In its extended form, yes. The gatehouse and outer walls have only just finished being painted as a matter of fact. The whole undertaking has been useful in keeping the inmates occupied, for the most part with making bricks and acting as general labourers. The cost-saving benefits are not inconsiderable."

"Very enterprising," commented Pills. "Would their time normally be put to such good use? In the absence of building projects, I mean."

"As much as possible. Unless necessity dictates otherwise we give convicts work in the same trades they had prior to incarceration. Salem is noted for its cloth and silk weaving, for example, and then there's ironwork, carpentry, and just recently we've begun to introduce carpet weaving as well. The government pays Captain Gordon and I a percentage of the profits derived from the sale of goods manufactured in the jail, so we have a vested interest in maintaining a healthy and productive population."

"A sensible arrangement, I'm sure," said Pills. "I'd be interested to learn more about your plans for medical care."

"Certainly, doctor. Your colonel looks like he's ready to depart, but I'll do my best to answer any questions you may have tomorrow."

William was walking back in their direction. "The captain has just been telling me about the first class stabling at our disposal," he said. "He's going to accompany us to Mr Arbuthnott's residence and then return here with the bâtmen."

"Then I'll bid you a good evening, gentlemen," said Isaac. "I hope you enjoy the fine meal that's sure to await you."

"Until tomorrow," said Charles, shaking Isaac's hand.

"Aye, good evening to you." said Pills.

Captain Gordon sat beside the syce driving the officers' cart and explained where they were going. "Shall I go in front?" he called across to William, who was re-tightening the girth of his saddle.

"Please do, captain. After you."

The syce clicked his tongue and reined the ponies back to the road. *Woodman*, *Foreigner* and *Cobweb* plodded behind, followed by the officers and their servants. The musicians watched them go, before looking to the jailor for guidance.

"Follow me, lads. Let's get you settled in," said Isaac. "I expect you'll be wanting your hands free to lead your horse," he added to Private Allan.

"Ah, yes. Thank you, sir. If you don't mind," the private replied, handing him *Bulger*'s leash.

*   *   *

"We need your casting vote," said an impatient Maurice when Charles wandered into the dining room for breakfast on Wednesday.

"Good morning to you too," Charles replied, taking a seat and asking the servant to bring coffee and toast. He didn't have the appetite for anything more substantial at this early hour. There was no sign of William or Pills yet. Maurice and Robert had already finished boiled eggs. "Apologies if I've kept you both waiting. I slept rather heavily."

"That's all right. Good morning," said Robert. "We've been up for a while and need to be leaving shortly."

Charles glanced at the clock on the wall. It was approaching a quarter to five. The Salem Cup, the principal race of the day, was due to start half an hour after sunrise at seven. "Of course. So then, what am I voting on?"

"Our strategy," clipped Maurice. "As you know, unless there are any surprise late entries, we face an all-Australian contest between *Cobweb*, *Woodman*, Mr Shaw's *Vaurien*, and Major Hutchieson's *Vandieman*."

"With *Vandieman* being the undisputed favourite, according to what Lieutenant Foord was telling me last night," noted Charles.

"Quite. Major Hutchieson isn't shy about expressing his confidence by all accounts, and not without justification. *Vandieman* has been the crack horse at meetings throughout the Madras Presidency for some time. We'd be foolish to underestimate his ability, even though he's to be ridden on this occasion by Mr Scott."

"Whose performance in the District Plate tends to suggest that he's unlikely to get the best out of *Vandieman*'s natural talent," added Robert.

The District Plate had been the first of yesterday's three races. Scott had finished the mile and a half in a distant last place on *Amber*, a chestnut Australian owned by The Exiles syndicate. Veterinary Surgeon Shaw, who Maurice had discovered owned a racehorse stud nearby, claimed a decisive win on the syndicate's Australian filly, *Molly Bawn*. He'd repeated that success riding an Afghan mare called *Gunga* in the Galloway Plate as well as the Oriental Stakes. In doing so, he gave The Exiles a clean sweep.

"The same can't be said of Fred Shaw though. There's no lack of skill or experience in his case," Charles cautioned.

"That's true. His horsemanship is beyond question," agreed Robert.

"One can't help but be impressed by his elegant riding style," Maurice conceded. "However, I suspect *Vaurien* is past his best."

The servant returned carrying a tray. Charles sipped the reviving coffee while Robert pressed on.

"As we see it, and bearing in mind it's a two-miler, there are a couple of ways we might sensibly approach the race. Maurice's preference is to let *Vaurien* and *Vandieman* lead, with us pushing from behind to tire them out before the closing furlongs."

"While Robert would rather we go out strong from the off and simply not give them a look-in at all," Maurice countered. "I'm inclined to believe that's the riskier option, albeit the more dramatic one. What do you think?"

Charles saw merit in both suggestions, but was far from convinced that *Vandieman* and *Vaurien*'s chances could be discounted so readily. Allowing either of them to set the pace would be like opening the door to the spectre of defeat. And then there was the question of his friends' motivation to consider. Not their desire to win for the sake of personal pride and regimental honour. That went without saying. Charles was wondering about the unspoken subject of profit. There were two races of interest this morning, and from the perspective of potential financial gain they needed to be weighed together.

The headline Salem Cup offered a prize fund of a thousand rupees, roughly equivalent to a hundred pounds, while the mile and a half Survey Purse was worth five hundred rupees. As was custom, prize money would be divided between the owners of the first three finishers in each race, with two thirds of it going to the winner. A trainer's cut was twenty per cent, and another ten per cent went to the jockey.

Robert would be riding *Foreigner* for Maurice in the Survey Purse, and was expected to win that with ease. Maurice was therefore the owner of two horses set to pay out, the trainer of three, and jockey of one. The implication being that he was virtually guaranteed a healthy return from today even if *Woodman* and *Cobweb* only took the second and third places between them in the Salem Cup. Robert and Charles, on the other hand, needed *Woodman* to win in order to do more than just cover their expenses, which for Charles included the race entry fee. If Robert had confidence in the bold, all or nothing strategy, Charles was happy to trust his judgment.

"Well, we didn't ride all this way to teach a lesson in subtlety," Charles replied, smiling. "I say attack from the front and give them no quarter. Let's show Salem how the 16th Lancers like to do things."

"I'm glad you agree," said Robert.

"Very well," Maurice nodded.

"And when you've left the others for dead and it's just you two charging for the finish, what then?" asked Charles, tongue in cheek.

"Then may the best man win," said Maurice.

Characterised by tight bends and firm, flat ground, the race course was a simple half-mile oval set in an otherwise featureless clearing not far from the Collector's Bungalow. By the time Charles arrived at a quarter to seven, Robert and Maurice were already warming up the horses and the band members were tuning their instruments. He'd ridden there in David Arbuthnott's carriage, accompanied by William, Pills, Captain Gordon, and the magistrate's Quaker wife, Eliza.

Charles made straight for the track. He wanted a few hushed words with Robert on his own. "How's our lad faring this morning?" he asked, patting *Woodman*'s neck.

Robert bent down from the saddle to make sure Maurice and the other jockeys couldn't hear his reply. "I've never known him so full of beans. Probably have to keep him in hand quite a bit just to make things sporting."

"Well don't be too generous," said Charles. "You and I need the bounty from this one. Give the subalterns a triumph worth celebrating, eh?"

"Count on it," Robert replied with a sanguine smile.

Although the course was far too out of the way to solicit the scale of attendance regularly witnessed at Bangalore and Madras, the Salem gathering was no less enthusiastic and just as well dressed. Corporal Thornhill scored the growing sense of anticipation with his opening tune of the morning, a rousing jig played in duet with Private Deare.

Charles returned to the spectators' side of the rail and joined the group talking to William and Pills. Almost all the faces had become familiar to him during the past couple of days. Amongst them were *Senhor* D'Souza, the demonstrative brother of the Portuguese consul-general in Calcutta, and an overtly Anglophile Mr Venatchetelliah, both of whom owned coffee plantations in the Shevaroy Hills.

"I don't believe you've met Major Hutchieson," Captain Gordon said to Charles, gesturing towards the corpulent, middle-aged gentleman who'd been in full flow of bluster about how *Vandieman* was going to dominate the race. Charles introduced himself.

"Pleased to meet you, lieutenant," replied the major. "It's damned decent of you chaps to tootle down from Bangalore to make up the numbers like this."

Charles was rankled by the patronising insult and could see William was too. Now wasn't the moment to punish it, but he couldn't resist laying bait. "I've heard great things about your horse, major," Charles responded. "No doubt you've encouraged all your friends to wager heavily on his success?"

"Indeed I have. If ever there was a safe bet, it's my *Vandieman*."

"We are about to find out," said *Senhor* D'Souza, directing attention back to the track and defusing the tension evident to everyone except the major. "*Boa sorte*, my friends, *boa sorte*."

The violin piece ended with a duelling flourish as the runners were called toward the post and people crowded along the rail. Colonel Henry Foord was acting as starter for the race as well as one of its stewards. His son, Montague, was watching from a few yards past the line. "Saved you a spot," he said, beckoning Charles over.

"Good man," Charles replied, offering his new friend a cheroot and lighting another for himself.

The lieutenant was the Salem District Engineer, responsible for an extensive road building programme and construction of the jail. A promotion to the rank of captain was expected to become official within the next few weeks. Though engineering held no interest for Charles, during their previous conversations he'd come to respect the obvious passion Montague had for his work. The colonel seemed to be an equally pleasant fellow, who, as Chief Engineer of the Madras Public Works Department, was also his son's superior. Charles had pondered what such a relationship might be like and whether being in the shadow cast by paternal reputation helped or hindered Montague's ambitions.

"My money's on *Woodman*, so I wish you the very best of luck."

"Thank you. Fingers crossed you won't be disappointed," said Charles, pulling his brass binoculars from their case.

Colonel Foord raised his service revolver to the clouds and waited for the horses to form up. *Vandieman* had the inside position and *Cobweb* on his right, *Vaurien* restless beside him, and *Woodman* at a disadvantage on the outside.

A heartbeat of silence.

Then the crack of the gun and an eruption of cheering.

Vandieman made a blistering start and surged to the front with *Cobweb* close behind. *Vaurien* spooked, jostling sideways into *Woodman*'s flank until Fred Shaw regained control. That lost Robert precious moments, but *Woodman* recovered ground before the first bend.

Approaching the back straight, Maurice glanced over his shoulder to see *Woodman* in last place. So much for strategy. They needed to improvise. He maintained his position on *Vandieman*'s tail and waited for Robert to catch up. By the top of the second bend, *Woodman* was sailing past *Vaurien* and Robert shouted ahead, "Here!" They completed the first lap with *Vandieman* still in front and *Vaurien* already feeling the pace.

Doing just enough to keep the pressure on the leader, Maurice let *Cobweb* settle down on his way through the bend and into the second run along the back stretch. He knew *Woodman* would be well served by being able to do the same.

"Aliwal! Aliwal!" called Maurice on the approach to the home straight. They hadn't agreed a signal, but Robert understood its meaning well enough. The captain was preparing to strike.

He launched his assault in the last furlong of the first mile. Robert matched it and both horses overtook *Vandieman* before the post. Now they could revert to something like the original plan and put space between themselves and the favourite.

"Seems *Vandieman* is about spent," said Montague, fighting to be heard.

"Well and truly!" Charles replied, taking his eyes from the track to search the thicket of top hats to his left. He found Major Hutchieson still urging his horse on, hammering the air with his cane, and determined not to accept the thorough trouncing that was now a foregone conclusion.

Cobweb and *Woodman* were head-to-head, Robert taking the outside line. By the middle of the third circuit, *Vandieman* was trailing by half a furlong and *Vaurien* by nearly two. Knowing he was out of the money, and that the scuffle at the start meant likely disqualification, Fred Shaw pulled *Vaurien* up short and left the others to it.

"*Cobweb*'s going strong. Can *Woodman* best him?" asked Montague.

Charles felt sure *Cobweb* was already going at full tilt, or as close to it as would make no difference, whereas Robert was still keeping *Woodman*'s head down. "Oh yes. You watch. Any moment now."

The stable companions thundered past the spectators for the penultimate time, round the bend, and then Robert at last gave *Woodman* free rein. Charles drummed his fist on the rail. *Woodman*'s acceleration down the back straight was so savage that Maurice couldn't possibly expect *Cobweb* to defend it. Extending a lead of two lengths to three and then more, *Woodman* had it all to himself and crossed the finish with Robert punching the sky.

Montague was elated. "By God, Charles, what an outstanding performance!" he said, shaking hands. "My congratulations to you and Mr Maillard on a victory so richly deserved!"

Other people standing nearby expressed the same sentiments. Charles thanked them all, relieved more than anything else that the race had gone his way in the end. As the clapping and cheers subsided, and the band began to play again, Major Hutchieson tapped Charles on the shoulder.

"A fine race, lieutenant. Your man rode well."

Whether that was meant as a genuine compliment from a good loser or snide contempt from a bad one, Charles couldn't tell. Neither did he much care.

"Fine indeed. My commiserations to you and your friends, major," Charles replied. "Let us hope they're the forgiving kind and that their faith in your advice will be restored in time. Henceforth, have a care to remember that one has to be extraordinarily brave or profoundly deficient in wisdom to bet against the cavalry in a horse race."

The major looked as if he was about to choke on the humiliation. He retreated in disgust, muttering under his breath.

Mr Brandt's brown Arab, *Ascalon*, made all the running during the initial mile of the Survey Purse half an hour later, but true to form Robert and *Foreigner* shot away on the last lap to win by a couple of lengths. The Pony Race followed, with *Shut-Em-Up* living up to the name given him by Isaac Tyrrell and taking first place with ease.

As soon as the ponies had cleared the course, Colonel Foord and Lieutenant Walker oversaw the installation of improvised grass-matting hurdles in the first quarter of each straight. Private Griffin accompanied their labours with a jaunty cello solo. The Hastumputty Hurdle Race was to be a two-lap affair and the final contest of the meeting.

"I'm not familiar with this trio," William Dickson confessed to Captain Gordon as they watched the horses being warmed up. "Which is fortune likely to favour, would you say?"

"Fred Shaw should make quick work of it on *Monarque*, although *Pathfinder*'s no defaulter and can't be entirely ruled out."

"And what of *Senhor* D'Souza?" asked Robert, back from the paddock where he and Maurice had left *Foreigner* in the care of the syces.

"I'm afraid *Last Chance* has little or none. He's only entered for amusement though, so it's of little consequence," explained the captain.

David Arbuthnott's stewarding and socialising duties had been keeping him busy all morning. Now they were all but over, he could begin to relax. He apologised to his bungalow guests for neglecting them, and offered his congratulations to Charles, Maurice, and Robert. "We have much to celebrate this evening, gentlemen," he added. "And I wonder, colonel, if the quartet might be willing to grace the party with their splendid repertoire?"

"Of course," William replied. "They'll consider it a privilege."

"Wonderful! Eliza is going to be most pleased. But now to the business at hand. My fellow Exiles and I are hoping Mr Shaw will have better luck against *Pathfinder* than he did against you chaps."

"Indeed we are," agreed Captain Gordon, as the race got underway.

Monarque held an early lead throughout the opening lap, with *Pathfinder* biding his time half a length back. *Senhor* D'Souza took the first two hurdles rather gingerly, but seemed to be enjoying himself despite keeping *Last Chance* off the pace. *Pathfinder* moved up on the leader as they approached the third hurdle, which both horses cleared without effort. Then for no fathomable reason *Monarque* suddenly bolted off the track, taking *Pathfinder* with him. The protests of the crowd drowned out the stream of blasphemy flowing from Fred Shaw and *Pathfinder's* jockey, Mr Bartlet.

Focused as he was on his own flight over the third hurdle, D'Souza was slow to react to what had happened, but once safely over the obstacle he recognised the opportunity and let *Last Chance* have his own way down the straight. He'd reached the bend before the truants were brought back under control. *Pathfinder* re-joined the course way ahead of *Monarque* and set about the chase. D'Souza's hesitancy over the fourth hurdle allowed Bartlet to close in as they galloped past the clamour and waving hats on their right. *Pathfinder* made a valiant effort to draw level, only to lose his way again in the closing yards. To the bewilderment of his rider, and the consternation of all those with wagers at stake, *Last Chance* clinched it by a head.

"It really isn't poor Fred Shaw's day," said Maurice, when *Monarque* eventually trotted over the line.

"But a plucky show from our *Portuga* friend," Robert noted.

Isaac Tyrrell was wandering over with *Bulger* on his leash. "Quite an upset, don't you think?" he said, gaining murmurs of agreement from everyone.

"Providence is certainly shining on anyone who took a wild punt!" David Arbuthnott replied.

"If only I'd had such foresight."

"Been lumbered with the puppy again?" Charles queried.

"Not lumbered, no, not in the least. In point of fact, I've just this minute purchased him from Captain Fitzgerald's man. After a little haggling, he settled for thirty-five rupees."

"A fair price, I'm sure."

"I'd have parted with more, but don't tell him I said so."

"I won't breathe a word. We'll all miss young *Bulger's* antics," said Charles, thinking of privates Allan and Deare and their fondness for the puppy.

"He's a character, sure enough. I imagine he'll make an ideal companion for my son, Fred, and can guard my cows too. The hyenas bother them something terrible."

"Ladies and gentlemen! Please gather round for the prize-giving," Captain Gordon called out several times to what remained of the crowd. It had begun to dwindle after the hurdle race as people left to start their working day.

Shoulder to shoulder and four rows deep, they formed an orderly semi-circle in front of a cloth-covered table placed by the rail. David Arbuthnott, Colonel Foord, and Lieutenants Walker and Edgecombe stood behind it, their backs to the course. On the table was an array of silverware, and envelopes containing all the prize money.

The magistrate delivered a brief speech about how the races reflected great credit on the town and everyone involved. He thanked his colleagues, the owners and jockeys, and all the people who'd given up their time, and in many cases their capital, to support what he sincerely hoped would become an annual event. After polite applause, he added, "May I also express particular gratitude to Colonel Dickson and his officers, not only for making the long journey from Bangalore and demonstrating impeccable sportsmanship, but for allowing us all to enjoy the music of the 16th Lancers' string quartet."

"Hear, hear!" someone shouted. "Encore!" requested another voice. The band obliged, accompanying the rest of the ceremony with an up-tempo selection played softly from a distance.

Colonel Foord invited Messrs Paynter and Brandt to step forward to receive their runners-up winnings from yesterday's District Plate race. Then the assembly cheered Fred Shaw to the table. With humble dignity, he accepted The District Plate itself on behalf of The Exiles syndicate, their achievement already engraved in its circumference.

"Might as well stay where you are, Fred," said the colonel.

The formalities were repeated for The Galloway Plate and The Oriental Stakes, the veterinarian eventually returning to the anonymity of the audience with all three trophies clutched to his chest. To avoid tarnishing Shaw's moment of glory with the low water mark of a third place, the winnings from the Hastumputty Hurdles were given to Captain Gordon to look after for The Exiles. Mr Paynter took the second place envelope, and was followed by *Senhor* D'Souza whose expression suggested he felt like something of a fraud. Handing over the prize money, a small silver cup on a teak base, and leading the onlookers in a round of applause, Lieutenant Walker put the coffee grower's mind at rest with a few reassuring words about the quality of the race to the finish.

Isaac Tyrrell recouped what he'd spent on *Bulger* with his windfall from the Pony Race, Mr Brandt collected the cash for *Ascalon*'s second place finish in the Survey Purse, and the one remaining trophy went to Maurice for *Foreigner*'s emphatic win.

"No shiny trinket for us by the looks of things. That's rather a shame," Charles said to Robert.

"I wouldn't be so sure about that," hinted Montague with a knowing chuckle.

David Arbuthnott addressed the crowd again. "Which brings us, ladies and gentlemen, to the awards for this morning's blue riband race. May I ask Lieutenant Agnew, Captain Fitzgerald once again, and Major Hutchieson to come forward."

Charles and Maurice approached the table, shook hands with the stewards, and waited for the major to join them.

"Major Hutchieson?" David Arbuthnott called out.

"He departed a while ago," someone replied from the back row.

"Ah, I see. Thank you. In that case we'll carry on and I'll make sure the major gets what he's owed later."

Maurice and Charles pocketed the envelopes they were handed and expressed their thanks.

"Remain a moment longer, if you would, gentlemen," David Arbuthnott instructed. Then, speaking half to the audience, he said, "Lieutenant Agnew, we have something special for you to take back to Bangalore." He paused before continuing with a raised voice. "It gives me enormous pleasure to invite my good friend, and our unstinting patron, Mr Venatchetelliah, to present the Salem Cup."

On cue, carrying eighteen inches of the very finest, solid silver craftsmanship, Mr Venatchetelliah smiled with pride as he elbowed a path to the front. Charles gazed in utter astonishment.

"I congratulate you most greatly, sir," said the benefactor, straining to lift the trophy into Charles's arms. "It is my heartfelt wish that you will consider this a worthy commemoration of *Woodman*'s magnificent success."

"Beyond measure, sir. My sincerest thanks to you," Charles replied, feeling his words were entirely inadequate.

The prodigious object he cradled was a cup in name only. Below twin cherubs sitting back-to-back on a tiered throne adorned with depictions of fruit and game, a pair of horse figurines reared forth from sweeping scrolls and foliage. The likeness of a wine ewer ascended above the equine Eden, with fighting bears in relief around its body, and handle segments twisting up from a horse's head to a harp-styled neck and elongated spout.

"Against such revered competition," Charles stumbled on, "success might have eluded *Woodman* were it not for Captain Fitzgerald's expertise, and Lieutenant Maillard's strength and skill. The glorious Salem Cup is thus a glory shared."

Mr Venatchetelliah asked Robert to come and stand with his friends, and then hailed for three cheers. Charles thrust the prize aloft with each huzzah.

As farewells were said and people started to disperse, the three officers examined the detail of their acquisition.

"Spectacular intricacy," Robert observed.

"A piece of art really. Quite beautiful in its own unique way," said Maurice.

"I am most overjoyed to hear you say that," beamed Mr Venatchetelliah.

"The quality of the work is absolutely first class. Made in Madras, presumably?" Charles asked.

"No, no, sir, not Madras. I spared no expense in commissioning it from the distinguished firm of Joseph and Horace Savory, of Cornhill in London. It has travelled far to reach its destiny in your hands."

Woodman and *Cobweb* trotted under the gateway arch and down the palm-lined avenue, Robert and Maurice leading the way back to the Collector's Bungalow. Behind them followed the Arbuthnott's carriage, and *Foreigner* tethered to a cart carrying the band and bâtmen.

"I think a few photographs are called for," said Robert, eager to record their victories for posterity.

"A fine idea and I'm sure Charles will agree," replied Maurice, who was looking forward to a light lunch and a relaxing afternoon.

establishment, it was always Tino that Goody relied upon to escort the troublemaker outside.

The weekly stipend he received swelled the savings hidden beneath the floorboards of his tenement room, but associating with Levi Goodman had proved far more valuable than even Tino expected. Through keen observation, he learned the craft of the croupier and how to imitate the speech, manners, and habits of the upper class in recreation. He studied their weaknesses too and listened intently to their naively unguarded conversations about business, politics, and women – their mistresses, their daughters, and their wives.

Tino Paranza traded in violence and depravity. But working for the Fenians had been a mistake.

The plan had gone dramatically wrong and would be demonised as an outrage of unexampled atrocity.

Breaking Richard O'Sullivan Burke of the Irish Republican Brotherhood out of Clerkenwell Prison had sounded like a good idea at the time. Not that Tino cared in the slightest about Richard Burke or his cause, but the money Michael Barrett had paid for Tino's assistance was ample inducement. All he had to do was store kegs of gunpowder during the week beforehand and provide some barrows for moving them on the day of the escape.

In their haste, the Irish had used too much powder and brought down a section of the exercise yard wall sixty feet wide. And not even at the right time of day. Burke and all the other prisoners were still in their cells when the blast went off.

The trouble was, the explosion also damaged some of the Corporation Lane tenements across the road, killed a dozen passers by and injured scores of others. Now Michael Barrett and his companions would be rounded up and interrogated before being tried and inevitably executed. None of them were likely to walk to the gallows without first putting the finger on their Italian-sounding storeman. Besides, even if he wasn't implicated by the Fenians, the local community was bound to learn of Tino's part in the crime. If they didn't lynch him themselves, they'd certainly turn him in.

Which left Tino with no choice. He had to leave. Not just Clerkenwell or London. He had to flee the country altogether and start again beyond the reach of British justice.

He plucked a crumpled newspaper from the gutter and cast his eyes across the front page. A military expedition to rescue British hostages had begun in Abyssinia, Prime Minister Derby had given a speech about the Reform Act, and construction of the Suez Canal was nearing completion in Egypt.

Wherever there are ships there are people, Tino thought, and wherever there are people there's money to be made.

*   *   *

What started with Carrin's idea to celebrate the inheritance of troop horses had evolved into an annual event and a cornerstone of Bangalore's social calendar. The Aliwal Ball, as it was now called, was hosted by the 16th Lancers' non-commissioned officers in commemoration of the regiment's part in the Battle of Aliwal during the campaign on the *Sutlej* in 1846.

The editor of the *Bangalore Herald* reported the 1868 event with his usual glowing rhetoric, saying that it, "*went off with great éclat,*" on Tuesday, 7th January, at the Public Rooms, and how, "*things could not have been arranged in better taste.*" Major General Haines had danced, Colonel Dickson had been chaired around the ballroom, "*and all seemed to appreciate the fun and to enjoy themselves thoroughly.*"

A popular success though the ball undoubtedly was, the shine had worn off for most of the officers. It just wasn't quite the same without Bill Wauchope, James and Magdalene Goldie, Carrin, and Augustus Dobrée.

When James Goldie learned that Magdalene was pregnant with their second child, he'd decided it would be sensible to take a period of furlough. Returning to England would make life more comfortable for his wife, and there were cousins eager to meet baby Mary. The family departed Bangalore last March, leaving Charles back in command of his troop. Subsequent letters from James confirmed they were all well and that Magdalene had been safely delivered of another daughter, whom they'd named Ethel.

Carrin had continued to suffer the effects of jungle fever and went on sick leave back to Kent in July.

In October, a demoralised and disillusioned Bill Wauchope elected to exchange commissions with a gentleman of the 6th (Inniskilling) Dragoons stationed in York. Captain Richard Renshaw arrived in thereabouts, but some departments have already begun relocating here from our last place by Whitehall Gardens. Anyway, best not keep Mr Wylde waiting, ma'am."

They carried on along several corridors until they reached the office of the Slave Trade Department.

"Mrs Munro is here, sir," said Victor through the half-open door. He stood aside and invited Sophia to enter the room, which stank of fresh paint and stale tobacco.

A slender, middle-aged man with an unflattering chinstrap beard and an irritated expression was seated behind a small desk cluttered with reports, maps, and charts. The window to his right looked out to a dark courtyard. William Wylde finished what he was writing before replying to Sophia's friendly greeting. "Good morning, madam," he said, with a perfunctory handshake. "Please do take a seat."

"I very much appreciate you sparing the time to see me," Sophia began. She was about to say more, but William was in a hurry.

"I received your letters, and certainly found your wish to document the Zanzibar trade noble in its intent. The thoroughness of your researches thus far is to be commended."

"Thank you."

"However, I must dissuade you of the notion that such an expedition would be practicable. Furthermore, even if it was, this department would be neither willing nor able to support the endeavour."

"May I ask why?" said Sophia, with terse exasperation.

"In brief, because the diplomatic situation between the Foreign Office, Her Majesty's Government in India, and the Sultanates of both Zanzibar and Oman is as delicate as it is complicated. And, as you know, Doctor Livingstone's current expedition in the area already has amongst its aims the observation of the movement of slaves."

"Aye. But to my knowledge a photographer isn't accompanying him, unlike the last time. And his priority is locating the source of the Nile, is it not?"

"Quite so, but..."

"Whilst mine would solely be the human traffic and its associated deprivations, the abolition of which is your department's *raison d'etre*. Do we not have a moral obligation to do all in our power to hasten the end of such suffering?"

"Yes, yes, but please understand. As worthy and honourable as such a crusade would be, now simply isn't an appropriate time to contemplate it. There is also the fact of you being a woman to take into consideration."

Sophia bristled with frustration, but William continued before she could launch a response.

"I mean no disrespect to your gender or your undoubted talents as a photographer, madam. It may interest you to learn that we undertook some research of our own before agreeing to this meeting, and I have no need of convincing on the latter point," he said, gesturing towards the portfolio case on Sophia's lap. "However, if the public were to discover that Her Majesty's Government had knowingly sent a woman into harm's way – to very likely meet a degrading and gruesome end at the hands of *Mahommedan* slavers – the political ramifications could be catastrophic."

She hadn't considered the political perspective, she admitted to herself. "I see, but then why agree to meet me? Why not simply reject my proposal in writing?"

"Because I wanted to look you in the eye and form my own opinion of your veracity and fortitude before making an introduction."

That came as a surprise, though Sophia tried not to show it. There was clearly more to Mr Wylde than her first impressions had given him credit for.

"An introduction to whom?"

"Captain Charles Wilson of the Topographical and Statistical Department of the War Office. TSD for short."

"And is he going to Zanzibar?"

"No. The Sinai Peninsula, I believe."

"Then I'm afraid I really don't understand," said Sophia.

*   *   *

"Good morning, ladies. May we offer you some tea?" said Charles Wilson when he opened the gate at eleven o'clock the following morning. A captain in the Royal Engineers, his brooding eyes and unkempt beard gave him a stern appearance incongruent with his friendly smile and casual demeanour.

"Frankly? Yes, that's about the sum of it. Which is where Hector Mackay enters the picture. No pun intended."

"A Highlander presumably?"

"Yes, indeed, he's from Lairg in the far north if I recall correctly. Hector's a great bear of a man, extraordinarily resourceful, and something of a linguist. He'd go along with you. Before he retired from the army, he was a sergeant in the 93rd Sutherland Highlanders and distinguished himself in the Crimea and during the Indian Rebellion. I've trusted my life to him on several occasions and wouldn't hesitate to do so again. First and foremost his role would be to protect your safety, but he'd also act as translator and would give your group the appearance of being led by a man. There would likely be times when you'd find such a ruse culturally expedient."

"That would take some getting used to, but we understand the necessity," said Sophia.

"When would all this happen?" asked Janet.

"You'd sail for Egypt in July, so we have a few months to plan and prepare, and you'd need to be in Bombay before the end of February at the latest."

Sophia looked at Janet again. Janet nodded.

"Well, it seems you have yourself a photographer," Sophia said to Wilson, standing up to shake his hand.

"Wonderful. That's settled then. More tea?"

CHAPTER THIRTEEN
THE ESTABLISHMENT, BANGALORE, INDIA
TUESDAY, 21ST APRIL 1868

The peal of the nine o'clock bells from Holy Trinity Church faded away on the soft breeze that aired Charles Agnew's room. He was lying on his bed, looking out the open window, lost in thought. His uniform was dirty and damp after the morning's mounted drills with his troop. They'd ridden well, but there was always room for improvement if he wanted them to live up to the high standards set by James Goldie. Bougainvillea swathed the whole bungalow in purple, and he wondered why such attractive flowers had no scent. It seemed a shame.

His attention returned to the letter from Harriet that had been delivered yesterday. It was the fifth time he'd read it.

1 Oxford Villas   *28th February 1868*
Oxford Street
Cheltenham

My Dearest Charles,

Today is Friday and I'm so dreadfully tired after a truly momentous week. Please forgive the brevity of this note, but fear for me not. My heart is overflowing with happiness.

On Wednesday, 26th February, at about three o'clock in the morning, you became the uncle of the sweetest, most beautiful baby boy in all creation. I hope you'll be pleased to learn that George and I have named him after you.

Little Charles and I are both doing well. He's blessed with a quite relentless appetite! I don't know how I would have coped without mother by my side – she's been a wonder – and George is being tremendous in caring for our every need. I do love him so very greatly. He's such an adoring husband and father.

He'd been informed that he was to command a party of invalided men departing India in June or July and likely reaching England by August or September. While Charles didn't entirely relish the thought of another long sea voyage around the Cape, it was a worthy duty and would be a break from the tedium of inaction. With it came the incentive of up to seventeen months of furlough, during some of which he would reside in Cheltenham and get to know his nephew and brother-in-law. There was no telling when another such opportunity might arise and he intended to make the most it.

Morgan knocked on the open door to attract his friend's attention. "Morning Charles. Can I tempt you to a hand or two of cards at the club?"

Charles folded the letter and stood up, brushing dust from his tunic. He'd tell Morgan all about Harriet's good news later. "You know well enough by now that I'm not a gambling man," he replied with a forgiving chuckle.

"Ah yes, silly me."

"But I'll happily join you for lunch later on."

"Excellent." Morgan turned to go, but then remembered something else. "Alec caught me earlier, by the way. Said he has a favour to ask you."

*   *   *

"*And will you,* Jessie Mary Arnold Marshall, *take this man to be your husband? Will you obey him and serve him, love, honour and keep him, in sickness and in health? And forsaking all others, keep only to him as long as you both shall live?*"

That more than half the pews in St. Mark's Cathedral were full on the morning of Wednesday, 10th June, was testimony to the regiment's high regard for Alec Innes. His bride looked angelic in the white dress made for her by Emily Orr, and someone said later they thought they'd seen tears of joy in his eyes when he heard the words, "I will."

Charles was deeply honoured to stand by Alec's side as his best man, and General Hubert Marshall had never been prouder than when he gave his daughter away. Jessie's younger sisters were bridesmaids and the epitome of sibling sweetness. And as for Jessie herself, when she walked back down the aisle as Mrs Innes, arm in arm with the man she cherished, she felt happier and more alive than at any time in her eighteen years.

John and Emily Orr, and Micky and Augusta Lavelle, had been conspicuous by their absence from the ceremony.

"Have you seen them anywhere?" Charles asked Morgan once everyone had filed outside to the soaring heat of the day.

"I haven't, no. Rather odd, don't you think? It's not like Micky to miss a *céilí*."

"Keep your eyes peeled for me, would you? We don't want the happy couple worrying. Hopefully they'll turn up at the club later."

"Of course," said Morgan.

The club, which had recently been formally inaugurated as the Bangalore United Services Club, was where General Marshall had arranged for the afternoon reception to be held. All those of suitable rank or title were invited. Everyone else returned to barracks. Carriages had been organised to convey the bride and groom, their attendants, and the most distinguished guests, the half a mile or so down the road from the cathedral. They passed Micky's house on the way.

Inside the Lavelle residence, Doctor John Orr had done all he could. It had not been enough. With her children and Emily at her bedside, Augusta drew her last shallow breath cradled in Micky's arms. He was inconsolable in his grief.

Three days later, Charles was clambering into a masulah boat on the same beach outside Black Town where the regiment first landed in India three years before. With him were twenty-eight men of the ranks no longer medically fit for service, along with the widows of two deceased troopers and their three children. The British vessel, *Copenhagen*, lay out in the Madras Roads ready to convey them home.

By the end of the week another shipment arrived in Bangalore from England and was delivered into the care of Quarter Master Fuller. This time the crates contained new saddlery, which brought a smile to Thomas Brown's face. It was replaced by a worried frown the next day when Veterinary Surgeon Tom Richardson reported an outbreak of malarial disease among the horses.

CHAPTER FOURTEEN
ALEXANDRIA, EGYPT
THURSDAY, 6th AUGUST 1868

"Mind your step there, lass. I've got you," said Hector Mackay. He held out his hand for Janet as she reached the bottom of the steamship's gangway. She took it gladly, pausing to savour the moment before setting foot on the pier. Africa.

Sophia was following behind and Hector extended her the same courtesy. Ordinarily she dismissed such unnecessary chivalry. It was the sort of thing she found obsequious and patronising, but it was somehow different with the big Highlander. There was an uncontrived sincerity in his conduct towards the women he'd been charged to protect, and even Sophia had come to grow fond of feeling looked after. She'd also noticed how Janet was drawn to the unmistakable warmth and kindness in his eyes.

Intimidatingly tall and powerfully built with a voice to match, Hector kept his hair short and his beard long. Both were red and turning grey. Lifelong self-discipline and moral rectitude made him a difficult man to read. Sophia couldn't be sure if he was as attracted to Janet as Janet clearly was to him, but she supposed time would tell.

Although it was only a few weeks since they'd first met Hector at the TSD stables, the twelve-day voyage from Portsmouth had provided ample opportunity to get acquainted. If not yet a close friend, he'd certainly become a most trusted companion. When they'd asked him to call them by their given names, he'd appeared deeply uncomfortable with the idea and so they let it pass. He still referred to them as miss and ma'am. Except when he called Janet lass, which was developing into a habit.

Through their onboard conversations, they'd learned more about Hector's early years in Strathnaver and how he'd joined the army to flee the gnawing poverty left behind in the wake of the Clearances. He spoke modestly about his military experience at *Alma, Balaklava, Sevastopol,* and Lucknow. Soldiering suited him, he said, and he'd been proud to serve alongside so many gallant men. He'd had a wife and daughter in India, but they'd died. Neither Sophia nor Janet pressed him further on that subject.

The uneventful passage from England had been a relaxing interlude between the excitement of preparation and the hardships they knew lay ahead. But they'd been far from idle. The Rock of Gibraltar, the many vessels they steamed past, and Malta's Valletta harbour where the ship took on supplies, all presented useful opportunities to refine their on-deck camera techniques.

Everything was much easier with a third pair of hands to help carry and set up the equipment. Sophia was pleased, and rather relieved, that once he'd been shown what to do Hector demonstrated a natural aptitude for preparing the glass plate negatives. It was a tricky process involving a flammable mixture of cellulose nitrate and ether, called collodian, and then a silver nitrate solution. Once exposed in the camera, each plate had to be varnished as well to permanently fix the image. While they worked, Hector shared his views on how they could go about recruiting local guides and porters in Baluchistan, and offered guidance about what would be considered appropriate female behaviour. He reminded them that their safety was his first concern and that he'd be grateful for their understanding and cooperation.

Before leaving London, with Wilson's help Sophia had persuaded Hector that his kilt and glengarry might not be entirely in keeping with the image their group needed to portray. She'd paid for new suits of clothes from a good tailor, along with a pith helmet and luggage befitting a gentleman traveller. Hector had acquiesced and was still adjusting to the constraint of trousers. Sophia had invested in a second camera and tripod as well. She intended to use it to increase their efficiency and breadth of coverage. It was also a safeguard against the single most vital item of equipment being damaged or stolen. Glass plates and chemicals, both of which they needed in great quantity, were supplied by the TSD and packed in special boxes. And now here the three of them were on the threshold of a strange country on the edge of an unknown continent, with the Mediterranean wind doing little to moderate the fierce, dry heat of summer. They walked along the pier, climbed its few steps, and stopped to take in the scene. Janet looked tiny standing beside Hector, and Sophia even more so.

Having disembarked in many unfamiliar lands in the past, Hector could imagine how enthralled they must both be feeling. He waited in watchful silence while they gathered their thoughts.

The bustling quayside extended around most of the wide crescent of the harbour, which had a great fortress guarding its western entrance. The sweet scent of dust consorted with the stench of seaweed and donkeys and men. Warehouses, some of them four storeys high, and the homes of wealthy merchants jostled for position between sacred mosques. The towers that stood beside them intrigued Janet. She asked Hector what they were. "They're minarets, lass. A fellow stands up there at the top and calls all the Mahommedan within earshot to their prayers. Five times every day they do that, so you'll hear it for yourself soon enough."

In the conversations that whirled around her, Sophia could make out French, Italian, German, English, and other languages besides. And then there was what she assumed was Arabic, which to her unaccustomed ear sounded like something from another world. "What a wonderfully cosmopolitan place," she thought aloud.

The Egyptian men all wore either a turban, fez, or what resembled a larger version of the British army's forage cap, shaped like a pill box. Their long, loose, cotton shirts were called a *galabeya*, Hector explained. There were black Africans too. Most were employed as servants of Alexandrian traders. Some were seafaring merchants and their own masters.

Sophia noticed that a few of the Egyptian women concealed themselves behind veils and were attended by servants, whilst the poorer looking majority left their faces visible. She wanted to understand why, but decided now wasn't the time to find out. They had their precious baggage to collect and a representative from the British consulate to find.

Henry Calvert found them first. He was wearing a cream suit over a white waistcoat, with a stiff-collared shirt and a black tie. There were damp patches under his arms. "Good morning, and welcome to Egypt," he said, removing his straw boater and shaking Hector's hand before Janet's and then Sophia's. "Vice-Consul Henry Calvert, at your humble service. One is terribly pleased to meet you all. Did you enjoy a pleasant journey? One does so admire your courage in venturing here at this time of year. A trifle warm, what?"

When she had the chance to speak, Sophia made the required introductions and thanked Mr Calvert for his timely arrival. "Perhaps you can tell me? What's that picturesque structure over there?" she added, pointing across the harbour at the fortress.

"Certainly, ma'am. That's the *Qa'it Bay* Citadel, which dates back to the fifteenth century. It's believed to be built on the site of the Lighthouse of Alexandria, one of the Seven Wonders of the Ancient World. One would be delighted to arrange a guided tour. Tomorrow perhaps?"

"How fascinating, thank you. Aye, I'd like that."

"My pleasure, ma'am. Now, may one suggest we secure your luggage and make posthaste for the consulate? One has transport ready and waiting."

The group's bags and boxes had already been unloaded. Hector supervised their transfer to the requisitioned cart, ahead of which was an open carriage that seated four. "I'll ride with the luggage to make sure it doesn't go wandering," he said, climbing up beside the mule driver who shifted over to make room. Sophia and Janet sat beside one another in the carriage, with the vice-consul opposite them behind the coachman. Henry opened a paper bag he'd pulled from his jacket pocket.

"May one offer you some lupin beans, or *tirmis* as they're called hereabouts?" he said, leaning forward with the bag.

"What does one do with them?" asked Sophia.

"One eats them, ma'am. Squeeze the outer skin between finger and thumb, and the bean within leaps out. They're a most wholesome way to stave off hunger between meals, one finds."

Sophia and Janet took a couple each and were pleasantly surprised by the smooth texture and creamy, slightly nutty flavour.

"*Allāhu 'akbar...*"

Janet turned in her seat to look up at the nearest minaret.

"*Allāhu 'akbar...*"

"That's the *mu'addhin* beginning the call for the *Dhuhr*, or midday prayer, miss. He's saying the god of Islam is the greatest," Henry explained.

"*Allāhu 'akbar...*"

"He doesn't sound very cheery about it."

"*Allāhu 'akbar.*"

"To the unaccustomed ear, it might seem that way at first. However, one has no doubt the evocative beauty of the songs will quickly become apparent."

Accompanied by a chorus of calls from one minaret after another, they trotted away from the quay and down a succession of Napoleonic avenues to the shabby consulate building on *Rue de la Bourse*. Sophia had imagined somewhere more ostentatious. Not that she cared about such things. She was just thankful for the chance to bathe and to sleep in a proper bed.

"Please consider yourselves our special guests," said the consul-general, Colonel Edward Stanton, from the head of the dining table that evening. "London has asked that we offer every assistance within our power to ease your transit to Suez. Rest assured, we'll be all too happy to oblige."

"You're most kind, thank you," Sophia replied, raising her glass. "This white is delicious, by the way."

"It's the '64 *Nuits-sous-Beaune*. I'm glad you approve."

The fish course was anticipated momentarily. One end of the table in the stateroom was set for nine. As well as Colonel Stanton, who Hector later commented seemed like a very good-natured fellow, there was Mrs Stanton, Consul George Stanley and his wife, and Henry Calvert. They were also joined by the vice-consul from Port Said, Doctor Herbert Zarb, who was visiting Alexandria on official business. Janet was curious about his accent and asked where he was from.

"I'm from Malta, and thus my native tongue is Maltese. Your accent is also very charming, Miss Steward, if I may be permitted to say so?"

"Aye, you may," Janet blushed. "Our ship stopped at Valletta on the way here, though only briefly. We were taken by its beauty."

"Thank you. That warms my heart. Let us hope fate returns you there again one day for a longer visit."

"Do you speak any other languages, doctor?" asked Sophia. "I imagine such talents would be useful in your line of work."

"Indeed they are, ma'am. I have some Arabic and I'm fluent in Italian and French."

"And English," Janet added with a smile.

"One tries one's best, yes."

The diplomatic staff were quite used to accommodating special guests from London, and to the need for discretion during their stays. That didn't deter judicious curiosity.

"Tell me, Mrs Munro," George Stanley began. "Does one have a particular itinerary in mind?"

"Well, I suppose we'll spend at least a couple of days here in Alexandria. We'd certainly like to take up Mr Calvert's offer of a visit to the Citadel. What was its name again?"

"Qa'it Bay," Henry reminded her.

"Aye, thank you. No doubt there are other historic sites to tempt our interest as well. And then I dare say we'd better be on our way to Cairo."

"Quite so, quite so. One assumes you plan to visit the Great Pyramid of Giza?"

"Another of the Seven Ancient Wonders," noted Henry.

"Oh, most definitely. Although the detour will add time and distance to our journey, it would hardly do to come all this way – to the land of the Pharaohs – only to miss the chance to photograph such an iconic monument."

"And the Sphinx," added Janet.

"Aye, and the Sphinx."

Hector's mind was occupied with more practical matters. He addressed Colonel Stanton.

"Sir, may I ask what we might expect from the consulate in Suez? And with whom we should make contact?"

"Of course, Mr Mackay. Please feel at liberty to ask anything at all. Our man there is Consul George West, and a thoroughly conscientious chap he is too. You may like to telegraph him with an update on your progress once you reach Ismailia. He'll arrange suitable lodgings upon your arrival in Suez, and expedite your onward travel via the first available steamer. He also happens to be the Suez agent for P&O, so is well placed to deal with such matters."

"Thank you, sir, I'm glad to hear it."

"Och, that reminds me," said Sophia. "I meant to send a telegram to London when we first came ashore. Is the telegraph office far?"

Herbert Zarb was quick to volunteer a reply. "Not far, ma'am, no. I'll be paying it a visit myself in the morning. Perhaps I might save you the inconvenience and take a message there on your behalf?"

"Aye, thank you, doctor. That would be much appreciated."

"At your service, ma'am."

*   *   *

The overland journey to the Red Sea took as long as the voyage from England.

When the dismal outskirts of Suez finally came into view, Sophia had to fight back tears of overwhelming relief. She was proud of what they'd achieved, but it had been far more arduous and challenging than she or Janet ever expected. They couldn't have done it without Hector, of that she was certain.

A sweltering, dust-blown train had carried them as far as Cairo, where they hired a covered wagon, the pair of mules that pulled it, and a willing but taciturn driver who spoke only Arabic. After careful consideration, they sent half their stock of glass plates and chemicals by rail to George West in Suez. It was a gamble, but they decided it represented no greater risk of loss or damage than bumping everything across the desert themselves.

Giza was everything Janet had hoped for, despite the incessant demands for *baksheesh* from the pestering hawkers and self-appointed guides. Sophia took the photographs she wanted, and they both enjoyed an exhilarating camel ride while Hector guarded the wagon.

Then came the four-day trial north-east across flat, featureless desert to Ismailia, the reputedly comfortable French settlement born of the canal project.

The rough track they followed for eighty miles was well established, but often indistinct thanks to the sand forever blowing across it from their left. One or other rear wheel sank up to the axle in the soft verges at least half a dozen times. It took Hector's great strength and the driver's persistence with the whip on the mules to get them moving again.

During daylight hours they roasted, while at night, beneath a spectacular clear sky and a waning moon, it was so cold Janet feared they'd all freeze to death. Sophia and Janet curled up inside the wagon. Hector and the driver slept on the ground beside it. The recalcitrant mules were tethered to one of the wheels.

Janet was astonished by how much water they needed to drink to counter the merciless heat. At the end of the second day, she talked to Sophia about it.

"I think Hector might be concerned about the water stock."

"What makes you say that?"

"Have you noticed how often he checks the barrels? And for every three or four times we take water, he drinks but once."

"Och, no, I hadn't noticed. We need to remedy that."

"Aye, we do. Let's agree to only drink when he does and to not take as much as we have been."

"Aye, agreed," said Sophia.

It was difficult. Splitting headaches soon accompanied a dragging lethargy, but Hector never complained so neither did they.

At Ismailia they telegraphed ahead to George West, as Colonel Stanton had suggested, saying they expected to reach Suez in four days. While they waited for a reply, clothes and bodies were washed, thirsts slaked, mules rested, and the wagon was replenished with water, food, and extra blankets. A telegram was delivered to their hotel the next morning.

BOXES SAFE MURRAY WAITING
PROCEED HOTEL BACHET PORT TEWFIK
G WEST

It sounded like the railway gamble had paid off. Sophia wouldn't know for sure if all the materials survived until she inspected them, but it was reassuring news nevertheless. As for Mr Murray, he'd just have to wait a while longer.

Most of the rest of that day was spent with one of the cameras. They took pictures of the town from the dunes that separated it from Lake *Timsah*, looking south across the lake itself, and north-east to where the yet to be completed upper half of the canal connected with it.

The Great Bitter Lake beckoned. After an early start and twenty-five easy miles, they reached its salt-encrusted south-west flank by the following evening. The prevailing wind was now at their backs, but Sophia cursed the havoc it played with the camera and the wet plate negatives. Nothing escaped the affections of the infernal sand.

Everyone slept well that night, but in the morning they woke to a worrying discovery. Two of their remaining four water barrels had sprung leaks. One was completely empty, the other about a quarter full. They drank as much as they could stomach from it and gave what was left to the mules.

"If we ration the remaining barrels we can make it last until Suez. One between the four of us and one for the beasts," said Hector, with his usual calm authority.

"That'll be half the amount we've been drinking every day so far."

"Aye, ma'am, we may get a wee bit thirsty. But we'll make it to Suez safe and sound, I promise you."

The driver didn't understand Hector's words, but could see the look of concern on the women's faces. He knelt down and began to draw in the dirt with his finger, making the shape of the lake and then adding a line beside it. That was the track they were on, running close to the shoreline. He pointed to where he thought they were. Sophia, Janet and Hector all nodded to show they understood. Then the driver drew another line, parallel to the first one. He looked up, smiling his toothless smile, and brought his cupped right hand to his mouth. "*Mayyah*," he said.

"Seems our friend here isn't as daft as he looks," said Hector, giving the driver a comradely pat on the shoulder.

They followed the next spur off the track and within half a mile found the parallel line. It was another track and immediately beside it was their saving grace.

"Must be the Sweet Water Canal," Hector deduced. "It's the freshwater supply for this whole area. My apologies."

"What on earth are you apologising for?" Janet asked.

"For not realising its whereabouts to begin with, miss."

"Och, away with you. We've found it now, that's the important thing."

"And you think we can drink from it?" Sophia checked.

"Aye, ma'am. I imagine it's the same stuff our barrels were filled with in Ismailia. This runs all the way to Port Said, I believe. We can follow the channel to Suez, and take from it what we need."

Which is what they did, keeping their barrelled water as a contingency against the unexpected.

The Great Bitter Lake narrowed into its diminutive sibling, the Little Bitter Lake, and past that the Suez Canal cut across the desert in a straight line to the southern horizon. The view was unchanging, but true to their promise to Charles Wilson they took a photograph every few miles anyway. As always, Janet catalogued each negative with the date, time, and her best estimate of their location.

At the entrance to the canal a couple of miles south-east of Suez town, Port Tewfik curled out into the bay like a welcoming hand. As the wagon rolled towards it, the shimmering expanse of the Red Sea became visible beyond the breakwater to their right.

"There's something I've been wondering about," said Sophia.

"What's that, then?" prompted Janet.

"How useful our photographs of the canal will really be to the TSD. It's crossed my mind more than once that Wilson might've devised this part of our journey just to acclimatise us. To test us, even."

"I don't know about that, ma'am," Hector responded. "But whatever the truth of it may be, I can tell you this: you've both acquitted yourselves admirably, and you have my utmost respect for doing so."

"Thank you, my friend. We're very grateful," said Sophia, the lump in her throat returning.

Janet squeezed Hector's arm.

*   *   *

Arranging for guests to stay at Hotel Bachet served George West's purposes well, though he made no profit from it.

Overlooking Port Tewfik's eastern basin, the hotel offered convenient access to the Suez road, railway station, and a telegraph office. Most importantly, the P&O landing stage and the consulate were also close by. It was an unpretentious place known for its cleanliness and comfort. Each of the dozen bedrooms had a generously proportioned unglazed window with louvred shutters. There were verandahs at the front and rear of the building at ground level, and another wrapped around three quarters of the first floor. It offered little in the way of shade, but a commanding view of the canal on one side and Suez Bay on the other.

A hulking great fellow with red hair and a bushy beard was standing up there when George walked over from his office. He caught the man's eye and waved in greeting. "Hello there! Are you Mr Mackay of the Munro party?"

"Aye, that I am, sir. May I know who's asking?"

"Consul George West. Good morning to you."

"Ah, good morning Mr West. I'll join you presently."

Hector wandered back inside and down the central staircase to the entrance at the south end of the hotel. The consul was waiting patiently by the steps outside.

"It's a pleasure to finally make your acquaintance, Mr Mackay," he said, shaking hands. "Is the hotel to your satisfaction?"

"Likewise, Mr West. Aye, indeed it is, thank you. I haven't seen Mrs Munro or Miss Steward as yet this morning, but no doubt they'll be up and about shortly."

"You're most welcome. And that's quite all right. I'm sure they must be weary after your journey."

"Aye, but in good spirits. I gather you're the man to talk to about finding passage on a ship?"

"Yes, that's partly why I'm here as a matter of fact. There's a steamer departing for Karachi tomorrow morning at ten o'clock, and another three days hence."

"I'd hazard a guess we'll take the one tomorrow. How soon do you need to know?"

"I thought you'd probably be keen to get going, good for you. By five o'clock this afternoon, if possible?"

"We can tell you now, Mr West," said Sophia, as she and Janet emerged from the lobby and introduced themselves. "Please forgive our tardiness. I'm afraid I rather overslept," she added.

"I quite understand. The hour is still early, so any apology should really be mine. Do I take it you already have a preference regarding a ship?"

"Departing tomorrow morning would suit us very well, I think. If that's agreeable to you, Hector?"

"Aye, of course, ma'am."

"Marvellous. Thank you," said George. "I'll make the necessary arrangements with the captain in that case. Am I correct in my understanding that you need to disembark on the western coast of Baluchistan, rather than Karachi?"

"Yes, that's right. Do you foresee any problems?"

"No, not at all. I'm sure that will be quite achievable."

"I hope so. Oh, and we owe you a great debt of gratitude for the safekeeping of our photographic materials. They were in my room when we arrived yesterday, and all in perfect condition."

"You're most welcome, ma'am. It's my pleasure to be of service, even if only in such small ways. Speaking of which, I have another duty to perform," he said, giving Sophia a handwritten note. "Mr Murray found me last night and asked if I'd deliver this to you."

Dear Mrs Munro,

I trust this finds you well, and eager for more adventure.
Mr West will be able to provide directions to the Café d'Italia on Rue Colmar.
Please join me for lunch there at one o'clock.
I look forward to meeting you and your colleagues, and making arrangements for the collection of your items.

Sincerely
Everett Murray

"Thank you, Mr West, you're very kind," said Sophia, as she read the message. "Presumptuous fellow, this Mr Murray. And items? What a peculiar turn of phrase."

"I'd venture his work makes him a creature of habitual discretion, ma'am," suggested George. "When you make your way into town, *Rue Colmar* is the fourth street on the right. You'll find the café at the far end."

"Since we're going there anyway," said Janet, "we could take some photographs of the town this morning and then return this way after lunch for a last few around the port. I'll need a wee bit of time to organise the plates before they're ready for Mr Murray to collect as well."

"Then we have a plan for the day," agreed Sophia.

"Well, I must be getting on too," said George.

"Aye, of course. Thank you once again, Mr West. If we don't see you again later, I'm sure we will in the morning," Sophia replied.

As George said farewell and went off in the direction of his office, Hector noticed the mule driver walking towards them. He'd slept in his wagon overnight, around the corner from the hotel, and was ready to return home to Cairo.

Hector shook the driver's hand. "*Shukran jazīilan.* Thank you very much," he said, with a broad, grateful smile. He gave the man the money he was owed.

The driver beamed in response. "*Ma' es-salāmah,*" he repeated to each of them in turn.

"He's saying goodbye. Go in peace," Hector explained.

Without further ceremony, the driver turned and left.

There was time for one more picture before their lunch appointment. Sophia and Janet positioned the camera for the composition they had in mind, while Hector prepared a negative. The *Café d'Italia*, on the corner opposite them, would be centred in the foreground. *Rue Colmar*, up which they'd just walked, would stretch off to the left. The telegraph office and a glimpse of the railway line would be on the right.

Sophia was just about to remove the lens cap when a good-looking young waiter stepped out of the restaurant. She waited for him to stop moving. He lent against a post on the verandah and lit a cigarette. Then he turned in Sophia's direction and noticed the camera. He stared at her with a blank expression. Sophia began the exposure before the moment was lost.

The ebullient owner of *Café d'Italia* was gracious in finding a safe corner for the camera equipment to be stored while his guests ate their lunch. The waiter Sophia had seen outside showed them to their table. He seemed friendly enough, although there was something about his smile that made her feel uneasy. The man they'd come to see was already there. He stood up to welcome them.

"Everett Murray. Pleased to meet you all."

Sophia wasn't sure what she'd expected, but Everett's charismatic presence didn't fit any of her preconceived ideas. He was probably around Janet's age, of average height and build, and not handsome by any definition. His clean-shaven, tanned face was narrow and angular, with high cheekbones, a prominent brow, and a large, slightly crooked nose. And yet there was a character to his features she found compelling. The look in his heavily lidded eyes, and the directness of his manner, suggested self-confidence that remained just the right side of arrogance.

Once the introductions were out of the way, and the attentive waiter had taken their orders, conversation naturally turned to the trio's experiences on the way to Suez. Janet did most of the storytelling. Everett was full of praise and thoughtful questions. Sophia wanted to know more about the enigmatic Mr Murray and decided there was no harm in asking.

"I'm curious, Everett. What exactly is it that you do? What brings you to this part of the world, for instance?"

"I suppose you might say I'm a professional traveller. From time to time I'm asked to act as a kind of unofficial intermediary between friends in London and friends elsewhere. As for coming to Suez, you're the reason for that."

"Och, well, my photographs at any rate. I'm not sure I entirely understand, but thank you for trying to explain."

"When are you all due to depart?" asked Everett as the food arrived.

"Tomorrow morning at ten from the P&O quay. And yourself, sir?" Hector replied.

"I see. I'm also leaving tomorrow, though not until later in the day. May I collect your negatives this evening, Sophia? We appear to be running out of time."

"The items?" Sophia said, playfully.

Everett held her gaze and smiled. "Quite."

"Yes, this evening is what we had in mind too. We're at the Hotel Bachet."

"Good. I'll be there by eight o'clock. Now, Hector, would I be safe to assume you still carry a *sgian dubh*?" he asked, referring to the traditional Highland short-bladed knife.

"Aye, sir. Never without it."

Janet looked at him with surprise. "I didn't realise you'd been armed all this time."

"Of course, lass. That you hadn't noticed is a good thing. Means nobody else is likely to have done either."

"I was just as much in the dark as you were," Sophia reassured Janet.

Everett opened the leather briefcase at his feet and took out what at first glance looked like a bunch of rags. "In case you ever need a less close-quarters means of defence... here, complements of Wilson," he said, passing Hector the concealed Beaumont–Adams revolver.

"Understood, thank you."

"And you'll be wanting these," added Everett, handing over a box of ammunition.

"Goodness me," said Sophia, when the penny dropped. "I do hope that proves to be a wholly unnecessary precaution."

"Aye, so do I, ma'am," Hector replied. "So do I."

Janet finished sorting the glass plates in Sophia's room by half past six.

All the negatives from Ismailia to Suez filled three of the specially designed boxes. One hundred and eight photographs in all. Each plate was in a separate brown envelope, on the outside of which were written details of the image it contained. That information was also recorded on two copies of a reference list. One would go with the plates back to England, the other would be kept by Sophia. Janet had sealed the boxes and labelled them for the attention of Capt. C. Wilson at the Topographical and Statistical Department, London. Once that was done, she'd repacked all the other plates they'd used into as few boxes as possible and sealed those too.

Now at half past seven after a light supper, Janet, Sophia and Hector were sitting outside on the verandah, quietly drinking glasses of porter beer while they waited for Everett Murray to turn up.

"How long did Wilson say this next voyage would take?" Janet mused.

"Likely ten or eleven days, lass. Barring any delays at Aden," replied Hector.

"Oh, aye, that's right. Well, I think I might go for a wee stroll this evening. It'll be a while before there's another chance to enjoy the simple pleasure on dry land."

"That's a good idea. I'll probably stay here though if you don't mind. I'm beginning to feel quite tired," said Sophia.

"Of course I don't mind. I'm looking forward to a good night's sleep myself."

"If you do go wandering, lass, I'll need to accompany you," Hector pointed out.

"Do you promise to be armed to the teeth?" she teased. "I shall enjoy your company either way."

The sound of trotting hooves heralded the arrival of a small trap with Everett Murray at the reins.

"Good evening, Everett," said Sophia, noticing her fatigue suddenly evaporate. "Will you join me for a glass? These two are deserting me in favour of a walk."

"Perhaps just one, thank you."

"You'll be pleased to hear that everything is ready for you, thanks to Janet's hard work."

"Your kind efforts are much appreciated," Everett said, with a subtle bow of his head in Janet's direction.

"It was no bother at all. I don't suppose we'll see you later, so I'll wish you a safe trip back to London."

"Aye, good luck to you, sir," added Hector.

"Thank you, and the very best of luck with the rest of your expedition."

*   *   *

Tino Paranza didn't understand why he'd been instructed to surveil the three Scottish travellers, but he didn't need to. Getting paid was all he cared about. It should've been a simple enough task, and a pleasant one. The two women were easy on the eye. Especially the spirited, dark haired one. He'd imagined taking her by force.

But now Tino had a problem to solve. Now he was hiding in a dusty warehouse, keeping watch on the hotel across the street from a ground floor window, and waiting for his opportunity.

He'd seen them arrive at Hotel Bachet and unload their baggage from a sorry-looking wagon. They'd all gone to their rooms early, so Tino had returned home to sleep as well. When he came back this morning, he saw George West talking to the soldier, and then to all three of them. West passed a note to the dark haired one. She'd frowned when she read it. The wagon driver spoke to them too before he left. West walked off in the direction of his office and the Scots went to their rooms again. They came back out ten minutes later with camera equipment and found a carriage to take them to Suez. Tino had gone on foot. He caught up with them on the outskirts of town where they'd stopped to take a photograph. He'd passed them without being noticed and went home to wash and change. Then he'd gone to his regular job at the restaurant where he worked most afternoons. He was still encouraging the owner to convert the back room into a discreet gambling joint.

Why had he gone outside for a smoke at just that moment? Why did he look at the camera instead of turning away? It was a stupid reaction. He didn't like being caught off guard.

But Tino had been lucky with their choice of lunch venue. It allowed him to eavesdrop on their conversation and get close enough to the dark haired one to smell her scent. He'd discovered the soldier carried a blade and a revolver, and most usefully of all that the Englishman was going to meet them at the hotel to collect photographic negatives. Whether or not his own image would be amongst them, Tino had no way of knowing for sure. If the Scots were leaving on a ship tomorrow, neither they nor whatever pictures they carried with them might ever make it back to London, whereas the ones being couriered by the Englishman almost certainly would. Tino couldn't afford to let that happen.

This evening had been both curious and a cause for optimism. He'd watched the Scots drinking outside the hotel, the Englishman arriving, and then the soldier and the redhead leaving. The Englishman and the dark-haired one had carried on drinking for a while, before going into the hotel together. He saw her appear at the window of the downstairs room furthest away. She'd closed the shutters. About an hour later, the soldier and the redhead came back. They'd stopped to look at the Englishman's pony and trap before going inside. The woman also had a downstairs room. She'd stood at her window for quite some time. The man had gone upstairs and paced back and forth on the verandah. Eventually he went to his room, presumably on the other side of the building.

A couple of hours had gone by since then, perhaps more, and Tino was cold and hungry. But then his patience was rewarded. The Englishman was walking down the hotel steps carrying three boxes. It would take him a couple of minutes to secure them in the trap and get the docile pony moving.

Tino ran to the door at the far end of the warehouse, out into the chill air and back around the building to crouch in wait below the window he'd been watching from.

The Englishman was on the reins now. The pony walked on.

Tino Paranza followed them into the night.

*   *   *

Twenty-two troop horses died from the mystery disease that spread through the stables. At the end of July, acting on advice from Veterinary Surgeon Richardson, Colonel Dickson had issued an order concerning the cleanliness of the grain bags:

> *Each bag between the hours of feeding is to be turned inside out and exposed to the sun and air. Every horse is to be fed from his own bag, the bag belonging to one horse is not to be used for any other.*

Whether that made any difference, nobody could be sure. By the middle of October the crisis ended as suddenly as it had begun. It left some of the troopers needing to share mounts until replacement horses were acquired.

Private Meehan was the regiment's only human casualty of the summer on 21st July. Alec Innes recorded the cause of death as an abscess on the liver. Two days after the man was buried, the gossip doing the rounds of the barracks was that poor Emily Hill had run away from her husband on account of his cruelty. Sergeant Major Hill, known as 'Gassy Hill' by the lower ranks, was widely regarded as a low, vulgar ruffian, so his wife's predicament came as no surprise to anyone.

On the morning of Tuesday, 18th August, a total solar eclipse turned day to dusk and brought Bangalore to near standstill between quarter past eight and ten to eleven. Save for the occasional passing cloud, the city's residents were treated to an unobscured view of the spectacle and the fleeting equality of shared wonder.

Sergeant Fox and Farrier Major White were awarded good conduct medals at a divisional field day on 19th September, and at the end of October an incorrigible delinquent by the name of Flood narrowly avoided a flogging. A court martial sentenced him to two years' hard labour, branding with a 'BC' tattoo on the left side of his chest to forever mark him as a man of bad character, and discharge from the service 'with ignominy'.

Everything else carried on more or less as normal, including the regular Bangalore Races in which Maurice Fitzgerald and Robert Maillard almost always competed.

Today, however, was not a normal day.

With the furloughed exceptions of Charles Agnew and Robert Whigham, all the senior officers of the 16th Lancers were boarding a train at Royapuram station that would return them to Bangalore. They were in a sombre, reflective mood. This morning they'd attended the funeral of their good friend, Captain Walter Bagenal, at St. Mary's in Fort St. George.

Walter had fallen ill a fortnight previously with what Alec Innes diagnosed as phthisis. Everyone else called it consumption. Alec recommended that Walter go to Madras where he could receive better care at the larger hospital in White Town. A week there had evidently been of no use and Walter passed away yesterday, Wednesday, 25th November. It was a devastating loss.

As of this morning Robert was now Captain Maillard, promoted without purchase to replace Walter in command of their troop.

"We should do what we can to help him in the coming weeks. It'll be a difficult time," said Maurice as the train moved away from the platform. He was sharing a compartment with Morgan Farrell, John Barker and James Kennedy.

"Indeed. I'm sure he'll appreciate that," agreed John.

"Did you know he has a younger brother?" said James.

"Who? Robert?" checked Morgan.

"No, Walter."

"I don't recall him ever mentioning one."

"A lieutenant in the 45th Foot. Served on that expedition to Abyssinia at the beginning of the year – thirteen thousand men to rescue a few missionaries held hostage by a bunch of savages. I overheard Walter saying how relieved he was that Beauchamp made it through unscathed."

"What's your point?" asked John.

James pondered the question. "I suppose it all just makes such little sense. One brother goes off to war and returns without a scratch. The other doesn't get even so much as a sniff at glory, yet dies in the prime of his life from some malevolent disease."

"I'm reminded of another sad tale I heard only last week," began Maurice. "When Robert, Charles, Pills and I were in Salem the year before last, we met a captain of the Sappers and Miners by the name of Montague Foord. A very fine fellow – as was his father – responsible for building roads and public buildings and so forth."

"I remember Charles speaking highly of the man," said Morgan.

"Quite. Seems that while hunting in the hills near Salem earlier this month he was mauled by a sloth bear."

"Fatally?" queried James.

"Well, no, and that's the thing of it. Turns out his native hunting guide tried to shoot the beast, but in his haste missed and struck Montague instead. Before he expired, the good captain scribbled a note exonerating the *shikari* from any blame."

"The Lord certainly moves in ways mysterious beyond my comprehension," confessed James, shaking his head.

"The Lord has a cruel sense of humour if you ask me," said Morgan.

CHAPTER FIFTEEN
WATSON'S ESPLANADE HOTEL, BOMBAY, INDIA
THURSDAY, 18th FEBRUARY 1869

"Hello. I'd like a room."

"How many nights will *madam sahib* be wanting?"

"I'm not sure yet."

"How many is madam sahib's party?"

"Just me."

"And madam sahib's name please?"

"Munro."

At any other time the hotel's unique cast-iron architecture would have called for a photograph. Its myriad columns, balconies, latticework, and shutters were a stark celebration of linear design and as frenetic as the city itself. Three penthouse apartments occupied the fifth floor.

But all Sophia wanted was privacy, refreshment, a steaming bath, and a long sleep. It was a few minutes past ten o'clock in the morning.

Sleeping would have to wait. There was a telegram she needed to send.

Two porters carried her luggage to a room that had a balcony overlooking the street. At the hotel's reception she'd requested a pot of tea, and hot water to bathe in. Both arrived as the porters left, courtesy of a train of servants that filed in and out with rapid efficiency.

Sophia closed all the shutters, locked the door, stripped naked, and poured the tea.

The sanctuary of her own space. Glorious, inviolate, unsullied space.

Nobody staring. Nobody shouting. Nobody touching. Nobody spitting.

The three-day passage from Karachi, on a decrepit steamship with too many passengers and not enough berths, was an ordeal Sophia never wished to repeat.

She couldn't remember ever feeling this dirty or exhausted. Or this lonely. She sank into the bath and closed her eyes.

Sophia woke with a start and cursed at having dozed off. The water was cold and she was shivering. It was nearly noon. She dried herself, and dressed in the only clean clothes she had left. Back downstairs, she asked the receptionist for directions to the *Times of India*.

Half a mile away, by Elphinstone Circle, Sophia found the elegant building without any difficulty. Fifteen arched windows separated by brick pilasters spanned its first-floor frontage. Iron bars protected the windows from intrusion at ground level and made it look like a bank or a prison. Three betel-stained steps led up to an arched doorway and into the lobby.

Charles Wilson had given instructions to use the newspaper's telegraph office to confirm her safe arrival in Bombay, and to trust in the integrity of its editor, Robert Knight. "He's a journalist, and vocally critical of the Empire," Wilson had said, "but no less dependable for those failings." It was hard to believe, Sophia thought to herself, that only seven months had passed since that conversation. Given all that had happened in the meantime, it might just as easily have been seven years. She wondered how Wilson and James the photographer were getting on in the Sinai.

At the enquiry desk inside, Sophia asked to see Mr Knight and said her name was Mrs Munro from London. A clerk hurried upstairs to convey the message. Robert Knight came to the lobby twenty minutes later.

"I understand you wish to see me, madam? I'm Knight. How may I help you?" he said, somewhat disdainfully, in a London accent. He appeared to be in his mid-forties.

"Sophia Munro. It's a pleasure to meet you."

"Likewise, madam." He waited for Sophia to explain what she wanted.

"I was led to believe you'd be expecting me."

"Not that I recall. I fear you have me at a disadvantage. What was it regarding?"

"Captain Charles Wilson at the TSD said I should find you, and that I'd be able to send a telegram from here."

"Oh, did he? I'm afraid our mutual friend omitted to mention any of this to me. But no matter. Come this way," said Robert, showing Sophia through to the second office on the left.

Two overworked Indian telegraphers sat at a desks with their backs to the door. Both were entirely immersed in the coded world of *dits* and *dahs* and seemed not to notice the intrusion. One of them was transcribing a message coming through on the southern line that connected Bombay with Bangalore and Madras, whilst the other, motionless save for the subtle movement of his hand on the Morse key, was sending on the northern line that stretched to Agra, Calcutta and Peshawar.

"Because we're Reuters' agent in India, as well as providing a telegraph service to the public, things tend to be a little busy in here," Robert explained, handing Sophia a telegram form and a pencil. "However, if you jot something down on here, I'll have it sent immediately. And no charge, of course."

"You're very kind, thank you." Sophia wrote out the simple message and handed it back.

TO TSD WAR OFFICE LONDON
ARRIVED SAFE BOMBAY
WATSONS HOTEL
WAITING INSTRUCTIONS
S MUNRO

Robert glanced at the words before prioritising it with the operator. Why would this woman need instructions from a department of the War Office? He was intrigued. "I'm guessing, by your brevity, that you have some experience with the telegraph?"

"Aye, some," Sophia replied. "How long do replies usually take from England?"

"It varies. You'll likely have something by early next week, but possibly sooner. The new Indo-European line will make a significant difference once it comes into operation, and there's talk of a plan to lay a submarine cable between Aden and Bombay. If that happens, both speed and reliability should dramatically improve."

"I see. Thank you again for your assistance."

"My pleasure. Now, may I offer you tea? I'd be interested to hear the story that brings you to my door."

Sophia hesitated. "Please don't think me ungrateful, but I'm afraid my need for rest outweighs my capacity for conversation this afternoon. Another time?"

"Of course. Thoughtless of me. Perhaps you'd accept an invitation to supper with my wife and I on Saturday?"

"Thank you for your understanding. Aye, I'd like that."

"Until Saturday then."

Sophia walked back to the hotel and ate a light lunch. In the darkened calm of her room, she undressed and climbed between clean, crisp sheets. Sleep would hold her in its gentle embrace for sixteen uninterrupted hours.

Sophia spent Friday unpacking luggage, sending clothes to the hotel's laundry, sorting through umpteen negatives, cleaning her one remaining camera, and drinking oceans of tea. She visited the newspaper building at the end of the afternoon, but no reply had been received.

The hotel's penthouse apartments each had a roof terrace. On Saturday morning, she used their height to take pictures in the four directions across the city. Steamers and fishing boats were coming and going in Bombay Harbour to the east. The *Bhendi* Bazaar and a new fountain dedicated to the Duke of Wellington could be seen to the south. Back Bay, shaped like an ear, was to the west and beyond it the vastness of the Arabian Sea. And to the north, the city's urban sprawl.

When she returned to her room after lunch, two envelopes had been slid under the door. One contained a scribbled note from Robert Knight. He and his wife, Catherine, were looking forward to receiving Sophia at their home this evening any time after five o'clock. He provided their address and some directions. It didn't sound far. In the second envelope was the reply from London she'd been waiting for. Her hand covered her mouth when she read it.

MURRAY AND NEGS MISSING
WAIT BOMBAY FOR COLONEL MEADE
BALUCH NEGS HIS HANDS ONLY
THEN FREE TO TRAVEL
WITH WILSONS GRATITUDE

Shocked and confused, Sophia's mind flooded with questions she couldn't answer. What had become of Everett? It was six months since Suez. Had he been missing all this time? What does missing really mean anyway? Who's Colonel Meade? Did possession of the Baluchistan photographs somehow place her in danger? How long would she have to wait?

Sophia looked around the room at the organised chaos of her belongings. The unlabelled boxes of glass plates were stacked in a corner. She knew which ones were which. Should she try to conceal them? Sophia decided there was little point and that her time would be better spent replying to London. "*RECEIVED AND UNDERSTOOD*" was sent to the TSD an hour later. It was only half true.

"Did you get a reply to your telegram?" asked Robert Knight as he poured Sophia a glass of wine.

"Aye, I did, thank you. And, by the way, please forgive me if I seemed impolite when we first met. I was just so awfully tired."

"There's nothing to forgive, I assure you. Having had the dubious pleasure of many a steamship voyage, I completely understand."

"Thank you. I'm feeling much revived now, and more my usual self."

"I'm glad to hear it," said Catherine, who was a year younger than Sophia. "Where were you before Bombay?"

"Baluchistan."

"Gracious! What possessed you to go there on your own? You must be terribly brave."

"Och, no. I was travelling across some of the country taking photographs for an ethnographic study I hope to publish. Two very dear friends, Janet Steward and Hector Mackay, were with me."

"Yet they didn't come to Bombay?"

"Sadly for me, no, but very happily for them. They fell in love during our journey together, you see, and decided to return to Scotland to be married. We went our separate ways at Karachi."

"Oh, how romantic! That's lovely. I imagine you must miss them?"

"More than I can say, aye. They make a wonderful couple though and I'm delighted for them. I do hope they're safe."

Catherine wanted to know more about Janet and Hector. Robert's curiosity about Sophia and her work was growing by the minute. They were both satisfied by the conversation that blossomed over the course of their meal.

Sophia talked about the physical and photographic challenges of the most recent expedition, and how she probably wouldn't be sitting there if wasn't for Hector. They'd found themselves in several difficult situations along the way, one of them quite terrifying, but Hector had always ensured their safety regardless of the risk to his own.

She also described how the TSD had been helpful with maps and contacts and advice. Though Sophia didn't mention anything else, Robert could guess the nature of what they might've engaged her to do on their behalf. He asked if she'd heard of Andrew Wilson and his 1855 journey across Baluchistan.

"Any relation to Charles Wilson? Do you know if he explored the coast?"

"No relation at all, no. Andrew wandered more to the north I believe. We were colleagues at the paper for a while after he returned," Robert explained before recounting what he could remember of the story.

Over the main course, Sophia's voyages on the *Great Eastern* with Janet thrilled Catherine and held a professional fascination for Robert.

"So when you said you had *some* familiarity with the telegraph, you were being just a little coy?" he teased.

"Well, aye, possibly. Or just grumpy. My apologies."

"No apology necessary. I wonder if they'll use the same vessel for the Aden to Bombay cable?"

"I suppose they might. Captain Anderson and his crew certainly have more experience at it than anyone else."

"And you said you were able to send one of the very first messages across the Atlantic? What a marvellous privilege!" said Catherine.

"Did you get a reply to that one?" asked Robert.

"Actually, no, though I didn't really expect to."

Sophia told them about Henry Moriarty, how he'd sparked her interest in the slave trade, and some of the tragic sights aboard dhows she'd photographed around the Arabian coast. Travelling with two cameras had definitely been the right decision when there were three people, but not so practical now she was working solo. She'd given one of them to Janet to take home with her.

They talked about the newspaper, how Robert had taken it over nine years previously, and his passionate views on the importance of maintaining a free press.

"None of what I've been talking about will find its way into the paper, will it?" asked Sophia.

"Of course not, no. You're a guest in our home. I wouldn't dream of exploiting what I hope will be a new friendship for the sake of editorial."

"That's a relief, thank you. I hope it will be too."

"I'm wondering though... well, two things in fact... have you ever considered writing, and would you be interested in me publishing some of your photographs?"

"Writing for the newspaper?"

"Yes, exactly. I'm sure my readers would be fascinated by the adventures of an independent young woman and the world she's experienced."

"Really? I'm flattered, I must say. May I give it some thought?"

"Certainly."

"As for photographs, I'd be delighted if they could be seen by more people."

By the following Wednesday Sophia had become so absorbed in exploring Bombay's wonders and wretchedness she could have forgotten all about Colonel Meade. She would have done if it hadn't been for the boxes in her room acting as a stubborn reminder of the telegram from London. There were eight of them altogether and she'd procured a large trunk in which to pack them ready for transportation. The colonel arrived at the hotel that evening and sent a note requesting the pleasure of Mrs Munro's company in the lounge bar at eight o'clock.

Sophia couldn't see anyone who fitted the bill amongst the handful of people in the room when she first walked in. Then she noticed a middle-aged man entering the hotel lobby from outside and heading towards the bar. He was wearing an extravagant pith helmet at a jaunty angle and carrying a swagger stick.

"Pardon me, sir," Sophia ventured. "Might you be Colonel Meade?"

The man hooked his left thumb in the fob pocket of his waistcoat and studied her intently for several unnerving moments. Though by no means tall or unusually built, he was overtly masculine. His walrus-like moustache and burnside whiskers were silvery grey and carefully groomed. It was his small eyes that disoriented Sophia the most. They were blue, but far paler than her own, and had a peculiar hypnotic quality. Like a wolf staring down its prey, she thought.

"That I am," he replied at last, extending his hand to shake. "Colonel Richard Meade. And you must be Mrs Munro." His accent was southern Irish, though Sophia couldn't quite place it. Neither could she recall ever meeting anyone so bluff and suave in equal measure.

"Aye. Sophia. I'm happy to make your acquaintance."

"Likewise. Let's take a seat, shall we."

The colonel ordered two glasses of brandy and set his pith helmet down on a table between a pair of leather armchairs. His hair was wavy, dark brown and heavily receded.

"So, what do you make of Bombay?" he asked.

Sophia laughed. She was glad the conversation was starting on a light and informal note, though it wasn't an easy question to answer. "I think it's a truly astonishing place. I'd never have believed anywhere could be as colourful and exotic as Alexandria, but Bombay confounds one's senses to the point of being overwhelming."

"Quite so. There can be few cities in the world with such a great variety of races, nationalities and religions."

The waiter sauntered over with the brandy.

"Forgive me, colonel. I confess to knowing nothing about you beyond your name and rank," said Sophia.

"Then we find ourselves in the same proverbial boat, other than that I gather you're some sort of photographer."

"Aye, that's right. Perhaps we don't need to know anything for the purpose of our meeting?"

"Perhaps not, though I see no harm in it. Allow me to volunteer a little, so as to put your mind at ease... I served in the army for many years, as you'll have deduced, and I've come to Bombay from *Indore* on my way to London and eventually Cork."

"Pardon my geographical ignorance, but whereabouts is Indore?"

"It's an unremarkable place about three hundred and seventy miles north-east of here. Anyway, I received a request to take into my care a number of... what do you call them? Negatives?"

"Aye, glass plate negatives."

"And to deliver them safely to the TSD. I don't question such things you understand, Mrs Munro. Obedience is an old soldier's habit."

"And quite a relief it'll be. To pass responsibility for them on to someone else, I mean. When do you depart?"

"The 26th, the day after tomorrow."

Sophia was tempted to ask if the colonel had any more information about Everett Murray, but she didn't imagine there was any reason why he would so decided against it. Instead, she explained about packing the boxes in a trunk in preparation for his arrival. "And I purchased a stout padlock to keep it secure," she added, handing over the key.

"Most thoughtful of you. I'll have the trunk moved from your room to mine later on, and then your involvement in whatever this is will be over. I'll also despatch a telegram in the morning to confirm the handover has taken place."

"That's quite all right, and thank you."

The colonel raised his glass. "Well, here's to you Mrs Munro," he said. "*Sláinte.*"

"*Slàinte mhath*," she responded with a smile.

"Now that our official business is as good as concluded, tell me about Suez and the journey to Alexandria. This will be the first occasion I've travelled by that route."

Sophia described as much as she thought would be helpful and explained how her only experience of being a railway passenger in Egypt was on the section between Alex and Cairo. The colonel was grateful for the information, though didn't seem enthused by what he heard.

"Will this be a permanent return home for you?" Sophia wondered.

"No, no, merely a brief furlough. I don't wish to be away from my dear wife and children for any longer than necessary, and I'm required back in India before the end of the year in time for the visit by His Royal Highness."

"His Royal Highness?"

"The Duke of Edinburgh. He intends quite a tour, I'm told. And what are your plans?"

"I've been asking myself that very question. I could go back to Scotland, but now that I'm here in India it would be a shame not to see more of it. I'd welcome your advice."

The colonel downed what remained in his glass. "I quite agree – a shame indeed. It's a vast country, as I'm sure you're aware, with a great diversity of landscapes and a rich cultural history. Your interest would be in its photographic possibilities, presumably?"

"Aye, in part at least."

"And would you be travelling with companions?"

"I'm not at the moment."

"That's unfortunate. The Ganges Plain would provide a bountiful artistic harvest – from Calcutta in the north-east to Delhi and the Punjab in the north-west. However, I wouldn't recommend attempting a journey across that part of the country on your own if you value your safety."

"What would you suggest instead?"

"Bangalore," he replied without hesitation. "I suspect you'd do yourself great service by going there to begin with. The climate is relatively agreeable and there's a thriving British community."

"Thank you. I'd been wondering about perhaps going in that direction. I suppose it would give me a chance to adjust a little more – to India, that is – and to take my time deciding what to do next."

"Good. Most wise. Then to help you on your way, permit me to write a letter of introduction to my good friend, Doctor James Ranking. I'm sure he and his wife, and indeed their charming daughter, would be happy to have you stay with them a while."

"Oh, that's very kind. Thank you, I'd appreciate that."

"Think nothing of it."

The waiter was instructed to fetch writing paper, envelopes, a pen and ink. While they were being found the colonel explained that since Bombay and Bangalore weren't connected by a railway line, the most comfortable option was to take a train all the way to Madras and then another one to Bangalore from there.

With the materials acquired, he composed a short letter to Doctor Ranking. The hotel would post it in the morning. He also a made a separate note of the address for Sophia, and then wrote a second letter for her to carry. It politely invited whoever should read it to provide her with any and all assistance.

"As a minor precaution against difficulty, this will render you help from any military or civil authority you might come across," he said.

Below his bold signature, it read:

C.Q. TURNSTONE

Colonel Richard J. Meade
Governor-General's Agent for Central India
The Residency, Indore

223

CHAPTER SIXTEEN
HETTY PEGLER'S TUMP, GLOUCESTERSHIRE, ENGLAND
MONDAY, 5th APRIL 1869

Charles turned his back on the darkness, ducked under the great lintel stone at the long barrow's entrance, and squinted as his eyes adjusted to daylight again. A low dry-stone wall revetted the mound where the path led into the tomb. Charles sat on it and took care lighting a cigar with his last match. He'd used half a dozen or more while trying to illuminate his exploration of the empty burial chambers that lay off the central passage.

Sheltering from the bitter wind howling unopposed across the ridge from the south-west, Charles contemplated the many questions that sprang to mind as he savoured the taste of the tobacco. Until an archaeologist had the temerity to come along and dig them up, for instance, who were the Stone Age people whose remains had been undisturbed here for millennia? What might their names have been? Had they ridden horses and put them to the plough? What sort of livestock did they breed? How did they dress to keep warm on days like this? If they ventured away from their community, where did they travel to and why? What gods had they worshipped? And, in the end, how did they die? It was astonishing, Charles thought, how a kind of memory of unknowable lives lived so long ago could survive in monumental stone, or in the name of this local landmark in the case of Hester Pegler, the wife of a seventeenth-century landowner. Charles wondered if he himself would be remembered by posterity.

Charles took out his notebook and pencil to jot down a few *aide-mémoires*. He was planning to write to Morgan and Alec about everything he'd been occupied with lately. Telegraph messages served their purpose well enough, but lacked the freedom of expression and privacy of a letter.

One of the things his friends already knew about from previous correspondence was that the voyage back to England on the *Copenhagen* had taken twice as long as the one out to Madras on the *Golden Fleece.*

While the ship was at the mercy of storms in the Indian Ocean, its cargo had shifted about in the hold and unbalanced the whole vessel. That necessitated a significant reduction in speed and detouring to Mauritius for unloading, repairs and reloading. Under other circumstances a sojourn to a tropical paradise during its warm and dry winter season would have been no hardship. When the *Copenhagen* arrived, however, the Mauritian population was still in the process of recovering from a devastating March hurricane. The death toll had been high, though no one could put a figure on it. Homes and businesses were left flooded and roofless, and spans of a railway viaduct had fallen into the Grand River. Indentured labourers from India rescued what sugar cane they could from flattened plantation fields, toiling for their British employers in conditions much the same as those endured by the freed African slaves they replaced. The harbour at Port Louis was a tangled chaos of dismasted ships and wrecked hulls, including those of the *Vigilant, Dresden* and the *Henry Ellis*. With so much else to contend with, it was understandable that the harbour master and his exhausted workforce had been in no rush to attend to the needs of the *Copenhagen*, which they resolutely ignored for weeks. Charles allowed the widows and troopers he commanded to spend as much time ashore as they wished during the day, but insisted that everyone, himself included, was back on board by nine o'clock each evening. Horse racing had resumed at the *Champ de Mars* course and theatres were re-opening, but for the most part the stay on Mauritius was a dull and frustrating experience. By the time the *Copenhagen* eventually disembarked its passengers at Gravesend on Monday, 2nd November, four and a half months had elapsed since leaving Madras.

HM's Journal for Alec, Charles noted. In April of the previous year, Queen Victoria had published *Leaves from the Journal of Our Life in the Highlands from 1848 to 1861*. The edited diary extracts were so popular with the public that the book sold out before the *Copenhagen* had even left Mauritius. Charles thought Alec might be interested in reading it. He would try to find a second-hand copy and either send it or take it back to India with him when he returned.

Having discharged his duty, and after a brief visit to the cavalry depot in Canterbury, Charles had made haste to Cheltenham to see out what remained of the year with Harriet and her new family. He was thrilled to be reunited with his sister again after three and a half years apart, and to see how she and her infant son were thriving. Charles and George Cracklow got along famously, which pleased Harriet no end, and Charles was quick to form an uncharitable opinion of George's overbearing mother, which pleased Harriet almost as much. Christmas was celebrated with a feast at the Agnews' Exeter Place residence, where Charles was treated to unexpected humility and admiration from his father, selfless pride as ever from his mother, and curiosity about India and his journeys from everyone. On account of his absence, it was apparent to Charles in a way that it wasn't to Harriet that their parents had aged beyond their years while he'd been away. James didn't have the same vigour that Charles remembered, and Catherine was becoming noticeably absent-minded and forgetful. They were both beginning to look frail.

Charles drew in another mouthful of smoke and noticed a kestrel soaring high above the plateau. He followed the bird's course as he exhaled and watched it dive out of sight towards its unsuspecting prey. His train of thought returned to Catherine.

He and Harriet had always known about their mother having been a foundling. They'd been told the tale as one of miraculous good fortune many times as children. On a freezing January night in 1805, a month-old baby girl was discovered by an unknown saviour in the passageway of 23 Cannon Street in the City of London. She was taken into the care of St. Swithin's Church a few hundred yards away, and baptised Catherine Swithin. Later, she was adopted by a wealthy merchant family and given their surname. And so it was as Catherine Swithin Hamilton that she eventually entered society and met James. When Charles and Harriet were old enough to consider the details of the story more critically, they would speculate between themselves about the circumstances of their mother's abandonment, who her parents by blood might have been, and what characteristics they'd inherited from them for better or for worse. They realised the truth would never be known, and that it might very well be better that way. Nevertheless, their theories and fantasies grew more elaborate over time. Charles was most fond of the notion that an unmarried Hamilton daughter, or perhaps a niece, had fallen pregnant by some dashing beau who'd reneged on all his promises and left the girl to face the consequences of their tryst alone. To save the poor mother's reputation and safeguard her future prospects, the patriarch of the family arranged for her to be hidden away in the country until after the baby was born. A servant was charged with the task of depositing the child outside the home of a trusted friend of the Hamiltons, and it was one of their servants who took the infant to the church. Charles imagined the rector of St. Swithin's asking the servant her name and being told it was Catherine. As good a name for a female child as any, he might've thought. And then after an appropriate period had gone by Catherine was adopted back into the Hamilton family, which had been the plan all along, thereby gifting her respectability and a life of privilege. She may even have known her mother like a cousin or a much older sister without ever realising her identity. For reasons that had never been explained, Catherine hadn't had anything to do with her adoptive family for decades, so there was no way of ever finding out what really happened.

Charles wasn't going to share this cognitive tangent with Morgan or Alec, but he would ask Morgan to tell Trumpeter Dolan to look out for a copy of *The Moonstone* by Wilkie Collins arriving in the post. Charles had nearly finished the novel and was sure William would enjoy its originality and intrigue. Dolan had been a sickly orphan of about twelve years of age when he came to the army from the Foundling Hospital in Bloomsbury. Most of the men had treated the boy with kindness, protecting him from the few that were otherwise inclined, and he'd been mothered by some of the wives. Charles had instinctively gravitated towards being William's mentor; encouraging his musical talent and helping him improve his reading and writing. Charles's empathy was influenced at least in part by what he knew of Catherine's childhood, and the lad's given name was an inevitable reminder of his older brother.

Charles had spent a couple of weeks in London during January, staying at the United Hotel on Charles Street in St. James's. He made a number of expensive visits to Hawkes on Saville Row, crammed in as many plays and operas as he could, and called upon his father's sister, Aunt Marianne, in Marylebone by way of familial courtesy. Charles had been struck by how different London seemed. Not because it had actually changed so much since the last time he'd seen it, though there was a new Liberal government and the Thames didn't reek quite like it used to, but because he was different. His time overseas had given him a new perspective on many things.

Charles scribbled *After India?* and took a final drag of his cigar. Crushing what was left of it into the earth with his boot, he began making his way south towards Uley Bury hillfort. He walked with limber strides, swinging his duck's head cane forward with every third step, and on occasion had to reach for the brim of his bowler when a gust threatened to carry it off.

The question he'd returned to more and more often of late was what did he want to do once the regiment completed its posting and came home from India? If he continued his career with the 16th Lancers he'd be back to traipsing between garrison towns, and that wasn't an appealing prospect. One alternative was to follow the example of men like Pills Macbeth and James Goldie, and extend his stay in India almost indefinitely by exchanging between regiments. Charles had certainly grown to love the sub-continent and there was plenty of it he'd yet to experience. On the other hand, how relevant was being a cavalry officer to his future? As things stood there seemed precious little chance of the regiment ever being called upon to put its training with the sabre and lance into practice. In the heat of grief's anger he'd joined the cavalry to emulate and avenge his brother, but without even a minor skirmish to fight, never mind a full-scale war, what was to be gained by clinging to that naïve ambition?

Charles was following the western circumference of the Iron Age earthworks, and he stopped to admire the dramatic view over the Severn Valley. *If not cavalry, what else?* Terraced into the hillside below him was a secondary rampart, its contours still a formidable defence, with dense woodland bare of leaves covering the steep slope further down. When the time came he knew he could take over his father's business interests and add to them with his own acquisitions, but that idea didn't inspire excitement. If he was honest with himself, Charles recognised, without Larne harbour and the Carnfunnock estate he had no enthusiasm for being a landlord. Perhaps horses could be the answer? The questions circled without resolution and he continued his walk.

From the southern bastion of the fort Charles could easily make out Stouts Hill on the far side of the village of Uley. A thousand yards away as the crow flies, he guessed. Home to the Browne family, the country house sat in twenty-two acres and was distinguished by its Georgian Gothic architecture, crenellated roofline, and unusual hexagonal window leading. Charles had been a guest at Stouts Hill since the day before. Moving on, he followed the fort's eastern flank, scrambled down a well-worn path through the trees, and strolled back into the village down Crawley Hill road. Charles stopped at The Crown Inn to purchase a box of matches and a glass of refreshing pale ale. Warming himself at a table by the fire, he added to his notes: *Aintree. Wetherby. Bath Ball. Uley concerts.*

Witnessing a horse called *The Colonel* romp to victory in the dramatic Grand National steeplechase on 3rd March had made a tiresome journey to and from Merseyside worthwhile. Although his fellow officers in Bangalore would have read about the result already, Charles would give Morgan a first-hand impression of the event and the grandstand chatter. He'd intended to remain in the north for a while and travel to Wetherby for the National Hunt Chase, but that race had been cancelled as a mark of respect for the men and horses lost in a calamity on the River Ure at the beginning of February. According to press reports, the York & Ainsty Hunt, led by Sir Charles Slingsby and accompanied by some gentlemen from the 15th Hussars stationed at York, had been chasing a fox northward in the direction of Newby Hall for about an hour by the time it reached the river. The fast-flowing Ure was at least fifty yards wide and had been swollen by late rains. Whilst their quarry swam across pursued by the hound pack, most of the huntsmen continued along the south bank towards the nearest ford. Slingsby and about fifteen others, however, decided to board the Nidd Ferry. Some of the 15th Hussars had been amongst them and Charles didn't intend to mince his words when telling Morgan what he thought of their foolishness. The small, flat-bottomed ferry was propelled by hauling on a chain and had a safe capacity for no more than half the number of horses that clattered aboard. When they started to kick each other and create a panic a third of the way across, the vessel capsized and hurled its passengers into the frigid water. All of the cavalry officers managed to swim to safety or were rescued by plucky onlookers, but nine animals drowned along with Slingsby and five other members of the hunt.

When Charles returned to Cheltenham after the Grand National, he was greeted by an invitation to the annual Easter Fancy Ball at the Assembly Rooms in Bath on Monday, 29th March. Nine hundred and fifty-four ladies and gentlemen danced the evening away with quadrilles, waltzes, and lively galops. Like Charles, most of the one hundred and seventeen officers from the army and navy wore their dress uniforms. A good proportion of the other guests entered fully into the fancy spirit of the occasion and attended in the guise of water nymphs, angels, seventeenth-century peasants and aristocrats, Spanish matadors, Highlanders, Cavaliers, an Indian Prince, the Knave of Hearts and other characters from popular fiction. The Browne sisters, Mary and Catherine, both widows in their mid-sixties and old friends of the Agnew family, wore gowns that retained their elegance and dignity despite being several seasons out of step with the latest fashions. Mary's late husband, Colonel Benjamin Browne, had served in the 9th Lancers, and Mary was interested to hear about Charles's time in India. She told him about a day of concerts taking place a week hence at the National Schoolroom in Uley, which aimed to raise funds for a new organ for the parish church of St. Giles. Charles offered to lend his voice to the choir if the sisters thought that might help, which of course they did. They insisted he stay at Stouts Hill for as long as he wished before and afterwards.

Charles found the sisters' hospitality as boundless as their conversation, and yet somehow mildly suffocating. After the light lunch that followed the first concert of the day, he'd made his excuses and escaped for the much-needed bucolic interlude from which he was now returning. He needed to wash and change before all the performances were reprised in the evening concert. It was at times like this that Charles most missed having Solomon Smith's assistance with shaving and the laying out of clean clothes.

Charles had been chosen to lead the choir's tenor section, which was comprised of the Reverend Alan Kingscote, the son of Queen Victoria's chaplain; Lieutenant Thomas Vizard of the 11th Dursley Rifle Volunteers, from Ferney Hill in the neighbouring village; and a young man from Hertfordshire called Frederic Broughton who was a tutor at the school and harboured an ambition to be a journalist. The bass section was made up of Captain Harcourt Bengough of the 77th Regiment of Foot, whom Charles knew from the year below him at Rugby; and General Sir William Codrington who'd risen to be Commander-in-Chief of the army during the Crimean campaign, served as a Liberal MP for Greenwich, and been the Governor of Gibraltar. Cordelia Vizard, one of the lieutenant's sisters, was joined in the contraltos by Ann Bengough, the captain's mother; Mary Codrington, the general's daughter; and several other ladies. There were nine sopranos, including Mary Browne; Alice Vizard, as painfully shy as her siblings; Ann Kingscote, the clergyman's wife; and, most notably, Lady Emily Kingscote, the Woman of the Bedchamber to Her

Royal Highness Alexandra of Denmark, the Princess of Wales. Emily was the same age as Charles, who thought her voice was particularly fine. During a break in one of the rehearsals she'd given a brief demonstration of the language of signs and finger spelling used by the Princess, which earned her the admiration of the whole choir.

The evening's entertainment was expected to attract a rather larger audience than the morning had achieved, but the programme would be the same and the encores even more enthusiastic. Songs would include *The Chough and Crow*, *Kelpie's Bride*, *The Distant Chimes*, *I Know a Maiden*, *Bird of Mine*, *The Gipsies Tent*, and a charming Codrington duet of *Blow Gentle Gales*. Lieutenant Vizard's solo rendition of *Cameron's March* was generally considered the most popular piece. The Browne sisters would also play the overture to Boieldieu's comic opera, *The Caliph of Baghdad*, in a harp and piano duet.

Charles pocketed his notebook and finished his drink. There was something else he wanted to tell Morgan and Alec about. Not some thing, in fact, but some one. Someone who had come to occupy a rather special prominence in his thoughts since the Bath fancy dress ball, and about whom there was certainly no need to write a reminder. As he set off on the last fifteen minutes of daydreaming back to Stouts Hill, Charles was humming the tune of a favourite ballad.

CHAPTER SEVENTEEN
THE RACE COURSE, BANGALORE, INDIA
MONDAY, 28th JUNE 1869

There was a full card at the Bangalore Cup. It was going to be a hectic day for John Orr. He was one of seven stewards, and had a gelding called *Confederate* in the main race.

His turf club duties would occupy him until late afternoon and he was enjoying being free of the sound of crying more than he cared to admit. Emily had given birth to their first son four months ago. They'd named him Sutherland, and he was teething already. Ten-year-old Katherine had been making her father proud with the tireless support she'd given her mother.

What was foremost in John's mind today, however, was doing everything in his power to give Micky Lavelle some small reason to smile again. More than a year had gone by since Augusta passed away and his friend was still lost in the darkness of mourning. With gentle tact, John and Emily had both persevered in encouraging Micky to get out and about and attend social gatherings. This was the first time they'd succeeded and John was determined to prove the tide of fortune was turning for the Lavelle family. He took Morgan to one side and asked for his discreet help.

"Timing is of the essence," he said. "The bookies are currently favouring *Zoauve* to win. He's the three-year-old owned by Messrs Blair and Fane of the Templars syndicate. They also have *Paragon* in the race, but he's no threat at all. And then there's my *Confederate*, entered as a four-year-old. As we speak, his odds are pretty long. But the going is good to soft, and that gives him an advantage over the younger competition. What I'm hoping you'll encourage Micky to do – before the stewards' inspection an hour from now – is have a flutter on *Confederate* to win. Perhaps a little something on *Zoauve* to place as well, just for good measure. Would you do that for me?"

"With pleasure," Morgan replied. "Wasn't *Confederate* four when you brought him over from Melbourne a year ago?"

"You have a good memory. He was called *Speculation* then."

"Ah, I see." Morgan smiled in appreciation of the doctor's chicanery and the noble motivation behind it. "I'm bound to ask, what's going to happen at the inspection?"

Veterinary Surgeon Tom Richardson had aged *Zoauve* as a three-year-old at the beginning of the month, but John knew the Templars hadn't obtained a certificate to that effect. Richardson died ten days ago, the 16th Lancers' first fatality of the summer and its sixth of the year so far, which left the syndicate in a vulnerable position. John planned to use his influence amongst the stewards to achieve a majority vote objecting to the horse's age when its teeth were inspected. Not that he would burden Morgan with any of this information.

"Suffice to say *Confederate* and *Zoauve* will both be starting as four-year-olds," John answered.

"Forcing *Zoauve* to carry more weight than he's used to?"

John just raised one eyebrow and harnessed a smirk.

Morgan laughed. "Say no more," he said.

"Thank you, I really am most grateful," said John, shaking Morgan's hand. "Now, I'd better be off to the parade ring. I'll see you later on."

Morgan found Micky keeping himself to himself at the stand rail where he'd staked claim to a prime vantage point near the winning post. The excited trackside atmosphere had yet to lift him from his dour and morbid frame of mind.

"I heard about the Innes family's tragedy," he said, after the usual greetings and small talk. "Terrible sad, so it is. Terrible sad."

With Alec acting as midwife, Jessie Innes had faced the conclusion of her first pregnancy with stoic courage and was safely delivered of twins a week ago. Baby Katherine was healthy. Baby Jessie only survived an hour.

"A bittersweet joy, that's for sure," said Morgan.

The field running in the opening fixture was approaching the last bend. Morgan took advantage of the distraction to steer the conversation in a more useful direction.

"Here they come," he said, pointing to his right. "Looks like it's turning into a two-horse race. Have you put anything on this one, Micky?"

"No. Keeping my powder dry till later, so I am."

"Same here. Who do you fancy for it? I've been hearing good things about *Paragon*," Morgan lied. He was keen to get the measure of Micky's knowledge.

"Aw, no, you have it arseways. He doesn't have the legs for this kind of ground. The wise money will be on *Zoauve*, so it will."

"Oh, I see. Thanks for setting me straight."

The crowd cheered as the first victory of the day was clinched by a head in the final yards.

"Did you know John Orr has a horse in it too?" Micky asked once they could hear themselves again.

"Does he? Which one?"

"*Confederate*. He's a *quare* fine beast, so he is, but likely an outsider today."

Morgan pretended to consult his race card. "Ah, yes. *Confederate*. Interesting odds. Worthy of a punt in the spirit of solidarity? I feel the luck o' the Irish is with us."

Micky agreed, though without much enthusiasm, and followed Morgan towards the bookmakers where they both put a few rupees on the next race as well.

Regaining their spot at the rail, they chatted idly while they waited for the next group of riders to come under the starter's orders. Micky asked if Morgan had heard anything from Charles recently.

"Oh yes, we correspond regularly. The most recent letter I had from him talked about all the races and balls he's been going to, and how he was singing in some choir or other to raise money for a church organ. He telegraphed last week about being on his way to London for the Royal Grand Caledonian Ball in St. James's. He was expecting to meet the *Khedive* of Egypt and the British Consul, a Colonel Stanton, while they were in England visiting Her Majesty."

"Having a fine time hobnobbing then. And he's keeping well?"

"As far as I know. He certainly sounds like he's enjoying spending time with his sister and her family. And apparently he's smitten, too, would you believe? Someone he met in Bath, I think, though he hasn't really said much about them or his intentions."

"Good for him. I'm very glad to hear it, so I am," Micky replied, just as the spectators surged forward. The race ended well for him, his arbitrary selection romping ahead to an easy win. He looked surprised and vaguely pleased about it.

A hand on Morgan's arm was accompanied by a jovial voice. "Mind your back there, lieutenant, coming through." Morgan instinctively moved forward out of the way and turned to see who it was. A white-haired gentleman with unusually long burnside whiskers was edging past. Morgan returned his attention to the track. The distinctive scent of bergamot and lemon perfume was lingering in the thick air.

It took a moment for his memory to catch up with his senses. Suddenly alert, Morgan scoured the mass of hats and faces trying to locate the man with white hair. He spotted him not far away with two women. He couldn't see their faces. One was plump and judging by the style of her clothes probably in her middle age. The other was petite and had wavy black hair cascading unbound from beneath a wide-brimmed hat.

"Can't be?" Morgan thought aloud. He made his excuses to Micky and pushed through the crowd to find out.

"Sophia?"

The woman shot an automatic glance over her shoulder and carried on walking. Recognition caught up with her three paces later. She stopped abruptly and turned around.

His complexion is darker, Sophia thought to herself. Rougher around the edges, but still a handsome rascal.

"Lieutenant Farrell of the 16th Lancers," she said with a straight face.

Her hair was longer and she was a little thinner in the cheeks, but her eyes and voice were just as enchanting as he remembered them.

"Stranger things do happen after all," he replied.

An expectant, curious, wide-eyed silence was broken by their laughter. Sophia stepped forward and offered her hand to shake. Or to kiss. Either would be fine. Morgan shook it gladly, but ventured no further.

"I have a bone to pick with you," Sophia teased, as if no time at all had gone by since their first meeting.

"Oh really? About what, may I ask?" Morgan grinned.

"About not replying to my telegram."

That vexed him. He reached inside his tunic.

"This one?" he said, showing her the crumpled envelope he always carried.

Sophia was taken aback and somewhat embarrassed. It was nearly three years since Newfoundland and he still had her message.

"I replied the very next morning," Morgan said. "And there was me wondering why I didn't hear from *you* again."

"Och, goodness me! Well, then I apologise for doubting you. I suppose your reply might not have reached Heart's Content until around the time the *Great Eastern* was departing again. It must've been lost in all the mayhem. What did it say?"

"That doesn't matter now. It's wonderful to see you again. Is Janet here too? How have you ended up in Bangalore?"

"It's a long story."

"I'd like to hear it."

Sophia gave him the potted headlines about returning to London, crossing Egypt, and the Baluchistan expedition. She explained about Janet going back to Scotland, and said she'd been staying with the Ranking family. Morgan was enthralled by her adventures, and told her as much. He was rather envious too.

"By happy coincidence, James has been a keen amateur photographer for many years," she continued, "so it's been marvellous having a kindred spirit to share ideas with. And I have him to thank for introducing me to the staff at the hospitals as well."

"The hospitals?"

"Aye, the general women's facility and the lock hospital. I've been volunteering some of my time at both in recent weeks. It's been quite eye-opening, I can tell you!"

"I don't doubt it. That's very charitable of you."

"Och, I just try to lend a hand where one is needed. Sometimes it's administrative duties, sometimes helping nurses in the wards. The other day I even assisted at a birth, which was the most wonderous experience! I've been shocked by the degrading treatment of working women in the lock hospital though."

Around a third of all the soldiers in Bangalore contracted syphilis, and one in ten had gonorrhea. In a vain attempt to combat such high rates of venereal disease, the army had been financing a so-called lock hospital in the cantonment for decades. By law, prostitutes had to be registered with the police and submit themselves to weekly physical examinations. If they were suspected of exhibiting signs of infection they'd be confined to the hospital for treatment. Their registration ticket would be confiscated until they were declared clean again. Between eighty and a hundred women tended to be registered, but they represented only a tiny fraction of the prostitutes operating in brothels all over the district.

"Women are even confined simply because it's their monthly time. The ignorance and indignity of it all is an absolute disgrace."

As much as Morgan admired Sophia's compassion, the topic made him feel deeply uncomfortable for a number of reasons. He was thankful for being blessed with the inscrutable face he found so valuable in a card game.

"And the hypocrisy!" Sophia carried on. "Even in the general hospital, loyal British wives suffer terribly with diseases passed on from the indiscretions of their husbands."

"I imagine that must have distressing implications for their children's care too?"

Sophia was impressed by his thoughtfulness. "Aye, you're quite right, it does."

They'd both become oblivious to people moving around their reunion, but the start of the blue riband race was imminent and spectators were flowing towards the rail with a noisy urgency they could no longer ignore.

"I wonder..." said Morgan, leaning towards her to be heard, "would you like to meet one of my friends?"

"I'd like that very much, aye. Lead on." She took his arm and they cut their way back towards the rail.

"I was about to send out a search party, so I was," said Micky when he saw Morgan approaching.

"It's my great pleasure to introduce Mrs Munro, who will, I'm quite sure, insist on you calling her Sophia."

"Indeed I will. I'm very pleased to meet you," she said.

"And this is Michael Lavelle," Morgan gestured.

"Micky, my dear, and I'm glad to know you."

There was nothing inscrutable about Morgan's face now. He'd lost interest in the race, but he'd made a promise to John Orr and would see it through. Once the runners were under way, he pointed out the horse in fourth place going round the clubhouse turn. "The one with the jockey in blue silks... that's *Confederate*. Micky and I have wagers on him," he told Sophia.

"Well, then I wish you both the best of luck! He's keeping pace so far."

Micky's expression had lightened with Sophia's arrival. Now the field was on the back stretch, he was almost animated.

The jockey kept *Confederate* in hand behind *Zoauve* and the two leaders all the way to the final bend, by which point they were done for. He let him go as they rounded on to the home straight and *Confederate* accelerated away.

"Go on, boy! Go on!" Micky was shouting.

When *Confederate* crossed the line two lengths clear, Micky pounded the rail with open hands. "Well blow me down, would you look at that!" he said, though nobody heard him over all the cheering. An unfettered smile had conquered his face. "Morgan was right, so he was," he said in reply to congratulations from Sophia. "Seems we do have the luck o' the Irish today."

Micky went off to collect his winnings, leaving Sophia and Morgan to talk amongst themselves. She asked about how he and the regiment had been faring in Bangalore, and told him of her plans to move on, at least for a while. She wanted to explore some of northern India with her camera, and was keeping a watchful eye on the newspapers for reports about the Aden to Bombay telegraph. Morgan expressed his admiration, though really he was unsettled by the thought of her vanishing again so quickly.

"Did you come to the races all by yourself, Sophia?" asked Micky with his typical directness when he returned.

"No, no, I'm with Doctor and Mrs Ranking, but goodness, I've quite lost track of time. They must be wondering where on earth I've gone."

Morgan cursed in his head. "Of course. Well, I hope I'll see you again very soon?"

"I hope so too." She took Morgan's hand in both of hers and held his gaze. "Let's not wait another four years until the next time."

Sophia said her goodbyes and rushed off in search of her hosts.

"A *quare* fine lady, so she is," observed Micky.

"*Quare* fine indeed," agreed Morgan as he watched her melt into the crowd.

CHAPTER EIGHTEEN
PORT SAID, EGYPT
WEDNESDAY, 17th NOVEMBER 1869

George West had always been an early riser. The solitude of the ebbing darkness before twilight was his refuge. It was only then, before the call to prayer and while the desert air was cool and still, that his mind found peace. When *mu'addhin* imposed on the silence, George took solace in watching the glowing birth of a new day on the Sinai horizon.

This morning his habit was rewarded with the amusing bonus of an embarrassment for the Ottomans and French. From where he stood on François-Joseph Quay, George had an unobstructed view of the long line of ships at anchor. They stretched far into the distance of the outer harbour on his left, and around eight hundred yards to his right towards the pair of timber obelisks that marked the entrance to the canal. He reckoned there were about fifty altogether, and every one of them was liberally decorated with bunting and the flags of nations. At the vanguard of the fleet yesterday had been *L'Aigle*, the French imperial yacht that carried the Empress Consort of Napoleon III, Eugénie de Montijo. In a couple of hours, at eight o'clock, it was to have the honour of being the first vessel to officially enter the new waterway. Except that the survey ship, HMS *Newport*, had stolen the glory by blocking the path through the narrowest section of navigable channel.

"Ha! That'll put their petticoats in a twist," George scoffed.

During the night, Captain Nares of the Royal Navy had somehow managed to slip past all the other craft to get in front of *L'Aigle*. It was a remarkable feat of seamanship that George imagined would earn both a reprimand and discreet applause from the Admiralty. Commendable though the stunt was, the British consulate would have to pick up the diplomatic pieces once Monsieur de Lesseps and Isma'il Pasha learned of it. Those would not be easy conversations.

George took out his notebook and scribbled a description of the scene for his personal diary. Since reaching Port Said two days ago, he'd filled many pages with observations, stories from colleagues, and his thoughts about how the opening of the canal would change things.

Isma'il Pasha was the uncompromising and imprudent thirty-nine-year-old khedive, or viceroy, of Egypt and Sudan. He was also the architect of the opening ceremony festivities. At the beginning of the month, he'd apparently ordered ninety-seven of Alexandria's most violent criminals to be summarily drowned at sea in sacks weighted with stones. Whether this was a genuine precaution against unrest or simply a show of Ottoman ruthlessness, George didn't speculate. Either way, such blatant disregard for a civilized judicial process would hardly do anything to improve the khedive's reputation.

Ferdinand de Lesseps, on the other hand, was regarded as an eminently likeable gentleman. The enterprising visionary behind the development of the Suez Canal also happened to be a cousin of Empress Eugénie. He called her the canal's guardian angel, because of her unwavering support for the project. After visits to Venice, Athens, and Constantinople, she'd arrived at Alexandria on *L'Aigle* with a forty-strong retinue twelve days ago. From there she travelled by train to Cairo, and spent time sailing on the Nile and viewing the pyramids. Monsieur de Lesseps had welcomed her to Port Said early yesterday morning.

The empress formally inaugurated the great engineering achievement at a majestic ceremony in the afternoon. Her confessor, Monseigneur Bauer, along with priests from a variety of Catholic denominations and a mahommedan *ulama* all blessed the canal in their own unique ways. In the evening, thousands of lanterns illuminated the festival fleet, bands played on many of the decks, and broadside salutes were fired with unrelenting enthusiasm.

Behind *L'Aigle* this morning was the khedive's *El Mahrousa* and the yachts of Emperor Franz-Joseph of Austria, King Wilhelm I of Prussia, and Prince Henry of the Netherlands. Just as sleek in the water, and no less elegant with its two masts and pair of aft-leaning funnels, was the P&O steamship *Aden*. It had crossed from Marseilles with a hundred and twelve First Class passengers and was to be the first commercial liner through the canal. Some of the British consular delegation would have the privilege of joining her for the trip to Ismailia and Suez.

George would be one of them and he was looking forward to being part of the whole grand occasion. Mostly though, he just wanted to get back to work. Lately he'd been preoccupied with the canal's implications for his P&O agency. He presumed that travellers would soon be able to book direct passage between Europe and India, avoiding the need for an overland journey to or from Suez or even the necessity of setting foot in Suez at all. If that proved to be the case, would the company still need an agent? George hoped so, but he was far from optimistic and had no idea how he'd replace the lost income if his services weren't retained.

Further back in the line of ships was HMS *Rapid*, evidently neither as daring nor brazen as the *Newport*, along with all manner of other craft carrying dignitaries and special guests. Amongst the names being bandied about, George recalled the Egyptologists, Auguste Mariette from France and Karl Richard Lepsius from Prussia, the Norwegian playwright, Henrik Ibsen, French artist, Jean-Léon Gérôme, and the French author, Théophile Gautier. Britain's engineering fraternity was represented by the likes of John Hawkshaw, the canal expert who'd been the saviour of the Suez project in 1863, as well as the celebrated railway engineers, James Falshaw, Benjamin Haughton, and Daniel Kinnear Clark.

Somewhere in the convoy on board the S.S. *Hawk* was John Pender, chairman of The British-Indian Telegraph Company. The *Hawk* would be laying the Suez end of the Bombay cable early in the New Year if everything went to plan.

Near the lighthouse at the entrance of the inner harbour, and therefore a long way down the order of precedence, were members of the press on the paddle steamers *Fayoum* and *Mehemit Ali*. George met some of them yesterday. There was Mr Shepherd from the *Times of India* in Bombay, Mr Simpson from the *Illustrated London News*, and an earnest but likeable fellow from a British engineering journal. George had neglected to catch his name. Henry Calvert mentioned over lunch that the *Fayoum* was ordinarily a pleasure cruiser used by ladies of the khedive's harem. There was light-hearted agreement that it now being home to a pack of journalists was most fitting.

The consulate building was half a mile away on the north-east corner of *Place Abbas*. George decided to collect the overnight telegrams before strolling back. It wasn't his responsibility, but since he'd been standing across the street from the telegraph office he thought he might as well. George glanced through the communications as he walked. The usual mundanity of consular business was peppered by messages relating to the festival, but one slip of paper caught his eye. It was from an unnamed sender in Suez for Doctor Zarb.

PREPARATO. PRIORITA?

Italian wasn't George's strongest language, but he understood "Prepared" and "Priorities?" Who was prepared, and for what? Why the anonymity? And, most importantly, why was Herbert Zarb involving himself in Suez matters? It was a puzzle George could make no sense of, and one that fuelled a nagging instinct.

Doctor Zarb had been the personal physician of Ferdinand de Lesseps for a long time, which George imagined meant he was often privy to sensitive information about the canal development. Now that Port Said was on the verge of becoming a much busier and more important place, conceivably more important than Alexandria, the doctor's sphere of influence as vice-consul was inevitably going to expand. George resolved to pay greater attention from now on.

In the lobby of the consulate, George handed all the telegrams to a clerk for distribution. He found Edward Stanton in a particularly cheery mood upstairs.

"Ah, good morning, George. Have you heard the news?"

"Good morning, colonel. About the *Newport*?"

"About the *Latif*?"

"I fear not. One of the khedive's corvettes?"

"Yes, that's right. It tootled off down the canal yesterday afternoon to perform a final check for obstructions and so forth, and then promptly ran aground!"

"How unfortunate!" said George, sarcastically. "I don't suppose the khedive is terribly pleased?"

"Indeed not. He and the Egyptian prime minister left their guests last night to personally supervise the vessel's recovery. I'm reliably informed he stormed out of the party swearing to impale every last one of the *Latif*'s officers for their incompetence."

"Charming *fellah*, isn't he."

"Quite."

"Did they succeed in re-floating her?"

"I haven't heard as yet, but I'd be surprised if they didn't. We should assume the fleet will get underway on schedule."

"In that case, we'd better be making our way to the *Aden* shortly."

"Ah, yes, it's getting to that time. I suggest we gather in the lobby in twenty minutes. Now then, what was that about the *Newport*?"

George explained. Colonel Stanton was not amused.

By mid-afternoon the *Aden* was halfway to Ismailia and averaging around four knots per hour. It would be dark by the time the anchor dropped in Lake Timsah. Spirits on board were high despite the slow progress.

"We live in historic times, gentlemen," said Colonel Richard Meade as he joined the group of British consular officials on the fore deck. Returning to India after his furlough, he'd been aboard since Marseilles.

"Indeed we do, colonel. A fine story to tell one's grandchildren, God willing," replied George West. "I'm glad to see you again. It must've been February when you were last in Egypt, was it not?"

"Likewise, Mr West. Yes, that's right. Time to get back to one's duties now though."

Exchanging handshakes and pleasantries, Colonel Meade reacquainted himself with Colonel Stanton and Henry Calvert, with whom he'd dined before leaving Alexandria for England, and was introduced to Consul Mr Perceval and Vice-Consul Doctor Zarb from Port Said.

"What's your opinion of the canal thus far, colonel?" asked Henry.

"A triumph of ingenuity over nature, that's for certain, though I confess I hadn't expected its navigation to be so fraught with difficulty."

Posts had been installed along the entire length of the canal to mark the port and starboard boundaries of the safe channel. More than a handful of captains failed to maintain a course within it and their ships grounded in the shallows. Since the task of getting them moving again was often laborious and time consuming, and with the snaking channel only being wide enough to accommodate single-file travel, passengers further back in the fleet had no choice but to exercise patience.

"It's a matter of better dredging, which will naturally take time to complete," explained George. "As I understand it, the intention is to create a wider and more consistent channel, thereby enabling the passage of ships north and south simultaneously."

"I see," said Richard. "Shame they didn't succeed in that before the opening. I should imagine it'll be long past midnight before those at the tail end reach our destination."

"I dare say you're right."

The *Aden* was passing between the east and west halves of the settlement of *El Qantara*. A steward stopped by the group to offer the men complimentary champagne.

"I noticed an Italian steamer not far behind us earlier. Rubatini is it?" queried Richard as he took a glass.

"The Rubbatino Company, colonel. They operate a mail and passenger service between Genoa and Alex," clarified Mr Perceval.

"Is that the same outfit that recently purchased land in East Africa?"

"Quite so, yes. A chap called... what was his name, Herbert?"

"Sapeto."

"Yes, yes, Sapeto, thank you. *Signore* Sapeto apparently negotiated with the Sultan of *Raheita* and managed to secure the Rubbatinos a sizable area around the Bay of Assab. Because of Assab's proximity to the shipping lanes at the southern end of the Red Sea, we believe they intend to use it as a coaling station, presumably to support an expansion of their operation into the Arabian Sea."

"A shrewd investment. I suppose the canal is bound to have an undesirable impact on their Mediterranean service?"

"Almost certainly, yes, while at the same time creating an opportunity to exploit the demand for travel to and from India," said George.

"And by having their own coaling station, they'd reduce their costs and be a commercial alternative to Aden," added Herbert.

"The beginnings of a new Italian colony perhaps?" wondered Richard.

"That's a distinct possibility, yes," said Colonel Stanton. He spotted a rain shower heading their way and suggested they all take shelter before its arrival. "It perhaps seems odd to experience a downpour when surrounded by so much arid desert, colonel. I'm told it has something to do with the climatic influence of Lake Timsah being an inland salt sea," Edward explained.

"Peculiar indeed," said Richard. "And what do we have to look forward to in Ismailia, do you think?"

"From what we can infer from the extraordinary scale of his preparations, and the vast sums of money he's borrowed to pay for it all, the khedive certainly has quite a party arranged," said Henry. "There's to be a grand dinner and ball tonight – if we get there in time – and all manner of entertainments."

"Interestingly, however, it seems he's chosen not to invite the sovereigns of other countries that share his faith. Like the Sultan of Morocco and the Shah of Persia, for instance," said Edward. "From which one might deduce that his priority is to impress particular European leaders instead."

"It's hard to imagine that going down well amongst the mahommedan nations," said Richard.

"Quite."

Once the rain had passed, the conversation was taken back out on to the deck. The ship ahead of them had grounded, and they watched the process of its recovery with amusement.

"Hardly bodes well for the future commercial success of the canal, does it?" Richard thought aloud.

"Which would not come as unwelcome news in London," commented Edward.

"The success of a Franco-Egyptian project not being in our best interests, you mean?"

"It's all a very delicate political game, of course, the final outcome of which is still far from certain," Edward replied. "It's no secret that the British government has been against the canal from the very beginning. For a while, a specific objection to the use of forced labour served to impede progress, but now we just have to wait for the heavily indebted house of cards to collapse. Until that happens, the canal represents a threat to British security and merchant trade. But when it does... well, then one might easily foresee a situation where control of the canal falls into British hands, and that would change everything."

When the *Aden* dropped anchor in Lake Timsah a little after eight o'clock that evening, the spectacle ashore mocked the imaginations and vocabulary of all who gazed upon it. George West wondered how the descriptions he would write in his diary could possibly hope to do any of it justice.

The multicoloured tents and camel caravans of visiting Arab chiefs were arranged on the bulge of land between Lake Timsah and the canal on Ismailia's eastern outskirts. On the other side of the town on the Avenue of Victoria, just across from Ferdinand de Lesseps' house, a temporary settlement of more than twelve hundred tents had been created.

Facing the lake at one end of the embankment was the khedive's palace. About eighty yards long, and two storeys high, it had taken only six months to build. On the dunes that separated the town from the lake, an enormous hall had also been constructed to seat the six thousand who'd be waited on by a thousand footmen wearing powdered wigs. Beside it was a separate dining room for those sovereigns considered worthy of an invitation. The khedive had imported all the furnishings from Paris, including chandeliers, mirrors, ornamental fountains, gilt chairs, and marble tables.

Bursting with enthralled guests and indifferent locals, the whole town was decorated with colourful streamers flowing from Venetian masts, elaborate garlands, triumphal arches, and every conceivable kind of flag. There were Bedouin fighting displays, and feats of Dervish daring with burning coals and scorpions. All illuminated from below by score upon score of oil lamps and flaming torches, and from above by breathtaking fireworks.

The spellbinding world conjured from the sand by Isma'il Pasha would beguile his guests until sunset tomorrow. Then they would return to reality by way of Suez, and George West would get back to work.

C.Q. TURNSTONE

PART FOUR

CHAPTER NINETEEN
THE ESTABLISHMENT, BANGALORE, INDIA
SUNDAY, 24TH JULY 1870

France had declared war on Prussia.

A week to the day since the news first reached Bangalore it was still the only thing anyone really wanted to talk about. Speculation was rife. Who would strike first? Where were decisive battles most likely to take place? What influence would cavalry and artillery have? How different might the borders between nations be when it was all over?

The direct telegraph cable connection between Britain and India was in its second month of operation. From Porthcurno near Land's End in Cornwall all the way to Bombay, it enabled transmissions to be received throughout India within minutes, which for eager audiences used to being often weeks behind the times was almost like watching history unfold first-hand. The marvel of immediacy had turned report gathering from Bangalore's telegraph office into something of a cantonment sport. The latest off the wire a few hours ago was that Napoleon III was preparing to travel to Metz to take personal command of his 'Army of the Rhine' and had appointed Empress Eugénie as Regent of France for the duration of his absence.

"We keep talking about Prussia, but strictly speaking," John Symes-Bullen pointed out, "the Frogs are mobilising to fight a whole coalition of northern German states, of which Prussia is merely the leading player."

"I'm not sure there's anything mere about Prussia, but you're quite right about the confederation," said Carrin.

"It seems to me," John continued, "for France to have any chance of victory it will need to create useful alliances with Austria, Denmark and the Italians, and I doubt it'll have much luck with any of them."

"And it'll need to make intelligent strategic use of what resources it does have," Carrin added. "That von Moltke fellow is a master tactician by all accounts, and I can't see the ailing Emperor being a match for him."

"I suppose Britain throwing her hat into the ring would be too much to hope for?" wondered Francis Drummond.

"On whose side?" baited Morgan with a straight face.

"Good lord, Morgan, what a question!" John exclaimed.

"He's just pulling your leg," said Carrin.

"Oh, I see," John laughed, realising the trap he'd fallen into. "But to answer Francis," he continued, "I can't imagine a time we'd ever countenance going to war with our German friends, and certainly not as allies of the old enemy the French. Neither does it seem likely Prussia would need to seek an alliance with Britain."

"One can't help feeling envious of all those on the verge of glory though, can one? Not when here we all are so far away and without an enemy to fight, I mean," said Francis.

"Well, we have the monsoon and cholera," Morgan smiled.

The four men were on the bungalow's verandah waiting for the afternoon's deluge to end, and for Charles to join them, before taking their carriage over to the Cavalry Officers' Mess. Henry Wilkinson's long-awaited return from furlough this morning was cause for a celebration dinner.

Henry would have learned by now of the cholera epidemic that broke out amongst the men of the 21st Regiment of Foot in the old barracks at the beginning of last month. So far it had been contained to only seventy-seven cases, of which forty had been fatal. As a precaution against greater calamity, the wives and children of the infantrymen had been moved under canvas on the Agram Plain behind the cavalry barracks.

Charles had arrived back in Bangalore in early January after a memorable journey from Southampton. Cabins aboard ships navigating the newly opened canal were as rare as hen's teeth, so he'd travelled via Egypt's overland route instead. He stayed at Shepheard's Hotel in Cairo and visited the pyramids just as Robert Maillard had once done. Suez lived up to all his lowest expectations.

He'd made financial arrangements to retain his room in the bungalow while he was away, as well as livery for *Woodman* and the continuation of Solomon Smith's stipend. His reunion with all three, and of course with Morgan and Alec and his other good friends, brought him more joy than he'd anticipated or could begin to explain. Charles supposed it had something to do with taking comfort in their familiar dependability when so much else was fluid and unpredictable.

Although he didn't go into details with Morgan or Alec, neither of whom pressed him on the subject, the sweetness of his romance in England had turned abruptly sour and he'd yet to find any consolation in being philosophical about it. It was also obvious that the 16th Lancers was a very different looking regiment to the one either Charles or Henry had known before they went away. In large part that was thanks to a complicated purchase dance initiated by Colonel Dickson, Captain Riddell and Captain Fitzgerald.

It began early last year with George Riddell deciding to retire with a view to reinvigorating the Bragborough Hall estate near Rugby. By the summer Maurice Fitzgerald was following suit, which in turn prompted Robert Maillard to leave India in August and take George's place in command of the Canterbury depot. James Kennedy left for the 3rd Dragoon Guards stationed in Colchester, exchanging places with a veteran of the Abyssinian campaign called Graham Hamond.

After consulting with Morgan via telegram from Cheltenham, Charles had purchased George Riddell's rank to become Captain Agnew. John Symes-Bullen purchased the rank of lieutenant from Charles, and Henry Graham the rank of cornet from John.

Charismatic William Dickson, who'd been on extended furlough to England since last March, announced his retirement only recently. That left the way clear, at last, for Thomas White to purchase the full rank of lieutenant colonel and obtain permanent command of the regiment. And so Henry Wilkinson could become a major, John Barker a captain, and William Hill a lieutenant.

John Barker and Major Hugh Burnell then added to the turmoil by choosing to exchange with William Shaw and John Bayley of the 7th Hussars, newly repatriated to Canterbury after a long posting in Peshawar on the wild North West Frontier.

Meanwhile, Pills Macbeth had moved on to the position of deputy inspector general of hospitals, reporting to John Orr; William Farmer and his family had returned to England; and Cornet William Barker was doing a fine job as the regiment's new adjutant. To his great credit, he was also acting temporarily as quarter master after James Fuller was forced into retirement by ill health.

Robert Maillard originally conceived The Establishment bungalow as a subalterns' chummery, and though Robert was sorely missed and two of its residents were now captains, Charles was pleased that its fundamental character remained the same. Carrin had been back from his convalescence at home in Kent since April and was looking all the better for it. He'd reoccupied his old room, left empty after James Kennedy's departure. Francis Drummond had been offered Robert's room, and John Symes-Bullen the one vacated by John Barker. Nobody seemed to know what had become of the pet monkey.

Charles reflected on some of this in a long letter he'd nearly finished writing to Harriet. He told her about how Yadhu Nayak had once tried to explain the Hindoo notion of *karma*, the principle of cause and effect. Every action in life has a consequence and every consequence can be far-reaching, Yadhu had said, like the overlapping ripples made by monsoon rain upon a lake. The purchase system is much the same, Charles wrote. One man comes to a decision, such as George Riddell, for instance, that on the face of it has nothing whatsoever to do with anyone else, but which goes on to directly influence the course of many other men's lives.

He wrote too of how much he'd come to like and respect John Symes-Bullen and Francis Drummond. They were only twenty-three years old, Francis being the elder of the pair by some five months, yet they tended to demonstrate a degree of maturity uncommon in privileged men their age. They were conscientious officers, excellent horsemen, and Charles was happy to have them both in his troop.

Cornet Drummond was even taller and broader than Charles, dashing and clean-shaven, and spoke with a confident Perthshire accent modified by a public school education. His father had been the Lieutenant Governor of the North-Western Provinces; one of his uncles was the 7th Viscount Strathallan; John Murray, the 4th Duke of Atholl, was one of his great-grandfathers, the present duke being the Secretary of State for India; and one of his great-great-grandfathers, William, the 4th Viscount Strathallan, was killed at the infamous Battle of Culloden whilst serving as a major general in Bonnie Prince Charlie's Jacobite army.

Lieutenant Symes-Bullen couldn't lay claim to quite such a distinguished pedigree, but he had inherited part of Catherston Manor just north of Charmouth on the Dorset coast. Several of his ancestors had apparently achieved senior positions in the navy, and one had been a justice of the peace. Charles could easily imagine John being suited to the judiciary himself. Blessed with a strapping build, but standing no more than five foot three in his boots, he had a wide nose and the kind of easy smile that was synonymous with a generous disposition.

Whenever giving serious thought to a matter, as he did often, he had the habit of removing his steel-framed spectacles and cleaning the small oval lenses methodically with his handkerchief.

The cacophony of rain fell silent as abruptly as it had begun, and Charles could hear Morgan calling his name. He set the letter aside and made for the verandah with hat and cane in hand.

"Still hypothesising about French and German battle plans, I see," Charles said as he lit a cheroot. The others were all poring over John's ten-year-old Edward Stanford map of Europe.

"I'm thinking of taking bets," winked Morgan.

"What say you, Charles?" asked Francis. "A wager on the outcome?"

"Mr Agnew isn't one for gambling," said Carrin, without any hint of criticism.

"Indeed I'm not. But if I was, my money would be on Prussia."

CHAPTER TWENTY
THE RESIDENCY, BANGALORE, INDIA
SATURDAY, 24TH SEPTEMBER 1870

"Sophia of Heart's Content fame?" Charles asked with a rhetorical smile as they shook hands.

Morgan was taking delight in being able to make what felt to him like long-overdue introductions.

Sophia laughed. "Och, am I preceded by a reputation?"

"Morgan may have mentioned your missions of science once or twice."

"Has he now?" she said, her eyes lifting to Morgan's. She liked what she saw in them.

"I hadn't expected you to be here, but I'm so glad you are," he said.

"Likewise, Lieutenant Farrell of the 16th Lancers," Sophia teased. Charles couldn't help noticing how she squeezed Morgan's arm as she said that.

They were in the shade of a stand of trees on the Residency's east lawn. Morgan and Charles wore their full dress uniforms with scarlet tunics. Sophia maintained her usual casual style, which elicited disapproving tuts from many of the women in attendance sweating beneath weighty gowns and tight corsets.

The grounds thronged with guests from across the spectrum of Bangalore high society, both military and civil. At the invitation of Colonel Richard Meade, now chief commissioner of Mysore and *Coorg*, they were all gathered for tiffin in honour of Major General Arthur Borton. The fifty-six-year-old veteran of campaigns in India and the Crimea had arrived from England the week before last to take command of the Mysore Division of the Madras Army. He was accompanied by his wife, Caroline, one of their daughters, and his aide-de-camp, Lieutenant Edward Duncombe Shafto of the Royal Artillery.

"What adventures have you had since last we saw each other? Did you go to the north as you'd planned?" Morgan enquired.

"How long has it been?"

"About fifteen months," he replied without needing to think about it. "Too long."

"Aye, too long," Sophia paused. "And aye, after another photographic project not far from here, I'm pleased to say I did go north. I travelled via Agra to Delhi and then onward to *Ambala* and eventually *Simla*."

"That must've been quite a journey," prompted Charles, for whom Sophia already seemed more like an old friend than someone he'd only just met.

"Oh, it was, and with so many wondrous sights along the way I'd need several lifetimes to photograph them all. I've only been back here in Bangalore with the Ranking family for a couple of weeks."

"How did you get on without Janet and her Highlander?" asked Morgan.

"Well, I knew it would be foolhardy, quite apart from rather impractical, to be exploring India alone, so a while ago I employed a retired havildar – a most gallant Hindoo gentlemen – as my assistant and translator. The difficulties of the trip would have certainly multiplied without him. I do still miss Janet and Hector, of course, but it's reassuring to hear from time to time that they're happy and content and in good health."

"I'm glad to hear that too," Morgan said sincerely.

"I've never been to Simla," said Charles, "but I understand it's not unlike Ooty in that it serves as a summer retreat?"

"And I've yet to visit Ooty," replied Sophia, "but if it's high up amongst forested hillsides, and with a climate even milder than Bangalore's, then aye, very similar."

"Indeed so, that describes it perfectly."

"Was that the reason for Simla being your destination? It being a retreat, I mean," asked Morgan, the dozens of far more interesting questions going round in his head having to play second fiddle to propriety.

"Not entirely, no. You see, my dear friend James Anderson, who'd captained the *Great Eastern*, sent word of a special party being planned for late June to celebrate the completion of the telegraph connection. The viceroy, Lord Mayo, was to be involved from his home in Simla, and James assured me that if I could get myself there I'd be made welcome."

"That was decent of him, and well deserved. You were as much a part of it as anyone, after all," complimented Morgan.

"Och, I wouldn't go so far as that, but it was a great privilege to be invited." A Residency steward offering tea served in delicate porcelain cups interrupted the conversation for a moment. Saucer in hand, Sophia continued. "The viceroy's official residence is a remarkable, if somewhat draughty, place called the *Peterhoff* on a sunny ridge that runs south from Simla town," she explained. "He and his two teenage sons were charming and generous hosts, their only demands of me being that I take their portraits and share stories of my travels. Naturally I was only too happy to oblige on both counts."

"Naturally," said Morgan.

"And how was the party?" asked Charles.

"Och, it really was quite something! The 23rd of June is a Thursday I'll long remember, that's for sure. In fact, thanks to the time difference between Britain and India, for those of us in Simla it carried on until the wee sma' hours of the Friday. You see, John Pender – he's the chairman of The British-Indian Telegraph Company – and his wife were holding a *soirée* at their home in Piccadilly. James was there, along with some of the other senior officers from the *Great Eastern* voyages, as well as the Prince of Wales, the Duke of Cambridge, Ferdinand de Lesseps, and even Lord Mayo's wife, Blanche." Sophia sipped her tea. "And, because of the way great distances simply vanish when under the telegraph's spell, it was as if we were right there in the room with them. Messages were flying back and forth around the globe at astonishing speed. The viceroy spoke to President Grant in the United States, President Grant spoke to the Prince of Wales, the Prince of Wales spoke to the khedive in Alexandria, the King of Portugal, and to the viceroy. Countess Mayo was even able to say hello to her husband and boys, which was a rather touching moment."

"How wonderful!" said Charles. "And were you able to send messages of your own?"

"Sadly not, no, but I was grateful to witness history being made and to photograph the viceroy playing his role in the drama."

"And you've had your own telegraphic dramas before," Morgan consoled with a brazen grin.

"Aye," Sophia laughed, "that I have."

Morgan was about to say something else, but the sight of John and Emily Orr emerging from the Residency's grand portico distracted his attention. Emily was opening a lace parasol. John was carrying a long, slender case.

"My apologies, will you excuse me for just a moment?" Morgan said to Sophia. "There's someone I need to speak to."

"Of course," she replied. "I'm not going anywhere."

Charles and Sophia carried on the conversation until Morgan returned a few minutes later with the doctor and his wife. He'd taken custody of the beechwood case, cradling it in one arm while he introduced Sophia to the Orrs. Then he turned to present it with pride to a mystified Charles.

"John was kind enough to look after this for me until the surprise could be sprung. Happy birthday, my friend."

"It's your birthday today?" checked Sophia.

"My thirty-fourth," Charles replied. The day had been passing quite contentedly without anyone mentioning its significance, and now he felt vaguely embarrassed at being ambushed.

"Well then happy birthday from me as well!"

John and Emily wished him the same and Charles thanked them all. "I think Morgan is eager for you to take a look," nudged John. "There are two clasps..."

"Ah, yes," said Charles, turning the case around to open it. "Goodness, Morgan!" he exclaimed when he saw the sabre and scabbard inside. "Thank you. What a fizzing gift, and an extraordinary piece of work! A *tulwar?*"

"A tulwar indeed, all the way from *Jeypore*. I'm glad you like it," Morgan replied with satisfied relief.

"Of course I like it. No more following convention with my old '53 Pattern!" Charles said, setting the case down and extracting the Indian-made weapon from its velvet-lined mounting. He tested the weight and marvelled at its balance.

"The blade is Damascus steel," Morgan explained, "which will hold a much better edge than our sabres do, and I gather the silver-inlaid leaf decoration on the hilt is called *koftgari*."

"It really is a thing of beauty, and I like the shape of the knuckle bow as well. It fits my hand perfectly."

"Almost like it was made for you," Morgan beamed. "Quite striking how curved the blade is, don't you think?"

"And it widens noticeably towards the tip – for added momentum in the draw cut I suppose. Thank you again. It's incredibly generous."

"Aye, very thoughtful," admired Sophia.

"My pleasure. You're most welcome," said Morgan. "The drinks will still go on your tab this evening, mind you," he added with a chuckle.

"Wouldn't have it any other way," smiled Charles.

"I've never held a sword. May I?" Sophia asked.

"By all means," Charles said, offering the hilt of the tulwar in her direction.

Sophia wrapped her fingers around it and took a step back as she swept her hand left and right. "Och it's so much lighter than I expected," she said, her eyes following the movement of the blade. "And what a curiously powerful feeling it is to wield something so deadly."

"A feeling every soldier must learn to master, I dare say," suggested John.

Sophia relinquished the sabre again and Charles returned it to its case. He looked forward to showing it off in the Officers' Mess later and was already trying to think of ways to repay Morgan's kindness.

"You mentioned another photographic project earlier," said Morgan, now eager to re-focus on Sophia. "What was that about?"

"Something different to my usual work for a change. You see, until around '65 there was an organisation called the Archaeological Survey of India, or ASI for short, which as the name suggests was dedicated to researching the country's antiquities. In its absence, last year the government invited anyone with the time and inclination to voluntarily list, and ideally photograph, whatever ancient buildings happened to be in their vicinity. Lord Mayo has since told me that the Secretary of State is in fact pushing for a reinstatement of the ASI, but time will tell. Anyway, it sounded like a worthwhile endeavour, so after doing a little research of my own I ventured sixty miles or so east of here to a village called *Avani*. I thought its four magnificent Hindoo temples, all countless centuries old, would make for an interesting photographic challenge."

"A challenge in what sense, my dear?" wondered Emily.

"In that the scale of the architecture and the extent of the iconography would very likely require ingenuity to capture with any kind of thoroughness. And that very much proved to be the case, because they took far longer to photograph than I expected."

"Are the temples dedicated to particular deities?" Charles asked.

"Aye, they are," Sophia said, intrigued by the question. "I can't recall all their names now, but I do remember another one – on a hill just outside the village – built to honour the goddess *Sita* who's said to have lived there. I photographed that as well."

"How fascinating. I'm quite envious," said Charles. "If memory serves, *Sita Devi* was the consort of *Lord Rama* and is associated with courage, purity and self-sacrifice."

"You know something of Hindooism then?" Sophia replied, impressed by his obvious interest in the subject.

"Only a little, if truth be told. A gentleman of that faith has been doing his best to educate me."

"Has he told you about the *Bangarapet* legend?"

"Bangarapet...? No, actually, I don't think he has."

"It's a wee place about fifteen miles to the south-west of Avani. Sita is said to have wandered barefoot around the area where the village now lies. According to the legend, as she did so the ground beneath her feet was transformed into a labyrinth of gold mines."

"What a far-fetched story!" said Emily, sounding more dismissive than she intended.

"And yet," Sophia continued, "the strange thing is, as I saw for myself, the fields of that district really are flecked with gold. I was told the local people have been gathering and trading it for generations."

"Far-fetched or not, either way I'm staggered I've never heard about an abundance of gold so close to home," confessed John.

"I suspect there's more of it in this great country than most people could imagine," said Richard Meade, overhearing the conversation as he approached. He was circulating amongst his guests with effortless diligence and social flair, but had been looking forward to spending time with this group in particular.

"Ah, colonel, good day to you. Yes, I dare say you're right," John replied. "You already know my wife, of course, but may I introduce..."

"Mrs Munro and I are already acquainted, Doctor Orr," interrupted Richard, tilting his pith helmet to an even jauntier angle and extending his hand to Sophia. "I'm very glad to find you safe and well."

"Likewise, colonel. I'm so pleased to see you again."

"Doctor Ranking has been looking after you, I trust?"

"With unfailing kindness, aye. Thank you again for sending me in his direction and for all your advice and assistance."

"Oh don't mention it. Time permitting later on, I'd very much like you to meet my dear wife – also an Emily," he said, with a courteous nod of acknowledgement towards Emily Orr. "I'm hoping you'll indulge us both with tales of your photographic expeditions."

"Of course, I'll be delighted to."

"Splendid."

"And may I offer my congratulations on your new appointment," Sophia added. "Quite a change from Indore, I imagine?"

"Thank you, it most certainly is. Although, after eight engrossing months, one might say I'm past the first bloom of novelty. But I'm forgetting myself. Forgive me, captain," said Richard, turning to address Charles, "How do you do? I'm Colonel Richard Meade."

"It's an honour to meet you, colonel. Captain Charles Agnew, at your service, and this is Lieutenant Morgan Farrell."

"The honour is mine, gentlemen, I assure you. Politics and administration may have kept me occupied of late, but only twelve short years ago I was in command of the finest native cavalry regiment in India. Meade's Horse, as it became known, saw its fair share of action around *Gwalior* amongst other places. So you see, I have good reason to hold the cavalry in the highest regard. Now, tell me, what do you make of the Prussian's use of heavy horse at Mars-la-Tour last month?"

"The 7th Cuirassiers charging the French guns, sir?" replied Charles.

"Quite. Under that von Bredow chap."

"A necessarily daring tactic by all accounts, which proved successful despite the toll of losses. What was it, almost half the force of eight hundred?"

"So I read, yes, that's right," chipped in Morgan. "The press has already immortalised it as Bredow's Death Ride."

"A chilling headline, but had they not shown the kind of devil-may-care courage every horseman aspires to," Charles continued, "it's reasonable to conclude the French wouldn't have been subsequently put to flight and the siege of Paris wouldn't now be in its fifth day."

"I agree," said Richard. "There will be those who call such engagements reckless. However, it seems to me that Bredow's use of topography, surprise and speed more than answered the doubters who question the value and relevance of cavalry on the modern field of battle."

"As we in the 16ᵗʰ Lancers hope to have the chance to reiterate further one day."

Sophia and Morgan exchanged a glance of furtive reluctance when Charles said that.

"Good for you, captain. Quite right too," said Richard. "One of the rewards of my present position is that I'm able to retain some involvement with cavalry matters, albeit in a rather different context."

"How so, colonel?" asked Morgan.

"The region's *Silladars*, that is to say our irregular native cavalry, have long needed reorganising to make them a more effective and reliable force. Their role has more to do with policing than battle, but it's a task I'm enjoying sinking my teeth into nevertheless."

"One of many, I'm sure," said Sophia.

"Very many indeed, from the likes of repairing irrigation tanks and prospecting new lines of railway, to judicial reform and extending primary education to the masses. There's much else besides, all of it the substance of what one might readily imagine a chief commissioner would be concerned with. However, the Kingdom of Mysore comes with a unique, additional responsibility that underlies all else."

"By which you're presumably referring to the young *rajah*?" queried John.

"In part, yes. As I expect you all know, we've been guardians of the region for almost forty years, but the vexed question looming over us is how Mysore should be prepared for reversion to the status of a native principality. I'm of the firm opinion that we should consolidate upon everything achieved by my predecessor, Mr Bowring, to the end that the province may be handed over to His Highness the 23ʳᵈ *Mahārāja* in perfect order. Guiding the young man on his long journey towards that day will be crucial to a successful transition."

"Pardon my ignorance, gentlemen. You're making it sound as if this mahārāja fellow is no more than a wee lad, or have I misunderstood?" asked Sophia, who guessed she might not be the only one wondering the same thing.

"He's only seven, in fact," Richard clarified. "I met him and his tutor, Colonel Malleson, for the first time earlier this month. His name is *Chamarajendra Wadiyar*, and a more intelligent, pleasant boy you'd be hard-pressed to find, nor one with such a precocious talent for the violin. Malleson seems to be doing a fine job of ensuring he receives a proper education, including encouraging him to vie in sports with companions of his own age."

"Then perhaps there's reason for cautious optimism?" Emily suggested.

"I believe there is, my dear, yes," said Richard. "Now then, I've monopolised the conversation long enough. With your permission, may I borrow your husband for a moment?"

"Of course you may, colonel," smiled Emily.

"Thank you. Before I do," said Richard, turning to Sophia, "there's a gentlemen over there on the south lawn whom I rather suspect you'll enjoy meeting. His name is Doctor Fitzgerald, and he's kindly volunteered to photograph some of my guests before this afternoon's monsoon descends."

"I rather suspect you're right, colonel, thank you," Sophia replied with enthusiasm.

"My initial suggestion was that he made his arrangements on this side of the building, but he was quite insistent the south would be better and I thought it best not to argue."

"I'd have insisted the same. At this time of day, you see, when the sun is high in the sky, having the subjects facing southward guards against the composition being marred by dark shadows."

"Ah, yes of course, that should've occurred to me. I'll remember for next time," said Richard. "Well ladies, and gentlemen, I do hope you all enjoy the rest of the day. Shall we, doctor?"

"After you, colonel," John replied.

"Perhaps we might reconvene in a wee while?" Sophia asked Morgan and Charles.

"We'll come and find you," replied Morgan, trying not to sound too eager in front of the others.

The courtesies of parting duly observed, Emily joined a clique of wives deep in cantonment gossip, Charles and Morgan went in search of refreshment, and Sophia headed to the south lawn.

"What I wanted a word with you about, doctor," explained Richard once he and John were on their own, "is the forthcoming Municipal Regulation Act and an opportunity it will present that I'd like you to consider."

"Very well, colonel. Please go on."

"In brief, the intention is that Bangalore's petta and cantonment municipalities will fall under the overall direction of a central municipal board, whose task it will be to coordinate improvement works and so forth across the city. Needless to say, the two separate districts would retain control of their own administration and finances. None of this is likely to happen before the spring, but it does mean I'll need to appoint an executive officer to lead the new board. With that in mind, I've been wondering if I could tempt you away from your hospital work?"

"This is most unexpected, colonel," replied John, taken aback. "It's very kind of you to think of me."

"Hardly kind, my dear fellow. In my view, you're simply the right man for the job. However, there's no rush. Take your time to cogitate on the idea and discuss it with your wife, and then we can talk on it further in a week or two."

"Thank you, yes, I'll certainly do that."

"Good, good. Well, if you'll excuse me, I'd better go and make sure the major general is being looked after."

John had an afterthought as Richard was walking away. "By the way, colonel, do you happen to recall if the Residency's library holds copies of Bradshaw's?"

"Bradshaw's? It does, yes, and invaluable they are too. Help yourself, by all means."

The four stewards trying to fulfil Doctor Fitzgerald's requests were demonstrating boundless patience. It wasn't that his instructions were unclear or onerous, or in any way impolite or disrespectful. He just couldn't quite make up his mind about how best to position everything they'd brought outside. It would be an important photograph and he wanted it to be perfect.

The scene was being set adjacent to the south terrace. Bamboo blinds hung unfurled between its slender Ionic columns and were tied in place around the handrail of the balustrade. To the left, arched windows were closed with louvred shutters. The vivid white of the Residency's stone and plaster made the delicate pinks, oranges, purples and blues of potted chrysanthemums and hydrangeas look all the more colourful. Two patterned rugs, hand-knotted in Bangalore, protected a large rectangle of carpet liberated from the foyer, upon which stood a pair of *chaise longues* separated by a chair with matching upholstery, and four footstools. Their placement had changed half a dozen times already.

"Rather you than me," jested Sophia as she neared the doctor. He was peering into his camera, its blackout cloth draped over his shoulders.

"I beg your pardon?" he snapped with obvious irritation before emerging into the light. The fifty-three-year-old's Dublin accent was as distinctive as the day he left over a quarter of a century before. His tone softened immediately when he saw the woman awaiting him. "Oh bless my soul, if I'm not mistaken you're the Mrs Munro whose photography I've heard so much about? Apologies for my rudeness, ma'am."

"Sophia, aye, and you must be Doctor Fitzgerald. The apology should be mine for creeping up on you like that."

"Patrick Gerald Fitzgerald and I'm delighted to meet you. Now, what was it you were saying?" He was dressed in a double-breasted frock coat as well-worn as his collar and tie. Salt and pepper sideburns and a walrus moustache tangled below a shock of receded silver hair. A bamboo swagger stick was tucked under one arm.

"Rather you than me," she repeated, gesturing towards the furniture. "I've always found groups of people by far the most difficult subjects of all. It's so often like trying to herd headless chickens."

Patrick laughed. "And so it will be today, to be sure. I believe I'm expecting sixteen adults and a few young children, and I don't mind confessing to you my uncertainty about the best approach," he said. After a moment's further thought, he added humbly, "Would it be an imposition to prevail upon your professional opinion?"

Sophia was accustomed to talking about her travels and showing her portfolio of work, but it was unheard of for another photographer, not even James Ranking, to seek her creative advice. She was deeply flattered.

"Och, no imposition at all, if you think I might help?"

"Indeed I do, thank you. I'm but a devoted amateur and can't pretend to have anything like your skill or experience," Patrick said with reassuring modesty. He offered her the blackout. "I was thinking four adults to each *chaise longue*, one on the chair of course, and five more standing behind," he explained as she took command of the camera, "with the children at the front on the rugs or stools."

Sophia was careful to notice all the details of the image inverted on the focusing screen, emerging from under the cloth now and again to check something in plain sight. She asked the doctor to sit on the chair and then stand behind a *chaise longue*.

"I do have a few thoughts," she concluded, hesitant about potentially causing offence.

"I hoped you would. I'm all ears," said Patrick.

"I'd be inclined to open the shutters of those two windows and roll up the blinds on this side of the terrace. Doing so will help to reduce the brightness of the background and create more useful contrast."

"Ah yes, so it will," he realised, immediately issuing instructions to the stewards.

"Aye, that's better," Sophia confirmed once they'd been carried out. "Although on second thought, could we lower the blind nearest the corner again – just by a few feet so its texture can be seen? And then, I think there'd be merit in the *chaise longues* being at slightly more of an angle. Shall we try that?"

"Consider it done," he said, and within moments it was.

"See what you think now," invited Sophia, handing back the cloth.

"Ha! Small changes, but what a tremendous difference they make!" said Patrick with sincere gratitude.

"Och, it's my pleasure. The rest will have to be played by ear once the guests are here, of course. When the time comes, I'd be happy to assist with the preparation of your plates if you wish?"

"That's most generous of you, thank you. However, I'm still loyal to the convenience of the waxed paper process and already have them at hand."

By the time Sophia first took up photography, wet plates had replaced waxed paper as the medium of choice for negatives. Despite that, many photographers in India preferred to continue with waxed paper, James Ranking among them, so she was fascinated to learn more from Patrick. They chatted about their craft, the advantages and disadvantages of different methods, and how revolutionary it would be if a dry plate were to be invented. Patrick was proud to tell Sophia about how some of his images of Lucknow and Cawnpore had been featured at the 1860 exhibition of the Madras Photographic Society, and how he was soon to take up a new appointment as the Garrison Surgeon in Bangalore. Sophia liked his warmth and humility, and respected the passion he had for their shared art. She hoped this would be the beginning of a long friendship. When Patrick asked about the *Great Eastern* and what she'd been working on since then, she was pleased to be able to recount her stories in a way that only a fellow photographer would be able to appreciate.

Their conversation was interrupted by an excited King Charles Spaniel bounding at their feet and the girl in a pretty white dress chasing after it without success. Her hair was tied with a ribbon and Sophia thought her to be about seven years old.

"I'm so sorry for the intrusion," said a tall woman walking towards them without haste. She was wearing a top hat and had the puppy's leash looped around one hand. The elegant simplicity of her navy blue dress was like a more formal version of what Sophia often wore. "Here boy! Come to momma!" she called, crouching down. The drawn out vowels in her accent suggested she hailed from the United States, though Sophia couldn't begin to guess where exactly.

"Oh, that's quite all right, Mrs Scott," Patrick replied. "May I introduce Mrs Munro?"

"You may, doctor, thank you. Please do call me Harriet."

Sophia appreciated that. "And my name is Sophia. It's a pleasure to meet you," she said. "What an adorable wee creature he is!"

Harriet had the puppy under control and clasped to her waist. "Isn't he just? That's the second time he's escaped me today, and I seem to have misplaced my husband as well."

"And is this your daughter?" Sophia asked. The girl was standing awkwardly at Harriet's side, head bowed in a shy silence.

"No, no, this sweet child is one of Colonel Meade's. My two daughters are over there somewhere." She handed the leash to the girl and set the puppy back down on the grass. "You run along now my dear, but keep a good hold of him this time."

"Might I ask, Harriet," Sophia began as the girl skipped away, "am I correct to assume you're American?"

"Proudly so, yes. Georgetown in my nation's great capital, Washington D.C., is where I call home. And I can hear that you're from bonnie Scotland like my darling Douglas."

"Aye, so I am."

"Sophia is an accomplished photographer, Mrs Scott," Patrick explained, "and has just been telling me about a daring expedition she undertook in Baluchistan."

"My goodness! Baluchistan? South of Afghanistan?"

"Och, the doctor is being too kind. I wouldn't say daring, and I was in good company, but aye."

Harriet insisted she tell the tale again. Sophia obliged, limiting her narrative to the highlights of the journey and an outline of the ethnographic study, but found herself feeling a little uneasy about how intently Harriet seemed to be listening.

Some of the other guests who'd been invited to sit for the photograph were beginning to congregate. Sophia was relieved to use their arrival as an excuse for bringing her storytelling to an early conclusion. Harriet expressed her admiration and thanks before going to speak to them.

"Used to be a Russian baroness, did you know?" Patrick asked Sophia quietly.

"I didn't. But forgive me, isn't she married to a Scottish gentleman?"

"Major Scott of the Staff Corps, yes. However, it's the second time around for both of them. Her first husband was Baron Alexander de Bodisco, the Russian Ambassador to Washington. The daughters she mentioned still go by the name Bodisco, and two of her sons live in Russia. One's in the diplomatic service like his father, I believe, and one's in the Tsar's Imperial Guard."

"Och, I had no idea," Sophia admitted, wondering if her ignorance had been taken advantage of.

Emily Orr wanted to know where she and the others should be for the picture, and overheard enough to get the gist. "The doctor's quite right, my dear," she whispered. "The poor woman was but a child of sixteen when the baron convinced her to marry, and he a man of fifty-three! Can you imagine?"

"I'd rather not," replied Sophia.

"Well, no, quite. Given the life she's had, it's a wonder she looks so much younger than her forty-six years. Wouldn't you agree?"

"Aye, I suppose so, but what an interesting life it must've been."

"One can be happy for her now though. The major is a few years her junior and quite the catch, but don't tell John I said so," Emily smiled.

Patrick's attention was returning to the task at hand. "Shall we find you somewhere to sit, Mrs Orr?" he said.

"Oh, yes, please do. Where would you like us all?"

Patrick led Emily to the *chaise longue* on the left and invited her to take the more comfortable end with a back to rest against. She would be on the far left of the photograph. Sophia remained by the camera as Patrick's second pair of eyes.

John Orr was asked to stand on the far right, and then Patrick set about filling in the gaps. He quickly discovered that Emily Meade, six months pregnant and wearing a voluminous crinoline, needed to sit almost sidesaddle and thereby took up space planned for three on the other *chaise longue*. To her left he sat his personal guest, Miss Louisa Garstin, the twenty-six-year-old spinster daughter of General Edward Garstin of the Royal Engineers. She was a tiny woman with a characterful face, but her dress easily filled what little room remained. So much for the equally proportioned plan, Sophia thought to herself.

James Ranking agreed to occupy the far left standing position behind Emily Orr's shoulder, and if he had an opinion about the photograph he was courteous enough to keep it to himself. In Patrick's mind, the scene was now bookended neatly by respected colleagues. He offered Elizabeth, James's matronly wife, the chair in the centre. She accepted it willingly without comment, while their self-assured daughter, twenty-four-year-old Isabella, stood to John Orr's right behind Louisa Garstin.

Patrick walked back to Sophia. "What was that you were saying earlier about chickens?" he joked with a sigh.

Sophia laughed under her breath. "It's shaping up nicely, and I see Colonel Meade is migrating this way with more camera fodder."

"Ah yes, perfect timing. That's Major General Borton and his wife and daughter, and it looks like the Bodisco girls have taken a shine to Lieutenant Shafto."

Patrick asked Arthur and Caroline Borton to sit together as befitted their honoured status, and to grace the left-hand *chaise longue* beside Emily Orr. The major general cut a most distinguished figure in his brand-new cream suit of clothes accessorised with top hat and silver-headed cane. He curled the ends of his moustache, which stubbornly retained the mahogany colouring of his youth. By contrast, the hair that remained below his bald pate, and the thick sideburns flowing beyond his jawline, were silvery-grey. From a distance, Sophia thought he looked rather slumped and uncomfortable. She couldn't tell if he was glaring with the impatience of a man suffering a bad stomach or the insecurity of a man suffering his own vanity. Neither was she at all sure if his wife's vacant gaze was practiced submission or the symptom of a deeper malaise.

The Bortons' stylish seventeen-year-old daughter, Mary Louisa, who gave the impression of being somewhat delicate and self-conscious, perched behind Emily Meade.

Edward Duncombe Shafto, smartly dressed in light tweeds and with his arms crossed over a swagger stick, was the twenty-seven-year-old son of a County Durham clergyman. One of his ancestors was said to be the Bobby Shafto immortalised in the nursery rhyme, *"Bobby Shafto's Gone To Sea,"* and Edward had inherited its protagonist's fair hair and good looks. He was given the position standing between Mary Louisa Borton, whom he thought of like a younger sister, and Isabella Ranking, with whom he was yet to succeed in engaging in conversation.

Harriet Scott had been hovering at the periphery. "Doctor Fitzgerald, perhaps I might join Mrs Orr?" she announced in declaration of her real intention to sit next to the major general. She didn't wait for a reply, leaving Emily, Arthur and Caroline no polite choice but to shuffle right and left to make room.

Olga, the elder and more independent Bodisco daughter, stood firm against the back of the chair occupied by Elizabeth Ranking. Mittie Bodisco, meanwhile, sat in quiet defiance on the rug at Arthur Borton's feet. Both siblings were the epitome of fashion. Olga wore layers of white lace and an extravagant bonnet. Mittie had chosen a dark riding outfit, the braided tunic of which resembled the Lancers' patrol jacket, and carried a crop in immaculate white gloves. Her top hat was identical to her mother's.

"And now Colonel Meade, if you'd be so kind as to stand behind the major general and his dear lady wife," invited Patrick. The colonel did as he was asked, hooking his left thumb in his fob pocket and keeping his pith helmet on so that history would be in no doubt about who was in charge.

"Come and sit with me, children," his wife called over to their three young daughters. The shy one in the white dress handed the puppy's leash back to Harriet Scott before sitting on a footstool between her mother and Louisa Garstin. The youngest fidgeted on another stool and was encouraged to keep still by Emily's hand on her arm, while Elizabeth Ranking made her right knee available to the third.

"Thank you for your patience, ladies and gentlemen," said Patrick, "I believe we are nearly ready."

"My husband and his daughters will be here presently," pointed out Harriet to mumbled consternation. She was trying to keep the puppy still on her lap.

"Ah, yes, thank you, Mrs Scott," Patrick replied.

"Might that be them?" asked Sophia, nodding in the direction of three figures approaching from the portico.

Without saying a word to anyone, Douglas Scott strode to the back of the group to stand behind his wife in the gap between James Ranking and Richard Meade. His oldest daughter, a plain young woman who'd evidently tried hard to mirror almost every aspect of her step-mother's attire, stood on the colonel's left and stared at the camera with hope in her eyes.

While the younger Scott sister was quietly arranging herself on the one remaining footstool in front of Emily Orr, Sophia asked Patrick for a quick word. "I'm afraid we have a wee problem," she said. "Or should I say, a rather large one."

Douglas Scott was an unusually tall and well-built man, with receded fair hair, a horseshoe moustache, and what Sophia considered to be a supercilious manner. The problem was that he completely dwarfed the colonel and Doctor Ranking, and disturbed the balance of the scene.

"Ah, yes, I see what you mean," said Patrick.

"Perhaps a chair on the left?" Sophia suggested.

"Thank you, yes, that's a capital idea."

A steward was sent to fetch a chair, and Patrick was diplomatic in inviting the major to be more comfortable sitting down at Emily Orr's right. He acquiesced with begrudging reluctance.

Returning to Sophia, Patrick asked if she thought the picture was missing anything. She'd been considering that very question for a while. "Well, if they were willing, perhaps the stewards could be in it as well – up on the terrace and in one of the open windows?"

"I like that suggestion, yes. I'll talk to them. It's a shame we can't capture the rich colours of their turbans though, isn't it?"

"Aye, indeed. And there's one other important piece of the puzzle conspicuously absent."

"Oh, really? What's that?" Patrick said, perplexed and surveying the assembly once more.

"You," Sophia smiled. "May I suggest on Lieutenant Shafto's right?"

"Bless my soul, are you sure you don't mind?" he replied.

"Of course not. If you load the negative, and content yourself with the f-stop and focus, all I need do is expose the lens. It would be my pleasure."

"My sincere thanks to Doctor Fitzgerald and Mrs Munro," said Richard Meade, addressing the guests as they exhaled with relief the moment Sophia replaced the lens cap. "You are all welcome to retire inside whenever you wish to continue enjoying the Residency's hospitality safe from the impending downpour."

"I really am most grateful for your assistance. Thank you once again," Patrick said to Sophia when he returned to her and the camera. "Will it turn out all right do you think?"

"Och, it's no bother at all, I've enjoyed working with you. And aye, I think it'll be a very fine memento of the day."

"I do hope so."

People were dispersing back to the east lawn or up onto the terrace. Major Scott strode off as vigorously as he'd arrived. Sophia made a point of catching Mrs Scott's eye before she strayed too far. "My compliments, Harriet. From the way you maintained your poise, I feel sure you must be quite practiced at sitting for photographers," Sophia flattered.

"Why thank you, my dear. Compared to the tedium of posing for one's portrait to be painted, which I've endured more times than I'd care to count, the brevity of the photograph sure is a blessing."

"I suppose it must be. Nevertheless, in my experience only a small minority are truly at ease before the camera and it is they who always make the best subjects."

"You're very kind."

"Not at all. Some people have it and some people don't. What's that phrase the French have?"

"*Je ne sais quoi?*" offered Patrick.

"Aye, that's it, *je ne sais quoi*. One of the best illustrations I've ever seen was the *amir* of Afghanistan, Sher Ali, and most of his entourage for that matter. They featured in some wonderful images taken by John Burke last year at Ambala," Sophia continued, flanking around towards what she really wanted to talk about. "Are you familiar with his work, doctor?"

"I am indeed, the man has a rare talent. And I agree with you, the camera certainly loved the amir."

"How ironic for a man such as he," commented Harriet.

Sophia let that lie. "As a matter of fact, I was only telling some friends earlier today about how I travelled through Ambala on my way to Simla in the spring," she said, lightly. "The viceroy mentioned the conference that took place there, and hence how Mr Burke came to be engaged to record the event for posterity." Sophia could see she had Harriet's full attention now. "From what Lord Mayo did his best to explain to me, it seems the dominant topic of the conference was the installation of British embassies in Afghanistan. The amir was open to the idea of them in places like *Candahar* and *Herat*, but entirely resistant to there being one in Cabool."

"Presumably for fear of being seen as a British puppet by his own people," suggested Patrick.

"Aye, the viceroy intimated as much. Amongst other things, I gather they also discussed Sher Ali's desire for British endorsement of his legitimacy as amir."

"And did I read something at the time about him wanting assistance in securing his northern borders?" asked Patrick.

"Aye, that's right," confirmed Sophia. "Interestingly, or at least I thought so, he expressed to the viceroy his view that, whilst sensible precautions should certainly be taken, Russian aggression was unlikely for some years to come. I wonder how many politicians in Westminster agree with him?"

"Not many, I'd wager," Patrick laughed.

Harriet remained silent.

"Aye, especially since his nephew and fierce opponent, Abdur Rahman, is under Russia's protection in Tashkent, and more recently – last October I think – Russia established a fortress on the Caspian coast of Turkmenistan."

"The work of that General Stoletov if I recall," said Patrick.

"Lieutenant Colonel Stoletov, in fact," piped up Harriet. "Nikolai is surprisingly timid and vacillating for a man in his position. The credit should go to his superior, Lieutenant General von Kaufmann, the governor general of *Turkestan*. Dear Konstantin – my eldest son is his namesake you know – is the real engineer of the Tsar's imperial expansion."

Harriet's admission surprised even Sophia, and neither she nor Patrick were quite sure how to respond. Harriet filled the silence for them. "I've had the good fortune to know many interesting people in my time, but I confess to never having paid much heed to political matters. Now, I must catch up with my Douglas before I lose him for a second time today, so if you'll both excuse me?"

"Of course," said Sophia. "It's been fascinating meeting you."

*   *   *

At the United Services Club on Wednesday evening, John Orr ordered a couple of drams of Jameson's and sat down in a quiet corner with Micky Lavelle.

"What was it you wanted to talk about?" asked Micky.

"Something I came across at the weekend that I'm sure you'll find of interest," John replied, pulling a copy of *Bradshaw's Illustrated Handbook to the Madras Presidency and the Central Provinces* from his breast pocket. He turned to the section about the *Kolar* district on page forty-seven and read aloud. "*Excursions to Marikuppam where gold dust is found, and the country, for 130 square miles, is said to abound with that valuable mineral.*"

CHAPTER TWENTY-ONE
40 MILES EAST OF BANGALORE, INDIA
MONDAY, 30TH JANUARY 1871

"'Tis a terrible thing, so it is," said Micky Lavelle, thinking aloud.

"What is?" wondered John Orr.

"That business with the poor Winchester girl."

"Ah, yes. Terrible. We can but hope she'll be found before any more harm befalls her."

"And that those *Lushai* tribes face a reckoning for what they've done," added Micky.

A week ago to the day, tea plantations in the *Cachar* district of Assam had been attacked and burned by a band of some sixty *Mizo* warriors from the neighbouring Lushai hills. Reports were sketchy, but already certain was that James Winchester, the manager of a British plantation at *Alexanderpur*, had been murdered and his six-year-old daughter, Mary, abducted into the jungle. A number of Indian workers had also been wounded or killed, and at least several were thought to have shared Mary's fate.

"The last I heard before we left," said John, "was that a detachment of native infantry had been sent to track them down."

"Easier said than done in that terrain, so it is."

The friends were side-by-side on the driving seat of Micky's four-wheeled trap. They'd managed to slip out of Bangalore unnoticed yesterday morning whilst most of the cantonment was occupied with Divine Service. Now they were only four or five miles from Bangarapet.

Pleasantly warm, with a soft breeze and almost no chance of rain, it was a good time of year to be travelling. As they had last night, this evening they'd stay in a dâk bungalow and keep themselves to themselves. Tomorrow they would continue onward to Marikuppam where they planned to spend a few days carrying out an initial geological survey. John's time was limited by work and family commitments, not least of which was Emily nearing term in her latest pregnancy, and Micky didn't want to be away from his children for any longer than necessary. Michael, Anne and David were at home with their devoted ayah. However, John and Micky had already agreed to return during the next cold season if this first trip proved worthwhile.

"Speaking of easier said than done, are you still confident we'll find what we're hoping to?" asked John.

"If there's gold to be found, we'll find it."

"And if there isn't after all?"

"Then we'll ship out to the Cape and join the diamond rush, so we will," Micky chuckled, flicking the reins and encouraging the two ponies to maintain their trot.

John laughed. "Perish the thought. Emily would never allow it!"

"How long will it take her to forgive you for missing tonight?" teased Micky. The famous Italian tenor, *Signor Giacinto Marras*, now in his sixtieth year, was hosting a musical *soirée* at the Public Rooms in Bangalore from nine o'clock.

"Oh, not long, but I dare say returning home with a little gold dust would hasten my redemption. Besides, she's going with Alec and Jessie Innes and will doubtless have a marvellous time without me."

The conversation meandered like the road they were following across the agrarian plain. After more than four months of siege, Parisian resolve had finally crumpled under a prolonged heavy artillery bombardment; an armistice had been negotiated and Prussian-led forces occupied the starving city at the weekend; John wasn't accustomed to being hunched forward on a sprung seat for long periods and his back was sore; the 16th Lancers' year had started with what Alec Innes said was their forty-eighth death, not counting wives and children, Private Walkley of G Troop succumbing on 10th January; it was commendable how the regiment had raised £682 last autumn for the relief of the sick and wounded on both sides of the Franco-Prussian conflict; Micky was proud of how well young Michael was doing with his schooling; Micky missed Augusta.

"Do you suppose she'd have approved of what we're doing?"

"Of course she would have," John replied without hesitation. "In all the time I had the privilege of knowing her, Augusta never failed to be the most ardent and vocal advocate for your endeavours."

"I was a lucky man, so I was."

John knew Micky well enough to be able to tell when he was flirting with melancholy. After a respectful moment of silence, he changed the subject back to their present enterprise.

"I've been giving some thought to what you were saying last night about collecting geological samples."

"Have you now?" said Micky, his mind still elsewhere.

"I appreciate you have a great deal of experience with this kind of thing, but I wondered if there'd be any benefit in having what we find evaluated by an impartial expert?"

"You have someone in mind?"

"Perhaps, yes. Doctor Alexander Hunter. He's a colleague of mine in the medical service and a man of many talents. Aside from being an excellent surgeon, he's the founder of the Madras School of Art and the Madras Photographic Society. Most importantly for our purposes, he's also a keen geologist."

"And you'd trust his discretion?" asked Micky.

"Certainly. I've no reason to believe we shouldn't."

"Grand then, grand. It'd be reassuring to have my findings verified, to be sure."

Their destination for the day was appearing ahead. Micky flicked the reins.

*   *   *

Friday tiffin at the United Services Club on 10th March played host to a double celebration. Two days earlier, Alec Innes had seen Jessie safely delivered of a girl they'd named Susan, and Emily Orr had given birth to Constance last Thursday. All four were thriving.

"It's very kind of Emily to spend so much time with Jessie at our place. Please do tell her how greatly it's appreciated," said Alec in a momentary gap between the congratulations of their friends.

"They're a support to each other, I'm sure," John replied. "Let's raise our glasses to them," he added.

"Aye, to Emily and Jessie."

"To Jessie and Emily, the stars in our firmament, without whom we'd most surely be lost. *Sláinte!*"

"*Slàinte mhath!*"

Charles and Morgan had just arrived and ordered drinks. They made straight for the doctors and expressed their happiness and relief at the good news.

"And did I hear you've just become an uncle again, Charles?" asked Alec after thanking the pair for their best wishes.

"Indeed I have, on Sunday in fact. Harriet had a daughter they've called Kate, and I'm told they're both in fine health."

"Bonnie and blithe. That's wonderful," said Alec, sincerely.

"Hear, hear," agreed John, shaking Charles by the hand.

"After the loss of Reginald last year, I must say I'm delighted providence is shining upon my sister once more."

"Reginald?" queried John.

"Her second infant. They've moved recently as well, only a hundred and fifty yards from Oxford Villas to Oxford Street in Cheltenham, no doubt to better suit the needs of a growing family."

"A toast to bright futures then," proposed Morgan, raising his brandy glass.

"And to our trio of March miracles," added John. "To Constance, Kate and Susan!"

They all joined in with that, drinks were downed, and another round was ordered from a steward. Discussion gradually turned to more mundane matters. John was looking forward to taking up his appointment as president of the Municipal Board next month. Carrin Churchward's room in The Establishment had been empty since last October and nobody was rushing to find a new occupant. He'd only stayed for six months after returning from his last absence and was now on another twelve-month furlough in Kent. The general consensus was that he'd not come back to India at all, and that was a shame. Everyone liked Carrin and he was missed. There was conjecture throughout the cantonment about how much longer the 16th Lancers would remain in Bangalore. Sooner or later the regiment would be required to exchange stations with the 18th Hussars in Secunderabad. The wise money was on sooner.

Alec was about to ask Morgan if he'd seen much of Sophia Munro lately, but Morgan was distracted by the sight of Micky Lavelle walking towards them. He was clutching a rolled-up newspaper and looked decidedly unhappy about something.

"Pardon the interruption, gentlemen," Micky began. "John, might I have a quiet word?"

"Of course. Shall we go outside?" replied the doctor, leading the way and wondering what had so perturbed his friend.

As soon as they had privacy, Micky came directly to the point. "I'm afraid you were mistaken about Doctor Hunter's discretion, so you were."

"I don't understand," replied John. "His letter of last month was even more helpful than we'd hoped. Did he not do everything he promised?"

"It was, and he did, but then he went and published the whole damned thing. See for yourself," Micky said, opening the copy of yesterday's *Madras Mail* and handing it to John.

John sighed with exasperated disappointment when he saw the already familiar words on the page. The letter described in great detail how Doctor Hunter had examined the box of chlorite samples John sent him, and how he didn't hesitate to confirm they contained both true gold and true coal, although the latter was of a poor quality. He went on to suggest a ton of extracted samples should be delivered to his School of Arts for washing. The constituent gold could then be sent to a Doctor Percy in London for further testing and valuation.

"What on earth possessed him?" John said, shaking his head. "I'm sorry, I really didn't expect Alexander would take such a step. Thank heavens I didn't tell him where the samples came from. I hope this won't cause us any difficulties?"

"Not between you and I, and you can't be blamed for another man's folly, but we'll need to be more careful from now on, so we will."

*   *   *

A mood of agitated expectation seemed to hang over the cantonment like a dark cloud all summer. It first appeared at the beginning of June when reports from the 18th Hussars in Secunderabad told of a cholera outbreak claiming thirty-five lives in only ten days. The more people speculated about how much time the 16th Lancers had left in Bangalore, and what perils might lie ahead, the more ominous the cloud grew. Everyone shared the sense that preparations needed to be made and affairs put in order.

An increasing number of officers and men were studying for both the Lower and Higher Standard Examinations in *Hindoostani*. Charles, Cornet Edward McCausland, and Private Riley were amongst them, and Captain Henry Robinson was found to have a rare aptitude for the language.

James Goldie obtained a three-month extension to the furlough that had kept him away since April. On 6th June, he and Magdalene and their three children, Mary, Ethel and Adrian, boarded a ship at Madras bound for Melbourne. They wanted Magdalene's parents to meet their grandchildren, knowing only too well they might never get another chance.

Before the month was out Richard and Eleanor Renshaw had departed on a fifteen-month furlough, and Major John Bayley was ordered to make his way to Wellington for a period of depot duty.

Henry Wilkinson was in command while Thomas White remained in England. Ever watchful over morale and discipline, Henry rostered the regiment to patrol the city's outposts. Henry wanted to keep the men busy and looking beyond their usual surroundings, but in part it was a way of making them ready for an inspection on 29th June by Frederick Haines – now Lieutenant General Sir Frederick Haines, the commander-in-chief of the Madras Army since May.

During the first half of July, John Orr found himself in the curious position of giving evidence to Captain Gompertz, the Bangalore cantonment magistrate. An enquiry was being conducted into what the press was calling a scandalous affray.

It transpired that Ensign Fred Lambert of the 21st Regiment of Foot had accepted an invitation from a Miss Van Ingen to visit her family's home, where he was promptly set upon and severely beaten by four men of the lady's acquaintance. Swearing vengeance, Lambert returned to the bungalow after dark a week later accompanied by Ensign William Frere, also of the 21st, and the burly sergeants Noakes and McInnes of the 16th Lancers. On seeing them approach, and believing them to be burglars, the father and three brothers of the lady in question rushed outside. At some point during the ensuing scuffle one of the brothers, Edwin Van Ingen, fired his fowling piece into Ensign Frere's side at close range and with another shot caught Ensign Lambert in the knee. As the nearest doctor known to be in the vicinity, John Orr was then fetched to attend the wounded officers. Frere barely survived, and Lambert was lucky to escape an amputation. In the trials that followed, Edwin Van Ingen was eventually acquitted of attempted manslaughter, and for trespassing Lambert and McInnes were let off with fines of five hundred rupees and fifty rupees respectively. No charges were brought against the other members of the Van Ingen family or Sergeant Noakes.

The gaping divide between the classes and a burgeoning preoccupation with mortality were cast in vivid relief during the third weekend of the month.

General Edward Garstin passed away in Bangalore at the age of seventy-seven and his funeral took place on the morning of Saturday, 15th July. The entire garrison turned out to pay its respects, along with much of the cantonment's civilian population.

Ahead of the gun carriage upon which the general's coffin travelled to its final resting place, the cortège was led by the band of the 16th Lancers playing Handel's *Dead March*. A pair of open landaus transported the general's family dressed in their mourning clothes. His widow, Mary, was accompanied in one by her eldest son, John, and his new wife, Isabella, as well as her eldest daughter, the widow Maria. The other Garstin siblings, Edward, Constance, and Louisa, rode in the second vehicle, and it didn't go unnoticed that Louisa was being kept company by Doctor Patrick Fitzgerald. Following behind on horseback were officers from the 16th Lancers, 23rd Brigade of the Royal Artillery, 21st Regiment of Foot, and the 27th and 39th Regiments of Native Infantry.

Agha Aly Asker, the Persian horse trader who'd once been commissioned by Sir Mark Cubbon to construct the grand Residency building, had his home and extensive stables about a mile south of the main barracks. From there it was another three quarters of a mile or so to the cemetery and for all that distance the men of the garrison were shoulder to shoulder on both sides of the road. Every minute on the minute from seven o'clock they heard a salute being fired by one of the 23rd Brigade's howitzers. It continued until the general was ceremoniously lowered into the ground.

Private Watson died the next day. A few members of his troop attended the hasty burial.

The cloud of tension finally burst on the morning of Tuesday, 26th September when a telegram from Madras confirmed what everyone had been anticipating: the 16th Lancers were ordered to proceed north to Secunderabad in November.

*　　　*　　　*

There were few better places in Bangalore to spend a Sunday morning than the *Lalbagh* Botanical Garden, at least for those for whom long-winded sermonising held no appeal. The ornamental paradise lay about two and a half miles south-west of The Establishment, not far from the eighteenth-century fort built by Hyder Ali, the garden's founder. Morgan and Charles had ridden there early on the first day of October on the pretext of needing to exercise *Lucifer* and *Woodman*, though really they just wanted to enjoy the tranquillity of its wide avenues for a while.

"Is that Sophia I see up ahead?" Charles asked.

Morgan stood up in his stirrups to get a better look. There was no mistaking the woman in the wide-brimmed hat walking alone by the lawn clock. "I believe it is," he replied, feigning indifference.

Charles wasn't fooled. "Forgive me for saying so, but it's a mystery to me why you haven't seen more of each other."

"It's not for any lack of wanting to on my part, I assure you," said Morgan.

"Or hers, I'm quite certain."

Morgan hoped his friend was right, but didn't acknowledge the comment. "It always seems to be that either I'm up to my neck in troop duties or she's busy volunteering at the hospitals."

"May I offer a suggestion?"

"If you must," Morgan smiled.

"I'll make myself scarce while you go and invite her to be your guest at my little shindig."

"That's actually a very fine idea. Are you sure you don't mind?"

"Making myself scarce? Not in the least. Don't worry your head about it. I'll go the other way and catch up with you later," said Charles, nudging *Woodman* into a trot. "Good luck," he added over his shoulder.

Bonnet macaque mothers watched from high branches and screeched warnings to their young as Morgan dismounted and led *Lucifer* in Sophia's direction. As had become their habit of late, the conversation began as if it was carrying on from where there'd left off only moments before.

"Have they given you all a definite date yet?" Sophia asked, reaching up to pat *Lucifer's* neck.

"Not yet, no, but it'll be sometime after the second week of November. Shall we go that way?" Morgan replied, gesturing towards the west gate.

"Aye," said Sophia.

They strolled in easy silence, sharing the simple unspoken pleasure of being in one another's company. Up ahead, a skulking purple heron emerged from a veil of reeds and took to flight with languid grace.

"I do love this garden," Sophia declared as they reached a towering white silk cotton tree. She sat on one of its buttress-like roots and removed her hat. "Did you know it's home to the country's largest collection of rare plants?"

"I didn't, but I'm rather fond of it too," admitted Morgan.

"And it offers artists such an extraordinary palette. I sometimes envy painters' freedom of expression. Perhaps the day will come when photographs will be just as colourful?"

"For your sake, I hope so."

Sophia just smiled at that.

Morgan changed the subject. "Have you heard about the entertainments our sergeants are planning for the end of the month?"

"No? Tell me."

"Five nights at the garrison theatre featuring the band and men of the ranks. They've already started rehearsing."

"By way of farewell performances?"

"That's their intention, yes, and they're all taking it very seriously. Now that Sergeant Noakes is out of custody, I gather he and Sergeant McDonald are even going to be swinging on a trapeze!"

"Goodness! That'll be something to see."

"If they don't break their necks it will," Morgan scoffed. "The last night will be for the benefit of the regiment's married folk, to help them pay their travelling expenses and so forth."

"Och, that's marvellous. Will you be going?"

"I expect I'll show my face once or twice..."

"But?"

"I'll be devoting most of my attention to the Masonic Ball on the 1st of November. Charles is organising it and I've promised to lend a hand."

"I thought you took a dim view of all that?"

"Oh, I do. However, in this case it'll serve well enough as the officers' party. Like you said, as a farewell. I was wondering if you'd consider joining me?"

The question sparked delight in Sophia's eyes, yet from the way her expression changed so quickly to one of despondent regret Morgan knew his hopes were about to be dashed.

"Och, I'm so sorry. I'd say yes in an instant, but I'll have left on my next photographic expedition before then. Probably on the 23rd in fact."

"Oh well, I quite understand," Morgan lied politely.

"Time never seems to work in our favour, does it?" observed Sophia, with more candour than either of them usually dared.

"It doesn't, no." Morgan used tethering *Lucifer* as cover for a thoughtful pause. "Where will you be going?"

"Way up north around Agra. Do you remember me telling you about the Archaeological Society of India?"

"Vaguely, yes, I think so."

"Well, Lord Mayo managed to resurrect it with Alexander Cunningham reinstated as its director general. Assisted by two other gentlemen, Archibald *Carlleyle* and Joseph Beglar, he's to lead a study of ancient buildings in three districts of the North West Provinces. Although I've not seen his work for myself, I'm told that besides being an archaeologist Mr Beglar is an accomplished photographer. My role will be to help Mr Carlleyle produce a photographic record of equal thoroughness and quality."

"Far exceeding equal, I imagine. That all sounds fascinating."

"Thank you."

"Presumably you'll be taking that havildar with you again?"

"Aye."

"Good, I'm glad. That sets my mind at rest a little."

"After today, I suppose it might be quite a wee while before we're able to meet again. I want you to know that I'm sad to think of it," said Sophia, her head bowed.

"Are you?"

Sophia lifted her gaze. "Aye."

"It saddens me too," professed Morgan, "but we will – meet again, I mean – I'll make sure of it."

Sophia stood up and kissed him on the cheek. It was the first time she'd ever done so. "We still have this morning. Let's walk some more," she said, taking him by the arm.

CHAPTER TWENTY-TWO
KODUR, 68 MILES NORTH OF BANGALORE, INDIA
TUESDAY, 28TH NOVEMBER 1871

Agnes Wisewould suffered under no illusions. She knew she wasn't the belle of Bangalore and would never be seen by society as anything other than lower class. These were burdens she carried with resentment, and for which the notion of them somehow serving the Almighty's great plan was a wholly inadequate explanation. Teaching at a church school and being *on the strength* of a cavalry regiment was small recompense, but at least afforded her a modicum of security.

Before this past week Agnes couldn't recall ever feeling free of the gnawing anxiety that followed her around like a malevolent pariah dog. But now, nine days into the six-week march, she was discovering a confident new sense of calm. The unlikely benefactors of her liberation were her experience with bullocks and a peculiar decision made by Major Wilkinson. The turning point had come on the second day.

The column stretched out for the best part of six miles, with twenty-one officers and four hundred and thirty-three men on horseback, a baggage train of twenty-eight elephants, forty-five camels and forty mules, as well as more than six hundred Indian syces, grass cutters and general servants. Following orders to not get in the way of them all, the eighty-nine women of the regiment set off from *Yelahanka* at three o'clock in the morning, a couple of hours before the main contingent. They were travelling in an unguarded convoy of *bandy* carriages loaded with all their worldly possessions and one hundred and thirty-four children, and made it to the campground outside a place called *Devanahalli* a little after sunrise.

Like so many other things in the army, including rations, uniforms and equipment, the cost of hiring transport was met by means of stoppages from a soldier's weekly pay. Most of the one-axled covered wagons were pulled by a single bullock and would set a family back the tidy sum of twenty-five rupees. A few were large enough to need a pair of animals and the quarter master demanded a higher price for those.

No one wondered how much eventually ended up in the hands of the Tamil men who owned and drove the bandies.

Prior to leaving Bangalore the majority of the wives had expressed horror at the thought of perching on the driver's seat and being at close quarters with a low caste, betel-spitting Indian man, whom it was natural, they demonstrated, to hold in vocal disdain. They'd sworn to each other, and to their husbands, that for the sake of dignity they would always ride in the covered part of the carriages. Agnes felt much the same as far as Indians were concerned, and like everyone else resolutely maintained her use of pejoratives rather than enquiring after her driver's name, but she had no intention of being confined or any more uncomfortable than necessary. She made a point of sitting up front, of being vaguely civil, and asserting her ability to play an active part in the driving. When the bullock needed to be led by the halter on steep or uncertain ground, Agnes took over the reins and stick. Some of the other wives began to follow her example and their squeamishness soon made way for a better view of the road.

Another of Hyder Ali's stone forts imposed itself on the centre of Devanahalli, and Tipu Sultan's birthplace was said to lie within a stone's throw of its walls. Seven miles to the north his *Nandidurg* summer retreat looked down on the wastes of the plain from the summit of a hill that resembled the shape of a sleeping bull. Save for these incidental claims to fame, Devanahalli was found to have few virtues worth extoling. However, no one had thought to provision the women with water before they left and the settlement was the only nearby source they could be sure of.

Knowing it would be mid-morning at the earliest before their tents and supplies arrived, and that grumbling about it while they waited would do nothing to improve the situation, Agnes had set about taking charge. She helped those with the most delicate constitutions to find relief in the shade of the bandies, and then recruited a small party of wives and drivers to join her on an expedition into the village. They returned safe to camp in less than an hour, only a few rupees poorer and with flasks full, sheep to slaughter and roast, and a cage of fowl for currying.

The women were outspoken in their thanks to Agnes for her guidance and initiative, but none needed to ask how she came to be so familiar with the practicalities of cross-country travel. They all knew her story, and had heard tell of countless others like it.

Agnes had never seen England, or even the ocean, but this was the third time she'd undertaken a journey between Bangalore and Secunderabad. She'd accompanied her first husband on the same march of relocation five years ago, and remembered only too well how arduous the route ahead was going to be. The handsome and ever-cheerful Private Hollier had caught her eye when the 18th Hussars arrived in Bangalore fresh from England in September of 1864. They married in the autumn the following year and reached Secunderabad on New Year's Day 1866. In spite of his energetic disposition, or perhaps because of it, Private Hollier died from a fever only a few short weeks later.

Bereft and distraught, not to mention furious with God, Agnes returned to Bangalore and her family home on St. John's Hill on the north side of town. It was there, one summer Sunday morning at St. John's Church, she began to entertain the attentions of Private Henry Wisewould of the 16th Lancers. Nearly a year to the day afterwards, on the 27th June 1867, they were married by the Reverend Gilbert Cooper in a simple service attended by a few friends, Agnes's mother, Sarah, and younger sister, Harriette. Her late father, Joseph Turner, had been a sergeant in the 15th (The King's) Hussars, and Agnes hoped her choice of a cavalry life would have made him proud.

The Wisewoulds had marked four anniversaries since then and Agnes still felt gratitude for having been saved from the prospect of a long and lonely widowhood. Henry was altogether different to Hollier. He played clarinet in the regimental band, even though his hearing was as poor as his ability to hold a drink, and was blessed with little in the way of humour, imagination, or ambition. He had a tendency to wallow in self-righteous indignation and could often be rather naïve, but Henry was a kind man, dependable and sincere to a fault, still alive, and mercifully undemanding of Agnes's matrimonial duty. So undemanding in fact that Agnes sometimes wondered if she ever stood any chance of bearing a child. The thought of pregnancy and childbirth petrified her though and she was in no rush. She was still only twenty-four after all.

Upon reaching the halt at Devanahalli, Major Wilkinson had ordered that the married men of the ranks were forbidden from sleeping in the married tents. And not just for that night, but for the whole of the rest of the march. It was a decision that baffled the officers just as much as everyone else and nobody was happy about it, except for Agnes. A handful of married NCOs paraded at the Officers' Mess tent and attempted to change the major's mind, but he couldn't be persuaded.

Ten square tents had been allocated to the families. They were separated from all the others on the left flank of the campground by a line of unhitched bandies, beneath which the drivers slept, and the herd of hobbled bullocks. In some unfortunate cases, tents were home to more than twenty people at a time even with the husbands absent. Agnes considered herself lucky to be sharing with only four other women and five children, and she slept better than she had in a long while.

Over the course of the forty-six miles from Devanahalli to Kodur, the routine and tempo of each day became more or less set and Agnes's tacit significance amongst the northbound sisterhood continued to grow. She was cherishing the companionship of the women, and the respect she was earning from them, as much as the moments of relative equality and genuine friendship they were all being gifted by the journey.

As they travelled ahead of the regiment early every morning, the wives enjoyed several hours of precious independence before the inevitable bombastic reunion with the men and beasts, and all the dust and stench and belligerence that went with it. Like a distant carnival, they'd hear the column long before they saw it. The great percussion of hooves, lyrical whinnies and trumpeting, the *tink-tink* of bridles and blades, raised voices sometimes in song, and the gurgling complaints of the camels. A somewhat quieter afternoon of leisure usually followed while the men hunted small game, before an evening spent cooking, eating, sleeping and preparing for the next departure.

Today's encampment had been established on an adequate, if unexceptional, site about a mile south of Kodur. With the intention of procuring supplies and avoiding boredom, small groups began drifting off in the direction of the village as soon as they were at liberty from their duties after breakfast. Henry suggested that he and Agnes follow suit and take his pet dog, *Nellie*, with them.

Self-sufficient and insatiably curious, *Nellie* had been trotting along beside the bandy and keeping Agnes company all the way from Bangalore. She was fiercely protective of her mistress and rarely let Agnes out of her sight. Agnes found it strange that Henry had chosen to name a mongrel bitch after one of his younger sisters, but she liked having *Nellie* around and kept such thoughts to herself.

At first sight Kodur seemed much the same as every other community they'd descended on. Thatched dwellings built of mud-bricks or stone congregated in haphazard fashion on one side of a main thoroughfare. Henry was quick to form the opinion that the residents they encountered were a surly lot and liable to chase them off at any moment. Agnes observed nothing to justify such paranoia and was relieved he had second thoughts about brandishing the bill hook concealed under his tunic. What passed for the village's bazaar was a disappointment when they found it, and had nothing left to buy worth having.

Since they were unencumbered, rather than returning to camp the same way they came, Henry decided to circle back via the north shore of the neighbouring tank. The lake was similar in size and shape to the one at Ulsoor in Bangalore, though far more pleasant in appearance with banyan trees tangled around its whole circumference. The mercury had risen notably in the past few days and the opportunity for a cooling dip was too tempting to pass up. Henry and Agnes undressed in the welcome shade of a banyan's canopy and tiptoed through leafy decay to the water's edge, still wearing their undergarments for modesty. With sharp intakes of breath and exclamations of delight, they waded in to waist depth and then submerged to their shoulders. To *Nellie* this all seemed like very strange behaviour. She feared for Agnes's safety and scampered back and forth, barking her alarm. Henry called her name, but his tone sounded more like a reprimand than reassurance and only made *Nellie* more frantic. She ran off in the direction of the village and vanished in the darkness of the trees.

It was after seven o'clock by the time Henry and Agnes trudged into camp, weary from a long walk they could have well done without. Henry put it down to them having taken an interesting detour. Agnes knew it was because he got them lost. They'd hoped *Nellie* might have found her own way back, but there was no sign of her. Henry thought the villagers had most likely tied her up. Agnes's patience had worn thin and she was glad her husband went off to snooze in a troop tent after dinner.

Henry was prodded awake about an hour later. His friend said that Major Wilkinson had sent some coolies up the road to make the next river crossing safe for the bandies, and that he and a few of the other married men were going to see what all the fuss was about. Henry agreed to join the reconnaissance. It was long after dark, but the sky was clear and the moon had only just begun to wane. They found the Indian detachment already hard at work cutting branches and binding them in tight bundles. On the near side of the *Chatravathi* River the road fell six feet at an abrupt forty-five degrees, which was far too precipitous for a bandy carriage. The bundles of branches were being stacked and pinned to lessen the declivity. The river itself was only about ten yards wide with a benign current, and never more than three feet deep, but its far bank was steep and sandy. The consensus was that the bullocks would struggle to get up it without assistance.

Wednesday's destination on the regiment's itinerary was *Palasamudram*, about seven miles away. Major Wilkinson anticipated delays at the river and sent the women off a couple of hours earlier than usual at one o'clock. He gave their husbands permission to go with them, on the strict condition they returned to their respective troops as soon as the bandies were safely across.

The Tamil squad had laboured relentlessly to complete the task in time. They were still there and the first to help when the lead bandy hesitated at the top of the bank, though they received not a word of thanks for their trouble. With a great deal of pushing and pulling and shouting, controlling the rate of descent then getting through and up the other side, all the carriages made it over without accident. Henry Wisewould wasn't so lucky. He'd gone into the river barefoot and nearly dislocated his left big toe under a rock. It swelled to twice its normal size and gave him much pain.

When Charles and Morgan came to the river some hours later they observed a corporal from Charles's troop trying to scramble up the bank. His horse, now standing motionless mid-stream, had stumbled on one of the branch bundles and unseated him into the water. Soaked to the skin, and humiliated by the jeers and laughter from the watching ranks, the corporal was looking for someone to blame. Several of the Tamil men were offering to pull him up the slope, but he pushed their hands away and struggled to the top on his own.

"Which of you lazy black bastards stacked those branches? I'll see you flogged!" he barked, taking the nearest of the labourers by the throat.

Charles dismounted and strode towards the fracas. "You there, corporal! Release that man this instant!"

Reacting to his captain's voice on instinct, the NCO complied. As he turned around, his face met the sting of a vicious backhand that sent him staggering backwards. The ranks grumbled their disapproval. Morgan had never seen Charles act with such anger and aggression before, and he jumped down from his horse to intercede before the situation escalated.

"Woe betide you or any other trooper I ever see or hear abusing these men again," Charles warned. "And lazy? Lazy be hanged! These fellows have worked all night, you damned fool! Now get back down there, retrieve your mount and get yourself across, or you'll be the one for a flogging!"

"But sir…" the scolded corporal began to protest, holding a palm to his cheek.

"On with it! And not another word," Morgan instructed. The corporal showed no contrition and muttered oaths of vengeance as he waded out to his horse.

"Jesus wept, Charles," Morgan said quietly to his friend, "a temper like that is liable to get you in trouble. I'm impressed."

By nine o'clock the regiment was installed just beyond Palasamudram, where an awkward combination of soft sand and loose rock confounded many attempts to secure tent pegs. Another large tank was only a hundred yards or so to the west, which at least made watering the horses and pack animals easier. Some of the officers spent the afternoon hunting a coalition of cheetahs and didn't see the messenger ride into camp carrying a letter from Madras for Major Henry Wilkinson.

"It's often said that a change is as good as a rest," Henry began, standing at the head of the table in the Officers' Mess tent before dinner, "and for a short while it seems I'm to have a rest from your fine company." Motioning to quell murmurs of consternation, he continued. "Earlier today I received a dispatch from General Haines with orders for me to proceed post-haste to Delhi, where I'm to participate in what's being called a Camp of Exercise taking place there from the middle of December."

Though they'd only heard vague rumours about plans for the gathering in Delhi, all the officers recognised what an exciting privilege the secondment was for Henry and greeted his news with a chorus of congratulations.

"Major John Bayley has been instructed to leave his depot duty at Wellington and rendezvous with our march at his earliest convenience. He will take over command until my return," Henry explained.

In the short time he'd been with the regiment before being sent to Wellington, John Bayley's admirable experience and steady manner had ingratiated him with his new colleagues. They'd all be glad to see him back again.

"However, since I will need to depart no later than the day after tomorrow to reach *Gooty* in time to catch a train to Bombay," said Henry, "I'm appointing Captain Whigham as your interim commanding officer. I trust you'll be happy to oblige, Robert?"

"Of course, major," Robert Whigham replied, half standing from his chair. "Thank you for the honour. I shall do my best to live up to it," he added with a respectful nod.

"I have every faith that you will," Henry reassured. "It probably won't be for more than about ten days, so just keep things rolling along and don't rush the river crossings. Monitor the situation with the helmet spikes as well, if you would. Losses are becoming far too commonplace."

Back in October the ranks had been issued with white pith helmets for the first time. Officially designated as Foreign Service Helmets, they resembled in design, if not ostentation, those that the officers had been wearing for years and could be fitted with a gilt metal spike in the Prussian style. It was becoming evident the accessories were no match for the carelessness of tired men.

"I certainly will," confirmed Robert, already thinking that simply revoking the order to ride with spikes would be the obvious solution.

"Are you able to tell us anything further about the Camp of Exercise, major?" enquired John Symes-Bullen.

The idea of conducting military manoeuvres to practice the art of war had been inspired in large part by the training methods employed by the Prussian army. Delhi would be the first time Britain had made a serious attempt at anything similar on a large scale.

"I share your curiosity, and the little I know comes from the general's letter. There are to be six weeks of exercises in all, but let me see..." said Henry, scanning the pages again for the pertinent facts. "Ah yes, he says the expectation is that more than twenty-one thousand officers and men will be involved, along with nearly six thousand horses and mules, and over fifty artillery pieces."

"That's what I call a party," quipped Morgan, raising his wine glass.

Ten days and seventy-three miles further north, the regiment made the difficult crossing of the *Penna* River at *Pamidi* where it remained for the whole weekend to rest and observe the Sabbath. Another dozen miles brought the column to Gooty on Monday, 11th December.

Tents were erected on good flat ground in the middle of a horseshoe of hills on the town's eastern boundary. It was a picturesque location for a camp, with grand views of twelfth-century fortress defences on the most prominent hill, but so sheltered that there was no respite from the oppression of stagnant heat. The closest water source was the district's only tank, an inconvenient three quarters of a mile away to the west, and it was found to be so foul with contamination that even the elephants thought twice about drinking from it.

Principal north-south and east-west routes crossed at Gooty, which had long made it important to merchants and warlords alike. Near its centre were a telegraph office and thriving bazaar, while a couple of miles to the north was the station on the Madras to Bombay railway. Major Bayley arrived there on the morning train, looking understandably haggard after some six hundred miles of locomotion, and wasted no time in relieving Robert Whigham of command.

The train also brought with it livestock and other goods going to market, and the most recent press. Copies of the *Madras Mail* were circulating around the camp by midday.

"Have you seen this contemptible bile?" Charles asked Morgan, handing him a newspaper when he returned from a saddle inspection. The *Bangalore Spectator* had syndicated a short piece, written in its typical backhanded style three weeks earlier, entitled "*Farewell To The 16th Lancers*". Morgan scanned it and read the offending section aloud.

"*...a body of men, whom it is the mistaken fashion with many to consider as of lax morals and unsteady habits...* Jesus wept! That sorry bunch of hacks have a rare nerve!"

"And no sense of irony. Such unprovoked vitriol really is outrageous though, don't you think?"

"Quite. There's nothing unsteady about our habits," Morgan said with a straight face, eliciting a raised eyebrow of disapproval from

Charles. "It'll certainly rain on the men's parade when they get a hold of it," noted Morgan more seriously.

"They already have, and they're incandescent," said Charles, pausing to light a cheroot. "With a view to shoring up dented morale," he continued, "and in part thinking about the atrocious state of the water here, I'm going to the bazaar after lunch to buy my troop a cart load of vegetables and beer. Would you care to join me?"

"That's a sterling idea," Morgan replied. "You're too good to them you know," he added with a smile.

Prolonged darkness muddled wits on the Tuesday morning until the explanation filtered through the ranks that a near total eclipse of the sun was taking place. Watching the phenomenon helped the last of the eleven miles to *Peapully* go by. The next thirty-nine through *Enugumarri*, *Dhone* and *Veldurthi* to *Chinna Tekuru* took five more days at the feet of a range of low hills on the regiment's right. Palmyras grew in abundance along the route and their sweet sap was fermented by the locals to create an intoxicating palm wine known as *toddy*. Responding to its unhelpful influence on regimental health and efficiency, Alec Innes instructed the column guard to prevent villagers selling the brew to the men. Jessie Innes was seven months pregnant and had remained behind in Bangalore at Alec's insistence. He was missing his wife and children and looked forward to being reunited with them as soon as he could take furlough.

After the customary Lord's Day of rest, a pleasant nine-mile leg in milder temperatures brought the lancers to *Kurnool* on Monday, 18th December. A slate bridge, built years previously by Agnes Wisewould's uncle, spanned an irrigation canal and beyond that the snaking *Handri* River defined the town's southern perimeter. Another bridge deposited the regiment in the urban centre, where the bastion of *Konda Reddy* Fort mocked their advance past the ruined white walls of deserted colonial bungalows and on to the banks of the *Tungabhadra*.

Major Bayley was frustrated to discover the bandies had yet to make the five-hundred-yard crossing despite a two-hour head start and the angry protestations of the women. Agnes had tried to reassure the drivers that the river was reliably shallow and sedate, but they were having none of it and refused to risk their bullocks unless more manpower was provided. The major ordered the officers and men to press on regardless, and promised the wives he'd send help. The next camp was only about half a mile north of the river, he told them.

The relative ease with which the army's horses and baggage train forded the Tungabhadra convinced the bandy drivers that it was probably safe enough, but Agnes was already taking action to force their hand. An audience of local men had gathered, all of whom made their livelihoods from the waterway, and Agnes badgered them until they agreed to take the women and children across in their coracles. The saucer-shaped craft, most between six and eight feet in diameter, were made of animal hide stretched around a bamboo lattice and proved far more stable than anyone expected.

Henry Wisewould returned a couple of hours later with the other husbands and a group of Indian servants. He found his wife standing on the north bank, with hands on hips and pride in her eyes, watching a line of bandies advance towards her. All the women cheered Agnes when the first of the bullocks lumbered onto dry land.

As the minutes passed and more bandies completed the crossing, it became obvious that the Wisewoulds' carriage had either met an obstacle mid-river or its driver had lost his bottle. It was stationary and threatening to tarnish Agnes's success. Ignoring his wife's pleas for patience, Henry blundered aboard a coracle and insisted on being conveyed to the bandy forthwith. He failed to comprehend the cause of the delay, despite the driver's best efforts to explain, and issued stern threats of violence ameliorated by promises of coin until the wagon somehow got moving again.

The encampment near Kurnool was home for two days, this time not for God's pleasure but for Major Bayley's. He ordered the troop captains to make a full inspection of horses and saddles, and sought the quarter master's assessment of the state of the baggage train.

One trooper, a member of the band called Marsh, had been thrown from his mount during the crossing of the Tungabhadra, though neither he nor the horse came to any harm and no equipment was lost. Other than some general wear and tear of the kind that had to be expected on a long march, overall the regiment was reported to be in a good state of affairs.

It was reassuring news for John Bayley. He was mindful of the fact that the Chatravathi, Penna and Tungabhadra had been but dress rehearsals for the two-mile wide *Krishna* River, which lay beyond the next halt at *Kyatur*.

When the head of the column caught up with the bandy convoy there just after eight o'clock on the Wednesday morning, Major Bayley issued an order that broke with convention and caused quite a stir. The family tents were not to be erected. Instead, all the married men were to accompany the bandies over the river immediately after breakfast, establish camp near *Bekkum*, and remain there until the regiment joined them on Thursday. An allowance of servants and the camels carrying the tents would have to go too.

Bayley's primary motive was clear enough. While the river would present little challenge to the horses, mules or camels, and none whatsoever to the elephants, the bullock teams hauling the baggage wagons were bound to have difficulty. To avoid the possibility of a manageable drama turning into chaotic farce, it was more important than ever that the women weren't in the way. By implication, the married couples would have a whole day and night together for the first time since Yelahanka a month ago. Whether or not that had factored in the major's decision-making was anyone's guess, but the married men were grateful either way.

Although the banks of the Krishna were steep on both sides, the flow of India's third-longest river was lethargic this far along its course and generally only three or four feet deep. Occasionally a bandy driver would earn a torrent of abuse from his mistress by straying into deeper water and causing baskets of wood, vegetables, and chattels to float off downstream, but for the most part the crossing was easier than anyone predicted.

By four o'clock the families' camp was settled on exemplary ground outside the village of Bekkum, surrounded by palmyras and date palms, well supplied with toddy, and out of sight and earshot of the officers.

It took all of the next day to get the baggage train across the river. For much of it, husbands and wives watched from the north shore where they strolled barefoot through the shallows, hand-in-hand, searching the sand in vain for precious stones. Sergeant Harvey reported that all was well amongst the married tents. All that is except for Sergeant Kent's young son, who'd been kicked in the head by his father's horse and was now in the gentle care of Surgeon Innes.

A Sunday and three marches north-west via *Venkatapuram* and *Thomalapalle* brought the regiment to *Kothakota* on Christmas Day, where celebrations were made with roast fowl and plum pudding washed down with gifts of beer.

On Tuesday, 26th December, at *Addakal*, it was ordered that the married tents should be pitched in the village's burial ground. Guy ropes were tied around headstones, children played amongst the graves, and no one lost any sleep about it.

The route then returned to a north-north-east heading, taking the column through *Janampeta*, *Bhuthpur*, *Jadcherla* and *Balanagar*. The road was better than it had been since the Krishna, as was the temperature, but game was scanty and supplies hard to find.

The curtain fell on the year 1871 at *Shadnagar*. Camp was established the customary distance from the village, with the married tents nearest the road in the shade of a grove of trees. A derelict timber shed stood adjacent, and inside it was found a decorated wagon bearing a curious wooden statue with huge painted eyes.

"Tell me, am I correct in thinking this is Juggernaut?" Charles asked one of the more senior syces when he went to see it for himself.

"*Jagannath*, sahib," the man replied. "The all-seeing Lord of the Universe, sahib."

CHAPTER TWENTY-THREE
SHAMSHABAD, 16 MILES FROM SECUNDERABAD, INDIA
TUESDAY, 2ND JANUARY 1872

Agnes and Henry Wisewould went into town seeking a Partridge, but returned with a Fox.

Charlie Partridge was Agnes's favourite cousin on her mother's side of the family. He had a bungalow in Shamshabad and Agnes was excited to see him and his wife again after so long. She would tell them all about the trials of the journey, introduce Henry, and gorge herself on all their news. She was particularly eager to hear about her beloved Uncle James, Charlie's father, who lived in Secunderabad and was a civil engineer of some repute.

Before they'd even had a chance to knock on Charlie's door, a jovial man with a thick Scouse accent and an overly familiar manner was calling to them from the neighbouring property. He looked to be in his late middle age, though dressed in the style of someone much younger, and said his name was Seymour Fox. Charlie had gone to Secunderabad for a few days, he explained, and wasn't expected home until tomorrow morning at the earliest. Agnes was all for simply thanking the man and returning another time, but Henry was reeled in by Fox's fraternal charm and had accepted the offer of some toddy before Agnes could do anything to stop him. One glass soon became three, and then Henry was inviting Seymour back to the tents to meet his chums.

That evening after dinner, Major Bayley let it be known he wanted the band to give an entertainment in the middle of the site such that all the officers and men might enjoy. He was mindful of the need for practice before their next public duty.

"Only another couple of marches to go," Morgan thought aloud as the strings drew out the opening bars of a familiar polka.

"And I for one am very glad of it," commented William Barker, the hard-working adjutant, emerging from the Officers' Mess tent to flop into a camp chair and join the audience.

"Same here," agreed Charles, "I'm sure we all are. Have you been keeping count, John?"

"Including this morning, there have been thirty-seven stages so far," John Bullen-Symes confirmed. "By the day after tomorrow I believe we'll have travelled a touch over three hundred and sixty miles."

"And we haven't lost anyone," said Alec Innes, filling his pipe. "Though I dare say there's still time," he added with playful eyes.

Morgan was about to comment on the clarinets sounding even worse than usual, but the group's attention became distracted by a raucous commotion in the Sergeants' Mess tent. Charles asked Francis Drummond to find out what was going on.

Like William Barker and the five others who also became lieutenants during 1871, Francis had been one of the last ever officers able to invest in the purchase of a promotion. It was all thanks to the Secretary of State for War, Edward Cardwell, and the reforms he'd succeeded in pressing through government. Amongst other modernisations inspired by lessons from the Crimean and Franco-Prussian wars, the purchase system had been abolished. Since 1st November, advancement now had to be earned rather than paid for. Exchanges between regiments were still permissible, and the value of an existing commission would be reimbursed to an officer upon his retirement from service, but Cardwell's interference remained a sore subject, and a divisive one, in the Officers' Mess.

"It appears some fellow from the town has had one too many pegs of brandy at the sergeants' expense," Francis reported back.

"The rummy cove! He must be either damned foolish or uncommonly brave!" Charles laughed. "Do we know who this fellow is and how he came to be here?"

"An old soldier by the name of Fox, as I understand it. Beyond that, none of the men seem to have a clue who he is or why he's here."

"Or none they care to admit," suggested John.

"Thank you, Francis. Ask Sergeant Noakes to arrange for this Mr Fox to be sent quietly on his way before any injury is visited upon him," Charles instructed.

The final camp was established ten miles along the road to the south-west of *Hyderabad* on Wednesday morning. All the tents were up by eight o'clock, the horses were watered and groomed by ten, and by noon spikes had been refitted to helmets and every uniform and saddle was as clean as it was going to get.

The general surgeon of Secunderabad made a brief inspection visit as a precaution against an epidemic of disease being brought into the cantonment. He found the regiment to be in remarkably good health, all things considered, and praised Major Bayley and Surgeon Innes for their achievement in having only five men on the sick list after such a long journey.

When Henry Wisewould completed his duties and wandered over to the families' area to see about some lunch, he was more than a little surprised to find an elephant and her patient Hyderabadi *mahout* standing outside Agnes's tent. Charlie Partridge and his wife and brother-in-law had come into camp on the animal, and were inviting Agnes to join them for an afternoon ride. Agnes introduced her husband to her cousin, and told Henry they intended to be back in camp by late afternoon. Charlie apologised for there not being enough room on the elephant for a fifth person, though he was sure Henry would understand.

"Dear Agnes tells me you encountered Seymour Fox yesterday and that he was the cause of some trouble. I'm most terribly sorry about that too," said Charlie. "The man's a notorious blackguard and a drunk, and I curse the day he came to live next door."

Henry offered polite sympathy and dismissed the suggestion of trouble with a white lie about no harm having been done. He confessed to being intrigued about Fox's notoriety.

"His story is quite well known around here," Charlie explained. "You see, back in '50 when he was a young infantry private, he set fire to the barracks in Bombay, would you believe! A court martial gave him ten years' transportation to Van Diemen's Land, and he's never forgiven Her Majesty for it. I do hope you've all checked your pockets."

Hyderabad was the capital of the largest princely state in India and had a predominantly Mahommedan population. It straddled the banks of the *Musi* River and was separated from Secunderabad, its much smaller sibling to the north, by a great lake named after a Sufi saint.

The first few miles of the final march on Thursday, 4th January 1872, offered tantalising glimpses of sophisticated Islamic architecture that made colonial Bangalore seem primitive by comparison. After crossing the *Afzal Gunj* Bridge from Hyderabad's ancient walled city into *Chaderghat*, the troops dismounted in the grounds of the British Residency.

"The Lord returned from the wilderness after forty days," mused John Symes-Bullen, "but it's taken us forty-four."

"He didn't have the bullocks though, did he," Morgan was quick to point out.

"And men can't live on toddy alone," said Alec Innes under his breath. Only Charles heard that, and it made him chuckle.

"It all looks very fine here, don't you think?" Francis Drummond observed.

"The Residency? Yes, indeed. Classically grand," said John. The home of the British administrator was a Palladian mansion with an imperious chiming clock, and no end of lamps to illuminate its neat lawns and winding pathways. The most striking feature of the building was the Corinthian colonnade of its two-storey portico.

"That too, of course, but I was referring to the place in general. If Secunderabad is only half as refined, we'll be in for a more comfortable time than we've been expecting."

The bands of 24th and 76th Regiments of Foot and the 5th Madras Native Infantry had been mustered to lead the cavalry the remaining distance to their new home. Everyone climbed back into their saddles as the drums began to roll, and Major Bayley gave the order, "Threes right," to initiate a right wheel out to the road in a column three abreast.

The main road forded a tributary of the Musi and brought the regiment to the eastern outskirts of Secunderabad, where scores of local people and members of the gentry were lining the last part of the route.

"Do you feel like some strange curio in a shop window, or is it just me?" Morgan asked Charles, who was riding beside him. They were crossing what appeared to be a parade ground and could see the curtain wall of their destination a couple of hundred yards away to their left.

"No, it's not just you. I can't tell if they're smiling at us in welcome or pity," replied Charles.

"As if they know something we don't," Morgan theorised.

"What do you think now?" Charles asked Francis, cocking his thumb towards the heart of the cantonment behind them. There was nothing refined to be seen, at least not from this far away.

"I think I may have been unduly optimistic," Francis replied with stoic resignation.

The bands played the regiment all the way to the horse lines outside the south end of the wall, before receiving Major Bayley's thanks and dispersing. Although there were no actual stables, simply a large paddock with hitching posts, stable duty was an immutable and well-practiced necessity. The NCOs kept the men at it for an hour in the mid-morning sun before Trumpeter William Dolan had the honour of sounding *Dismiss*, just as he'd done on board the *Golden Fleece*.

The wives arrived hours earlier to claim their allocated married quarters in the *parcherry*, the little village of cottages to the west of the parade ground. Henry Wisewould hadn't counted on it being quite so far from the horse lines, more than half a mile he guessed, and quite tired himself out carrying his saddle all the way there. He was pleased to find the bandy already unpacked and Agnes inside their humble two-room dwelling with the floor swept and breakfast ready.

The officers, meanwhile, had been welcomed by mounted staff from brigade headquarters and were getting acquainted with the new surroundings with help from the adjutant of the 4th Madras Native Cavalry, Lieutenant Warner.

The mud wall enclosed a rectangular compound, about three hundred yards long by two hundred wide, built on a north-west to south-east alignment that followed the lie of the land. It was sandwiched between two cemeteries, one a hundred yards to the north and the other immediately south of the horse lines. The main *picquet* gate was in the south wall and smaller gates punctuated the west and north walls. The western gate led to one of only two wells, and the regimental hospital three hundred yards away. Alec Innes and his medical colleagues went to inspect it. Over the eastern wall Riding Master Thomas Brown found an area of mostly flat ground adequate for his Riding School.

The six buildings of the old infantry barracks were arranged in the form of a square at the centre of the compound. Double verandahs faced out from the square, away from the stench of the urinals in the middle, and towards the variety of low buildings that clung to the perimeter. There were wash houses and latrines, stores and cook houses, the orderly room, sergeants' quarters, library, and a racquet court next to the canteen. The barrack rooms themselves were long and narrow, well ventilated, and large enough to avoid overcrowding, but it was woefully obvious why the filthy, decrepit buildings had been condemned for years.

Secunderabad was a cantonment of two halves, Lieutenant Warner explained, and the dividing line between them was the High Road that ran straight as a lance for two miles from east to west.

On the south side was a row of brigade offices, guard rooms, arsenals and commissariat stores. To their rear was the officers' district, a four-hundred-yard strip as long as the High Road of nothing but bungalows set in spacious gardens. As had been the case in Bangalore, some were subaltern chummeries, some housed individual officers and their families, whilst others were repurposed as messes or used by civil administrators. Further south still were the crowded streets and bazaars of the indigenous population.

North of the High Road lay the general parade ground and past that, amidst forest groves and criss-crossing roads and streams, were tanks, cemeteries and barracks spread over an area of around six square miles.

"With regard to the European regiments stationed here," said Lieutenant Warner, "including your good selves, there are more than twenty-five hundred officers and men altogether."

"In the order of fifty per cent more than Bangalore," calculated John Symes-Bullen.

"If you say so, John," Morgan teased.

"And what's the composition?" asked Major Bayley.

"Well, sir, there's the 24th and 76th infantry, the bands from which you've already had the pleasure of hearing, a heavy artillery battery, one battery of horse artillery and two of field artillery. The heavy battery is half a mile from the general parade ground. All the rest are three miles to the north in the cantonment at *Tirumalagiri*."

"I don't believe we knew about another cantonment," admitted Charles. "Is it similar to where we are?"

"Not really, no," evaded the lieutenant. "It's on higher ground and all quite new. Replacement cavalry barracks are being constructed up there as well, so with any luck you won't have to be in this old place for too long."

"And what about your lot and the 5th Native Infantry?" wondered Morgan.

"The 5th are your most immediate neighbours over there on the south side of your parade ground," replied Warner, pointing. "The 4th Native Cavalry, with whom I'm proud to serve, are a couple of miles to the north-west. And then we also have three companies of the Madras Sappers and Miners, and three more Native Infantry regiments: the 3rd, 24th and 29th."

"Therefore, a total force of some five thousand or so?" queried John.

"Yes, something like that."

"We appreciate your patience in giving us our bearings, lieutenant, thank you," said the major.

"My pleasure, sir. Now I'm sure you must all be keen as mustard to find bungalows and get settled in, so allow me to show you the way."

As the regiment strived to establish its presence in the cantonment during January, the familiarity of old routines provided reassuring certainty to officers and men alike while much else was in flux.

Dysentery exploded through the ranks even before the baggage train had been fully unpacked. "Be thankful for small mercies, laddie," Alec Innes would say to doubled-up troopers losing control of their bowels, "at least it's not the grim business of Corporal Forbes." The 18th Hussars had been decimated by cholera during their time in the same barracks and Alec feared its return. He tested water from the nearby wells and was dismayed to find they were both significantly more tainted than Bangalore's worst.

"You gentlemen have all heard me repeat this often enough in the past," he said, addressing the officers in their new Mess bungalow, "but the importance of proper filtering and boiling of the water cannot be overstated. The wells outside the barracks are bad in the extreme."

Major Bayley instructed the troop captains to be vigilant and ensure their men understood. Alec was grateful, though he knew it was going to be a losing battle. People would forget, especially when intoxicated or in a hurry, and were never likely to go to much trouble over water used for washing, cooking, or the horses. Other wells served the bungalow district, which in theory meant officers stood a better chance of avoiding sickness. In practice, officers relied on *bhistis* to fetch and carry water just as much as the ranks did, and Alec had little faith in the Indian servants' appreciation of contamination risks.

"I find it hard to imagine that the rations at our disposal are doing much to aid the men's health either," said John Symes-Bullen. "Or ours for that matter. The lean goat and stringy buffalo served here in the Mess is hardly any better than what I hear they're getting in the barracks' canteen."

"I suspect it's exactly the same, but with a better class of vegetable," said Morgan. "Isn't that right, George?" he added, directing his question to Quarter Master Graham.

"More or less, I'm afraid," George replied. "As you know, the main difficulty regarding supply is the nearest railway station being some ten days away. Rest assured though, I'm doing all in my power to procure sufficient victuals for our needs and I'm hopeful the situation will improve."

"We have no doubt of it, George, and I'm sure we all share your hope," defused Charles.

"Quite so, quite so," said Major Bayley. "In the meantime, some of us can look forward to lavish feasting at the prime minister's expense."

"The prime minister?" queried Francis.

"Sir Salar Jung, prime minister of Hyderabad State, no less. He's summoned us to a *soirée* at the Nizam's palace the day after tomorrow."

John Bayley's chosen party rode towards Hyderabad during the late afternoon in the company of Lieutenant Warner, his commandant, Colonel Buchanan, and more than a dozen officers from other Secunderabad regiments, most of whom had been to the palace before and now viewed such engagements with apathy. Outside the British Residency they exchanged saddles for *howdahs* and continued on elephants guarded by a force of the Nizam's infantry.

"Have you heard from Sophia lately?" Charles asked Morgan as their animal's silent gait rocked them from side to side.

"I'm not expecting to whilst she's busy with the archaeologists. If I had any idea where a letter might find her I'd write one, but I don't so I haven't. What about you? Have you told Harriet about our new abode?"

"Not yet, no," replied Charles. "I confess I'm at something of a loss about what to say. Did I tell you she's moved again?"

"Not that I recall. Still in Cheltenham?"

"Yes, to Clarence Square on the prestigious Pittville estate this time. It's a popular area for ex-India men, so I expect George is amongst friends there."

The procession was following the main road south into the old city from the Afzal Gunj Bridge. It threaded two glorious archways to pass the *Laad* Bazaar, the towering minarets of the *Charminar* and an enormous seventeenth-century mosque, before turning right and entering the grounds of the *Chowmahalla*.

Climbing down from their rides and leaving the escort of soldiers behind, the group was greeted by a member of the prime minister's staff who led them into the southern courtyard. It was a magnificent space, about a hundred yards wide by a hundred and twenty long, half of which was taken up by a rectangular pond ornamented with nine fountains and surrounded by palm-lined gardens. A neoclassical palace stood on each side of the courtyard. Designed with Corinthian columns to the north and south, and Ionic columns to the east and west, their symmetry was connected by Doric colonnaded arcades.

The officers were shown to the south-west arcade, cast in reviving shade by the setting sun, and prompted to sit on cushions arranged beside low tables on the rug-covered stone. Tea was poured while passing introductions were made to the *nawabs*, ministers and leading merchants already in attendance. Once such formalities had been observed, servants arrayed the tables with a rainbow of aromatic Hyderabadi dishes and courteous imitations of bland British fare. In the courtyard, tulwar-wielding male dancers circled to the relentless driving rhythms of *Marfa* drums.

"The Marfa began with cavalry in the Nizam's army during the last century, so it may hold some appeal for you gentlemen," suggested a slim man in early middle age who'd strolled across to the gathering from the *Afzal Mahal*, the palace at the south end of the courtyard. Dressed in the unpretentious style of a Mahommedan statesman, a dark grey *shalwar kameez* and white *topi* cap, he was of no more than average height, with a small chin and a smile as generous as his moustache. "*Aadab*. I offer my respects to you," he said, cupping his right hand to his forehead as he bowed. "My name is Mir Turab Ali Khan, though you may know me as Salar Jung. It is my honour to make the acquaintance of officers from Her Majesty's 16ᵗʰ Lancers. I am most grateful to you all for accepting my invitation."

Major Bayley stood and thanked the prime minister, expressing polite interest in the origins of the music before introducing his officers one by one.

"Please forgive His Royal Highness, the Nizam, for not being here in person to receive you," Salar Jung requested. "The hour is late for a child of only five years, as I'm sure you will understand." With that he bade all the British guests a very good evening and transferred his attention to the panjandrums further down the arcade.

"He seems a pleasant fellow," Francis commented to Lieutenant Warner. "The product of an English education?"

"I don't believe so, no, but an eminently capable man with a fine intellect nevertheless."

"Prime minister for nearly twenty years," interjected Colonel Buchanan, "and co-regent until the Nizam comes of age. He's dragged Hyderabad State into the nineteenth century with all manner of admirable reforms, and to his enduring credit he kept the city's sepoys loyal during the rebellion in '57."

"Hence the knighthood a couple of years ago and the favourable treatment he tends to receive from the press," said Warner.

In keeping with the cultural diversity and religious tolerance for which Hyderabad was famed, there was a brief interlude in the entertainment while Hindoo musicians replaced the drummers and dancers.

Supported by the harmonic drone of a *tambura*, the lyrical melodies being plucked on a fretted *veena* were accompanied by percussion from a *ghatam* and a *mridangam* double-sided drum. The Carnatic repertoire was more familiar to all the officers recently arrived from Bangalore, and more conducive to relaxed conversation.

"Getting used to all this palatial luxury would be no hardship," Morgan contemplated out loud as he eyed another helping of a flavourful rice and mutton dish.

"I've always thought you have a princely demeanor. I'm sure you'd make a fizzing nawab," jested Charles.

"There's all that praying though, isn't there."

"And the abstinence from alcohol."

"Ah, yes, and that. Perhaps I'll sacrifice my high standards and stay in Secunderabad after all."

"How are you chaps finding the place?" asked Colonel Buchanan, overhearing the name of their station. "Rather different to what you've been accustomed to, eh?"

"But we've appreciated the warm welcome from your regiment, colonel, and indeed from the others," Charles replied diplomatically, with a nod of thanks to Lieutenant Warner.

"Our pleasure," said the adjutant.

"I gather the 18th Hussars left you a poor inheritance, though of course they'd been having a rough time of it," the colonel ploughed on.

"I don't think I'd be speaking out of turn if I said the barracks leave a great deal to be desired," Charles replied. "We understand they've even been declared unfit for use?"

"Oh yes, many times," confirmed Buchanan.

"Is where you're located more favourable?" asked Morgan.

"Saints preserve us from this damned weird music!" blurted out one of the artillery officers at the obnoxious volume of someone unaware of their own hearing loss. "Don't you chaps find it intolerable?"

"I can only speak for myself, but I've developed quite a fondness for it," reproached Charles in an even tone. "And it must be said these musicians are particularly accomplished in their art."

The officer scoffed and Colonel Buchanan returned to Morgan's question. "More favourable, lieutenant? I should say so! The buildings are past their prime, but we're quite fortunate on the whole. Conditions everywhere north of the High Road tend to be better, particularly up at the new entrenchment at Tirumalagiri."

"We're already looking forward to moving in that direction," Morgan admitted.

"And sooner rather than later," Francis added.

Charles nodded his agreement. "We've been in a similar situation before though in Bangalore when we had to wait for the Agram barracks to be completed. Our patience was rewarded in the end and I'm sure it will be again."

"That's the spirit, Mr Agnew," commended Lieutenant Warner.

Captain Whigham was one of those nominated to stay behind in Secunderabad. He'd not been best pleased about it, but when the

Hyderabad party returned in the morning they found him in an uncommonly good mood.

"The adjutant received a telegram from Madras earlier," Robert explained, "with orders for me to proceed to Wellington's convalescent depot by the 17th and relieve a Captain Stevenson of the 21st Regiment of Foot."

Major John Bayley offered his sincere congratulations, recognising the secondment was an inadvertent reward for Robert's leadership during the march from Bangalore. "As I can testify after my own recent experience of duty in Wellington, the climate, water and society there will all be a tonic for you."

"Lucky beggar," Morgan whispered, double-taking at Charles when he received no response. There was a look in his friend's eyes he'd seen before. "Have you just turned a corner with something?"

"Perhaps," said Charles, surfacing from a distracting flow of rushing thoughts. "I'm going to have a word with John."

Morgan rode back to their bungalow in the afternoon to find Charles already there and engrossed at his desk. "Did you get what you wanted from your conversation with the major?"

"I did, yes," Charles replied, his Perry nib hovering mid-sentence. "He's agreed to give me temporary command of Robert's troop."

"In addition to your own?"

"Of course."

"Then you're going to be busy for a while!"

"That's precisely my intention," said Charles with a contented smile. "You remember me saying yesterday about not knowing what to write to Harriet?" he added. "Well, I do now."

Charles didn't like Secunderabad any more than anyone else, and wasn't relishing the prospect of years in its dust-blown feculence, but he'd reached a consciously constructive decision. In the letter he was composing to his sister, he said there was no point being maudlin about circumstances beyond his control and that he intended to immerse himself in making the best of things instead. Deputising for Robert Whigham and doing all he could to maintain the welfare of the men was part of that. There was the Secunderabad Lodge, overlooking a tank not far from the east end of the general parade ground, and continuing his Masonic progression. He'd resume his Hindoostani studies with conviction, and after the palace excursion he was hopeful that Hyderabad would be a haven of culture and entertainment.

On Thursday, 25th January, the telegraph brought word of Mary Winchester's rescue. Four days previously the right wing of the Lushai Expedition, under General Brownlow, had besieged the village of *Sailàm* where the girl was being held captive. A brief artillery bombardment forced the Mizo population to capitulate and negotiate peace terms. The campaign's civil officer, Police Superintendent Captain Thomas Lewin, reported that young Mary was found unharmed, smoking a pipe in the village chief's hut, but no longer speaking English.

Major Henry Wilkinson rode into the barracks a fortnight later, immediately resuming command and praising John Bayley for the fine job he'd been doing. A celebratory dinner was hastily arranged in Henry's honour.

"It is my profound pleasure to be back with the regiment once again. Thank you all for your kind words of welcome and your curiosity about Delhi," Henry began, speaking to his fellow officers in the Mess while they waited for the first course to be served. "There'll be time enough this evening to answer all your questions about that, but first I'd like to get something else less savoury out of the way."

He was referring to another syndicated newspaper article that had outraged the barracks the day before. Originally published by the *Bangalore Herald* at the end of January, it read:

> *"We are sorry to hear from Secunderabad that the 16th Lancers do not much appreciate the change of stations. Surely this gallant regiment could not have expected to pass the whole of their Indian career at such a delightful station as Bangalore, or have forgotten that in the natural course of events they must undergo the same vicissitudes of an Indian career as others who have not had the good fortune to spend their first six years here."*

"We needn't dwell on how, or from whom, the *Herald* came by their information," Henry continued, "but it goes without saying that I never wish to see such derogatory hearsay in print again. For the sake of our good name, let us all redouble our efforts to be the watchdogs of regimental discretion."

Agreement rumbled around the room. Sensing the need to prompt a change of subject, the adjutant raised his brandy glass and proposed a customary toast. "Gentlemen! To the 16th!"

"The 16th!" everyone replied in unison, rapping their knuckles on the table.

"Now don't maintain the suspense any longer," dared Morgan. "Regale us with what happened at the Camp of Exercise."

"Very well, Mr Farrell," Henry surrendered. He outlined the scale and complexity of the organisation involved and how, just as in the bloody campaigns he'd experienced first-hand in the past, even the best plans never survive long on the field of battle. "Rather inevitably some of the mock engagements closely resembled actions of 1857, most notably the capture of the ridge covering Delhi. But aside from tactics of attack and defence, valuable lessons were learned about supply and discipline, signalling, reconnaissance and surveying. In the fullness of time there's much I intend to apply to training here."

"Training of the ranks, sir?" queried William Barker.

"The ranks, yes. And all officers too," replied Henry.

John Orr telegraphed Alec Innes on Valentine's Day. Jessie had given birth to a healthy son that morning, he said, and she was recovering well in Emily's care.

"Have you decided what you'll call the boy?" wondered Henry Wilkinson as he shook Alec's hand in the adjutant's office.

"Aye, Hector, after my brother."

"A fine, steadfast name. Please do give your wife my best wishes when you see her."

"Thank you, sir, I will."

Henry handed Alec the furlough authorisation he'd just signed. It gave the doctor leave to return to Bangalore on private affairs for a period of four months. "We'll see you in June," he said.

A full complement of medical staff was re-established two days after Alec's departure when Assistant Surgeon Kemp transferred from the Royal Artillery's 9th Brigade. G Battery had been stationed at Tirumalagiri for some time, so he didn't have far to come to the comparative squalour of the old cantonment. Accustomed as Kemp was to the Secunderabad climate, even he was troubled by the early arrival of the hot season. It was almost as if it stalked him down the hill to be the spectre at the cavalry's feast.

With the sweltering heat came the flies. Men in haste quenched raging thirsts with untreated water, dysentery cases multiplied, and the inescapable swarm revelled in an orgy of feeding and reproduction. By the second week of March they'd become an angry black infestation and the *chowrie* sellers in the bazaar were running out of horsehair. Trumpeters Dolan, Flaggen and Sewell were promoted to lance-corporals, and Baker, Reynard, Robinson and Warr to lance-sergeants. All of them swatted and cursed in irritation as they sewed new stripes on to the right arm of their tunics.

It was too blasted hot for anyone to be bothered with pranks during the first morning of April, least of all Agnes Wisewould who was beginning gainful employment again. She spent a couple of hours first thing tutoring Mrs Johnson's children, for which she was to receive fifteen rupees a month, and then sweated two and a half miles north to *Bowenpally* to do the same for the children of Lieutenant Colonel *Hight* of the 29th Madras Native Infantry. The long walk there and back increased her monthly fee to twenty rupees, although the supplement hardly compensated for the torrid exertion.

"I gather you're no fool after all and went and passed the lower standard Hindoostani exam," Morgan said to Charles when their paths crossed outside the orderly room a little after midday. "My heartiest *mubarak!*"

Charles smiled. "*Shukriya.* It was quite straightforward really. I'll take the higher standard as well before long."

They talked for a while about mundane troop matters, the infernal temperature and flies, and how they might spend the afternoon, but Charles seemed preoccupied and agitated. Morgan hadn't failed to notice how tense and out of sorts his friend had become in recent days.

"Have you been burning the candle at both ends more often than is good for you?" Morgan asked with gentle directness.

"No, I don't believe I have. Why?"

"It's just you haven't been your usual spirited self of late. I've been wondering if you're quite all right?"

"Oh, I see," replied Charles, surprised by how much Morgan's observation caught him off guard. "Possibly a touch under the weather. Lots on my plate of course, but I'm fine, really."

Charles wasn't fine, and after another fortnight he couldn't hide it or pretend otherwise any longer. His self-imposed workload, the torment of the heat, and the misery of recurring episodes of fever had worn him down and left him wretched and fatigued. Assistant Surgeon Kemp diagnosed the mild symptoms of malaria with a promise they'd get worse before they got better. Charles felt like he was letting the regiment down, but didn't argue with the recommendation that he take some furlough on medical grounds.

"I'd go to *Matheran* hill station near Bombay if I were you, Mr Agnew, sir," suggested Kemp. "It's smaller than the likes of Ooty or Simla, though not so far away, and as a summer retreat just as tranquil and fortifying. There's an excellent sanitorium and several good hotels. Go for a couple of months. Actually no, on second thoughts, go for four."

Henry Wilkinson was quietly understanding and reassured Charles that both his troop and Robert Whigham's would be in safe hands while he convalesced. The major signed off the furlough to begin on 23rd April and Charles returned to the bungalow to give Morgan the news.

Exhausted by the journey to get there, Charles arrived in Matheran on Wednesday, 8th May. He received a telegram from Morgan that evening. The temperature had soared to between 103 and 107 degrees in the shade during recent days, his message said, and this afternoon Private Hardy Johnson died suddenly of sunstroke. Charles knew Johnson well. He was a quiet, methodical old soldier, liked by all, and now the regiment's first loss in Secunderabad. There were more dangerous things than dysentery and malaria, everyone knew that, but even Charles hadn't reckoned on the sun being one of them.

More telegrams came from Morgan throughout May. The most shocking, on the 20th, reported that at eight o'clock the previous evening Assistant Surgeon Kemp had also succumbed to the effects of sunstroke. If even experienced medical staff could be cut down in their prime, Charles pondered, what chance did the common soldier have?

Corporal Chapman, the band's bombardon player, went the same way as Johnson and Kemp on the 23rd and Private Jennings the day after that. Mrs Sullivan, taken by consumption, and five children were buried before the month was out.

CHAPTER TWENTY-FOUR
THE LAVELLE RESIDENCE, BANGALORE, INDIA
FRIDAY, 7th JUNE 1872

"It's the thunder that frights, but the lightning that smites," recited John Orr, craning heavenward and marvelling at the celestial extravaganza.

"My father used to say that too, so he did," Micky recalled with fondness.

"Perhaps God is upset about something?" contemplated Emily.

"But which one my love? Jehovah, Zeus, Indra? There are so many to choose from after all," goaded John in affectionate jest.

"Stop it you naughty man!" Emily laughed, squeezing her husband's hand.

"In New Zealand the Māori call their thunder god *Tāwhirimātea*. Ah, but what's the difference? Gods are spiteful and capricious and all as bad as each other," scorned Micky with an expression as dark as the moonless sky.

The three of them had come out to the verandah to be entertained by nature's great spectacle. They watched the flashes and forks, the pregnant clouds glow silver and fade, and felt the rumbling salvos echo in their bones. It was near and far in every direction all at once, the air thick with the sweet tang of ozone. There was no rain, not yet, but the storm had been incessant for three days and nights in a row and heralded the imminent arrival of the south-west monsoon.

Tearing themselves away from the drama and turning to go back inside, they caught Micky's three youngest children at their bedroom window, eyes transfixed and mouths gaping. Realising they'd been spotted, the siblings ducked out of sight and scampered to their beds to pretend to be asleep.

Emily laughed. "Bless their souls. One can't blame them for wanting to watch such a mesmerising show."

"There's no harm in it, sure enough. I'll leave them to their mischief tonight," said Micky. "I expect Michael's watching out the back there as well. He'll be turning fifteen this month, you know. A man already."

"And a credit to you and his mother," said John.

"Thank you. Augusta would be *quare* proud of them all, so she would," Micky replied. "But anyway now, let me refill your glasses. I'd like to return to what we were talking about over supper."

During the previous cold season, Micky had broadened the scope of his geological survey in the Kolar district to include the area around *Oorgaum*, a couple of miles north of Marikuppam. He was convinced beyond doubt that he was on to something significant, and since returning to Bangalore a few months ago he'd been compiling detailed reports about his discoveries and how they might be exploited. He'd invited John and Emily over to update them on his progress and to seek their counsel.

"The way I see it," he began once they'd made themselves comfortable in the drawing room, "there's no sense going any further until three important issues have been resolved, namely finance, security and our claim on the land."

"As far as staking a claim is concerned," John replied, "given my relationship with the commissioner, I believe we can have a certain confidence that obtaining a mining licence will be no more than a formality."

"That's reassuring to hear. We'd need exclusive rights of course."

"Naturally. The Mysore government would expect a share of the value of whatever comes out of the ground, so cooperation will be in its interests. I'd suggest keeping our powder dry on that account for the time being."

"Very well," Micky agreed. "The question of money is the thorniest one in my mind. That is to say, how might we go about raising sufficient funds to pay for all the plant and machinery and manpower needed to mine on a worthwhile scale?"

"I've been giving a lot of thought to that as a matter of fact," said John. "From my researches it seems the gold fields of California, Nevada and Australia have all done well in securing substantial British investments, but are often yielding disappointing returns. If a more lucrative alternative were to present itself here in India, investors would be bound to clamour for it."

"Fools not to," said Micky.

"There was an article in the *Calcutta Examiner* last year talking about the possibility of finding gold in Assam, which gets to the heart of the matter rather well," John continued, unfolding a press clipping he'd been keeping in his pocketbook. "*An El Dorado like those of California, Victoria, and New South Wales is a great want of this country,*" he read aloud. "A great want indeed."

"Gold has always been found in Assam's rivers though," Micky pointed out. "Any hopes of serious production in that region are fanciful, so they are."

"Quite, and therefore whilst Assam sticks to its tea plantations the opportunity remains for Kolar to fulfil the desire for an Indian El Dorado."

"Forgive me, darling," Emily interjected, "that answers the question of why but not of how."

"Ah, yes, thank you, my love. Remiss of me." John smiled and sipped his Jameson's. "For starters, we're fortunate to have so many well-connected friends and moneyed acquaintances amongst the gentry here in Bangalore and Madras, and I have a few people in mind in particular..."

"Only for starters?" interrupted Micky.

"Not to diminish their importance, but yes. You see I've been thinking that making contact with investment brokers in London could be the secret to success." John checked his notes before carrying on. "There's a Mr P. Watson on Old Broad Street and a Mr W. Tregellas on Bishopsgate Street, both of whom appear to have excellent reputations, though no doubt there are others as well."

"I can see the potential merit in that idea," said Micky, pausing for thought. "I suppose using the services of a broker would save us wasting time and effort – time better spent in Kolar – and improve our odds of securing the best deals."

"My thoughts exactly," said John, pleased that Micky was open to the suggestion.

"I think this leads us towards the other issue I mentioned: security." Micky sat forward in his chair. "Thanks to our experience with that Doctor Hunter fellow, it's fair to say we've already learned a lesson or two about trust and discretion..."

John was still embarrassed by the Doctor Hunter fiasco. He nodded in agreement, but kept quiet while Micky continued.

"...not least that the fewer people involved the better. Obfuscating our real interest by referring only to the profusion of coal may also serve our purposes quite well. The physical security of a mining operation would need to be dealt with, but it's also crossed my mind that there's a wider perspective to consider."

"A wider perspective?" queried Emily.

"Well now I don't want you both thinking I'm putting the cart before the mule, so I don't, but if Kolar is as rich in gold deposits as my work suggests then feasibly any mining there could have significant economic and political repercussions."

"Ah, yes, I take your point," said John. "I'd wager it might even draw unwanted attention from already covetous eyes in St. Petersburg."

"It's a good job Harriet Scott is up country with her husband then," Emily commented.

"Harriet Scott?" asked Micky.

"Baroness de Bodisco, as was."

"Oh yes, I catch your drift now. Fortunate for sure."

"There's something I'm not quite clear about," confessed Emily. "Whether it's a broker in London or a speculator here in India, how will such people be convinced about the value of a mine in Kolar?"

"We'd provide them with evidence in the form of geological samples and my technical reports," Micky explained.

John could see his wife was pondering something. "What is it, my love?"

"Just that... well, wasn't it Little Boney who said a good sketch is better than a long speech?" Emily replied, quoting Napoleon Bonaparte. "What if all the reports and samples were accompanied – and brought to life, so to speak – by photographs of the mining locations?"

"Am I not blessed to have such a clever wife?" crowed John with unmistakable sincerity. "I think that's a thoroughly marvellous idea!"

"I agree, a *quare* fine proposal indeed," said Micky.

"Presumably you're thinking of Mrs Munro?" asked John.

"She's easily the best qualified, yes. I realise we have other dear friends who enjoy taking pictures, but Sophia's experience – and talent in my opinion – are unrivalled. And besides, her involvement might be a way to kill two birds with one stone."

"I don't follow," said Micky, frowning.

"You said a mining operation would need security – someone to provide a deterrent from interference. Would Morgan Farrell not be ideal? Sophia could write and suggest it."

"He would so, were he not in Secunderabad. But why would Mrs Munro write to him?"

Emily raised her eyebrows and John laughed. "Come off it, Micky," he said, "surely you must have noticed by now?"

*   *   *

Charles regretted that he'd not have the chance to thank Assistant Surgeon Kemp for suggesting Matheran. His physical constitution had been revived in its lofty haven by rest, better food, and daily doses of quinine powder dissolved in arrack. Even if runneth over was an exaggeration his cup was certainly close to brimming again. The best part of three months had been rather too long for his state of mind though. Every telegram bearing bad news had torn at his conscience, and in the absence of duty and stimulation he'd wrestled with melancholy spawned by boredom. For all that Charles was now ready to throw himself back into regimental life, he knew his eagerness was being tempered by a nagging anxiety about Secunderabad's evidently perilous environment.

The return journey was a chore made all the more wearying by the season. With every passing mile the saturated cloak of the monsoon clung tighter around the world like a spiralling fever, pressing down a little heavier, smothering more completely, and pinching all existence into oppressive confinement between the muted red of the earth and the dull grey that obscured the sky. When the rain fell in torrents as predictable as parade ground drills it washed away everything but the tyrannical humidity.

Save for pretty little Ethy Kilminster's release from a long illness, and Private Michael Hair being slain by sunstroke whilst on escort duty in Hyderabad, there had been a merciful hiatus in the loss of life during June and July. Charles had no way of knowing what had been happening since he departed Matheran, cut off as he was in neither one place nor another with a telegraph office or an address to write to. When he rode into Secunderabad on the morning of Wednesday, 21st August, and Morgan welcomed him at the bungalow, weeks of news charged en masse.

325

A month-old telegram from Harriet in Cheltenham told of her joy at the birth of George Cracklow. Thomas White, who'd remained in England, retired from service at the beginning of August, enabling Henry Wilkinson to be promoted to lieutenant colonel. Private Shaw had been buried on the 6th, and on the 18th James Goldie's baby son had passed away in *Bellary*. Charles would send congratulations to Harriet straightaway, and write to James and Magdalene with his deepest condolences.

"And Henry's throwing a dinner for the whole regiment this evening," added Morgan.

"The *whole* regiment?" queried Charles.

"Apparently so. To celebrate his new rank and give a speech, I expect. He's had a big marquee put up in the barrack square."

"Well, that's something to look forward to then. I want to thank you, by the way, for keeping me posted about goings on while I was away."

"No trouble at all. You're feeling well again, I take it?" said Morgan.

"Oh yes, fit as a butcher's dog. But what about you? You've been conspicuously silent on your own account."

"There's been nothing to say of any interest, just the usual routines. Until yesterday, that is," Morgan replied. "I received a letter from Sophia..."

"About time too!" joked Charles.

Morgan laughed. "Oh, we began corresponding a while ago after she made it safely back to Bangalore. She's staying with the Ranking family again."

"I'm glad to hear it."

"Anyway, I need to talk to you about this latest letter. The thing is, she's asking me to consider taking furlough so that I might join her on a sort of expedition."

"What a fizzing opportunity! And you will, of course?"

"Well, she was a bit vague, but it seems Micky Lavelle is doing some kind of survey work in the country east of Bangalore and could do with an extra pair of hands. You know, someone to keep an eye on things. I'm not entirely sure what use I can be to him, but Sophia is going along as his photographer so needless to say I'm interested. What do you think?"

"I think you're long overdue using any of your furlough entitlement and most definitely deserve an interlude from this place. Besides, one should never look a gift horse in the mouth," said Charles, shaking his friend's hand.

Three days after all the troopers sweated in the airless marquee and listened to Lieutenant Colonel Henry Wilkinson explain how proud he was to command the regiment, Private Folkes and one of Quarter Master Graham's children were laid to rest. Private Staines died from dysentery on the 26th and Private McKee on the 29th. The hiatus was over.

On Friday, 30th August, Henry Wilkinson hosted a dinner for all the officers and their sweethearts, which doubled as a farewell to Morgan. His request for a period of furlough on private affairs had been approved and he was to leave in the morning. The band was instructed to provide entertainment, and its members duly trudged to the Officers' Mess through a monsoon downpour. Henry gave them permission to shelter under the bungalow's portico, but it was generally felt that playing for nearly three hours whilst soaked to the skin would have been better rewarded by a nip of brandy.

Before dawn on the following Monday, Henry led the regiment across to the general parade ground for a morning of manoeuvres in drizzling rain. Events began inauspiciously when Private Madden was thrown from his mount with one foot stuck in its stirrup. The horse galloped off dragging him at its side and he was only saved from a certain death by the stirrup leather breaking under strain. The eventfulness of the day continued in the afternoon when all the families in the married parcherry were ordered to send away their cooks and servants for at least forty-eight hours. Cholera had broken out in Secunderabad's bazaar district.

By the time a telegram was received from Morgan confirming his arrival in Bangalore, Private Griffin was suffering through the final days of his battle with dysentery. He was a popular soldier, much admired for his talents as a performer. He'd played cello in the band, travelled to the races at Salem as part of the string quartet, been a leading light of regimental theatre productions, and, as interlocutor on board the *Golden Fleece*, a willing slave to the fashionable demand for minstrelsy. When friends gathered at his bedside on the 11th September, he sang his favourite *"Oh, What A Blazing Row!"* in a delirium of sepsis and organ failure before sinking into the black and implacable ocean of eternity.

Ten days later, Private Golding met a similar fate. He was twenty-three years old, a flute player in the band, and known to be much given to drink.

On Tuesday, 24th September, glasses were raised in the Officers' Mess on the occasion of Charles Agnew's thirty-sixth birthday and the end of the monsoon.

CHAPTER TWENTY-FIVE
OORGAUM, INDIA
SUNDAY, 6th OCTOBER 1872

Morgan could barely keep his eyes off Sophia. His mind was jumping around like a maniacal macaque, thoughts darting from one thing to another, there and then gone. Monkeys were aplenty on the boughs overhead and in the illuminated glades beyond the shadows. When they grinned and screamed it was if they knew what Morgan was thinking and were mocking his infatuation.

Riding at a leisurely walk, Sophia was a length in front on an Afghan grey that might easily have passed for the twin of Morgan's horse. He'd purchased the geldings for a song in Bangalore, choosing sturdiness and companionable temperament over youth or performance. He was still marvelling at how Sophia rode astride in loose-fitting trousers rather than sidesaddle in a skirt, at the visible form of her thighs and the way their shape was accentuated when they squeezed the flanks of her mount.

Oorgaum nestled in the fertile lee of a forested meridian that rose like a spine from the surrounding plain. When they all arrived yesterday, Micky had driven his heavily laden bullock cart to a clearing where he'd camped on his last visit. It was a discrete distance from the village, but close to a stream and the area where he intended to focus his search. Five tents were erected in a spacious semi-circle with Morgan's at one end next to Micky's. For the sake of habitual propriety Sophia's was placed at the other end, separated from her companions by a mess tent and a store.

This morning Micky was going to be busy organising his equipment and negotiating with a group of local labourers, so Morgan and Sophia had decided to leave him to it and explore the vicinity. They were heading north-east through redolent constellations of banyan, teak and sandalwood, luxuriant waves of fronds flooding the chaos of roots and tumbling into their path like breakers.

Although Sophia had demonstrated herself to be an adept horsewoman, which impressed Morgan no end, she was unaccustomed to long hours in the saddle and had travelled most of the way from Bangalore at Micky's side on the cart. The ride through the groves was the first time she and Morgan had ever been completely on their own, out of sight from not just their friends and wider social circles but also the scrutinising eyes of society in general. Though neither of them voiced it, they were both acutely conscious of their seclusion and the intimacy of experiencing it in comfortable silence.

Sophia's long calico tunic covered her hips and was belted at the waist. It clung to the damp skin of her shoulders. The thought crossed her mind that despite having chosen clothes for reasons of demure practicality they were probably leaving little to the imagination. The idea thrilled her. She hoped her intuition was right about Morgan enjoying the view.

After a mile the track delivered them back into the light and to an outlying cluster of the settlement. Sophia was intrigued by what she saw rising above the thatched roofs and she guided her horse towards it.

"Just like the one Charles is so fond of in Ulsoor," Morgan remarked as he dismounted near the temple's east entrance.

Sophia watched the way he moved, how he rolled up the sleeves of his collarless shirt and casually tilted the brim of his bowler. A carbine was slung across his back.

"Aye, I've been there too. This one bears such close resemblance, I'd hazard a guess it's similarly dedicated to Someshwara," she said, returning her attention to the architecture. "Built during the time of the *Chola* Empire, that's for certain, but judging by the less extravagant iconography it's likely much older than Ulsoor's."

A multitude of bas-relief figures adorned the lower level of the *gopuram*, some obviously human or animal, others neither entirely one nor the other, whilst life-size statues of curvaceous female deities guarded the portals to the first four of the six upper tiers.

Hearing the creak of stirrup leathers, Morgan turned to revere Sophia's lithe elegance as she stepped down from the saddle and removed her hat. It was the wide-brimmed one she always wore on expeditions, and often in between, defiantly unconventional and yet altogether congruous with equitation.

They tethered the horses and Morgan followed Sophia through the monument's central passage. A stone pillar rose some eighteen feet from a square base at the threshold of the temple courtyard. "They call this a *stambha*, a connection between heaven and earth," Sophia explained, admiring the proportions of the obelisk.

"I wonder if it works like the telegraph?" jested Morgan, putting his ear to the column and tapping its surface. "No, seems not," he said with a straight face.

Sophia laughed. "Let's go this way," she proposed, gesturing towards the cloistered south wall.

As they began their circumambulation they could hear voices coming from the direction of the main shrine tower, some chanting mantras, others in conversation. Sophia ran her hands over the stonework and paused to study one particular carving, tracing its outline with her fingertips. "Isn't it wondrous to imagine how many people have walked where we're walking, stood where we're standing, and even touched this very image just like I'm doing now? Generation upon generation through century after century."

"And touched hands like this?" Morgan replied, daring to entwine his fingers with Sophia's.

"Aye. Like this," she granted, looking up into his eyes and prolonging the divine sensation.

The moment was interrupted by a gentle tugging at the hem of Sophia's tunic. It was a girl of six or seven, small for her age, exuding the kind of confidence that comes with unconditional thoughtfulness for others. A vermilion *bindi* decorated the space between her eyebrows. She smiled at Sophia and held out her offering, bangles tinkling as they slid down her thin arm. The gift was a red hibiscus, liberated from the shrine with the best intentions, its prominent stigma thrusting forth from between curling petals.

"Och, thank you, my dear! That's so kind," Sophia responded, joining her palms together in thanks before accepting the flower. The girl's smile widened, understanding Sophia's reaction if not her words. She returned the *namaste* and then ran back to her mother.

"You've made a friend," Morgan commented.

"What a sweet gesture. I wonder what prompted her to do that?"

"A mark of respect for a kindred spirit, perhaps?" suggested Morgan, quite seriously.

Sophia took his arm, lost for the right words as they walked on.

Though cicadas were absent from the forest orchestra at this time of year, the evening around the campfire was accompanied by the thrum of other insects, avian cantatas, and the heckling repertoire of the resident primate population. The unmistakable sawing roar of a leopard could sometimes be heard in the far distance.

"Mind you don't forget to check your tent for cobras and other beasties before you retire for the night," said Micky, speaking across Morgan in Sophia's general direction after their meal.

"Aye, as I did last night and this morning. Fear not, this isn't my first waltz," she replied with a grin, taking no offence at having the obvious stated for her benefit. She knew he meant well.

"How do you plan to proceed tomorrow?" Morgan asked Micky, still uncertain about exactly what useful purpose he was going to serve.

"The last time I was here I found three auriferous strata..."

"Three what?" Morgan queried, chuckling at his own ignorance.

"My apologies. That is to say, layers of gold-laden rock in three locations."

"Oh I see. You were saying..."

"My intention is to begin a sinking into one of those strata to better estimate the scale of the potential yield," Micky continued.

"To what sort of depth do you anticipate having to go?" asked Sophia.

"'Tis hard to judge, so it is, but fifteen to twenty feet would be my guess. Truth be told, the full value will be impossible to determine until a proper shaft is excavated and that's beyond my means for the time being."

"Unless you find so much with your test hole that money becomes no object," Morgan pointed out.

"Wouldn't that be a blessing!" Micky replied. "And on such an optimistic note I'm going to wish you both a good night. I have an early start in the morning, so I do."

"Sleep well," said Sophia. "Watch out for those cobras," she added with a wink.

Micky laughed and wandered off to his tent.

Alone again, Morgan and Sophia lost themselves in story-telling and easy silences. Sophia described something of her life before widowhood, how her husband had been a successful merchant of wine and spirits in Perth, and of his untimely death in an accident on the Tay. Morgan asked after Janet, talked about Dromquinna and his parents, and was delighted that Sophia had steamed so close by Kenmare Bay and remembered its beauty.

"That little girl at the temple earlier..." said Morgan, setting out on a more sombre train of thought after a while. "She reminded me of some of the children of the regiment. The poor ones lost of late, I mean. Having witnessed the dreadful heartbreak of grieving parents, men and women ordinarily as hard as nails, I have to say I don't know how you do what you do at the hospitals with such equanimity."

Sophia moved along the log until they were hip to hip. She lent her head against Morgan's shoulder. "Even after all this time, you still manage to take me by surprise," she said with quiet tenderness, plunging them into another piquant silence, longer and more expectant than the last.

They could hear Micky snoring softly. Morgan added wood to the fire.

"Do you still have it?" Sophia asked when he returned to her side.

"Have what?"

"My telegram."

"Without airs or graces hearts content? Of course I do."

Sophia smiled. "I'm glad. But I have a bone to pick with you."

"Another one?" Morgan teased.

"You never did tell me what your reply said."

Morgan pulled his wallet from an inside jacket pocket. "Lucky I kept a copy then. Otherwise I might've forgotten all about it."

"Rascal!" she scolded with mirth, nudging him in the ribs.

He unfolded his handwritten note, dog-eared and water marked, and passed it to her.

"*HUZZAH CABLE,*" Sophia read aloud, tilting the page to make out the words in the firelight. "*HEART CONTENT ONLY WHEN PATHS CROSS AGAIN.*" That was unexpected. "Goodness! What a touching thing to send," she said, trying to comprehend its full meaning and implications. "*SAFE TRAVELS,*" ended the transcript. "I do so wish I'd received this at the time." Sophia took a moment to compose herself. "And how's your heart now?"

Morgan knelt on the ground in front of her and placed her hand against his chest. "Judge for yourself," he smiled.

Sophia thrust the fingers of her free hand into Morgan's hair and pulled him forward. Seven years of hoping and wanting ignited in their first exquisite kiss and blazed with a ravenous ferocity that left them wild-eyed and breathless. Morgan was still kneeling, Sophia straddling his lap, his arms around her waist, her hands holding his face, their foreheads touching. "Don't you dare sleep in your tent tonight," she whispered, laughing with relief and renewed desire.

*   *   *

Whatever Eleanor Renshaw's personal feelings were about coming back to India after more than a year in England, she remained tight-lipped. She and Richard, now a brevet major, had arrived in Secunderabad at the beginning of the month to find a regiment barely recognisable from the one they'd left behind in Bangalore.

At Henry Wilkinson's invitation, Richard joined John Bayley on a ride out to a low hill that lay about a mile to the east of the barracks. From the open ground at the top, Hyderabad could be seen quite clearly in the distance to the south-west.

"What do you make of it, gentlemen?" Henry asked, the high arch of his eyebrows as ever giving the false impression of superciliousness.

"The view?" queried Richard, solemn-faced. "Quite impressive, I suppose."

"So it is, but I meant the climate," Henry clarified.

"Noticeably cooler, with a worthwhile breeze," observed John.

"Ah, yes," said Richard, "certainly more agreeable than from whence we've come."

"I'm glad you both agree, because it's my intention to relocate the ranks here at the earliest opportunity." Henry nudged his horse forward and turned to face his colleagues. "This plateau is well-suited to encampment, as you can see, and would serve perfectly well for parade drills and so forth."

"Is there a water source?" John wondered.

"I'm sure we'll find one, or set some coolies to digging a well or two," Henry replied. "In any case, the bhistis can always bring water up from town."

John's horse sighed and nodded its head.

"Forgive me if I'm being a touch slow on the uptake, Henry," ventured Richard, "but why do you want to move the men here at all?"

334

"To improve their health. To save lives, in fact. We have a responsibility to preserve the fighting strength of the regiment after all," said Henry, shifting in his saddle. "I've been studying the records kept by Surgeon Innes and found that 1869 was our worst year for deaths. A dozen men perished that year. However, during our first nine months in Secunderabad we've already lost the same number, and that's before accounting for any of the wives or children."

"A morbid balance sheet, to say the least," noted Richard.

"Quite. Hence why I've been petitioning the government about the urgency of the need to complete the new Tirumalagiri barracks," Henry explained. "In the meantime, I'm seeking permission from headquarters for a temporary camp here in the cleaner air. It will mean a longer ride for officers coming and going whilst on duty, but I'm confident such a minor hindrance will not be met with complaint."

"I'm sure it won't," said John. "Will the married men move as well?"

"The sergeants will have to, of course, otherwise we'll have anarchy, but I'd foresee the married ranks staying where they are in the parcherry. I believe vacating the main barracks needs to be the priority."

"That may prove unpopular," predicted John.

"Perhaps, but as Lydgate once wrote, one can't please all the people all the time," Henry replied.

"Easy for a monk to say," scoffed Richard.

William Dolan had flourished in his role as the colonel's trumpeter and as a cornet player in the band. He'd grown to maturity in the cavalry, becoming a skilled rider and a lance-corporal in the process, but as far as anyone knew he hadn't a single relative or friend outside the regiment. When a combination of fever and dysentery killed him in the early hours of Sunday, 13th October 1872, Alec Innes recorded his age as twenty years. Charles was deeply affected by William's death. He attended the funeral and read a short passage from one of the lad's favourite books.

After the deaths of Private Hughes and Private Blades during the following ten days, the Secunderabad toll exceeded 1869 by twenty-five per cent. That was enough to persuade headquarters about the wisdom of Henry Wilkinson's proposition. On Friday, 25th October, the condemned barracks were evacuated and a camp established on the chosen plateau.

CHAPTER TWENTY-SIX
SECUNDERABAD, INDIA
WEDNESDAY, 13th NOVEMBER 1872

"...this constant advance of Russia creates new dangers to our Empire in the East," John Symes-Bullen read aloud from a syndicated *Saturday Review* article. *"The chief of these dangers, and it is a most serious one, is the effect which the proximity of Russia will have on the imaginations, the hopes, and the ambition of the natives of India. Our rule in India depends in a large degree on the universality of the impression among the people that there is no use in thinking of contending with us."*

"Like the ruse of a finesse in whist? That's an interesting point of view," commented Francis Drummond.

"Rather more than just a point of view, I'd wager," John replied, glancing at Francis over the rim of his spectacles. "They then make the point that: *If, after advancing to the borders of India, Russia were at war with England, and obtained some temporary success, which no reasonable man will pronounce impossible, the seeds of a new Indian mutiny might be sown, germinate, and shoot into leaf with inconceivable rapidity."*

Like many earnest debates that had taken place in the Officers' Mess over the years about faraway military expeditions, discussing the potential implications of Russian expansionism provided a modest dose of vicarious adventure. It was a way of clinging to the hope that one day they'd have their fair share of the real thing. The catalyst for this particular conversation was the movement of Russian troops towards Khiva during September. A thirty-four-year-old colonel by the name of Vasily Markozov had begun leading a force eastward from the Caspian coast with the objective of taking the city on behalf of the Tsar.

"I recall reading a piece that approached the topic from another perspective. Let me see if I can find it," said Charles, flicking through the pages of a weeks-old journal. "Yes, originally from *The Times*, here it is: *...admitting that, in certain contingencies, the proximity of the Russians to our Indian borders might facilitate inconvenient agitation among our subjects, it is* *very questionable whether any neighbouring Power could be more troublesome to us than that which now reigns in Khiva."*

"The Khan of Khiva is no doubt a petty despot who fully deserves to be punished," John interjected, quoting from the *Saturday Review*.

"Is that Feruz Khan?" queried Francis.

"The very same," Charles confirmed. *"The Times* goes on to suggest: *The Khanats are the home of Mahomedanism of the most intense and fanatical type."*

"Of course, all of this reiterates the strategic importance of Afghanistan," said John.

"One can't help wondering if it'll be the stage for more drama in the future. In which we might get to play a part, I mean," hoped Francis.

Paymaster Thomas Dynon was sitting on his own in the corner and only half-listening, but the mention of Afghanistan drew his attention. "Pray that you're never called upon to do so if I were you, Mr Drummond."

"What makes you say that, sir?" Francis asked.

"Because I remember what it was like riding through the hellish defiles of the Bolan Pass in '39," replied Thomas, his tone severe. "None who were there will ever forget the Baluchi snipers, the terrible problems we had with supply, or how everything unravelled after the capture of *Ghuznee*."

"It would be different a second time around though, would it not? Lessons learned and all that," Francis assumed.

"Afghanistan was a tragic disgrace back then, and if we ever go back it very likely will be again," Thomas said with certainty as he stood up. "Perhaps I've just lived too long and seen too much," he added as an afterthought. "If I was still blessed with youth like you gentlemen, I think I'd forget about soldiering altogether and go to seek my fortune in South Africa or America. There's a piece here about New Rush to inspire such flights of fancy in fact."

"New Rush?"

"In the Cape Province. See for yourself," Thomas replied, handing Francis the newspaper he'd been reading. "Meanwhile I have duties to attend to, so if you'll excuse me, I'll wish you all a good day."

Francis unfolded the page and scanned the dense print to find what Thomas had referred to. He summarised it for the others. The article described how a workforce of nearly fifty thousand men was extracting a vast quantity of diamonds from a honeycomb of trenches many scores of feet deep.

"As rushes go, not such a new one any more then," John mocked, "but I'll grant you it does sound a most tempting enterprise."

"Apparently something like sixty per cent of the miners are migrant black Africans living in insanitary, segregated shanties," added Francis.

"And dying in them too, I shouldn't wonder," said Charles.

"We should recruit some. They'd feel right at home in Secunderabad," suggested William Barker with no hint of jest.

"Steady on, that's a bit much don't you think?" bristled John.

"Not particularly, no," William replied.

"I hear the band are off to Tirumalagiri tomorrow to play the 24th Regiment out of barracks," said Charles, deliberately changing the subject.

"Indeed they are," nodded William. "Privates Palmer, Pyke and Dyer have claimed their discharge and are leaving for England with them. Mrs Hayes is probably wishing she was too, poor woman."

No better off for the move to higher ground, Corporal Hayes died last Wednesday. His wife and their four children now faced a precarious future.

"When tomorrow?" wondered Francis.

"I believe the band's presence is required by half past two in the morning."

"That'll go down well," John laughed. "Private Wisewould and others will no doubt be quick to whine about the inconvenience."

"He was complaining to me only last week about the unfairness of Sergeant Doherty not dismissing him from Riding School," recalled Charles. "Something to do with Wisewould's reluctance to break an awkward horse to the lance."

"Did you indulge him?" John asked.

"Only as the path of least resistance. I spoke to Doherty and asked him to reconsider his decision. We have more important things to occupy our minds at the moment."

Charles was thinking of Henry's hilltop experiment, its day-to-day practicalities, whether or not it was proving worthwhile, and the growing discontent amongst the ranks. The married men were known to be especially unhappy about the long slog on foot to and from the parcherry.

As Christmas loomed closer, it was becoming clear to everyone that camping on the plateau was making little difference to the health of the regiment. The surgeons were as busy as ever and another two men had been lost.

Private Garratt was a minister's son who'd achieved an almost legendary reputation in the ranks for his dissipated behaviour. He departed the world on Tuesday, 17th December. Private Morris, on the other hand, was a likeable, unassuming man possessed of great physical strength. The circumstances of his demise five day later were out of the ordinary and a cause for wider concern. The story going around was that he'd left camp the night before in search of toddy, but for reasons as yet unknown had ended up being tied to a tree and beaten by a group of locals. He was still alive when members of his troop freed him in the morning, but hadn't lasted long. With a view to quelling any collective urge for reprisal, Alec Innes let it be known the toddy was to blame for Morris's death rather than the blows from his attackers.

Henry Wilkinson remained steadfast in his belief that camping in the clean air was preferable to being confined in the stench of the old barracks, and that the welfare of the men would inevitably improve with time. The men, however, unaware of Henry's lobbying efforts on their behalf, were losing faith in his judgment and beginning to display open dissent. Two mornings after Garratt was buried, the whole of D Troop refused to remain at stables for Henry's inspection on account of being kept waiting too long. They packed up their kit and marched off back to their tents, hooting the colonel as they passed.

More than seven and a half years after first being appointed a bâtman in Colchester, Solomon Smith still served Charles with unwavering loyalty and discretion. After lunch on Monday, 23rd December, he delivered a message received in the telegraph office that morning and was pleased to see it brought a smile to his captain's face.

"A relief to know Lieutenant Farrell is safe, sir," said Smith. "Happen John Gantz will be glad of it too. If you don't mind me telling him, that is?" he added.

"Indeed. Thank you, Solomon. And yes, of course, do tell Gantz. I'm going to the Lodge later, so I won't be needing anything else today," Charles replied.

"Right you are, sir. I'll return in the morning as usual then."

Charles read Morgan's telegram again:

BACK IN BANGALORE. ALL WELL.
RESIDING AT MICKYS. WRITE SOON.
STRUCK GOLD WITH S.

Whether the last line was meant literally or as a euphemism, Charles could only guess, but he was delighted for his friend either way. Hearing good news from Morgan gave his spirits the lift they needed. For the first time in a long while Charles allowed himself the luxury of optimism about the future.

PART FIVE

CHAPTER TWENTY-SEVEN
SECUNDERABAD, INDIA
FRIDAY, 24th JANUARY 1873

Of all the countless letters Charles had sent to Harriet over the years, this one was by far the hardest to write.

He said nothing of how he was shivering as he put pen to paper or of how he suspected he'd be burning in an inferno of fever before the day was out. Neither did he mention this morning's burial of the remains of Private Joe Gilbert, a quiet fellow who'd worked as a barman on watchman's corner of New Cut in Lambeth before taking the Queen's shilling, nor the four others who'd died since the New Year: Privates Mann, Martin, Linghan and Cross.

He asked after George and the children, his parents too, and described how the regiment had marched back to the old barracks on 2nd January. He left out the parts about how the men of the ranks had grown heartily sick of being camped up on the plateau, of Henry Wilkinson's disappointment, and the short shrift Henry received from the married couples when he interrupted their belated Christmas dinner in the parcherry on the 15th.

There had been a garrison review on the general parade ground on 16th January, during which Sergeant Major Marr and Sergeant Doherty were awarded good conduct medals. That was something positive to tell Harriet at least.

But Charles was procrastinating about getting to the point of the letter.

He was utterly demoralised and at the end of his tether about the futility of his life in India and the desperate suffering of the ranks, a suffering that seemed devoid of function or any hope of reward.

When the words began to flow and he committed them to the page, he felt a vague sense of relief.

It may come as something of a surprise, though I hope not an unwelcome one, that after a great deal of careful consideration I have concluded that the time has come for me to retire from the army.

Whilst I am entirely resolute in my decision, and will have the consolation of the value of my commission to look forward to, I cannot deny feeling some regret that my military career is to end with an inglorious early retreat back to private life – as a damp squib without the merit of any worthwhile accomplishment or legacy.

It will take some time to arrange, but I promise to telegraph you when I have a firm itinerary.

Charles read over the letter again and then added a postscript about how he was also writing to their father. It would be a much shorter note and lacking the candour he shared with Harriet.

He knew he needed to tell Morgan of his intentions as well, but that could wait for another day. Charles gave both letters to Solomon Smith to take to the post office, before returning to bed and pulling a blanket tight around his shoulders.

On Monday morning Alec Innes confirmed what Charles already knew full well. The cycle of chills and sweats, combined with bouts of crippling nausea, were symptomatic of malaria's recurrence.

"Just you take things easy for a wee while and you'll be fighting fit soon enough," said Alec, lightly. "Cross your fingers it's only a brief episode."

"I'll do my best, but I confess I've really had enough of all this," Charles replied.

"You've survived worse."

"I don't mean the illness. Well, that too of course, it's wretched. I meant being here, in the army, in this country, wasting my time and serving no purpose. As a matter of fact, I've decided to resign my commission and return to England."

"Have you now? I see..." Alec's expression darkened. He filled his pipe in silence while he mustered his thoughts. "And have you cast your decision in stone by telling the colonel?"

"Not yet, no, but I intend to this week."

The flame Alec held over the bowl flared and receded and flared again as he puffed the tobacco into a satisfying glow.

"In that case, before you do, may I give you an alternative course of action to ponder upon?"

"My mind's made up."

"Aye, no doubt, but humour me a moment," Alec insisted. "You see, I was going to take some furlough later in the year so that I might keep abreast of how Mr Maillard and the depot troop are faring in Canterbury, and to visit my parents while there's still an opportunity. My father will be turning eighty-one next month."

Charles was about to say something, but Alec raised a quieting hand and continued.

"If I brought those plans forward, perhaps you could come with me? On medical furlough, that is, rather than en route to retirement. It would give you a chance to regain your strength again, to spend time with your family and friends, and to reflect further upon your future. By the time you returned here, if indeed that's what you chose to do, the new barracks at Tirumalagiri would almost certainly be finished and the status and health of the regiment would be greatly improved."

"I appreciate the kind offer, but I went away on a medical certificate before and now seem to be no better off for it."

"Aye, so you did, but how long's it been since you last set foot on British soil?"

"Oh, about four years, I suppose."

"Well, there you are then. There's no substitute for the comforts of home when it comes to restoring a man's constitution and perspective."

"True enough, I'm sure. I'll give it some thought. That's as much as I can promise for the time being," said Charles.

"Good, good. Let me know what you decide."

Being all too aware that the illness plaguing his body was also affecting the clarity of his mind, Charles was far from hasty in his deliberations. More than a week went by before he spoke to Alec again and requested a medical certificate. He would go on furlough as suggested and revisit the idea of retirement at a later date. Charles reasoned he had nothing to lose. Alec was quietly pleased and set about making the necessary preparations.

Three days later Francis Drummond announced he too was taking furlough, on private business rather than health grounds, and could travel with Alec and Charles if they were agreeable.

"My Uncle James – more properly Rear Admiral Drummond of Her Majesty's Royal Navy – has managed to obtain an invitation for me to attend a Royal Levée at St. James's Palace on 26th May," Francis explained in the privacy of Alec's office.

"My congratulations," said Charles.

"Aye, a great honour indeed," added Alec.

"Thank you. It seems my uncle is to receive a knighthood in the Queen's birthday honours on the 24th, so we'll be having quite the time of it! I'm supposed to be sworn to secrecy, but one can't imagine there's any harm in telling you chaps."

"We won't breathe a word," Charles winked.

*   *   *

Anne Lavelle, now twelve years old and at the threshold of the first confusing throes of adolescence, had developed something of a crush on Morgan since he came to stay at her father's home. When he smiled and thanked her for conveying the telegram through the house so swiftly, Anne blushed and curtsied and was lost for any words she believed might sound even remotely grown up.

The message from Charles said he was taking furlough to England, departing Bombay aboard the troopship *Serapis* on or around 7th March, and asked if Morgan would be back in Secunderabad beforehand.

"Not on your life, chum!" Morgan said to himself as he read the words. Glad as he was for Charles having some time at home, he had no intention of returning to Secunderabad any sooner than absolutely necessary. More than anything, he didn't want to be apart from Sophia.

Their relationship had been an open secret whilst they'd been camped at Oorgaum. Micky could hardly fail to notice, and he gave them the benefit of his worldly understanding by never raising the subject in conversation. It was unavoidably different in Bangalore with Morgan at Micky's and Sophia at the Ranking's. They spent as much time together as possible, but being once again prey to society's expectations of proper conduct meant it was never enough.

A reunion with Charles in Secunderabad this side of his furlough wasn't on the cards, but another notion was springing to Morgan's mind that would serve the same end and others besides. He talked to Sophia about it as they promenaded around the Lalbagh Botanical Garden before lunch.

"What if we travelled back to England as well? On the same ship as Charles, I mean. We could take Micky's mining reports and your photographs to the people he's talked about in London, and then find ourselves a quiet place in the country for a few months."

"That's a tremendous idea!" said Sophia.

"I'm so pleased you think so."

"And how wonderful to think of us being alone again!"

"I think of little else."

Sophia squeezed Morgan's arm. "I'd love the chance to visit Janet and Hector," she beamed, her imagination whirring, "and I suppose it's about time my ethnographic work from Baluchistan saw the light of day."

"Most definitely. Let's discuss it with Micky this afternoon and then I can send Charles a reply."

"Aye... och, but wait, didn't Charles say he was going by troopship? Wouldn't that preclude me? What with not being *on the strength* of a regiment?"

"Ah, yes, I hadn't thought of that," Morgan realised. "But I bet if you asked for his help Colonel Meade could swing an exception for you – some sort of special dispensation."

"Perhaps, aye. I hope you're right. Let's talk to Micky first before we cross that bridge."

Micky was in full agreement about the advantages of Morgan's suggestion, but wanted John Orr to have a say before anything was settled. He asked the doctor and his wife to join them for supper that evening.

"That all sounds like a splendid way to proceed," said John when Sophia outlined the plan. "And will you carry mineral samples to London as well?"

"You took the words right out of my mouth," laughed Emily Orr, feeling somewhat envious of Sophia's opportunity and simultaneously proud that she was looking so happy.

"I was about to mention that, so I was," interrupted Micky. "There needn't be many of them, so as not to be a burden, but providing the brokers with physical evidence from Oorgaum would be a great support to our cause if you're willing?"

"No bother at all as far as I'm concerned," said Sophia.

"Willing and able, of course," Morgan confirmed.

"Grand, thank you," replied Micky. "Excuse me for a moment," he added, leaving the table.

"I'd be quite happy to raise the troopship question with the commissioner if you'd like me to?" John offered to Sophia.

"That's most kind, thank you, but I think I'd like to request Richard's help in person."

"As you wish. I'm sure he'll be amenable."

Micky returned from his study carrying a pair of soft leather pouches and gave one each to Sophia and Morgan. "We'll sort out the broker samples at a later juncture, so we will. In the meantime, these are for you..."

"Och goodness, Micky!" exclaimed Sophia when she opened the pouch and saw the quantity of crude gold within. "But you've already more than reimbursed us, have you not?"

"This is but a small token of my gratitude for all you've done and are intending to do. The value is hard to judge, though I'm confident it'll amount to a useful sum in London."

CHAPTER TWENTY-EIGHT
WATSON'S ESPLANADE HOTEL, BOMBAY, INDIA
WEDNESDAY, 5th MARCH 1873

"Morning. My name's Innes. Room 108. Are there any messages for me?"

"Good morning, sahib. One moment please," replied the young man at the reception desk. With unhurried efficiency he plucked an envelope from one of the pigeon-holes on the wall behind him. "This came a very short time ago, sahib."

Alec took the proffered telegram and was expressing his thanks when he heard a familiar voice call his name. He turned to see Morgan entering the lobby with Mrs Munro by his side.

"I had no idea we were to have the pleasure of your company as well," said Morgan, shaking Alec's hand. "I'm not sure if you're already acquainted with Sophia Munro?"

"Aye, the doctor and I have met before," Sophia explained before Alec could get a word in. "It's good to see you again," she added.

"Indeed we have, and likewise Mrs Munro."

"Och, none of that now. Sophia, please."

Alec laughed. "Very well. Sophia. And when you said 'as well' just now, Morgan, I take it you're expecting to rendezvous with Charles but he's omitted to tell you about Francis Drummond and I? We didn't know you'd be here either."

"Francis too? And all three of you are going on the *Serapis*?"

"Aye, that's right."

"And there was me thinking we'd be stuck with only Charles for company all the way back to Portsmouth," Morgan joked.

"In his defence he hasn't been at all well of late, as you're no doubt aware."

"Actually, no, I wasn't. He kept that quiet. Is it the malaria again?"

"Aye. He seems to be over the worst, thankfully, but it's taken its toll."

"Where is he now?"

"Still asleep probably. We didn't get here until the wee sma' hours last night. I'm not long up myself."

"Then let us not keep you from your breakfast," said Sophia, gesturing towards the restaurant.

"Thank you, but tea would suffice for now. Will you join me?"

"Certainly, aye. We could do with some refreshment."

Sophia led the way through to the deserted lounge bar and chose the same leather armchair she'd occupied four years ago during her meeting with Colonel Richard Meade. He'd been only too happy to facilitate Sophia's passage aboard the troopship, saying something about someone in the navy owing him a favour.

"Is your family travelling with you, Alec?" wondered Sophia after tea had been ordered.

"Sadly not, no, but they'll be following on in a month or two. It's for the best though. Wee Hector had his first birthday just last month, you see, and my darling Jessie is with child again."

"Congratulations!" said Morgan.

"Aye, that's terrific news. When's she due?"

"Thank you. Around the end of August, God willing, so it's still quite early days."

A steward set down a tray and while he poured three cups Alec opened his telegram. A subdued smile formed beneath his moustache.

"More good news?" asked Morgan.

"Aye, from the adjutant. It seems that while Charles and Francis and I were making our way here I was being promoted to surgeon major."

"And not before time!"

"Good for you, Alec. Hard earned and well deserved, without a doubt," added Sophia.

Alec took a sip of tea before lighting his pipe and relaxing into the upholstery. "But what about you both? Have you been here long? How are things in Bangalore?"

Morgan and Sophia arrived the day before yesterday. They'd checked in to separate rooms, but had hardly left Morgan's until this morning.

Sophia related a half-truth about showing Morgan around some of the city, this being his first occasion in Bombay, and talked about her intention to visit an old acquaintance at the *Times of India*. Bangalore was the same as ever, she said, and all their friends were in fine health.

"Did you have a straightforward journey?" Morgan asked, shifting the focus of conversation.

"It was a bugbear, naturally, but no more so than any other in this country," replied Alec. "Getting to *Wadi* Junction took five days with carriage and horses, and I dare say would've been twice that had we used bullocks. Then fourteen hours or so on the Great Indian Peninsular Railway brought us to *Bori Bunder* station. We were rather relieved to find the hotel is so nearby."

With an unobstructed view of the lounge doors, Sophia was the first to notice Charles and another gentleman entering the room. "Poor man, my goodness," she whispered with sympathetic alarm as she moved to stand.

Morgan followed Sophia's lead and immediately understood her reaction. "Jesus wept!" he said under his breath, raising eyebrows at Alec in disbelief.

From his gaunt features and the sagging fit of his morning suit, it was obvious even from a distance that Charles had lost a great deal of weight. At closer quarters a peculiar yellow tinge was apparent in the whites of his eyes.

"What time do you call this?" Morgan asked, relying on humour to mask his shock and concern.

Charles neither rose to the jest nor countered with witticism. "I'm glad you could make it," he replied with warmth, but none of his usual vigour. "And hello Sophia. I do hope you've been keeping well. May I introduce Lieutenant Francis Drummond..."

"Good day to you, ma'am. How do you do?" bowed Francis on cue.

Sophia made her usual correction, Charles and Francis were brought up to speed with the conversation, and more tea was ordered and poured. Morgan wanted to ask after his friend's health, but decided to wait until he could speak to Charles on his own.

"I'm curious, Francis," Sophia admitted, "are you by chance one of the Drummonds of Strathallan?"

"That I am, and proudly so. You know the estate?"

"Aye, though it's been a long while since I was last there to enjoy its beauty."

"Then allow me to extend an open invitation for you to be my guest at the castle – to you all, in fact."

"That's most kind, thank you. I'd like that very much indeed."

"Excellent, I shall look forward to it," said Francis. "And speaking of curiosity, does anyone happen to know how the name of our vessel is pronounced? *Se-rapis* perhaps, or more like *Serra-pis?*"

"Carrin steamed on her about three years ago," recalled Charles. "I think he pronounced it *Serra-pis*, in the Greek style, but I may be mistaken."

"That's how I heard the name spoken this morning," said Morgan.

"This morning?" queried Charles.

"Sophia and I walked across to the harbour earlier to take a look. The ship's been there since the 18th of last month apparently, and they've nearly finished coaling. We bumped into Alec on our way back."

"And what were your first impressions?"

"Painted all white, she's certainly a lady who knows how to stand out in a crowd," said Sophia with admiration.

Morgan smiled at that. "And did you notice the green band running around the hull?"

"Aye."

"Like a pretty ribbon tied about her waist," suggested Morgan, seeing the frisson he hoped for in Sophia's eyes. "I haven't been off dry land since we first landed at Madras," he continued, turning back to Charles, "but I'd hazard a guess the *Serapis* is longer than the *Golden Fleece* by about a third. All in all, she certainly looks striking from the outside."

"Have you taken her portrait?" Charles asked Sophia.

"Not yet, but I'd like to before we embark."

"I might take a gander at her myself this afternoon."

"May I accompany you?" asked Francis.

"By all means. You too, Alec?"

"Thank you, but no. Perhaps tomorrow. I have some letters to write and an appointment with an afternoon nap."

"Am I correct in saying you've travelled the Suez route before, Charles?" wondered Sophia.

"In part, yes, although that journey ended at Madras rather than Bombay. A P&O paddle steamer called the *Ripon* went between Southampton and Alexandria, and then the *Surat* – also of the P&O line – steamed from Suez. So this will be my first time on the canal, and I don't mind telling you how excited I am at the prospect."

"I quite understand. It'll be my first time on it too."

"And not stopping at Suez itself will be a blessing," added Charles.

"Aye, it certainly will be!"

"You chaps must be famished, aren't you?" asked Morgan in hope as much as expectation. "Shall we see about some food? A sort of early lunch for Sophia and I, and a late breakfast for you three?"

"Great minds..." said Alec. "Lead the way."

CHAPTER TWENTY-NINE
GULF OF SUEZ
THURSDAY, 20TH MARCH 1873

The Reverend John Westropp staggered at the starboard rail and hurled an empty black bottle over the side.

"*But unto you that fear my name*, said the Lord," he raved at the distant shadows of a Sinai dawn, hands outstretched in supplication, "*shall the sun of righteousness arise with healing in his wings!*"

"I'd venture there's many a soul aboard this 'ere lobster pot could use a healing touch, Padre," Boatswain Second Class George Baldock soothed as he approached along the fore deck.

"Then let them come to the light of the Lord and praise His name!" preached Westropp, slurring his Limerick vowels.

"As they surely will, Padre, as they surely will," George placated, beginning to guide the man by the shoulders. "Now how about we get you below to your cabin? I can arrange for breakfast to be brought to you. Or perhaps you'd rather rest a while?"

Forward of the ship's single funnel on the raised bridge of the quarterdeck, First-Lieutenant Atwell Lake was halfway through a four-hour shift as officer of the watch. The *Serapis* was steaming at a steady nine knots and now north of the village of *Ras Ghareb* about three miles off to port. A southbound steamer had been sighted an hour ago at five o'clock, though too far away to identify. There was a course correction coming up and Atwell had neither the time nor patience for a half-cut clergyman making a spectacle of himself. He'd sent George Baldock to offer the Reverend some kindness before the weather deck began to fill with folk seeking their first fresh air of the day. It was a relief to see the companion stairway door closing.

"Pardon us, sir. My apologies. Thank you, ma'am," said George, hurrying his incoherent charge stumbling past Morgan and Sophia waiting to ascend from the saloon deck landing.

They'd left their respective cabins whilst most of the other First Class passengers were still asleep, and had met to start the thirteenth full morning of the voyage with a breezy promenade. They knew it would likely be the only opportunity for private conversation all day.

"That damned fellow's a disgrace," complained Morgan, ducking out into the chill to be greeted by the scent of the desert carried on the air. He held the door for Sophia.

"I feel rather sorry for him," she said. "Let's wander towards the stern first, shall we?"

"Certainly," Morgan agreed as Sophia took his arm. "Why sorry for the wretch?"

"Alec was telling me about him the other day. According to the ship's surgeon, Mr Richardson, he was a navy chaplain until just recently. On HMS *Flora*, I think Alec said, a depot vessel stationed at Ascension Island and then the Cape, which sounds to me like a very lonely kind of existence. The story seems rather vague, but apparently some form of improper conduct led to the Reverend being discharged from service and sent home to avoid a court martial."

"Sermonising while under the influence, perhaps?"

Sophia stifled a laugh. "Rather more serious than that, I fear. Whatever the reason, he's clearly a deeply troubled young man and I can't help feeling sympathy for the unfortunate state he's in."

Morgan didn't share that sympathy, but admired Sophia's compassion nevertheless. By the time they'd completed a third circuit the deck was being warmed by the sun, members of the crew were trimming the braces, and more people had emerged from the fore and aft stairs. Amongst them were Charles and Alec strolling towards the stern to smoke, Major Richard Blundell of the 3rd Hussars in overall command of the troops on board, Henrietta Blundell in overall command of her husband, and Lieutenant Francis Burton of the 1st Bengal Cavalry arm in arm with his wife, Isabella.

"I'd like to go and speak with the Burtons, if you don't mind?" said Sophia when she noticed the couple.

"Not at all, I quite understand. I'll be sure to bump into you later on for chaste conversation conducted at a more respectable distance," Morgan smiled.

"I should hope so too," replied Sophia, squeezing his hand as they parted.

Isabella Burton befriended Sophia even before the *Serapis* had slipped its moorings in Bombay harbour at eight minutes past ten on the morning of Friday, 7th March. The starboard rail had thronged with passengers eager for departure, including Sophia who happened to find herself standing next to a courteous staff officer. He'd introduced himself and his wife, and Isabella in turn introduced their three-month-old daughter, Nellie Violet. The baby had her father's placid disposition and her mother's eyes, an unusual shade of blue that appeared almost like amethyst in a certain light. She cooed and laughed and gurgled sweetly, and was never any trouble.

As Sophia discovered later via Morgan, the gentlemen aboard tended to label Isabella a fiery Irishwoman. But what they called fiery, Sophia recognised as joyful originality, intelligence, and independent-minded spirit. And as for being an Irishwoman, it was true her accent came from her father's family in Dublin. Indeed, that was where she and Francis were married, but she was proud to have been born in *Kamptee* near *Nagpur* in India. As petite as Sophia, with a round face and the warmest of smiles, she had a rare knack for deciphering the peculiarities of human behaviour.

Isabella was rapt by Sophia's tales and asked question after interesting question. The story about taking photographs of slave ships was given added colour early one morning in the Gulf of Aden when the sail of a dhow was sighted on the port beam. Isabella had been curious about why Sophia wasn't capturing scenes aboard the *Serapis*. She'd considered doing so, Sophia admitted, but it made a relaxing change not having to think about plate preparation for a while. Isabella empathised completely.

A thousand and sixty-nine passengers embarked from Bombay, forty-six of them officers and their families, and a female photographer, accommodated in First Class. Most of the rest, including eighty-eight women and a hundred and eighty-nine children, were crammed cheek by jowl in the stuffy and poorly illuminated troop deck at the bottom of the hull. When smallpox, measles and scarlet fever all manifested down there in the heat and the filth, they showed neither mercy to the vulnerable on whom they preyed nor respect to distinctions of class as they spread upwards through the ship.

The first to go was William Edwards from the troop deck, aged thirteen days, at six o'clock in the morning on Thursday, 13th March, the sixth day of the journey. His tiny remains were committed to the deep at seven bells that afternoon.

Three days later, a little before eight o'clock on Sunday evening, Nellie Burton passed away in her parent's First Class cabin.

Francis Burton hid his grief behind a wall of stoic silence on Monday morning as he listened to the Reverend Hamlet Millet recite the funeral prayer over the shroud without once needing to read the words. Sophia held Isabella's hand as she sobbed and Nellie's body vanished beneath the waves of the Red Sea somewhere off the Sudanese coast.

Sophia was continuing to do what little she could to console her friend, spending time with her when she needed female company and leaving her and Francis on their own when all they needed was each other.

The ship's present speed was matching the force of the gentle following breeze so closely that at the stern it was as if there was no wind at all. The perfect conditions in which Charles and Alec could savour their tobacco.

"No sign of Mr Drummond yet?" asked Morgan when he joined them.

"Morning. He's up and about, but went in search of sustenance," Charles explained.

"Aye, and we'll be doing the same in a wee bit," added Alec.

"I'll come with you when you do, I'm starving. Another fine morning, eh?"

"That it is, and I imagine we might reach the canal before the day's out," said Charles.

"I don't know what all the fuss is about, but so long as it makes you happy, Charles, that's all that matters," Morgan teased. "I must say though, it's good to see you looking more like your old self again," he added.

"Thank you. I'm certainly feeling much better."

"All this sea air will be doing you wonders," said Alec.

Second-Lieutenant William Freeland relieved Atwell Lake as officer of the watch at eight o'clock and increased the ship's speed to ten knots. Suffolk-born William had the respect of the crew for his seamanship and fairness, and the appreciation of the passengers for his calm and friendly manner. Privately, he was impatient for the next time he'd be home in Hampshire to kiss Mary and celebrate their second wedding anniversary.

A little before two bells, William observed a group of officers from First Class pointing landward from the port rail. He left the quarterdeck to speak with them, satisfied that he could spare a few minutes with Boatswain John Brodie taking the helm.

"Good morning, gentlemen. What have you spotted?"

"Oh hello, lieutenant," replied Morgan, outside again after an adequate breakfast.

"A settlement, we think, at the mouth of that wide valley over there," said Charles. "Do you happen to recognise it?"

"Ah yes, I see it, sir. It's a place by the name of *Zaafarana*, and serves as a useful landmark on our course. We must be only fifty miles or so from Suez now."

"Ever been there yourself?" wondered Francis Drummond.

"No, sir, and I doubt it has much going for it. Mind you, further inland, at the foot of those mountains to the south, I believe one can find ancient caves and the monasteries of St. Anthony and St. Paul."

"Christian monasteries in Egypt? I had no idea," said Charles.

"Oh yes, sir. Coptic Orthodox. Dating back something like sixteen centuries."

"How extraordinary! Thank you, lieutenant."

"My pleasure, sir. If you'll all excuse me, I should probably be getting back to the quarterdeck."

Zaafarana remained visible for nearly an hour, by which time the crew was mustering by divisions on the fore deck with heads bowed as Lieutenant Freeland read the morning prayers.

"Now that's odd, don't you think?" said Morgan after the crew dispersed to their duties.

"What is?" Charles and Francis replied in unison.

"Well I've not seen them do that before. Look. They're getting at the thickest of those ropes kept at the bow."

"Hawsers, I think they call them," said Charles. "They're used for mooring and towing. I agree, very odd indeed."

"Same thing's happening down at the stern," Francis reported, shielding his eyes from the sun's glare with one hand.

"And now Captain Grant has come down from the quarterdeck and is having words with Major Blundell," noticed Morgan.

As soon as the major became available to talk to, Charles went over to ask if he knew what was going on.

"Slight change of plan," said Richard. "It's come to the captain's attention that there are insufficient victuals on board to keep us all fed and watered as far as Port Said. He's therefore decided to make an unscheduled stop at Suez to re-supply rather than ploughing merrily on up the canal."

"That's disappointing," said Charles with pointed understatement. "One might've thought he had ample time to procure the necessary before we left Bombay."

"Yes, quite. In his defence, I'm sure the captain had endeavoured to do just that and was simply let down by supply. On the bright side, however, it does present the opportunity for an evening ashore for any officers desiring a change of scenery."

"I suppose it does. I'll pass the word around. You'll be keeping the ranks confined to the ship, presumably?"

"Oh good God, yes! Can you imagine the chaos and carnage if we let them off?!"

William Freeland handed over to Third-Lieutenant Godfrey Eliot at noon, just after another steamship was sighted heading south. By one o'clock Suez Bay was visible off the starboard beam and Isabella Burton was persuading her husband to go ashore when the time came. It would do him the world of good, she told him, and she was perfectly content having their cabin to herself. Sometimes tears needed to be shed alone.

Morgan had hoped all the First Class passengers would choose to visit Suez so that he and Sophia could have a deserted saloon deck all to themselves. Failing that, they could disappear into the town on their own and be like a couple again for a few hours. However, as much as Sophia appreciated Morgan's train of thought, she insisted on remaining behind to keep Isabella company if needed.

"Och and besides, I've seen more than enough of Suez before," she said, leaning against the fore deck's starboard rail. "I seem to remember the food being good at a little Italian place on *Rue*... I think it was *Rue Colmar*. If it's still in business, you might like to try it."

"*Rue Colmar?*"

"Aye. The *Café d'Italia*. It's easy to find."

"And you're sure I can't change your mind?"

Sophia just smiled at that. "Nearly there, look."

With masts bare and steam lowered, the ship had slowed to a crawl for its approach to the docks.

"I thought it would be bigger," said Morgan.

"What would be?"

"Suez."

"Och, no. That's just Port Tewfik ahead. You can see the entrance to the canal to the right of it. Suez proper is away over there," Sophia explained, turning to point over the port bow.

By ten minutes to three o'clock, the *Serapis* was secured to the transport buoy in the arsenal basin and at six bells the accommodation ladder was being lowered towards the quayside. In the other half of the dock, the basin dedicated to commercial shipping, Egyptian stevedores were hard at work loading the P&O steamer *Golconda* with supplies. For passengers standing at the port rail on the *Serapis*, its position obscured their view across the bay towards the town.

British Consul George West observed the new arrival from his first-floor office window overlooking the arsenal basin. He watched the parties of weary-looking army officers in lounge suits, top hats and bowlers, coming ashore in their threes and fours to hire transport into town. Aside from the *Serapis* being unexpected there was nothing particularly unusual about any of it, but as a matter of habit George scribbled a brief description in his personal diary.

As dusk retreated beyond the western desert and oil lamps mounted a weak resistance against the darkness in boulevards and crooked alleys, Francis Drummond understood why Charles had shown so little enthusiasm for traipsing around Suez. It struck him as being like the seediest parts of Secunderabad, but with none of their charm. At least he'd be able to boast of seeing it in years to come, he said to himself, and exploring somewhere different for a few hours had still been preferable to the tedium of the ship. Neither Morgan nor Alec appeared any more enamoured.

In the absence of other dinner venues deemed worthy of patronage, and with everyone willing to trust Sophia's recommendation, the group retraced their steps to *Rue Colmar*. They'd happened upon the street earlier in the day and Morgan had pointed out the *Café d'Italia* on one corner.

When they stepped inside he couldn't help wondering if the place had gone downhill since Sophia was there. The décor was plain and functional at best, though clean enough, and the waiter who showed them to a corner table was polite and friendly. Of course, Sophia had praised the food, not the appearance, and Morgan was hungry enough to give it the benefit of the doubt.

Only a couple of the dozen or so other tables were occupied. Three young men having an animated conversation in Italian were about to tuck into bowls of pasta at one of them. At the other, an older duo with black fingernails and oil-stained overalls refilled their shot glasses from a bottle of ouzo and drank a toast.

The waiter delivered a complementary appetiser of freshly baked bread, thinly sliced and drizzled with olive oil.

"May we see the menu," requested Francis.

"*Scusa, signore*. Only small café. Today we make *tagliatelle con sugo di pomodoro, scusa*... pasta with tomato sauce," replied the waiter, gesturing towards the table of three men, "or mackerel or rabbitfish, how you say?... grilled... with potatoes."

"And what are they having?" asked Morgan, nodding at the Greeks' table.

"Pizza, *signore*."

"I'll have that, I think."

"*Sì signore*."

"The mackerel and potatoes for me," said Charles.

"Aye, same here," agreed Alec.

"I'm intrigued by the rabbitfish," said Francis, "but the pasta looks rather good. Yes, the pasta."

"*Sì signori*. And some wine?"

"A bottle of your best red would be fine," Francis answered on behalf of the whole table.

"I wonder if any of our shipmates had better luck finding entertainment? We haven't seen anyone since that artillery captain hours ago," commented Morgan when the waiter left.

"Perhaps the beauty of Suez was just too overwhelming and they've all gone back to the boat to calm down?" Charles suggested with an unflinching straight face.

"Aye, that'll account for it," laughed Alec.

"What ship?" interrupted one of the Greek men.

"Are you speaking to us, sir?" queried Francis.

"What ship you from?" the man repeated, his tone and expression implying genuine interest rather than rudeness.

"The *Serapis*," said Morgan, "bound for Portsmouth from Bombay."

"*Serra-pis* good name for good ship, yes?"

"Indeed. And you gentlemen? Which vessel are you from?"

"*Golconda*. We engineers. Suez, Bombay, Suez, Bombay, all the time we go."

"We've been there. To Golconda, I mean," said Francis.

"On ship?"

"No, no. The place. Near Hyderabad. There's an ancient fortress."

The engineers didn't understand. "You like ouzo?" the other one asked. "Come, drink ouzo with us."

"That's very kind. Perhaps later after our meal," Francis swerved.

"I'll have a drink with you," Morgan agreed, partly out of courtesy and partly curiosity about a liquor he'd not tried before.

The waiter bringing the order saved Morgan from a fourth glass. He thanked the engineers and shook their hands, none the wiser about most of what they'd talked about, but having laughed more than he had all day.

"Jesus wept, that's strong stuff!" he said, returning to his seat and breathing aniseed fumes.

The food exceeded expectations, proving to be as delicious as it was filling. More customers drifted in during the course of the meal, some to eat, others to pass the time with a drink, all of them men articulating a variety of Mediterranean languages. Francis ordered a third bottle of wine, Charles lit a cheroot, and the conversation continued its effortless meandering path between reminiscence and aspiration.

"I miss singing," said Charles, thinking aloud. "It's been an age since the last time."

"Small mercies," laughed Morgan.

"I remember you and Mrs Haines on stage in Bangalore with that opera singer," said Alec. "You were very good as I recall. What was her name?"

"Madame Anna Bishop. And thank you," replied Charles. "I think we sang *Memory* that night."

Alec was filling his pipe when his attention was drawn to a suave individual in a black shirt and crimson waistcoat shaking hands with the owner behind the bar. No older than Francis, Alec guessed, he turned to acknowledge the greetings of the three Italians before swaggering over to the Greeks' table. A whispered discussion ensued that Alec couldn't make out. One of the engineers pointed at Morgan as if making a suggestion.

"*Scusa, signore,*" the man in the waistcoat addressed Morgan. "Our mutual friend believes you're the kind of discerning gentleman who might appreciate games of chance."

"Does he now? And perhaps I am," Morgan replied cautiously, "but what business is that of yours?"

"Forgive my intrusion, *signore*. Allow me to introduce myself. My name is Tino. I am the croupier here. We have card tables and a roulette wheel in the back room. Very discreet, for invited guests only, you understand."

"This is more like it," perked Francis.

"All you gentlemen would be welcome, naturally," Tino emphasised.

"What do you say to some roulette, Morgan?"

Morgan was thinking he didn't trust this croupier fellow any further than he could throw him, but what harm could a few low-stake spins do? "Well I suppose the hour is still early," he said. "How about you, Alec?"

Alec eyed his pocket watch. It was a few minutes past nine o'clock. "Aye, I'll waste a few rupees with you. Or will it be pounds here?"

"Indian rupees, English and Egyptian pounds, Italian and Ottoman lira, French francs... many currencies flow through Suez, *signore*, and all may be won here."

"Before you ask," Charles said to Morgan with a knowing smile, "no, I won't. However, I'll be happy to watch you lose a fortune if you're of a mind to."

"Good man," Morgan replied. "I'll let you carry my winnings."

Followed by two of the three Italians, Tino showed the officers and engineers through a door by the bar, down a short passage, and through another door into the intimacy of the windowless gaming room. Time and money had evidently been invested to create an ambience in which players could relax and feel secure, though neither could mask the smell of rancid tallow and stale tobacco smoke. Faux damask decorated the walls with dark green floral motifs, chairs upholstered in ruby leather clustered around baize-clad tables, and the chandelier above the roulette table was sufficiently modest for no one to notice the wear in the imitation *Sultanabad* rugs.

"Just us?" Morgan asked rhetorically.

"*Sì, signore,* but others may wish to chance their luck later."

Once brass gaming tokens had been purchased for cash at a fair rate of exchange, more drinks were served and Tino took his position by the wheel on the black side of the table. Arranged facing him were one of the Italians, an engineer, Morgan, and Alec farthest away. To his right sat the other engineer, then Francis and the second Italian.

"And where would you like me to be?" asked Charles.

"Not playing, *signore?*" Tino queried.

"Merely spectating. If you have no objections?"

"As you wish, *signore.* Go where you please, of course, but may I suggest here on my left at the end of the table?"

"By all means. Thank you."

Francis and Morgan opened with trivial stakes on groups of four and six. Alec chose a middle dozen, and the Greeks and Italians all placed similarly conservative bets. The first spin ended on thirteen, which yielded returns of two-to-one for Alec and five-to-one for Morgan. The Bank was about even. Play continued in the same tentative manner for a while. Wins balanced losses, and laughter and good-natured banter were the most notable features of the game.

When the Greek engineer to Tino's right risked more serious stakes on three pairs, the atmosphere in the room changed immediately. Charles noticed a look pass between the croupier and the Italian facing him, who promptly made a bet as liberal as the Greek's. The other Italian went a step further with a selection of pairs and single numbers. Not to be outdone, the engineer beside Morgan wagered even more heavily. Francis was tempted to follow suit, but thought better of it when he saw Alec and Morgan holding fast with threes and fours. The spin brought an eight-to-one win for Alec and a complete loss for everyone else.

It seemed to Charles that a new and aggressive phase of the game was underway, dominated by a devil-may-care kind of extravagance on the part of the Italians as if it wasn't their own money they were throwing around. After only a few more spins, the engineers were having to buy additional gaming tokens they couldn't afford, and Francis was becoming reckless with those he had left.

The intensity was interrupted by one of the waiters entering the room with more drinks. The Reverend John Westropp followed him in, unsteady on his feet and in a bullish mood.

"*Scusa*, Tino, *scusa signori*. This gentleman would like to join you."

Morgan cursed under his breath. "What's he doing here?" he mouthed at Charles in exasperation. Charles shrugged.

"Evenin' one and all. Have you room at your table for a humble man of God?"

"*Sì*, Padre," Tino replied, spotting the dog collar and nodding to the waiter. "There is always room here for honest men."

"Is this really a suitable place for a man of the cloth, Reverend?" Morgan challenged.

"*He that is without sin*," retorted Westropp, taking a large sip from his whiskey glass, "let him call me a sinner!"

"Whatever you say, Reverend. Shall we continue?" prompted Morgan.

The Greeks looked perplexed.

"Allow me to cash you in, Padre," invited Tino.

"Thank you, my son."

Westropp ordered more whiskey from the waiter. Even with Alec's patient assistance, it took him as long to successfully perch himself on the vacant stool opposite Charles at the bottom end of the table as it did for the bottle to arrive.

The game recommenced and it became apparent right away that the Reverend had no intention whatsoever of pacing himself. He placed sizeable stakes all over the positions within his reach. The other players continued where they'd left off and Tino smiled when the spin favoured the Bank.

The Italians initiated the next round and between them staked a swathe of the table nearest Westropp. He slurred a grumble at that and downed more whiskey. Alec and Morgan placed their bets. The engineers both reverted to lower risk choices.

"May I reach any numbers on your behalf, Reverend?" offered Francis as he committed to a couple of rows of three.

"Ah sure that'd be a kindness. Thank you, my son. Find me four lucky pairs away down at that end, and may the good Lord guide your hand," Westropp replied, passing tokens to Francis with clumsy hands.

"Unlucky that time, Padre," said Tino when the ball dropped into eleven.

Charles could've sworn Francis had staked ten and eleven for the Reverend, but Tino had already raked the tokens before he could glance to check. Must've been mistaken, Charles thought to himself.

Wagers followed the same pattern for the next spin, with the Italians all but blocking Westropp, Francis helping, and everyone else going their own way. This time Charles paid closer attention. Francis was staking three pairs for the Reverend: two and three, four and seven, and eleven and twelve.

Tino hurried the players to make any final bets and launched the ball around the track. He began to rake the table in the same instant the ball dropped. "Red seven," he announced. "No winners."

"Wait a moment. The Reverend had a stake on seven," Charles pointed out with calm certainty.

"No, *signore*, he did not. The bet was on the row of four, five and six."

"He damn well did!" agreed Francis. "I placed his stake on the four and seven pair myself, and you saw me do it!"

"No, no *signori*. The stake was on the row."

"Oh, here we go," scoffed Morgan as he watched the Reverend get down from his stool and stumble round the table.

"Cheat a man of God, would you now?" Westropp accused the croupier. "If this fine officer," clapping Francis on the shoulder, "says it was on the seven, then may the Lord strike you down if you say otherwise."

"Take your seat, Padre, and place a new bet if you want to stay in the game." There was an edge to Tino's voice none of the guests had heard before.

"You'll be handing over my winnings first."

Tino ignored him and continued stacking tokens.

"We all saw the bet. Give the man what he's owed," asserted Charles, growing angry at the obvious injustice.

"Aye, come on now," agree Alec.

"I owe him nothing."

Westropp erupted at that, pushing the croupier in the chest and throwing a whiskey-emboldened punch that stood no chance of connecting.

Tino's reactions were sober and swift. He grabbed the Reverend by the lapel of his jacket and punched him hard in the mouth, knocking him down.

Whilst the engineers and Italians did nothing, Francis and Alec moved to help the clergyman. Morgan was rushing the other way to restrain the croupier, but Charles was closer and slammed a vengeful right hook into Tino's jaw.

When he saw the croupier's hand go to his hip pocket, Alec knew what was about to happen. In the instant the weapon appeared, he knew too that he was powerless to stop it.

"Knife!" a voice shouted too late.

Tino jabbed the stiletto blade twice in quick succession, each piercing wound like a whispered kiss. He barged Morgan aside as he fled the room. The Italians ran too.

Westropp was out of control and had lost all awareness of what was happening. Without needing to be told, the Greek engineers carried him out flailing and incomprehensible.

"Alec," said Charles, "I think I need your help."

Charles had sunk to his knees and was clutching the top of his abdomen with both hands. Dark red rivulets were oozing between his fingers.

"I'll get him!" Francis yelled as he ran to the door after the croupier.

"Halt there!" Alec called after him, already laying Charles down and applying pressure to his wounds. "Never mind that, just find a carriage quick sharp! We need to get Charles to the ship. Go!"

Morgan supported his friend's head on his lap and searched for hope in Alec's eyes.

A torturous ride through the night at breakneck speed brought the companions back to the *Serapis* half an hour before midnight to the sound of seven bells. Charles was carried to the sick berth and officer of the watch, William Freeland, was told about what had happened. He in turn informed Captain Grant, who ordered John Brodie to go ashore and wake up Consul George West.

"He's one of yours, so I won't involve myself unless you need me to," William Richardson, the ship's surgeon, said to Alec.

"Thank you. Have you laudanum aboard?"

"Aplenty..." William replied, extracting a bottle of the opium tincture from a cupboard. "Iodine and chloroform too if you need them."

"Get this down you, Charles," Alec instructed gently. "I admire how you're bearing the pain in silence, but this will ease it."

"We've been friends a long time," said Charles.

"Aye, we have, and true friends at that."

"As my friend then, rather than my surgeon, don't make game of me with your next answer." The strain in his voice betrayed the agony he was trying to conceal.

"You have my word. What's your question?"

"Is this a grim business?"

Alec hesitated, not wanting to admit the truth even to himself. "Aye lad," he said. "I'm sorry to say, it may very well be."

Charles nodded in acceptance, swallowed the bitter laudanum, and closed his eyes.

CHAPTER THIRTY
PORT TEWFIK, EGYPT
FRIDAY, 21st MARCH 1873

"Sleep is a privilege of the rich and the old, *Giorgio* my friend," said the Italian vice-consul, offering his hand in greeting, "but we are still young and poor, are we not?"

Descended as he was from a noble landowning family in Naples, *Cavaliere* Alessandro de Goyzueta, the Marquis of *Toverena*, could hardly be described as poor, but George West was grateful for his promptitude and laughed along.

The Italian consulate building was only a short walk away from *Rue Colmar*. George had telegraphed a couple of hours ago requesting Alessandro's presence.

"Quite so, quite so," George lied on both counts. "Napping is the secret, I've always found."

"Napping?"

"*Pisolino* is your word, I think?"

"Ah *sì, sì.*"

In their diplomatic roles, George and Alessandro had collaborated on Suez and canal-related matters many times before and were accustomed to sleepless nights. Mutual trust and a close personal friendship blossomed after they discovered a shared interest in geographical studies.

"Anyway, thank you for coming. I wasn't expecting you so soon."

"*Prego, prego.* Your message said most urgent."

"Time will likely be of the essence, yes. In fact, now you're here, we should get aboard the *Serapis* right away. I'll explain what little I know as we walk."

Surgeon William Richardson reported to the quarterdeck a few minutes before two o'clock.

"We're going to have a busy night, Godfrey," he remarked to Third-Lieutenant Eliot, who was on shift as officer of the watch. "There's been a death on the troop deck."

"Please God, not another infant?"

"Thankfully, no. Private Henry Maidmens of the 65th Regiment of Foot. Will you record it in the log?"

"Certainly. What time?"

"A quarter to two is close enough. I don't know his age, I'm afraid."

"Right you are, sir. How's that cavalry officer faring?"

"Poorly the last time I checked. Speaking of which, looks like the consuls are here to talk to him," said William, pointing out the two men who'd just climbed the accommodation ladder. "I'll show them down to the sick berth."

"Will your patient be able to speak to us, surgeon major?" George asked Alec after the necessary introductions had been made and explanations given.

"Aye, he's awake at the moment, but don't expect him to be entirely lucid. I'd like to stay with him if it's all the same to you gentlemen?"

"We quite understand, thank you. And yes, of course, you have your job to do as well. Am I correct in saying you were also present at the *Café d'Italia* when the incident took place?"

"Aye, I was."

"Then I suggest we take depositions from you and the captain at the same time. Is that all right with you, Vice-Consul de Goyzueta?"

"*Sì, sì.* What is the saying you have? *Due uccelli...*"

"...with one stone. Yes, my thoughts exactly," George confirmed.

The supplies that necessitated the ship making a stop at Suez amounted to nearly seventeen hundred gallons of water in eight enormous oak *tuns*, sixteen hundred pounds of vegetables, and over two thousand pounds of fresh beef. Though the water equated to a relatively incidental addition, the quantity of beef exceeded what had been loaded at Bombay by over twenty per cent, and the vegetables by more than fifty per cent.

Supervision of the loading process fell to Fourth-Lieutenant Frank Harston when he took over from Godfrey Eliot at four o'clock, and everyone on board was woken by all the banging and shouting. Paying no attention, Morgan and Francis paced back and forth along the weather deck in contemplation and agitated impatience as they waited to be allowed to visit Charles again, and for their turns to give statements.

Like most of the other First Class passengers, Sophia hadn't long drifted off when Charles was carried aboard on a wave of commotion that roused people from their bunks. Half-dressed outrage and speculation mingled with concern on the saloon deck. Sophia escaped it to keep Morgan company for a while in the crisp night air laden with the scents of machine oil, coal fires and rotting fish. She listened in distress as he vented his anguish, and offered what reassurance she could. When he noticed how much she was trembling, Morgan insisted she return to the warmth of her cabin. He wanted time to think and would come and find her in the morning.

"The consulate gentlemen would like to speak with you next, Francis," said Alec, in need of a pipe. "They've moved from the sick berth to the captain's state room, and asked if you'd be so kind as to meet them there."

"Very well. How's Charles?"

"He's been asking if you two are quite all right and unharmed, and I assured him you were. He's resting now. One of the assistant surgeons is keeping an eye on him whilst I come up here."

"They kept you talking a long time," noted Morgan.

"Aye. The Italian vice-consul asks most of the questions and is being very thorough and conscientious. He seems like a good fellow. They both do, in fact."

Francis went below to give his deposition. Alec and Morgan made a circuit of the deck.

"What are the odds of them finding the croupier, do you reckon?" asked Morgan.

"Slim, probably. Then again, Suez is a small place so you never know."

"And how is Charles really?"

"In a bad way, but a wee bit more comfortable than he was. The bleeding has reduced a great deal."

The sun had breached the bounds of darkness and was painting the western hills in rich amber shades. As their carriage rolled towards Suez, the horse trying to keep pace with its own trotting shadow, George and Alessandro knew they were in for a long day.

Even though he held the more senior diplomatic rank and the *Serapis* was a British vessel, George had encouraged Alessandro to take the lead in their joint investigation. It was clear that at least three Italians were involved in last night's drama at the *Café d'Italia*, and Alessandro stood a much better chance of gaining the cooperation of the local Italian community than George did. Neither of them was in any doubt that the croupier who'd introduced himself to the cavalry officers as Tino was in fact Tino Paranza, about whom they'd both had a variety of suspicions for some time. He'd be in hiding somewhere, so the most urgent task this morning was identifying and arresting his accomplices, the two Italian *bonnets*. Secondary to that was finding the Reverend Westropp and taking his deposition.

As for the Greek engineers, they appeared to have been no more than witnesses and speaking to them was therefore today's lowest priority. Logical though that was, George was also mindful of needing to tread carefully around anything to do with the P&O company. Nearly three years had gone by since he lost the agency contract. He wanted to avoid any accusations of sour grapes on his part, whilst also keeping the door open to the possibility of winning the contract back in the future. The P&O *Golconda* was due to depart for Bombay in the next few hours, and if she went with the engineers on board before they'd been interviewed that would be quite all right with George.

When they left the *Serapis* at four bells, the consuls told Atwell Lake they expected to return before noon. As he waited to see if their prediction would prove correct, his longer than usual watch was passing in relatively uneventful fashion. The mortal remains of Private Henry Maidmens were sent ashore at quarter past eight to be interred in an unmarked grave in a Suez cemetery. Twenty-five minutes later the P&O *Golconda* left the commercial basin to begin its journey south.

After three bells at half past nine, Atwell trained his telescope across the now unobstructed view of the town. A carriage was making its way towards Port Tewfik on the causeway road. By four bells Consul West and Vice-Consul de Goyzueta were back aboard.

"Hello again gentlemen," said Atwell, descending from the quarterdeck to meet them. "Earlier than expected and you've found our stray passenger, I see."

A burly member of Alessandro's staff was holding the Reverend John Westropp by the arm. To keep him upright rather than as precaution against abscondment, Atwell thought to himself. The clergyman was evidently still intoxicated. His torn clothes were soiled with vomit stains and gutter filth, and he was mumbling the words of the twenty-third psalm.

"Hello lieutenant," George replied. "Yes, the Reverend was all too easy to track down in the end. Please place him under arrest and do what you can to sober him up. We wish to conduct an interview as soon as he's in a vaguely fit state."

"Certainly, sir. I'll have the gentleman confined to his cabin under guard and get the galley to brew some extra strong coffee. I dare say you could both use a cup as well?"

"*Grazie mille*, lieutenant," Alessandro replied.

"Indeed we could. That would be splendid."

"If you make your way down to the dining saloon, I'll arrange for a spot of breakfast too," said Atwell.

As George and Alessandro were going down the companion stairs, Sophia was about to head up them.

"Mrs Munro, if I'm not mistaken?" George checked as their paths crossed on the landing.

"Och, Mr West! Aye, how are you?"

"I'm very well, thank you. It's a pleasure to meet you again after all this time, although I'm sorry it's not under happier circumstances. Are you acquainted with Captain Agnew?"

Alessandro and Sophia were introduced, and Sophia explained that she and the cavalry officers were all friends travelling to England together. There'd been no change in Charles's condition. "May I ask if you gentlemen have had any luck finding the croupier?" she added.

"Not as yet," George confessed. "However, we've just brought the Reverend Westropp aboard for questioning, and we're hopeful the two Italian suspects will be apprehended before the day is out."

"Well, I wish you both every success in your search. Perhaps I'll see you a wee bit later then?"

"Thank you. Yes, I do hope so," said George.

On the weather deck, Sophia leant on the port stern rail and peered out past the breakwater at a steamship approaching through Suez Bay. When Morgan came to find her she explained what George West had said, and they watched as the P&O *Pekin* docked in the commercial basin five minutes after half past ten.

When the British and Italian consuls left the ship having extracted nothing of use from an insensible Reverend Westropp, a single lingering note from the ship's bell was signalling the end of William Freeland's first thirty minutes as officer of the watch.

A quarter of an hour later the *Serapis* slipped its moorings and by five minutes to one o'clock was entering the Suez Canal under steam.

The next six hours saw two further watch changes, transit through the Little Bitter and Great Bitter Lakes, sight of another steamer heading south, and an inexorable decline in Charles's health. He was sweating profusely and struggling to catch his breath. Alec didn't dare give him any more laudanum.

In the vanishing twilight at ten minutes past seven o'clock, Frank Harston stopped and secured the vessel for the night on the east bank of the canal at milepost forty-nine and a half.

After sitting with Charles and Alec for a while, Morgan invited Sophia to join him on the weather deck again.

"Always at its most wondrous out at sea and here in the desert," she mused aloud, looking up at the spectacle of the cosmos as Morgan wrapped a blanket around her shoulders.

"A beautiful night, for sure. It's a pity Charles can't be moved, else he could marvel at it with us."

"I can't help thinking how none of this would've happened if I hadn't suggested that dreadful café."

"It's not your fault. Not in the least," Morgan replied with heartfelt conviction. "I've been wrestling with similar thoughts... what if this, and what if that... like what if the ship hadn't needed to stop at Suez in the first place? What if I'd not accepted a drink from those Greek chaps and gone along with the idea of playing roulette? And most especially what if I'd been a damn sight quicker around the table? Perhaps I could have got to the croupier before Charles did?"

"And then it might be you injured in the sick berth."

"Rather me than Charles."

"Och, don't say that."

"I mean it. Anyway, the point I wanted to make is that I've come to realise how fruitless it is to entertain such questions. The only person to blame is that blackguard croupier. What's happened has happened, and no amount of debating how it might've been otherwise is going to change that."

Most of the passengers were preparing for lights out when the coarse chug of a steam launch pulling alongside disturbed the tranquillity of the canal. Atwell Lake asked Captain Grant to come up to the weather deck and ordered the accommodation ladder to be lowered. At twenty-five minutes past ten o'clock a party of seven came aboard, led by a stocky young man wearing a fez, full beard, and a Savile Row lounge suit. George West introduced him as the Governor of Suez, Mohamed Tewfik Pasha.

The affable eldest son of Isma'il Pasha, and heir-apparent to the Khedivate of Egypt, spoke English fluently and hoped his personal intervention would underline how seriously the *Café d'Italia* incident was being taken by the Suez authorities.

"I am most grateful to the British and Italian consuls for the attention they have given this matter," Tewfik Pasha said to Henry Grant, with a nod of acknowledgement towards George and Alessandro. "And as you see, captain, they have brought two suspects for identification."

The Italian pair stood in shackled silence, their bloodied and bruised faces glaring arrogant defiance. One of their two guards was the same man who'd restrained the Reverend Westropp earlier.

"Thank you, governor. I'm sure all the officers involved will appreciate you taking the time to involve yourself like this," Captain Grant replied.

"Would it be possible for Surgeon Major Innes and Lieutenants Farrell and Drummond to join us here on deck?" asked George West.

"Certainly. Lieutenant Lake here will see to that now. In the meantime, perhaps Governor Tewfik Pasha would care for some tea in my state room?"

"Thank you, captain. I would be glad to accept your kind hospitality."

"Aye, that's them," said Alec minutes later, reiterating what Morgan and Francis had already confirmed.

It was all Morgan could do to stop himself unleashing his anger on the two prisoners.

"Thank you, gentlemen," said George.

"*Sì, grazie,*" added Alessandro. He instructed the guards to return the *bonnets* to the launch.

"By his absence, I take it your search for the other miscreant has yet to yield results?" Francis asked.

"We are hopeful he will be in custody within the day," replied Alessandro with more confidence than George believed was warranted. "And how is Captain Agnew now?"

"Not long for this world," Alec replied with undisguised sorrow.

"I'm truly sorry to hear that, truly sorry indeed. I will take my leave of you now, and bid you gentlemen *buonanotte* and farewell."

Tewfik Pasha and Captain Grant were emerging from the companion stairway. George had a quiet word alone with Alec, Morgan and Francis before the opportunity was lost.

"If he hasn't already done so, Paranza will more than likely attempt to make his escape up the canal. If I discover anything about his whereabouts during the next twenty-four hours, I will telegraph a discreet message addressed to you, Surgeon Major Innes, at Port Said."

"Thank you, Mr West. That's most thoughtful," said Alec.

"I only wish it was within my power to do more. Good luck to you all, gentlemen," George said with unambiguous sincerity as he shook each of them by the hand.

In the fortieth minute of Saturday, 22nd March 1873, Sergeant George Watkins, aged thirty-two years, of the 56th Regiment of Foot passed away in his troop deck hammock.

At the two bells of one o'clock, Alec urged Francis, Morgan and Sophia to gather around Charles in the sick berth. The time for goodbyes was upon them.

"Becoming your friend has been one of the great privileges of my life, and I thank you for it," said Sophia with tears in her eyes as she cradled Charles's hand in both of hers. His skin was cold and peculiarly translucent, grey and clammy like a Bangalore summer sky.

Charles smiled weakly, his voice faint. "Thank you, my dear, and likewise. Keep this rogue out of trouble for me, won't you?" he replied with a glance in Morgan's direction.

"Aye, I'll do my best."

"I believe he loves you."

"I believe he does. And I him."

Sophia released his hand and grasped Morgan's, holding it tight.

Francis was trying to remain appropriately taciturn. "It's been an honour to serve with you, Charles," he said.

"And with you, Francis. You're a fine soldier and a good man. Have we left Bombay yet?"

Francis cleared his throat. "We left some days ago. We're on the Suez Canal now."

Charles didn't respond to that. His breathing was becoming shallower by the moment. Alec checked his pulse.

Morgan bent down close to Charles's ear. "Ready for another adventure?"

No sound came when Charles opened his mouth to laugh. "...Reluctantly this time... so much for glory... but I'm at ease with my fate... I must ask something of you."

"Anything."

"Will you see that... Harriet and her family... are taken care of... and my nephew... Charles... has my cane?"

"It will be my pleasure. Consider it done."

"Thank you... and tell her... at the end... I spoke of how... I always... treasured my little sister."

"I will. And I'll make you another promise. If your murderer can be found, I'll see he's brought to book."

"My sabre... is yours," Charles half-nodded and tried to lift his arm. Morgan took his hand and shook it for the last time at twenty minutes past the hour.

"Doctor Alec..." Charles called out, before his final breath left his body like a long sigh.

CHAPTER THIRTY-ONE
LAKE TIMSAH, ISMAILIA, EGYPT
SATURDAY, 22nd MARCH 1873

"Then we concur?" Alec checked as he cupped handfuls of the basin's blood-tainted water over his forearms.

"We do, yes," confirmed Surgeon William Richardson. "Death was the result of organ failure caused by prolonged internal haemorrhaging of the hepatic portal vein. I'd say the poor fellow was doomed from the moment of the first strike."

"Would you care to theorise about the necrosis around the wounds?"

"That was rather odd, wasn't it? I can only think the blade must've been coated in some sort of caustic substance, which then acted upon the tissue. It was more noticeable around the fatal wound than the secondary liver puncture."

"Aye, I think so too. Soap, perhaps?"

"Possibly, yes. That might explain it," said William, tying off the last of the rough sutures that formed a Y-shape down the front of the torso.

"We can but speculate. Thank you again for being a second pair of eyes during the post mortem. I greatly appreciate your assistance."

"Oh, that's quite all right. I'll have some sailcloth brought up and help you sew him into his shroud. And if you don't mind me saying so, it's about time you had some sleep."

"Thank you, and I don't mind at all," Alec replied, "but I need to see him laid to rest first."

The *Serapis* had been at a single anchor about a hundred yards from the dunes on the south side of Ismailia since nine o'clock. A little after the eight bells of noon, Sophia watched from the port rail as a boat was lowered and rowed to shore. Besides the four able seamen at the oars, it carried Charles's corpse accompanied by Morgan, Alec and Francis in their full dress uniforms, two men from the 56th Regiment of Foot with the body of George Watkins, and the Reverend Hamlet Millet with his redundant Book of Common Prayer. Isabella Burton was returning the kindness of condolence and put a comforting arm around Sophia's shoulders.

The cemetery was less than a mile away on the north-west outskirts of town. The remains of the two men were interred beneath the sand in graves hastily dug by the oarsmen, and the words of a brief joint service spoken over them. The funeral party returned to the ship at ten minutes past two.

At quarter past, Atwell Lake ordered the anchor weighed and the *Serapis* proceeded under steam to resume its northward course along the canal.

*   *   *

More than four hours of uninterrupted sleep had done George West the power of good, but news of the death of a distinguished servant of the Crown didn't go well with his breakfast.

Lieutenant-Colonel Thomas McHutchin, a deputy superintendent in the Mysore Commission under Colonel Richard Meade, had passed away on the P&O *Pekin* after a long illness. He'd been going home to the Isle of Man for a restorative eighteen-month furlough with his family. George made his way across to the commercial basin and boarded the ship to pay his respects. As the resident British consul, he was expected to facilitate the remains being brought ashore for burial with the dignity they were due.

At his office window after the funeral, George trained his telescope along the weather deck of the *Pekin* as it slipped its moorings. Leaning on the rail at the starboard bow was a man he was certain he recognised. A man he hoped he'd never see in Suez again. A man who couldn't have purchased a ticket if George had still been the P&O agent.

George went directly to the telegraph office across the road on the arsenal basin quay, where he was a handed a telegram from Ismailia reporting the death of Captain Charles Agnew during the night. Pocketing the tragic message, George composed two of his own to be sent to Port Said. The first, anonymous and for the attention of Surgeon Major Innes on board the steamer *Serapis*, read:

ITALIAN PATIENT REQUIRING ATTENTION
PO PEKIN
BOUND PORT SAID MALTA SOUTHAMPTON

The second was to Vice-Consul Doctor Herbert Zarb, instructing him to secure the arrest of a *Pekin* passenger called Tino Paranza on a charge of murder.

If Zarb complied, then Paranza was bound to expose his role in the organised extortion and corruption that blighted Suez. However, since Zarb wasn't foolish enough to risk implicating himself, it seemed far more likely to George that he'd simply concoct an excuse for inaction. Without an ally in Port Said, Paranza would have to stay on the ship until Malta, which might give the officers of the 16th Lancers a chance to catch him. Either way, George reasoned, the outcome would favour justice.

When he returned to the consulate building, George sat down at his desk to begin writing a detailed report about the *Café d'Italia* drama for the British consul-general in Alexandria, Colonel Edward Stanton.

*   *   *

The *Serapis* spent a quiet night stationary on the canal about five miles north of El Qantara.

After the funeral at Ismailia, Alec, Morgan and Francis had retreated into grief and restless sleep in the privacy of their own cabins. They emerged again early on Sunday morning in need of food and fresh coffee. Morgan and Sophia sought out the comfort of each other's understanding company on the weather deck.

At dawn a diver had been sent down to begin clearing a blocked seacock valve in the hull, a task as unpleasant as it was arduous. Whilst he worked, a French steamer passed by heading south, the ship's crew mustered by divisions, prayers were read, and hawsers were secured to a pilot tug named *Edmond*, which had arrived to tow the ship along the final stretch of the waterway.

William Freeland oversaw the *Serapis* being secured to a buoy off one of the islands in Port Said's Isma'il basin at quarter past five in the afternoon. The diver resumed his labour for another few hours, passengers listened as *mu'addhin* called the faithful to the *Maghrib* prayer at sunset, and coal lighters and other supply barges came alongside. A steam launch brought telegrams and mail, amongst them an anonymous message for Surgeon Major Innes.

"Mr West was as good as his word," said Alec, when he joined the others in the dining saloon. He handed the telegram to Morgan, who in turn showed it to Sophia and Francis.

"The *Pekin* was the one that arrived at Suez not long before we departed, wasn't it?" asked Francis.

"Aye, it was. Lieutenant Eliot has just been explaining to me that Port Said's commercial basin is over on the town side of the harbour, and that's where all P&O ships dock."

"And if it turns up whilst we're still here?" Sophia wondered.

"Then the hunt will begin with finding out if he gets off or stays on board," replied Morgan.

By half past eleven a total of eighteen hundred pounds of beef, eight hundred pounds of vegetables, ten water *tuns*, and two hundred tons of coal had been received from the barges. Most of the passengers were settling down for the night, but Sophia couldn't sleep for thinking about Morgan's ominous talk of a hunt and what peril he might put himself in during its pursuit.

Atwell Lake set the diver to work again at four in the morning on Monday, 24th March, an hour and a half before the rest of the ship began to stir in response to three chimes of the ship's bell and summons to the *Fajr* prayer drifting across the harbour from unseen minarets.

There was no sign of the *Pekin* when Morgan stalked outside before breakfast, or after it. The navy crew was kept occupied cleaning the ship, another dozen *tuns* of water were craned aboard, and the diver kept diving.

At half past one the pleasant Mediterranean breeze was replaced quite suddenly by a force nine blowing from the south. It brought with it a heavy sandstorm that compelled everyone to shelter below decks and blasted Port Said for nearly three hours before vanishing into the Sinai. The bustle of harbour activity resumed, and the diver surfaced to announce that the troublesome valve was finally clear of its obstructions.

The *Serapis* steamed into the outer harbour at dusk and turned north-west in open water, the melodic calls to the *Isha* prayer fading away astern. Still nothing had been seen of the P&O *Pekin*.

Other than an occasional heavy swell, calm seas and comfortable weather blessed the next four days of the voyage. The crew mended old clothes and made new ones. A mishap led to part of the patent log – the device used to measure the ship's speed – being lost overboard. It was quickly replaced with a spare. Gunner George Thompson of the Royal Artillery's 18th Brigade and invalided Private John Spooner of the 76th Regiment of Foot were committed to the deep, and many steamers and barques were sighted heading east and south. One of them, on Wednesday morning, was the steamship *Kromahtah* carrying cargo from London to Singapore and Bangkok. It had sustained the loss of a screw blade and serious damage to its drive shaft, rendering it in need of help to get back to Malta for repairs. Captain Grant obliged and a lifeboat was despatched carrying hawsers with which to tow the stricken vessel.

"Hello there, Mr Freeland. Would you mind satisfying my curiosity about something?" Morgan asked William on Friday evening. The second-lieutenant was making a circuit of the weather deck during an uneventful shift on duty as officer of the watch and was glad of some conversation.

"I shall certainly do my best."

"I was wondering if our speed has slowed since we started pulling the other ship?"

"Strangely enough, no. We've been steaming one or two knots faster than before, in fact. All being well, we should reach Malta tomorrow."

"I'm relieved to hear it. So if a P&O steamer departed Suez after us, we'd probably still be ahead of it?"

"Possibly. Which one are you thinking of?"

"The *Pekin*."

"Oh I see. In that case, there's every chance it will have overtaken us by now. Newer P&O ships like the *Pekin* can best the *Serapis* by at least a couple of knots per hour."

The Maltese coast was sighted off the port bow at twenty minutes past eleven on Saturday, 29th March, and by two o'clock passengers were gathered at the starboard rail to watch their arrival at Valletta. The ship passed the sixteenth-century bastions and curtain walls of Fort St. Elmo, its straw-coloured limestone glowing like warm honey in the afternoon sun, and entered the haven of the Grand Harbour. The *Kromahtah* was cast off at half past the hour to be attended by local tugs, and within another ten minutes the *Serapis* was safely secured to the buoy of mooring number nine.

Morgan had been perched at the starboard bow with a borrowed pair of field glasses. "It's here," he told Sophia. "Five ships along. I'm going ashore to make enquiries. Would you like to come with me?"

"Of course I would. Mr Baldock tells me the wee ferries darting about are called... *dghajsa tal-pass*, I think he said. We can hail one from the top of the accommodation ladder."

Like the arteries of the harbour, countless dozens of the sculled boats carried people and luggage between ships and shore. Twenty-one feet long with a swooping bow, tall stemposts fore and aft, and a sailcloth awning over the stern half for shade, their construction abided by proud traditions. Each boatman stood in the middle of the craft and faced forward to push on the oars, expressing his individuality through the colour of the hull and the way he'd decorated it with floral designs and the protective Eye of Horus.

Conveyance the fifty yards to land took only a minute, and Morgan tipped the oarsman for directions to the P&O office.

"Reminds me of Alexandria," commented Sophia as they weaved their way along the arc of the wharf.

Beneath the city wall, flat-roofed warehouses and the balconied homes of Maltese merchants neighboured grander architecture occupied by shipping companies. All of them looked out across the harbour and were built in Valletta's characteristic limestone. Ships moored at right angles to the wharf's briny steps, pairs of stern hawsers sagging slack in the water. Mountains of cargo, in crates and sacks and barrels, were being loaded and unloaded by hand and cart and crane by flat-capped stevedores wearing brown waistcoats over sweat-marked cream shirts. Sailors and passengers came and went in horse-drawn carriages driven by men in wide-brimmed, bowl-shaped hats, and negotiations could be heard in every language of the Mediterranean. The aromas of hot oil, anise, and sweet date pastry wafted from the stalls of the *imqaret* sellers, and blended with smells familiar to working harbours everywhere, like the coal heaped on lighters and burned in furnaces, horse dung, decaying kelp, and fishing boats.

When Morgan and Sophia found the right building, the P&O clerk told them the *Pekin* arrived yesterday. Half a dozen new passengers were due to board, but only three had disembarked.

"Two of them were British artillery officers returning to the garrison in the fort, sir," he said. "The other was an Italian gentleman, I think."

"It's important. Please check. What was his name?" Morgan asked with obvious impatience.

"Certainly, sir. One moment..." the clerk replied, turning a page and running his finger down a passenger list. "Yes, here it is, sir. The gentleman's name was Paranza."

Sophia could see by the look in Morgan's eyes that he wouldn't be travelling any further on the *Serapis*. She knew too that he'd insist on her continuing the journey to England without him.

Back on the weather deck, Alec and Francis were waiting for them. Morgan explained what they'd discovered and his intention to remain on the island to track down the nefarious croupier. His entire demeanour had transformed into that of a commander with a singular objective.

"Francis," he began, "I need you to escort Sophia safely to London in my stead."

"An unnecessary duty, and one to which I've agreed to submit only because Morgan assures me it will allow his mind to rest a little easier," Sophia interjected.

"I understand, and you may both rely on me without question," replied Francis.

"And Alec," Morgan continued, "I promised Charles that his nephew would have his cane and that I'd see Harriet and her family taken care of. To that end, would you deliver the cane and something else to her in Cheltenham on my behalf?"

"Aye, I will, and gladly."

"Thank you. I'll give it to you before I go."

Morgan went to his cabin to pack a bag with spare clothes and essentials, and to change into his full dress uniform. He clipped the scabbard of Charles's tulwar to his sword belt and tucked his pith helmet under one arm. It was time to be a Scarlet Lancer again. Sophia, Francis and Alec were at the rail near the accommodation ladder when he reappeared.

"I hope you find him. Good luck," said Francis.

"Aye, and look after yourself while you're at it," Alec added. "I'll inform the officer of the watch you've disembarked."

"Thank you, my friends. Alec, this is for Harriet," said Morgan, handing over the gift. "You'll find the cane in Charles's berth."

The three men shook hands and then Alec and Francis made themselves scarce to give Sophia and Morgan a moment alone.

"Where will I be able to contact you?" he asked.

"I'll stay at Hatchett's Hotel in Piccadilly."

"Very well. I'll telegraph news when I can."

"Do what you must here, but promise you'll come safely back to me in London."

"I promise," he said, pulling her into an impassioned kiss and not caring who saw it.

CHAPTER THIRTY-TWO
PORTSMOUTH, ENGLAND
WEDNESDAY, 9TH APRIL 1873

Princess Beatrice was five days away from her sixteenth birthday. She would celebrate her special day wearing black at Osborne House on the Isle of Wight. The youngest of her mother's children, and well known to be her favourite, the princess was embarking from Gosport with Queen Victoria on Her Majesty's Yacht *Alberta*. Fitted with twin paddle wheels and funnels, three masts, and a comfortable deckhouse near the stern where members of the royal family and their entourage could shelter from the elements, the steam tender was less than half the size of the *Serapis*.

"Now there's a woman who knows a thing or two about mourning," Atwell Lake thought aloud, in part about the mother of a bright toddler called Henry who'd died from measles last evening on the troop deck. He was the sixteenth fatal casualty of disease, and the final death of the voyage. Three other mothers were bereaved the day before. Edward Atkinson, aged two, was buried at sea in sight of the Needles. The remains of Ann Kirkham, four, and John Hosman, just one, were to be sent ashore with Henry's for interment this afternoon.

It was half past noon and the officer of the watch was standing with a group of First Class passengers at the stern rail of the *Serapis*, now moored to Portsea dockyard's main transport jetty. Sophia, Francis and Alec were amongst them. Copies of this morning's *Hampshire Telegraph and Sussex Chronicle* had been brought aboard with other newspapers, and people were reading about the royal itinerary to which they were now bearing witness. One column over on page two, in an inaccurate report about Charles and the events at Suez and Ismailia, they also read of their own arrival yesterday. Telescopes were being passed around so that glimpses might be caught of the sovereign as she went by three hundred yards away across the harbour.

"A *dreich* day to be on a choppy Solent," said Alec, commenting on the bleak skies and chilly sea breeze that brought April showers, and drained all the warmth and lustre from the English coastline.

Following a mid-morning instruction from the harbour master, twenty minutes earlier the ship's masts had been dressed with signal flags and ensigns by way of a fluttering royal salute. All the other vessels in the dockyard had done the same, including a sister troopship, the S.S. *Jumna*, there since Saturday and ready for a refit, as well as the *Asia, Camel, Echo* and *Elfin*, the *Fire Queen, Grinder, Manly, Pigmy* and *Skylark*, the *Staunch, Vernon, St. Vincent*, and the *Vigilant*; names that spoke of the masculinity of colonial acquisition and oppression.

A little after one o'clock yesterday afternoon, a couple of hours after the *Serapis* had been piloted to its mooring, the Reverend John Westropp and a Mr Hooper were taken from their cabins and discharged under guard to the asylum wing of the Royal Naval Hospital Haslar in Gosport. Hooper had served as chief engineer on the Mediterranean fleet's HMS *Pallas*, and was marched on board at Malta. It was widely believed that the clergyman had gone quite mad.

The rest of the day had been spent getting out the baggage in preparation for disembarkation this morning. The able-bodied from the troop deck were sent off first, followed at half past ten by the invalided men going by railway to the enormous military hospital at Netley near Southampton. Some of the officers with families left the first chance they had, but most of First Class chose to remain aboard until after the rush had subsided.

Major Richard Blundell was far more absorbed in the news of the day, a novelty after being at sea, than in the progress of the *Alberta*. Further down the page, amongst other naval and military reports, a curious piece caught his eye.

"Captain Grant... it says here that a large portion of one side of our hull was coated in a new hydraulic cement paint before the *Serapis* set off to collect us from Bombay?"

"Yes, major, and remarkably anti-corrosive it is too. Invented by a Captain Crease of the Royal Marine Artillery, if memory serves. I expect we'll get a full coat in due course, as no doubt will *Jumna* and the other troopships."

"Really my darlin', do pay attention over here," chided Henrietta Blundell. "'Tis not every day one gets to wave at the Queen, is it now?"

Her husband folded the paper, looked toward the elegant craft steaming southward in the distance, and led the army and navy officers in a salute.

As the *Alberta* disappeared from view the armour-plated turret-ship, HMS *Monarch*, entered the harbour after the successful completion of sea trials, and the *Serapis* crew was put to work removing soiled bedding from the troop deck.

"I suppose we should be making our way to the railway station," Francis said to Sophia and Alec, who nodded their agreement.

Similar suggestions began to cascade from one set of travelling companions to another, and Captain Grant seized the moment to encourage departure. Everyone thanked him and his officers for their kindness and professionalism, and wishes were extended to all for safe onward journeys.

"May my husband and I accompany you as far as the station?" Isabella Burton asked Sophia. They'd already pledged to write to one another. The Burtons were bound for Liverpool where they'd board a City of Dublin Steam Packet ship to cross the Irish Sea.

"Och of course, I was hoping you would," Sophia replied.

"Will you be going to London as well, Surgeon Major Innes?" asked Francis Burton.

"Not yet, lieutenant, no. I need to pay an official visit to Netley Hospital first, and then I have another important duty to perform."

*   *   *

It had taken Morgan a fortnight to track down his quarry in Valletta, and cost nearly all his patience.

Resting during the heat of the day in a quiet room in an out of the way *Floriana* boarding house, he'd searched by night and came to know every alley, street and square in the maze of the capital. He'd scoured all the establishments he could find that might appreciate the talents of an Italian-speaking croupier. There were private members' clubs, like *Casino della Borsa* in the top floor of the Exchange on *Strada Reale* and *Casino Maltese* in the Treasury building on the west side of *Piazza San Giorgio*, and so many cafés, gambling dens, restaurants, brothels and theatres that they'd all started to look the same. In the end he'd spied him serving drinks in a seedy cellar bar halfway along the notorious *Strada Stretta*.

Now it was a few minutes past four in the morning on Easter Sunday, 13ᵗʰ April, and a full moon was descending across a clear sky. Morgan had spent the past two and a half hours failing to be inconspicuous further down the slope of the cobbled street on the corner of *Strada Teatro*. He'd been keeping the entrance to the bar under surveillance, whilst humouring the drunken taunts of soldiers and sailors, and fending off the persistent solicitations of local Catholic prostitutes. When they next went to take Communion, they'd arouse priests with confession of their sins and be rewarded with a lenient Hail Mary penance and a blessing.

Only four yards wide, but over seven hundred long with flights of stone steps at intervals, *Strada Stretta* cut through the heart of Valletta. To some, that's exactly what it was. The view from top to bottom was a chaos of louvres and balconies, bay windows and oil lamp-illuminated awnings, three and four-storey buildings pressing in from both sides like the walls of a sewer. Patrons flowed down from the fort and surged up from the harbour, imbibing at inconvenient tables and tumbling in and out of double wooden doors set in latticed arches. Laughter often spilled into violence, whilst duelling singers partnered folk ensembles playing the calfskin *żaqq*, tambourine and fiddle to accompany every conquest and humiliation. Like a charnel house for discarded morals, the street flouted convention, catered for every imaginable appetite and peccadillo, and was a law unto itself. Agnostic about class and gender as much as race and religion, anyone from anywhere was welcome if they had money to spend. *Strada Stretta* was light and colour and illusion, temptation and liberation, sanctuary and debauchery. It was the perfect habitat for Tino Paranza.

Morgan's pulse quickened when he saw Paranza exit the bar, light a cigarette, and push his way down the street. Morgan hid in the shadows of a vacant doorway and watched him turn left into *Strada Teatro* and go by, before following at least thirty yards behind. Paranza flanked the southern edge of *Piazza San Giorgio* and turned right on to *Strada Reale*, skirting *Piazza Regina* and continuing downhill past the Cathedral of St. John with its twin bell towers. Strolling over *Strada Britannica*, Paranza took aim at the statue of St. Francis of Assisi on the corner of the church and flicked the stub of his cigarette from between thumb and middle finger. It found its mark, showering the saint's stone cassock with glowing tobacco embers.

In sight of the diminutive Church of *Santa Barbara*, Morgan knew they'd be at *Porta Reale*, the city gate, within a couple of minutes. Perhaps the croupier had been living down in the suburb of Floriana all this time as well? The streets were deserted now. Morgan increased his pace.

Moonlight silhouetted Paranza as he walked under the great vaulting arch of the gateway and on to the bridge that spanned Valletta's three-hundred-year-old defensive ditch. He stopped abruptly and turned around, immediately recognising the man in the scarlet tunic he knew had been following him.

"Seeking trouble, lieutenant?"

Morgan emerged from beneath the arch. "You murdered my friend," he said, circling slowly to his left. "I'm here to take you to the Governor's Palace, where you're going to surrender yourself to the British authorities and answer for your crime."

Paranza laughed with derision. "You really think that's going to happen?"

"No. But I'm honour-bound to offer you the chance."

"Fuck your honour. And your friend. He got what he deserved."

"Have it your way."

"Go home Irishman, or you'll get the same," menaced Paranza, taking the stiletto from his pocket, stepping forward and flicking open the blade.

Morgan didn't move.

"Too gutless to use that?" jeered Paranza, gesturing at the tulwar hanging from Morgan's left hip.

Morgan remained poised. Silent.

Irritated and dismissive, Paranza rushed an impatient lunging attack. Morgan instinctively dodged right, parrying his foe's wrist with one hand and grasping the lapel of his waistcoat with the other. He yanked him forward to meet a bone-shattering Kiss o' Kerry.

"*Bastardo!*" Paranza shouted, clutching his bloody nose and retreating to recover his composure.

Morgan unsheathed Charles's Indian sabre, deliberately dragging out the sound of the blade scraping against its scabbard. Paranza smiled at that and rushed forward again with knife held high.

As the killer came within range Morgan thrust the tulwar up and forward in a sharp flash of movement. The draw cut cleaved flesh and bone from left clavicle to sixth rib, slicing through lung in an eruption of gore.

Paranza could neither speak nor scream. He stumbled forward, dropping the stiletto and reaching out to the waist-high parapet with his right hand. He propped himself against it, half turning to face his executioner.

Morgan saw surprise in the man's eyes, a flicker of hope, then the utter despair of realisation as his strength left him and he slumped forward over the barrier.

Tino Paranza spent the last seconds of his life plunging sixty feet into the darkness of the abyss. His mangled, mutilated corpse would lie unnoticed for days in the rubble at the bottom of the ditch, rotting amongst three centuries of foul detritus. Carrion for rats.

CHAPTER THIRTY-THREE
CHELTENHAM, ENGLAND
SATURDAY, 26TH APRIL 1873

The twenty-minute brougham ride from Lansdown railway station wasn't long enough to ease the knot that had been tightening like a noose in Alec's stomach all the way from Bristol. He patted his breast pocket for the dozenth time.

It was a pleasant spring morning on the edge of the Cotswolds, dry and bright, and warm for the season by English standards. Still acclimatising after the heat of India, Alec was dressed for winter.

Charles had spoken about his sister so often and with such fondness over the past eight years, it was almost as if Alec knew Harriet like the kind of close acquaintance he and Jessie might regularly invite to dinner. But they'd never met, and Alec was conscious he'd need to guard against conducting himself with undue familiarity. He wished Jessie was with him.

The driver reined in the horses on the south side of Clarence Square and knocked on the roof to signal their arrival. Alec stepped down to the pavement and admired the leafy elegance of the location. The square's residents overlooked a small park enclosed by railings and planted with birch, oak, ash and sycamore. The paths that crossed its lawns curved like a whipping Saltire and in places were white with drifting sloe blossom.

"Thank you, sir," said the driver, accepting Alec's coins and appreciating the extra tip. "That's number four, right there, sir," he added, pointing with his crop.

The Cracklow family home was a four-storey mid-terrace, faced with ashlar on the ground floor and white stucco above and below. An ornate wrought iron balcony spanned the first floor, and pilasters soared toward the low pitch of the roof. Five steps led up to the front door, painted black to match all the others around the square. The housemaid, twenty-eight-year-old Ann Symonds, opened it just as Alec was reaching for the knocker. She bade him enter, and took his bowler and coat. He didn't relinquish the cane he was carrying.

"Do come in surgeon major," boomed the man waiting in the hallway. In his early forties, with tidy sideburns and pronounced crow's feet extending from knowing eyes, his black lounge suit was new. "Thank you for telegraphing. I'm Captain George Cracklow. Pleased to meet you, sir."

Alec shook his hand and returned the courtesies. In common with many artillery officers, it was obvious George had suffered partial hearing loss and was under a degree of misapprehension about the volume of his own voice. The interior of the house was as grand as the outside, with mahogany architraves and bannisters, plaster friezes ornamenting high ceilings, wallpaper in the latest style, polished parquet, and modern gas lamps.

"We'll take tea in the drawing room, Ann," George instructed, showing Alec to the first door on the left.

As soon as Alec stepped through it and saw Harriet standing to greet him, his knot began to unravel. The family resemblance between her and Charles was striking, and it took Alec quite by surprise. With hair pinned high, she was wearing a long-sleeved black silk dress over a modest crinoline. It accentuated her pale complexion. Her smile was understandably reserved, though there was no mistaking its friendliness. In her tear-tired eyes Alec could see a tempest of heartbreak, confusion and longing.

"Welcome, dear Alec, welcome," said Harriet, taking his hand. "It is all right if I call you Alec, isn't it?"

"Aye, of course, ma'am."

"My brother always referred to you as Alec in his letters, and never with anything but the highest praise and admiration, so you see I've rather grown accustomed to thinking of you that way."

Alec was deeply touched to discover that Charles had mentioned him. "I might say the same of your name, ma'am, and the names of your husband and children too, for that matter," he replied. "May I offer you and your parents my sincerest condolences for your loss."

"Thank you. They're in London this weekend, but I will be sure to tell them all about your visit when next I see them. And I'm terribly glad you feel as I do, so I'd very much prefer you calling me Harriet. It's rather like we're old friends, don't you think?"

"Thank you, and aye, it is indeed," agreed Alec with relief.

"And now friends united in sorrow," interjected the dowager Cracklow, neither rising from her chair nor trying to conceal the snide bitterness in her voice. George's mother, Suzette, once the young and glamourous jewel of a family of Mayfair milliners, was in her sixty-eighth year and had been his lone parent since he was only seven weeks old in *Jaunpur* in northern India. She lived at 5 Oxford Parade with her reclusive spinster sister, Rose Gill, just across the road from Oxford Villas where George and Harriet began their married life. Harriet had hoped the move to Clarence Square, a fifteen-minute carriage ride away, would deter her mother-in-law from paying such frequent visits. She'd been disappointed.

"Tragically so, aye ma'am," replied Alec, with a subtle bow towards the silver-haired figure in heavy black lace.

George moved to placate her with the formality she expected. Out of unconscious habit, he twisted his gold signet ring back and forth as he spoke. "Surgeon Major Alec Innes, may I introduce my mother, Mrs George Cracklow. And Mother, this is..."

"Yes, yes, thank you, my boy," she interrupted. "Tell me, Mr Innes, are you a good surgeon?"

"Mother! Really!" admonished Harriet.

"I've had the misfortune to know army doctors who were no better than butchers," said Suzette as if Alec wasn't there.

Alec humoured her rudeness with barbed diplomacy. "I'm happy to make your acquaintance, ma'am. I believe I've helped more than I've hindered over the years. And my mind is resolutely open to the latest medical science, which has thankfully made great advances since the days of Waterloo."

Suzette mumbled a begrudging acknowledgement and returned her attention to her grandchildren. Five-year-old Charles Cracklow, who was the image of his father, was sitting cross-legged on the floor forming letters on a small blackboard. His sister, Kate, a couple of months past her second birthday, had inherited her nose and mouth from Suzette and her eyes from Harriet. She was toddling around with a small hand mirror and seemed endlessly entertained by her pretty reflection. Neither child showed much interest in the visitor, but Charles was polite and cheerful when Harriet introduced them.

"Your Uncle Charles wanted you to have this," Alec explained, handing the duck's head cane to the boy.

"Thank you, sir," replied Charles, evidently puzzled. He sensed from the way the object affected his mother that it held some strange significance he was too young to understand. It was as long as he was tall, and the eyes of the duck were almost completely worn away. Harriet made him promise to take special care of it.

Coals flamed in the marble fireplace, warming the north-facing room. George invited Alec to take a seat and make himself at home. "Our other son, named after my father and I, is in the nursery having his nap," he explained. Sixteen-year-old Rose Andrews, the nursemaid, was keeping an eye on him. "Ten months old already and growing fast," George said with beaming pride.

Ann the housemaid knocked on the door and entered carrying the tea tray. As she filed out again, Amelia Curks, the children's nurse, came in to take Charles and Kate upstairs. She was a couple of years older than Ann, and made sure she didn't forget it. Tensions amongst the servants were arbitrated by Mrs Partridge, the cook, who presided over the running of the house from her domain below stairs. Having attained the age of forty-two, she stood for no nonsense from the younger women.

George took a pipe from the mantelpiece and pressed tobacco into its bowl. "Smoke if you wish, Alec, by all means."

"Aye, thank you, I will," he replied, following suit.

"I have so many questions about what happened to Charles, I confess I don't know where to start," Harriet admitted.

"I'll do my best to answer them, but perhaps I might begin by explaining why I've come?"

"Thank you. Yes, of course, please do," she said, taking a sip from a dainty porcelain cup.

"Well, I'm really here on behalf of Lieutenant Morgan Farrell. I'm assuming his name is familiar to you?"

"Charles's best friend, yes. My mother and I met him in Colchester the day you all left for India. No ill has become of him, I hope?"

"No, no, he was in perfectly good health the last time I saw him. He requested my help in keeping three promises I witnessed him make to Charles. Passing on his cane to your son was the first of them."

"Oh I see. That's so kind of you to take the trouble."

"No trouble at all, I assure you. In his final moments, Charles expressed how much he'd always treasured you as his little sister – those were his words – and he asked Morgan to tell you as much."

Harriet broke down in sobs of grief, for which she tried to apologise when George offered her comfort. "Would you mind fetching those articles from your study, my love?" she said to him as she dried her eyes. "The first we heard of what happened was via *The Times*, but subsequent reports have been so carelessly inaccurate, inconsistent or downright contradictory that it's maddening," she added, speaking to Alec.

"The papers are nothing but sordid gossip-mongers and should never be trusted," opined Suzette.

"Yes Mother, thank you," Harriet snapped.

George returned presently with a sheaf of newspaper clippings, which he arranged in chronological order on a side table.

"Allow me to show you, Alec," said Harriet, "and perhaps you'll be able to sift fact from fiction for us."

"Certainly," he replied, following her to the table.

"This one was the harbinger of our despair," Harriet remembered, touching the crumpled excerpt from *The Times* on Friday, 28th March. "It uses the harrowing phrase *'stabbed by the hand of an assassin'*, since oft repeated. And then here's the *Western Morning News* from the same day, which incorrectly states your regiment as being the 16th Hussars, not the Lancers. They couldn't even get his age right. He was thirty-six not thirty-seven. And it says Charles was returning home invalided. But that's not true, is it?"

"No, it's not, at least not in the sense used by the army. He'd been suffering with malaria for some time, and had become quite run down, but he was travelling on medical furlough to recover not as an invalid unfit for duty."

"Thank you. That's a reassurance," said Harriet. "And thus, he must have changed his mind about retiring? He talked about his intention to do so in his last correspondence from Secunderabad," she added, taking a letter from her purse to show Alec.

"Aye. I'd convinced him to reserve judgment until after he was feeling better."

"If only more people in this cruel world were blessed with friends like you," Harriet smiled with sincerity, before attending the papers again. "The next day, as you see here, the *Cheltenham and County Looker-On* reiterated what we already knew, but at least had the decency not to muddle regiments. Then we heard no more for a fortnight until *The Morning Post* published this from its correspondent in Malta, dated ten days earlier on 4th April..."

Alec picked up the column. Its salient points, which he read aloud, were that Charles had been going home to "*take command of the depot at*

Canterbury", that he was "*cowardly stabbed by an Italian at the Café d'Italia in Suez*", and that his "*remains were conveyed to Malta where they were interred with military honours.*"

"Oh dear. Aye, I can quite see how you'd be confounded by this one. Cowardly stabbed at that place in Suez is correct, but the rest is make-believe and lazy journalism."

"So, Charles wasn't buried on Malta?"

"No, at Ismailia in Egypt. Morgan and I, and another friend, Lieutenant Francis Drummond, were there. The fellow interred on the island was a soldier from the 109th Regiment of Foot."

"Ismailia?" Harriet repeated, to fix the name in her memory.

"Aye."

"What was his name, the other soldier?" wondered George.

"Private Hammon. Eric Hammon, I think," Alec replied.

"Three days later, a week ago Thursday, *The Standard* had this longer article, but how much of it is conjecture I can't tell," Harriet continued, handing Alec the other clipping.

"They have it correct about Suez being a *miserable hole*," said Alec as he read on. "And it's true that the *Café d'Italia* had a roulette table, that Charles only watched when the rest of us played, and that he detected the croupier cheating another player. There was an altercation and, aye, I'm sorry to confirm he did receive two stab wounds to the abdomen from a stiletto blade."

"Thank you for your honesty. For all that the truth may be difficult to hear, it is like a salve for my heart," said Harriet. "*The Standard* goes on to say that Charles was taken back to the ship and placed in the hands of the surgeon. Is that a reference to you?"

"Aye. I was with him throughout, and the ship's surgeon, a Mr Richardson, provided kind assistance."

Harriet took Alec's hand in hers again. "Thank you for all you did for him. Now I must ask, because I must know... did my brother suffer?"

Alec chose his next words with care. "It would be false to imagine the injuries he sustained were entirely painless, but I can say with absolute conviction that he bore his burden with great courage, and everything was done that could be to try to save him and ease his discomfort."

Harriet nodded, tears welling, and squeezed Alec's hand in gratitude.

"The last report we're aware of is this from the *Western Daily News* a week ago today," intervened George, "which to my mind is the most vexing of all."

Alec shook his head and tutted as he read it. "Aye, vexing beyond words. Firstly, the *Serapis* did not have to *lie in the roads off Suez, whilst other vessels were working through the canal* – it docked at Port Tewfik to take on supplies. Secondly, this part about an attempt being made to pass off on Charles *some spurious coin in exchange for English money* is a fabrication that can only be attributed to guesswork on the part of someone who wasn't there, and he wasn't stabbed in the back as we left the café. This also seems to be suggesting that the croupier was arrested along with his accomplices, which is utter tripe."

"And towards the end where it says Charles died from his wounds *an hour or two later?*" Harriet dared to ask.

"No, I'm afraid that's not accurate either," replied Alec, determined not to be drawn further about timings for Harriet's sake.

She nodded her understanding of his unspoken meaning and finished her tea. Ann was instructed to bring a fresh pot, whilst Alec answered more questions and refilled his pipe.

"My father has said he is making an application to the Secretary of State for War for a grant of the value of Charles's commission," Harriet revealed. "And I understand our family friend, Major Gavin, the Member of Parliament for Limerick, will be raising a question in the House about the events in Suez."

"Our local MP, Henry Samuelson, has also pledged his support," added George.

"That's encouraging," Alec responded, "although I must caution against too much optimism regarding the War Office. Since Mr Cardwell changed how things are done, I'd be inclined to doubt his willingness to reimburse commissions in unusual circumstances such as these."

"Worth trying, I suppose," said Harriet, somewhat deflated.

Suzette chose to break her deafening silence. "Doctor Innes. You said earlier that Lieutenant Farrell made three promises, yet you have recounted only two of them."

"Thank you for reminding me, ma'am. You are quite correct," Alec replied, not rising to her sniping tone. He turned to Harriet. "Morgan's other promise was to fulfil Charles's wish that he would see you and your family taken care of. Before he disembarked at Malta, he gave me this to deliver to you as a token of his commitment to that vow..." Alec took the leather pouch from his breast pocket and placed it in Harriet's hands.

"Oh, good heavens! George, look at this!" Harriet exclaimed when she saw the gold inside.

"My Lord! A small fortune!" bellowed George.

"Quite possibly, aye."

Suzette rustled forward in her chair, eager to see what all the excitement was about.

"Lieutenant Farrell is evidently a man of honour and great generosity, but why did he leave the troopship at Malta in the first place?" George queried.

"Morgan believed Charles's murderer – the croupier – had escaped to the island. He stayed there to attempt to find the scoundrel and bring him to justice."

Harriet's spirits rallied again hearing that. "Have you received any word since?"

"Not as yet, but I'm hopeful we will soon."

"I shall pray for it, and for your good health and prosperity and that of your family. Thank you again for being such a loyal and steadfast friend to my brother."

"That's kind of you. It was always my pleasure."

"You'll stay for lunch, of course," insisted George, "but to where are you bound from here?"

"I'll be taking the railway to London and then onward to Canterbury, where I intend to pay the regimental depot a visit at the cavalry barracks. There are officers there, like Captain Robert Maillard, who knew Charles well."

*　　　*　　　*

Breathy panpipe melodies and innocent laughter echoed between the half-timbered buildings of the Buttermarket. Alec approached the square along Burgate, where he found Mr Punch entertaining a crowd of children with his swazzled rasp, the violence of his marital strife, and a variety of shenanigans with Pretty Polly and a peculiar Italian clown called Scaramouch. In the middle of the square, a maypole was already entwined in the colours of the dance. Alec's imagination was captured by intricate stonework and iconography to his right, and for a fleeting moment Christchurch Gate reminded him of a Hindoo *gopuram* in Bangalore. Canterbury's streets were festooned with bunting and flowers to celebrate the May Day festival, the beginning of summer, and for once the weather perfectly matched the occasion.

Another kind of commemoration was foremost in Alec's thoughts. Following New Military Road past the artillery and infantry, and then going south along Broad Street, he'd taken his time to savour the scents of the meadows, the sound of birdsong, and the warmth of the sun as he walked the half mile or so to town from the cavalry barracks.

Turning left off Buttermarket, Alec wandered the narrow Mercery Lane, on to St. Margaret's Street and found the building he was looking for a few doors down on the right. Four fluted Doric columns proclaimed the importance of what had once been a fish market, but was now the premises of G.M. Horan Monumental Stone Works. Glancing back the way he'd come, Alec could see the Cathedral's transept tower rising above rooftops of thatch and red tile. He removed his hat and stepped inside.

CHAPTER THIRTY-FOUR
THE WORLD'S END, TILBURY, ENGLAND
TUESDAY, 6th MAY 1873

Morgan stood at the riverbank and squinted into the azure haze. He was casting his mind back to the last time he looked south across the Thames, when the regiment had been embarking aboard the *Golden Fleece*, and to all that had happened since.

The low roofs of Gravesend and the higher ground beyond them were hardly more than a smudge in the distance. They seemed to take on the same grey-brown dullness of the great river. The tower of St. George's Church was the only distinctive landmark. Not far from Morgan's sentinel position, the decayed timbers of an old landing stage rose from the water like broken teeth, and two hundred yards away to his left the red brick bastions of Tilbury Fort sat squat and indefatigable. The morning tide was halfway between ebb and flow, revealing a muddy shore strewn with rocks, slick with green slime, and discarded fragments of upstream existence. The waterway itself was as busy as always. Steam ferries shuttled from one side to the other like the weft on a loom, passing between cargo vessels laden with exports and imports, and ships taking passengers away to new lives in the far reaches of the Empire and bringing survivors home to rebuild old ones.

All of it looked just the same, and yet so much had changed. Morgan was watching the scene, but not really seeing it. He was preoccupied with the future and memories of the past.

Three days ago would have been Walter Bagenall's thirty-second birthday. Morgan wished the gentle man from County Carlow had been alive to buy the drinks in the Officers' Mess, and that he'd had time to find himself a wife to celebrate the occasion with him. Augustus Dobrée could have been there to raise a glass as well. He'd be twenty-eight now, a captain perhaps, and likely as deserving as ever of good-humoured teasing. Morgan missed them both. And there was Charles of course. They'd shared a cabin all the way to Madras and a railway carriage with John Orr from there to Bangalore, the place that still felt like home. There'd been the fraternity of The Establishment with Robert Maillard and Carrin and the others; they'd raced and hunted and paraded, and sampled the dubious delights of the bazaar; they'd confided in each other, conspired in elaborate practical jokes, and been entertained at dances, parties, and theatrical performances; Charles had sung, been a best man and a best friend. The funerals had far outnumbered the weddings. The long march north to Secunderabad was a chore, the destination a disappointment.

One shining thread had run throughout everything, and that was Sophia; from their first chance meeting at the tavern behind him, and the telegraphic flirtations sent, received and missed between continents, to their reunion and the eventual wonder of their togetherness in the camp at Oorgaum that had for so long seemed as elusive as it was inevitable. Morgan's thoughts returned to her as he turned his back on the Thames and headed to The World's End, still fighting its losing battle against the elements.

He'd arrived at Tilbury the previous evening, paid for a room at the tavern, and then gone to the railway station's telegraph office. His message to Sophia at Hatchett's Hotel confirmed his safe arrival and said he'd meet her there by this evening. His breakfast had been served with her swift reply:

HEART CONTENT AGAIN
STAY WHERE YOU ARE
WILL COME TO YOU

"I bet a nice cup o' tea would set you right, wouldn't it, sir?" predicted Hannah Whitton with easy familiarity and contorted vowels when Morgan walked through the door dressed in his scarlet tunic. He laid Charles's sabre on a table by the smouldering fireplace and took a seat.

"And another gentleman left this behind, sir," said Eliza Whitton, handing over a dog-eared copy of Saturday's *Allen's Indian Mail*. "If you need to pass the time, sir," she added with a smile.

The identical twin sisters were sixteen and worked as barmaids for their enterprising parents. They'd been particularly attentive to Morgan since he became a guest. He thanked them for their kindness and accepted both the tea and the newspaper with gratitude.

There was a carelessly inaccurate mention of Charles, Alec and Francis all having obtained furloughs only last month. It was announced that a Lieutenant Farrell of the 16th Lancers had been promoted to the rank of captain following Charles's death, which gave Morgan no pleasure to read. An advertisement for life assurance quoted more than twice as much for policyholders living in India as for those in England. A fatal encounter with a man-eating tiger was reported near Hyderabad. Lea and Perrin hailed the appetite-improving value of their Worcestershire sauce, with a bold caution against accepting imitations. Sir Bartle Frere was going on a mission to Zanzibar to negotiate with the sultan there about the suppression of the continuing trade in African slaves. Morgan thought he might show Sophia that last article later.

A few other customers came and went, none of them staying long, and the twins were mostly occupied with cleaning. Morgan caught amusing snippets of their conversation as they worked. Without needing to be asked, Hannah brought more tea when he finished the first cup.

Morgan was beginning to consider going for another walk when the tavern door opened and Sophia stepped inside. He was on his feet before she'd even removed her hat. They rushed to each other's relieved and longing embrace, and Sophia held Morgan's face to kiss him again and again.

"Here I am, keeping my promise," Morgan said at last.

"So you are, thank God."

"Thank the captain of a certain merchant steamer for needing only meagre inducement to grant me discreet passage."

"I thank him too." Sophia squeezed Morgan's arms. "Please tell me you're all in one piece and quite all right?"

"And Bristol fashion. Weary, I'll admit, and I need a bath and a good tailor, but well enough. But what of you? Have you been in Piccadilly all this time?"

"Aye, for the most part. I delivered the mining reports and samples to the broker, along with my photographs, and sold the gold Micky gave me. It fetched a handsome price."

"Good, I'm glad. Have you heard from Micky since?"

"I telegraphed to tell him about the broker, but haven't had a reply yet. Alec came to visit as well. He was on his way to Canterbury and we met for lunch. He'd been to see Harriet in Cheltenham, where he gave her your gold and told her about what Charles had said before he passed away. She expressed her very dear thanks to you."

"Alec's a good man. I'll have to visit Cheltenham in person and pay my respects. Did Francis look after you as he promised he would?"

"Aye, he was unfailingly gallant, and once we reached London he travelled on to Scotland. I'd like to take him up on his offer of hospitality at Strathallan Castle at some point, perhaps en route to or from visiting Janet and Hector."

"That's an excellent idea, and then I can thank him whilst I drink his whisky. Thank you for indulging me and accepting his companionship, by the way."

"It was no bother. You said a merchant steamer."

"The *Alice*, yes, bringing cargo from the Malabar coast. She'd stopped at Valletta for supplies and I thought it wiser to travel incognito on a merchant vessel like her than a troopship. The *Crocodile*, one of the other sister ships of the *Serapis*, was there a couple of days before I departed on the 26th April."

The Whitton twins had been eavesdropping from across the bar and chose their moment to come over and enquire about Sophia's refreshment needs.

"A glass of French white wine would be most welcome, thank you," Sophia replied. "Is the landlord here still a Mr Farr? George Farr, I think it was?"

"No, missus. Mr Farr left some years past," said Hannah.

"'Tis our father now, missus. Charles Whitton is 'is name," added Eliza.

"And I'll have a pot of that fine ale of yours, please girls," requested Morgan.

He showed Sophia to his table and they pulled chairs together so they could sit side by side. The twins brought their drinks.

"What are your plans now you're back? Aside from bathing, tailoring and Cheltenham, I mean," Sophia asked, holding Morgan's hand.

"I was rather hoping we might make plans together," he replied. "We talked before about a quiet place in the country."

"I'd like that, aye." Sophia's eyes lit up and she kissed his cheek.

"In that case, after Scotland, how would you feel about going over to Ireland? We could sail from Glasgow. I think it's about time I reacquainted myself with Dromquinna, and I recall you saying how much you admired Kerry's beauty."

"I'd love to, thank you. And, aye, I did. It would be wonderful to see it properly."

"Here's to showing you where I grew up then..." said Morgan, raising his ale for a toast.

"To Dromquinna and new beginnings. *Slàinte mhath!*" Sophia replied, touching her glass to his tankard.

"*Slàinte!*"

"If they're still there, we could meet the Burtons in Dublin on the way."

"Certainly."

Sophia had been avoiding the topic of Malta up to now, but the tulwar laying on the table in front of her was too symbolic to ignore. "Did you find him?" she asked, knowing there was no need to elaborate.

Morgan rested his free hand on the scabbard. "I did, yes, and I kept that promise too."

Sophia nodded her understanding. "Then let's drink to justice, and to absent friends."

"Justice, and to the best of them. To Charles Agnew."

HISTORICAL NOTE

The following words are inscribed in stone in the south aisle of Canterbury Cathedral:

IN MEMORY OF
CAPTAIN
CHARLES AGNEW
WHO DIED BY THE HAND OF AN ASSASSIN
IN EGYPT
22ND MARCH 1873

THIS TABLET IS ERECTED TO HIS MEMORY
IN TOKEN OF THEIR REGARD
BY HIS BROTHER OFFICERS OF THE
SIXTEENTH QUEENS LANCERS

There are countless other monuments in the cathedral to soldiers who lost their lives in service of the Empire during the 19th century. In that context, surrounded by battle honours and the names of the fallen, the word 'assassin' might appear unusual. I was certainly intrigued when it caught my eye during a visit to Canterbury on a rain-soaked Sunday in the spring of 2015. I couldn't resist finding out more, and so began a journey of research into the life and death of Captain Agnew, the British in India, and the wider political turmoil of the era. Along the way I discovered the equally fascinating tales of the telegraph network, Micky Lavelle, the Bodisco family, and the embryonic intelligence service.

Above all else, by piecing together the available evidence, I wanted to tell the unknown story of Charles Agnew with as much historical integrity as a work of fiction can allow. I hope I've served him well.

In case you've been wondering, he really did paint that statue in Bangalore (and quite possibly the one in Leicester Square Gardens too.) The unclaimed £100 reward in Bangalore in 1866 would be equivalent to around £12,000 today.

413

Morgan Farrell, Sophia Munro, Janet Steward, Yadhu Nayak, Hector Mackay, Everett Murray, and Tino Paranza are entirely fictional, but with only those exceptions all the named people in the book are real-life characters (as are the horses, *Bulger* the bullmastiff puppy, and *Nellie* the mongrel.)

All the cavalry officers would have employed personal servants, known as bâtmen, chosen from within the regiment. In the absence of records on the subject, I gave Solomon Smith and John Gantz the jobs on behalf of Charles and Morgan.

Wherever possible, physical descriptions are based on contemporary photographs, paintings, and written accounts. I've tried to portray them all in a respectful and sympathetic manner without diminishing the likely reality of their Victorian-era attitudes and prejudices about gender, race, and class.

My depictions of Levi Goodman, Dr Herbert Zarb, and Seymour Fox break that self-imposed rule since history has already shown them to be disreputable. In the case of Dr Zarb, the British consulate had a fund set aside for the aid of seamen who fell sick and found themselves stranded at Port Said. The Maltese doctor was convicted of embezzling £173 from that fund in May 1873 (equivalent to around £19,000 today).

Throughout the story, I've tried to balance the dual objectives of portraying the period accurately and not wishing to applaud what historian, Eric Hobsbawm, called, *"...the fundamental racism of nineteenth-century civilization..."* In Madras, for example, White Town and Black Town (later renamed George Town) were the official names in use during the 19th century. There have been occasions when I've chosen to pull my punches regardless of the language and behaviour documented by contemporary commentators. Many of the story's characters use the word *coolie* when referring to Indian labourers or servants, but as Sathnam Sanghera points out in *Empireworld* (Viking, 2024), the term, "derives from 'kuli', meaning 'hire' or 'wages' in the Tamil language," and is, "unlikely to be a label that… labourers would have chosen for themselves. It was often taken as a racial slur when the British used it."

Sir William Denison's low opinion of 'the native Indian' is laid bare in his self-indulgent two-volume memoir, *"Varieties Of Vice-Regal Life."*

To the modern reader, 'assassination' probably conjures up images of a sanctioned killing for political or religious reasons. In Victorian

Britain, however, although use of the word 'assassin' was habitually reserved for descriptions of upper class deaths, it tended to be quite interchangeable with 'murderer' and usually had the same, less conspiratorial, meaning.

Based on the timing and wording of the initial reports in the British press about Charles Agnew's death (beginning with *The Times* on 28th March 1873), it might be deduced that, if not a sub-editor at *The Times*, it was either George West or Colonel Edward Stanton who first introduced the word 'assassin' to Charles's story. Whoever it was, they have my thanks.

Sicily is home to a unique form of martial art called *Paranza Corta*, which is based around the use of thin-bladed 'stiletto' knives. A *liccasapuni* ('soap licker') is a variant of the weapon with a long, folding blade, which would be coated in soap to cause permanent scarring.

Although Tino Paranza is a fictional character, he's inspired by the real-life Italian (or Italian-sounding) murderer of Charles Agnew. Who he was and what happened to him remains a mystery.

The circumstances of Charles Agnew's death, and the events that immediately followed, are based on documentary evidence – in particular the log of the *Serapis*.

The log records the Reverend John (Thomas Edmund) Westropp's drunkenness in Suez on the night of Charles Agnew's stabbing, his arrest shortly after Charles gave a deposition to George West, and his later discharge to the care of the Haslar Military Hospital. Other documentary evidence supports a hypothesis that Westropp was present in the *Café d'Italia*, although we'll never know for certain. The nature of the improper conduct that prompted his dismissal from service as a navy chaplain is unknown, but it seems clear he struggled with alcohol. Westropp had a BA from Trinity College Dublin, and was curate at a number of churches in Norfolk, Somerset and Huntingdonshire before and after his time at sea. In 1881 he became the vicar at Witham Friary in Somerset, where he established a village library and reading room, and in November of that year, at the age of thirty-six, he married a lady four years his senior called Mary Gordon Mules. They didn't have any children. He died at the age of fifty-four in March 1900. His successor at Witham Friary noted that Westropp had been in failing health for some time. Mary died in July 1943 at the age of 102.

According to the Kipling Society, Rudyard Kipling's character, *Mrs Hauksbee*, *"was almost certainly based on"* Isabella Burton, who travelled to England from Bombay on the *Serapis* with her husband. A little later in her life, she *"was a friend of the young Kipling, and acted with him in various theatricals."*

Micky Lavelle's amorous alligator story, and some of the detail of the excursion to Salem races, came courtesy of Isaac Tyrrell's memoir, *"From England to the Antipodes & India - 1846 to 1902, with startling revelations, or 56 years of my life in the Indian Mutiny, Police & Jails."*

In keeping with the British nomenclature of the era I've referred to the conflict of 1857 using variations of the Indian or Sepoy Mutiny, Rebellion or Uprising. However, it is now more appropriately called India's First War of Independence.

John Orr and Micky Lavelle were indeed friends, possibly even business partners, and Dr Orr is thought to have accompanied Lavelle on exploratory visits to the Kolar gold fields.

A group portrait in Bangalore, photographed by Dr Patrick Gerald Fitzgerald in 1870, and now kept in the archives of the British Library, shows how John Orr and his wife, Emily, moved in the same social circles as Colonel Richard Meade, Major General Arthur Borton, Major Douglas Scott, and Dr James Ranking. Their children and wives are in the picture as well, including Mrs Scott who'd previously been married to the Russian Ambassador in Washington, Baron Alexander de Bodisco. The precise date of the photograph is unknown, but we can be certain it was taken some time after the first week of September that year, since Arthur Borton didn't arrive in Bangalore until then. The location is the Residency, now called *Raj Bhavan* (a transliteration of the Hindi for "Government House"). Louisa Garstin, also pictured in the photograph, married Dr Fitzgerald in October 1871. She was twenty-seven years his junior. They had three children together and later lived in the Bedminster district of Bristol.

Some of the words spoken by Colonel Richard Meade in chapter twenty are paraphrased from a report he wrote in 1872-3 about the history of the administration of Mysore, and also from the narrative of his biographer, Thomas Henry Thornton, in *"General Sir Richard Meade and the Feudatory States of Central and Southern India"* published in 1898.

Colonel William Dickson's speech to the regiment before the flogging of Private Davis in chapter eight are quoted from Henry Wisewould's diary.

The Someshwara temple visited by Sophia and Morgan in chapter twenty-five is really located in the town of Kolar rather than Oorgaum.

By all accounts, Michael Fitzgerald Lavelle was a popular figure in Bangalore. The press called him 'The Gold King of Kolar'. His friends called him 'Micky'. He applied to Sir Richard Meade of the Mysore Government for a mining license in August 1873. After long negotiations, in February 1875 he was granted an exclusive contract with a twenty-year lease on an area of land around Marikuppam. The Mysore Government would earn a 10% royalty on all gold mined there. He had early success, but soon realised the task was beyond his means without significant investment in plant and manpower. But Micky was nothing if not canny. In March 1877 he sold his lease to the concisely-named '*Kolar Concessionaires Soft Corporation and Arbuthnot Company of Madras*', founded by Major General George De La Poer Beresford of the Madras Staff Corps – another Irishman. It's thought they paid £10,000 for the lease (equivalent to around £1.2 million today). Micky died at home in Bangalore in September 1895 at the age of sixty-four. Lavelle Road in modern-day Bengaluru is named after him. Kolar developed into India's largest gold mine and remained in operation until February 2001.

Francis Colebrooke Drummond, who returned to England on the *Serapis* with Alec Innes, left the 16th Lancers at the end of 1874 to join the 7th Dragoon Guards stationed in Norwich. In June 1875, at St. John's Church in Ballachulish, Scotland, he married Marcia De La Poer Beresford.

To make it possible for Morgan Farrell's fictional character to be in the regiment, Lieutenant *Ion* Turner was excluded from the story. With his wife, he travelled to India aboard the *Golden Fleece*. He was promoted to the rank of Captain after the death of Charles Agnew, and retired from service in June 1875 receiving the full value of his commission. Morgan Farrell's horses, *Lucifer* and *Gunner*, were in reality owned and raced by Mr Turner.

By the time Charles Agnew reached Suez in 1873, around 70% of all the shipping through the canal was British. To pay off the enormous debts he'd managed to accumulate, in 1875 Isma'il Pasha sold his country's share in the canal company to the British government for £4 million (equivalent to around £440 million today). The purchase caused something of a scandal at the time, because Prime Minister

Benjamin Disraeli didn't tell Parliament about it until after the deal was done.

Captain Charles Wilson was appointed Director of the Topographical and Statistical Department of the War Office in 1870. The TSD's role was to study the strength, organisation and equipment of foreign armies. It may not have been until this time – after his return from the 1868-9 Sinai expedition – that he and the three staff assigned to him began their work in the old stables off Spring Gardens. This is one of only two instances in the story where I've knowingly taken a minor liberty with the historical chronology. The other is in chapter fifteen when Sophia Munro stays at Watson's Esplanade Hotel two years before it actually opened for business.

The Royal Engineers first started receiving instruction in the art of photography in 1856 at their school in Chatham. General Sir Robert Napier used it to document the Abyssinia Campaign of 1867-8, a project that was sanctioned by the Royal Geographical Society *"in the cause of the Empire."*

During the Sinai ordnance survey expedition, James MacDonald took more than three hundred photographs of geographical and ethnographic interest.

Later in his career, Charles Wilson was Chief of the Intelligence Department on the 1884 expedition sent to relieve General Gordon at Khartoum, Director-General of the Ordnance Survey from 1886 to 1894, and Director-General of Military Education from 1895 until his retirement three years later.

The Intelligence Branch of the War Office replaced the TSD on 1st April 1873. The modern-day British Security Service (MI5) and Secret Intelligence Service (MI6) are its organisational descendants.

Thanks to advances in science, medicine, human rights, and social equality, the modern developed world undoubtedly offers a more comfortable existence than the Victorians could have ever imagined. That said, we'd be naïve to lose sight of the motives behind the corporate and political struggles to control territory, trade, and natural resources that continue to this day. Neither should we be blind to the causes and effects of modern-day slavery, which is estimated to exploit around 50 million people worldwide. In far too many ways that should matter, not much has changed in a century and a half. And, as the coronavirus pandemic demonstrated, disease is an invisible enemy that will always be blind to wealth and status.

It wasn't until 1897 that a British doctor called Ronald Ross identified malaria parasites in the stomach tissue of mosquitoes. He was working in the Indian Medical Service at Secunderabad when he made the discovery, and would go on to receive a knighthood and a Nobel Prize.

Sophia Munro would have been exceptionally unusual in Victorian Britain, but there is historical precedent for her unorthodox lifestyle. Sophia's character is inspired in part by Lady Florence Caroline Dixie, who was a traveller, war correspondent, writer, and feminist in the second half of the 19th century. Another notable inspiration is the Austrian round-the-world traveller, writer, and ethnographer, Ida Laura Pfeiffer. There are many examples of innovative female photographers from that era too, including Julia Margaret Cameron, Lady Clementina Hawarden, Mary Steen, and Harriet Tytler.

Sophia and Janet's experience on board Brunel's *Great Eastern* is a re-imagining of William Howard Russell's time on the Atlantic cable voyage with Robert Dudley. Dudley produced watercolour illustrations of the ship and its cable-laying operation, which later appeared in Russell's book, *The Atlantic Telegraph*. Russell was an Irish reporter with *The Times*, and one of the first modern war correspondents. Among other conflicts, he covered the Crimean War and the Indian Mutiny. Some of the words spoken in this story by Janet Steward, James Anderson and Henry Moriarty are borrowed from Russell's account.

The *Serapis* was refitted in 1875 and became the royal ship for Prince Albert's voyage to India. Howard Russell accompanied the Prince of Wales as his Honorary Private Secretary and filed reports for *The Times* throughout the seventeen-week tour. For his service, Russell was knighted by Albert, then King Edward VII, in 1902. The ballroom in Bangalore's Raj Bhavan, commissioned by Colonel Richard Meade, was named The Serapis Room in honour of the ship.

Prince Albert was initiated into the Freemasons during a tour of Sweden in 1868 and by 1874 had progressed to the honour of Grand Master of the United Grand Lodge of England. Masonic lodges in India were constituted as multi-racial and cross-class fraternities, in which no distinction would be drawn between members "*on the score of religion or creed.*" There were 40 lodges across the country in 1860. Today, India has in the order of 23,000 masons belonging to around 470 lodges.

The records of the Masonic Lodge in Secunderabad for 1873 note, *"The news was received of the death of Bro. Agnew, a member of the Lodge and P.M. of Lodge Bangalore. This worthy Brother having died on his way home, it was resolved to put the Lodge into mourning for a month and to hold a Lodge of sorrow. This was done on the 23rd April. At this ceremony the Rev. Bro. Liston assisted and was afterwards thanked for his help. The brethren from Lodges Mayo and Deccan were also thanked for their attendance."*

Morgan Farrell's fictional family home is a real place. Dromguinah House in Kenmare, County Kerry, in the south-western corner of Ireland, was home to Daniel O'Connell McSwiney and his wife Anastasia Farrell. They were killed in the Straffan railway disaster in 1853. Daniel's maternal grandfather was called Morgan. Towards the end of the 19th century, Dromguinah House was purchased by an Englishman who anglicised the name to Dromquinna. It's now a luxury hotel and wedding venue.

I've used a combination of place name conventions, usually favouring the Victorian British for well-known locations such as Bangalore, Madras, Bombay and Jeypore (now Bengaluru, Chennai, Mumbai and Jaipur respectively) and the current Anglicised versions for smaller towns and villages that otherwise might be difficult to find on a modern map.

British India established the 'Baluchistan Agency' in 1877 after community leaders signed a treaty the year before in which they accepted British colonial mediation in their disputes. Prior to the treaty, maps of the region show Baluchistan (or sometimes Baloochistan) as a distinct country in its own right. It is now a region within Pakistan.

Harriet Scott – previously Baroness de Bodisco – and her second husband, Douglas, moved to Scotland after his retirement from the army as a Major General in 1879. Mittie, the youngest of Harriet's six children, went with them. Harriet died at Portsmouth in June 1890 at the age of seventy-six. Her third child, Konstantin (known as 'Costa'), followed in his father's footsteps and became Chamberlain to Alexander III, the Tsar of Russia, six years later. His younger brother, William, served in the Russian diplomatic service. Waldemar, Baron Alexander de Bodisco's son by his first marriage, was secretary of the Russian legation at Washington and later the Russian consul-general. In 1867, he was present at the negotiations that resulted in the Alaska Treaty.

The Agnew family's application to receive the value of Charles Agnew's commission was refused by Edward Cardwell, the Secretary of State for War, in July 1873. A captain's commission in the 16th Lancers was worth at least £3,225 (equivalent to something like £350,000 today).

Harriet Agnew had five children. Reginald, born in 1870, and Edward, born in 1874, both died before their first birthdays. Catherine Agnew passed away in 1877 and within a year Harriet suffered yet another tragic loss when her husband, George Cracklow, died in February 1878 at the age of only forty-six. The homes they shared at 1 Oxford Villas (now 35 London Road), 7 Oxford Street and 4 Clarence Square in Cheltenham are still there. Letters that George Cracklow wrote home to his mother, Suzette, during the Indian Mutiny have become an oft-cited primary source for historians of the period. Harriet and her three surviving children led eventful lives, but that's another story.

After relocating the family to Exeter Place in Cheltenham, James Agnew did end up having to sell Larne harbour and the surrounding lands of Curran and Drumalis. James Chaine paid £20,000 for the property in 1866 (equivalent to around £2.4 million today) and went on to turn the harbour into a highly profitable business. James Agnew died in 1880 at the age of eighty-six. Exeter Place was off Grosvenor Street in Cheltenham, but no longer exists.

The Carnfunnock estate is now known as Carnfunnock Country Park and is open to the public. Although Cairncastle Lodge was demolished in the 1930s, the original walled garden and ice house remain among the park's many attractions.

Between 1869 and 1889, Jessie and Charles Alexander Innes (or 'Alec' as I've called him throughout the book) had eleven children. Two of them died at birth or in early infancy. In October 1874 at Secunderabad, they named their sixth child Charles Alexander. He would go on to become the Governor of Burma, Chairman of the Mercantile Bank of India, and Chairman of the Mysore Gold Mining Company (operating the Kolar gold fields started by Micky Lavelle). He was knighted in 1924.

Jessie Innes passed away in Islington in May 1909 at the age of fifty-nine. Alec survived her by eleven years and died aged eighty-eight at his home in Charmouth, Dorset. Lynwood Cottage is still there. It became a holiday home called Dolphin House for a while, but has since returned to being a private residence. The medals Alec's father won for his part in the battle of Waterloo were said to be his most treasured possessions. Alec and Jessie's lives are commemorated on a brass plaque in St. Andrew's Church in Charmouth.

Henry Wilkinson trained his men in the signalling skills he learned in Delhi, and in December 1873 eight NCOs attended a Camp of Exercise in Bangalore to demonstrate their effectiveness. Over the course of 1874 and 1875 the regiment moved to the new cavalry barracks at Tirumalagiri and the health of the men improved. The 16th (The Queen's) Lancers returned from India in 1876 to the cavalry barracks in Canterbury. During its eleven-year deployment overseas, the regiment lost a total of ninety-eight men and an unrecorded number of wives and children. With only a few exceptions, Charles Agnew among them, all those deaths were the result of disease or heat stroke. The cavalry barracks in Canterbury have long since gone.

Charles Agnew's final resting place at Ismailia is lost to history. Neither is it certain who arranged the memorial to him at Canterbury Cathedral. Robert Maillard is a likely candidate, but I like to imagine it was Alec Innes.

The World's End is still serving beer in Tilbury.

IN REMEMBRANCE

Private J. REYNOLDS	6/7/1865	Private W. WATSON	16/7/1871
Private J. CLAYPOLE	25/9/1865	Private J. THOMPSON	28/10/1871
Private L. EARNSHAY	9/2/1866	Private J. FOSTER	9/11/1871
Private W. LEACH	22/2/1866	Private R. HALL	22/11/1871
Private T. DARLING	29/5/1866	Private T. GIBBONS	16/1/1872
Private R. COOK	13/6/1866	Private H. JOHNSON	8/5/1872
Private E. RUSSELL	17/6/1866	As-Surgeon R.D. KEMP	19/5/1872
Private J. SMITH	10/7/1866	Corporal C. CHAPMAN	22/5/1872
Private R. ELLIOTT	15/7/1866	Private E. JENNINGS	24/5/1872
Farrier J. McCARTHY	29/7/1866	Private M. HAIR	15/7/1872
Private I. WARE	3/8/1866	Private R. SHAW	5/8/1872
Corporal W. BRICE	20/8/1866	Private T. FOLKES	24/8/1872
L-Sergeant J. COURTNEY	27/8/1866	Private J. STAINES	26/8/1872
Private I. MADIN	4/3/1867	Private C. MCKEE	29/8/1872
Private S. PARSONS	6/4/1867	Private J. GRIFFIN	11/9/1872
Private C. DRUMMOND	16/4/1867	Private F. GOLDING	21/9/1872
Private B. SANDERSON	4/5/1867	Private T. GUILOR	26/9/1872
Private G. KIPPS	3/7/1867	Trumpeter W. DOLAN	13/10/1872
Lieutenant A.C. DOBRÉE	2/8/1867	Private H. HUGHES	18/10/1872
Private J. PHIBS	30/10/1867	Private J. BLADES	23/10/1872
Private P. DOYLE	3/11/1867	Corporal R. HAYES	6/11/1872
Private G. MARTIN	16/12/1867	Private W. GARRATT	17/12/1872
Private C. WOODS	29/12/1867	Private M. MORRIS	22/12/1872
Private B. JOPLIN	30/1/1868	Private J. MANN	1/1/1873
Private C. JONES	24/3/1868	Private C. MARTIN	14/1/1873
Private J. MEEHAN	21/7/1868	Private M. LINGHAN	16/1/1873
Captain W.P. BAGENAL	25/11/1868	Private J. CROSS	19/1/1873
Private A. GRAY	5/2/1869	Private J. GILBERT	23/1/1873
Private O. COX	10/3/1869	Captain C. AGNEW	22/3/1873
Private T. McANALLY	20/3/1869	Private A. ESSON	26/3/1873
Q.M. Sergeant R.T. WARD	19/4/1869	Private J. MILLS	27/3/1873
Private T. NASH	23/4/1869	Private J. LEE	11/4/1873
Veterinary T.J. RICHARDSON	18/6/1869	Private J. RICKETTS	10/5/1873
Corporal W. HARRIS	5/7/1869	Sergeant R. ADDISON	17/6/1873
Private W. GLEESON	30/7/1869	Corporal W. BOLAND	6/7/1873
Private H. EDWARDS	15/8/1869	Private J. DAVIS	28/8/1873
Private J. PRESTON	23/8/1869	Private J. HIGGS	21/10/1873
Private V. McARDELL	7/9/1869	Private T. TYRE	4/11/1873
Sergeant Major G. SMITH	10/12/1869	L-Corp. J. CROOVES	20/1/1874
Private E. MARTIN	26/3/1870	Private R. MUNRO	15/3/1874
Farrier A. PAGE	29/5/1870	Captain T. DYNON	31/3/1874
Sergeant A. COAKLEY	13/6/1870	Private C. FAUTHORP	19/1/1875
L-Sergeant F. KAYCOLE	22/7/1870	Private J. PENNY	17/4/1875
Private T. DAMANT	23/7/1870	Private W. EVANS	2/6/1875
Private J. ATKINSON	25/7/1870	Private G. STEVENS	5/9/1875
Private J. THOMPSON	11/10/1870	Private J. MARNEY	7/9/1875
Private C. DUCKWORTH	29/12/1870	Private H. WEBB	29/10/1875
Private W. WALKLEY	10/1/1871	Corporal H. GLADWELL	1/11/1875

ACKNOWLEDGEMENTS

I'm indebted to the following people, all of whom provided invaluable assistance during the research for this book: Captain Mick Holtby, former Curator, and Robert Osborn, Assistant Curator, at the Queen's Royal Lancers & Nottinghamshire Yeomanry Museum; Chris Latimer, City Archivist at the Stoke-on-Trent City Archives; Fawn Walters, Archive and Library Assistant at Canterbury Cathedral; Claire Young, for transcribing Thomas Parnham's copies of the 1865 *Golden Fleece Gazette*; Members of the Record Copying team at the National Archives in Kew; John Falconer, formerly Lead Curator (Prints, Drawings and Photographs) at The British Library; Beatrice and Maree Garner, for transcribing and editing Henry Wisewould's diaries; Penny Hutchins, Head of Archives, and Lucy Blackburn, Archive Assistant, in the Templer Study Centre at the National Army Museum in Chelsea; and my father, Richard, for his infallible knowledge of Britain's railways.

A select bibliography may be found at threeswrite.com

For reading, feedback, advice and encouragement, I'd like to thank Sam Manicom, Birgit Schünemann, Helen Lloyd, Emma White, Caroline Shotton, Saranya Dhasarathan, Professor Robert Tulloh, Deirdre Molloy, Emma Adams, Simon Read, Ayla Hutchings, Karen Delmege, Dr Hazel Went, Steve Conabeer, Isabel Rye, Catherine and Lex Cochrane, Ted Simon, Rebecca King, John Hatch, Sára Ficken, Kathryn Hinton, Natalya Forbes, David Stidworthy, David Ashenden, Neil Hinchliffe, and Damien Borlase.

Thanks also to Dean Harmer, Lynn Evans, Ellie Glen, and Lewis Harold at Aitch Creative for the stunning cover design, and to Richard Hinchliffe at Brindle for making the book a reality.

Above all, EmmaLucy Cole has my love and gratitude for her wise counsel, Egypt and Arabic expertise, and for continuing to believe in what might be possible.

C.Q. Turnstone, 2025

ABOUT THE AUTHOR

Before studying for a Masters in Imperial and Global History at the University of Exeter, C.Q. Turnstone spent most of his career specialising in digital marketing and event management.

Originally from Hertfordshire, he's lived in many different places. Scotland will always be where he feels most at home.

Avarice of Empire is his debut novel.

Follow C.Q. Turnstone on social media @threeswrite and subscribe to his email newsletter on the web at threeswrite.com

www.ingramcontent.com/pod-product-compliance
Lightning Source LLC
Chambersburg PA
CBHW031737180726
48283CB00005B/1545